The DOOM *of* FALLOWHEARTH

The first arachyura flung itself at him from out of the dark so hard it impaled itself on his sword, running itself through. Logan kicked at it repeatedly, its writhing limbs still trying to claw at him as more of its kin swarmed forward from all sides. He got it dislodged and thrust hard into the open maw of another, right between the pincers, ichor gouting across his sword.

He withdrew the blade and turned the movement into a slash that burst the eye clusters of a third. He felt a surge of exhilaration as he fought, an angry defiance he hadn't known in a long time. He wasn't going to die here, in the dirt and the dark, down among these monsters. He'd live, as he always did. This would be just another story for the fireside.

BY THE SAME AUTHOR

WARHAMMER 40,000: CARCHARODONS

Red Tithe

Outer Dark

WARHAMMER 40,000

Dawn of War III

The Last Hunt

Blood Of Iax

WARHAMMER: AGE OF SIGMAR

Scourge of Fate

The Bone Desert

WARHAMMER 40,000: WARZONE FENRIS

Legacy of Russ: The Wild King

NON-FICTION

British Light Infantry in the American Revolution

Battle Tactics of the American Revolution

DESCENT™
JOURNEYS IN THE DARK

The DOOM *of* FALLOWHEARTH

ROBBIE MACNIVEN

First published by Aconyte Books in 2020

ISBN 978 1 83908 025 8

Ebook ISBN 978 1 83908 026 5

Cover art by Jeff Chen

Map by Francesca Baerald

Distributed in North America by Simon & Schuster Inc, New York, USA

Printed in the United States of America

9 8 7 6 5 4 3 2 1

ACONYTE BOOKS

An imprint of Asmodee Entertainment Ltd

Mercury House, Shipstones Business Centre

North Gate, Nottingham NG7 7FN, UK

aconytebooks.com // twitter.com/aconytebooks

This book is dedicated to everyone who has supported – and continues to support – my crazy writing dream.

The Barony of Forthyn
Ruined Tower
Blind Muir Forest
Fallowhearth

PROLOGUE

Darkness in the heart of the light, light in the heart of darkness.

The figure in the traveling cloak stood where she had not been a half-second earlier. The mist that had borne her to this place retreated, crawling down her body, and away into nothingness.

She gasped. The night air was cold and clear in her lungs, snapping her fully awake and banishing the last vestiges of the mist shroud from her mind. Her heart was racing in her chest. She felt sick. Was it always like this?

She looked around, noticing her surroundings properly for the first time. She knew instantly where the mist had taken her. The bone yard. Graven headstones surrounded her in neat rows, carved with branches, skulls and the other morbid icons of the god of death. Just a few months ago, such a place, wrapped up in the cold dark of night, would have given her pause. Now, though, there was a thrill to it. From this place of death, still and silent, good could yet flourish. She had convinced herself of that.

She drew back her cloak and hefted the heavy book in her hands. She'd sworn she would return it to its rightful owner. That was what she was doing tonight. It was why she had summoned up the hex nebulum, the mist shroud, why she had used it to slip past the guards, under the gates and through the town unnoticed. But first she had to know. She had to try. Just one incantation, and then she would give it back and beg forgiveness. She found the page, murmuring a simple oculus spell to enable her to read the words in the darkness.

The Black Invocation.

She hesitated. This moment was irreversible. If she did this, she knew her life could never be what it once was.

Was she being too hasty? Perhaps. But there was something wrong in this town, something creeping and scuttling and crawling, something malignant. Something with no concept of mercy. She could fight it with this power, though. She didn't even have to call upon her guards, upon the townsfolk, those honest people who would be expected to die for her. She simply had to raise the bodies of those whose spirits had long passed on. The evil would be overcome, and all without a single life lost. Surely that was worth the price she was about to pay? Surely that was worth giving up her inheritance, breaking the ancient laws. Distorting nature itself.

Besides, there was no other way she could be with her teacher. She loved her. It was an emotion she wouldn't give up, not now that she really knew what it meant. The life she had been given wasn't the one she wanted. She would make a new one, with her, starting tonight. She would give up her privileged existence, one she had never cared for, and start anew. Her teacher would understand. She knew she felt the same way.

She turned towards the crypt.

It was one of several that dotted the shrine's graveyard, a low stone structure with an iron door wrought in the likeness of rows of exposed bones. The gate was secured with a heavy padlock. She stepped towards it and raised her hands, her eyes closed. She felt the night's cold, drew it within, softly speaking words she'd carefully memorized. Part prayer, part incantation, each breath now turning to a frosty billow before her.

Ice clenched and hardened around the lock, spreading from her fingers. There was a dull crack as metal froze and warped. Finally, a splitting sound and the heavy thud of frozen metal striking dirt. The lock had cracked and broken apart.

She eased the gate open, trying to ignore its rusty protests. Within, five stone caskets lay undisturbed. The forebearers of the Fulchard family, interred together. She stepped back without entering, raising the book, settling it in the crook of her arm.

What she was doing might be a form of desecration, but it was necessary. Once she knew she had mastered the Black Invocation, she would no longer need the book. She could raise an army and save this town. Then, truly, her teacher would realize her worth. There was good in even the most forbidden of magics. Light in the dark. That was what she'd show everyone.

She began to speak, her voice low, taking care with each syllable. The words seemed to shudder and coil across the page before her. She felt a wind stir around the headstones, moaning through the small, open crypt. The power of Mortos, elemental death, rising to greet her.

But there was something off. It only took her a few lines to realize it. She faltered. One word, mispronounced. A frown crossed her face. She paused. Remember what you've been taught, she told herself. Remain calm. One wrong word doesn't end the world. A few might.

She began again. And again, a wrong word. Then another. Panic started to grow inside her, made worse by the fact that the heavy book seemed to be getting lighter in her hands. With a rush of horror, she realized that it was starting to dematerialize. Even as she tried to race through the arcane lines and bind the magic around her to the words, the pages began fading, growing incorporeal even as she gripped it.

The locus reditus! She was a fool! When she had first stolen the book and hidden it in her bed chamber, she had cast a location binding spell on it, a simple little hex that would return the book to where she had concealed it. She had feared that some servant or maid might discover it and take it away. In her decision to return it to its rightful owner tonight, she'd completely forgotten to unbind the spell. Now the book was vanishing right before her eyes.

"No," she began to murmur, then louder. "No, no, no!"

Her concentration was gone. But it wasn't too late. She knew the hex nebulum off by heart. She could still slip back into the castle, retrieve the book from where it had now returned, break the binding enchantment and leave. Return it to her lover. Make amends. As the last of the book vanished and she found herself clutching nothing but air, she attempted to marshal her thoughts once more.

But it was too late for that. She knew it the moment she heard the sound, cold and rasping, from nearby. What was done, was done. She had chosen her fate and there would be no going back now.

From inside the crypt she heard a low, slow scrape – the grinding of stone on stone, followed by a crack that reverberated through the suddenly quiet graveyard.

One of the crypt's coffins had just been opened.

CHAPTER ONE

For years now, Logan Lashley had fervently believed that his days of trouble were behind him. He had made a promise to himself – generally the only person he kept promises to – that the misadventures which had marred his youth would never be repeated. That was all in the past now, settled, nothing more than a source of free tavern ale from easily impressed merchant burgesses and city aldermen. He was retired, and glad of it.

There had been other promises too, most of them related to that first one. That he would enjoy his wealth. That he would never again draw his sword in anger. That he would never risk his life to save another being, living or near-dead. That he would finally get over his fear of spiders. That there would be no more adventures.

Adventures, misadventures. The differences were, in Logan's long experience, illdefined. Was his current situation – attempting to affect an air of outrage as the town guard took their time over his travel pass – an adventure or a misadventure? He feared the latter. Ever since he had awoken three weeks earlier to the clatter of the letter-carrier outside and discovered that scrap of paper slid beneath his townhouse's front door, a sense of foreboding had been stalking him. That mark, roughly scrawled on a scrap of hide parchment, always spelled out "trouble."

The man-at-arms standing by the town gate looked again from the travel pass to Logan, and back to the pass. He was typical of this cold, inhospitable corner of Terrinoth, a squint-eyed, patchy haired, pox-scarred brute in old chain mail and a worn leather hauberk. Logan was close enough to smell his stink – stale sweat and staler alcohol, mixed with the oil recently applied to his armor and the crude head of the heavy billhook hefted over his shoulder. The man sniffed, paused to scratch behind his ear like a dog and finally handed the pass back to Logan.

"Welcome to Highmont, Master Gelbin," he grunted, sounding anything but welcoming. He gestured to the second guard beside him, and the man released the bridle of Logan's horse. He'd been holding onto it as though afraid Logan was suddenly going to spur the thickset piebald past the gatehouse and into the town's alleyways. Imagine that. Logan Lashley, hero of Sudanya, Master of Sixspan Hall, held under suspicion! It would have been an outrage, if Logan had been traveling under his real name and if he had indeed not just been considering making a break for it.

No need for that, at least not yet. The men-at-arms parted, and Logan drew his cloak tight against the late morning chill before easing Ishbel in under the portcullis. Beyond it lay a narrow dirt street, sloping upwards, thick with townsfolk going to and from the noonday market stalls. The buildings crowded along the way, crooked and jostling. They were dark timber and pale wattle and daub for the most part, three or four stories high, many with thickly thatched roofs, a few with slate. Signs hung above narrow doorways declaring the trades practiced on the ground floors – a tailor, a cobbler, a dairy-seller, a physician.

Compared to the vast cloister streets of Greyhaven or the great monument city of Archaut it wasn't much, but Logan supposed the sight constituted civilization for this part of Terrinoth. Highmont was the capital of Forthyn, the most north-easterly of the baronies and the seat of its ruler, Baroness Adelynn. It was, in Logan's opinion, like Forthyn in general, a cold, windy, muddy place, and a damn sight less pleasant than either his townhouse in Greyhaven or his country estate on the edge of the Greatwood. It reminded Logan of the sorts of place he used to frequent in his younger days, which begged the question why he had come here at all. The slip of paper weighed heavy in his pocket.

He urged Ishbel up the street, the townsfolk hurriedly parting before him. For the most part they were strange-looking compared to the people he had grown accustomed to, living in western Terrinoth. They were shorter, burlier, fond of thick animal pelts and closecropped hair. Even here, in the heart of the barony, the influence of the northern clans was clear. To Logan, Highmont had the air of an outpost on the edge of the wilderness. Gods only knew what Upper Forthyn was like.

He passed a cluster of market stalls, catching the scents of fresh vegetables. Several sellers called out to him, clearly noticing his wealthy attire, but he ignored them. Past the stalls he had to duck beneath a low-hanging tanner's sign. Ahead, the turrets and crenellations of Highmont citadel, perched on the crag that formed the hill-town's peak, were just visible over the rooftops. He turned right along a side street after the tanner's workshop, easing Ishbel past half a dozen human tapmen and several Dunwarr dwarfs unloading casks from a pair of wagons. He didn't get much further.

The narrow passage was blocked by seven or eight figures, and more were gathering. They appeared to have spilled out from the back door of a thatched three-story tavern building. Logan heard raised voices, rebounding from the hunched buildings leaning over the street. He eased on Ishbel's reins. He'd barely been in Highmont for ten minutes. The last thing he needed was to get caught up in a tavern scrap that had spilled out onto the street.

Most of the figures ahead were men-at-arms, clad in mail, hauberks and sallets and carrying an assortment of polearms. One, presumably the ringleader, was wearing a tabard bearing the heraldry of Baroness Adelynn – an azure field emblazoned with a rampant roc, its golden claws and feathers a contrast to the stinking drabness of the surrounding street. The man in the tabard was the one speaking, addressing a figure at the center of the group.

"You think I'm an idiot? This is obviously a forgery! I should have you arrested right here and now, filthy adventurer!"

Logan didn't need to get much closer to make out the figure Tabard was addressing. He stood a good head taller than the men surrounding him, a rough hide pelt drawn round his broad shoulders, those heavy features set in a look of resignation. A spear was slung over his shoulder, and a long, curved dagger was sheathed at his waist. With a flicker of recognition, Logan realized the figure was an orc.

"I know your kind are dull, but are you deaf as well?" Tabard was saying, reaching out to push the orc's shoulder. The hulking figure held the man's gaze but didn't react. Tabard laughed, and the other men-at-arms joined in. A few of the tavern's patrons had stepped out to watch the confrontation, and the tapmen behind Logan had paused their unloading. Tabard, clearly relishing his growing audience, held up the scrap of paper he'd been carrying in one hand and dropped it into the dirt at the orc's feet.

"We don't want your kind around here, adventurer," he spat. "Not in Highmont, or in Forthyn. You bring trouble with you wherever you go. That's not a reputation Highmont needs in times like these. We'll take you to the main gate and see you on your way. Unless you've got other plans?"

The threat was clear, as was the orc's response, delivered with a level of clarity in the common tongue that visibly surprised the guards.

"If I fight, I kill. And I do not wish to kill you."

For a second everyone was silent. Then Tabard laughed. The rest joined in as he half turned to address his spectators.

"Well, great Kellos burn out my eyes! Some adventurer you are! Coward, more like!"

The orc remained silent. Tabard spun back abruptly, raising his gauntlet to strike. Logan's voice stopped him before the blow fell.

"Kruk, by all the gods, what do you think you're doing?"

The assembly froze and Logan, unnoticed until then, felt all of the tension packed into the narrow street switch to him.

Fortuna watch over him, but it was too late to go back now. He glared at the orc.

"Come here this instant, Kruk," he snapped, gesturing angrily. Nobody moved.

"You know this knave, sir?" Tabard asked slowly. Logan looked at him as though only noticing him for the first time.

"Gods, man, know him? Kruk here is my strong-arm. I sent him on a simple errand with my travel pass and here he is, carousing in a tavern. Typical! I do hope he hasn't been causing you any trouble, Captain…"

"Kloin," Tabard said slowly, looking him up and down. That's right, Logan thought. Take it all in. The knee-high riding boots, white doeskin britches, the fur-trimmed traveling cloak. Logan's attire might show a few days' wear and tear, but the quality was obvious. He was clearly a man of means and status. Not the sort of visitor worth antagonizing. Hopefully.

"Well met, Captain Kloin," he said, maintaining the practiced, arrogant tone and accent of a west Terrinoth noble. He had them on the back foot, and he had to keep it that way. He casually tossed his reins to another of the men-at-arms and dropped down from Ishbel's back. Then, lip curled, he parted the gathering and plucked up the scrap of paper Kloin had thrown at the orc's feet. As he bent forward, he made sure everyone got a glimpse of the bejeweled pommel of his sword and the fine blue-dyed cloth and silver trim of his tailored Rhynnian doublet.

"I should have known he would misplace this," he said as he stood back up, brandishing the grubby paper in the orc's face. "I told you to be careful!"

The orc remained impassive, gazing stoically back at Logan. He turned to Kloin.

"My pass, if you wish to see it, though it seems to be somewhat illegible now, I'm afraid. I'll have to procure a new one from the town watchmaster."

He made a show of the mud-smeared paper, letting the men-at-arms wonder whether he'd seen Kloin throw the pass in the dirt earlier. That seemed to do it. Kloin nodded.

"My apologies, sir. We didn't realize he was your strong-arm. We thought he was another vagabond looking to cause trouble. We've had too many of those here lately."

"An entirely understandable mistake," Logan said brusquely. "My thanks for finding him for me, captain."

As he spoke he made brief eye contact with the orc, before remounting Ishbel and taking back her reins. He snapped his fingers, summoning the orc from the midst of the men-at-arms.

"Come, Kruk! We've wasted enough time as it is. If I am late for my appointment with the master of the roc hatcheries, you will be sharing the horse's feed again for the rest of the week!"

After a moment's hesitation, the orc fell in alongside Ishbel. Logan fished in the heavy-looking purse hanging from his saddle's pommel and tossed a silver crown towards Kloin, which the captain caught deftly.

"A token of my thanks, for your assistance," Logan said, touching his spurs to his mount's flanks. "Rest assured I shall put in a good word with the baroness when I next sup with her."

He'd made it a good ten paces, the orc still sticking by his side, before Kloin answered.

"Sir?"

Logan fought the urge to dig his spurs in, wondering if he'd overdone the act. He twisted in the saddle.

"Captain?"

"Be careful," Kloin said, examining the coin. "These are troubled times in Forthyn. Some of the good people of Highmont may not be quite as… accepting of outsiders as I am. Adventurers aren't welcome."

Logan managed to summon up a smile, silently damning the arrogant, unwelcoming bastard. "Don't worry, captain. Neither of us intend to outstay our welcome."

He said nothing to the orc until they had turned up the next street and then paused in the shadows of an alleyway. Logan dismounted, tied the uncomplaining Ishbel to a hitching post at the alley's entrance, and paused to check the street beyond was quiet before turning to the orc looming behind him.

"I believe this is yours," he said, fishing into his cloak's pocket. He drew out his travel pass, then the dirty one he'd taken off Kloin, and beneath it found the scrap of paper that had brought him halfway across Terrinoth. On it, written in a heavy but legible hand, was a short note. *Remember Sudreyr. The White Roc Tavern, Highmont*. Beneath it was a signature, an X bisected by a vertical line – the mark of a pathfinder of the Broken Plains. Logan held the paper out.

"You came," the orc grunted, looking down at the note he had written without taking it.

"And lucky you are, too," Logan said. "Fighting seven men-at-arms all at the same time is a bit much at your age, Durik."

The orc lunged. Before he could react, Logan found

himself being crushed in a fearsome bearhug. He wheezed, accidentally inhaling the orc's musky armpit, and gave the big pathfinder a pat on the back.

"Easy there, '*Kruk*,'" he managed. Durik broke the hug and held Logan at arms' length, golden eyes surveying him in the alleyway's fetid gloom.

"You have grown old, little rogue," he said. "And you are still a skinny wretch."

"That's skinny, *rich* wretch to you, pathfinder," Logan corrected, returning the unclaimed letter to his pocket. "I was quite happily enjoying my retirement before your little message. All this way just for insults. I see you haven't changed!"

Durik laughed at the faux outrage and gave Logan a meaty slap on the shoulder. "And you still talk too fast! It will be just like old times."

"That's what I'm worried about," Logan said. "Are you going to tell me just what 'it' is? Why did you bring me all the way out here? And how did you find me in the first place?"

"How did Pathfinder Durik, chief scout of the Guk'gor tribe and first master of the Wilderness, find you?" Durik echoed, bearing his tusks in a grin. Logan pouted.

"Then at least tell me I haven't traveled all this way just to swap old stories, O great pathfinder? Actually, no. Please tell me that's exactly what I've traveled all this way for, and that there won't be any sort of harebrained adventure that's finally going to finish us both off?"

"It's a job," Durik answered.

"I rather feared it would be."

"If you feared, you would not be here, little rogue."

"What does it involve?"

"I will show you. Get back on your horse."

Logan huffed but did as the orc suggested, untying Ishbel as Durik fondled the horse's muzzle and fed her an apple he produced from a tusker-pelt satchel. Ishbel crunched noisily as Logan clambered into the saddle.

"If we get accosted by any more pea-skull men-at-arms, let me do the talking," he said. "How you even managed to gain entry to a town like this is beyond me."

"The plains and forest and mountains are my domain," Durik said, making way so Logan could walk Ishbel into the street. "But even in a town like this, it is easier to travel unseen than you might think. Make for the castle."

"The castle," Logan repeated in surprise. "You couldn't even lay low in a tavern by the east gate without being hounded by a pack of guards. How far do you think you'll get up the esplanade?"

"I have a letter," Durik said.

"The one that oaf of a captain assumed was a forgery? The one that's now crumpled and caked with mud? How did you get a travel pass within the walls anyway? The town watch doesn't exactly seem welcoming to humans, let alone an old Broken Plain nomad with more scars than teeth."

"I was summoned here," the orc replied simply.

"You were summoned to Forthyn?" Logan asked, his voice colored by his surprise. They were climbing the street once more, passing a small yard where a set of wheelwright's apprentices were hammering iron strakes. Logan had to force himself to keep his voice down.

"Who summoned you?" he demanded.

"Baroness Adelynn."

"The ruler of one of the twelve baronies of Forthyn summoned you, a Broken Plains orc, express to her citadel?"

"She summoned a master tracker and a hero of the lost city of Sudanya," Durik corrected.

"Well no wonder those men-at-arms thought the letter was a forgery. Kellos's flames, what have I gotten myself into?"

Durik said nothing, walking alongside Ishbel. A sudden thought occurred to Logan, one that caused an unexpected mixture of both worry and hope.

"Is Dezra here?" he asked. "Or Ulma?"

"I sent the same letter to all of you," Durik said. "The little alchemist responded first. She arrived here three days ago and left yesterday to Upper Forthyn. She is traveling ahead of us."

"For the love of all the gods, what is there for us in Upper Forthyn? It's the only place I can image that's more inhospitable than here. And what about Dezra?"

"The sorceress has not responded," Durik said. "I fear my letter did not find her."

"Not such a mighty tracker after all, then?" Logan asked. Durik said nothing.

To the left of them the street had opened up into a square of leveled ground, set before the arching windows and impressive clock tower of what Logan took to be Highmont's main guildhall. The space was occupied by the afternoon market, an artificial town in miniature – open-sided wagons and portable stalls formed little streets and alleyways, bedecked in pelts and rugs, dashed through with colorful silks and exotic embroidery. The air was pungent with the smells of fresh meat and fish, spices and manure, and filled with the chatter of hagglers, the cries of sellers and the lowing of cattle from the livestock pens. It was, Logan considered, the perfect spectacle of a noisy, smelly, dirty provincial town.

They were forced to make way for a fresh herd of tuskers being driven down the street, the undersides of their shaggy red pelts matted with muck, their breath steaming in the cold sunlight. They were being chivvied along by a pair of northern clansmen, both youths, their foreheads marked with blue woad. They brandished sticks at the beasts and shouted at them in a language Logan didn't understand. He saw the trio of town guardsman standing by the entrance to the square eyeing the boys darkly, and was abruptly thankful of their presence – if Highmont's men-at-arms were considering their dislike for the northern clans they were at least too busy to be doing the same towards the likes of Durik. Logan set Ishbel back on the street after the herd had passed by, grimacing at how their hooves had churned the dirt and dung into a quagmire.

The upper slopes of the town lay ahead. Highmont sat upon a steep hill that gave the town its name – the high mont, or mound. The streets closest to the wall that circled the hill's base were, typically, the poorest. The higher a traveler climbed, the wealthier the neighborhoods he found himself in. Here, in the shadow of the pinnacle crag that bore the town's citadel, the houses were wider and more regular, with slate roofs and exterior wall carvings decorated with rocs and drakes or hunting hounds and deer. A few were even built from stone. The crowds were thinner, and Logan noted a more genteel style of dress – nothing to match his own quality, of course, but garb more befitting the denizens of one of the baronial capitals of Terrinoth. A few passers-by even nodded to him, though they gave Durik a wide birth. For the most part, orcs in Lower Forthyn served as bodyguards, enforcers and hired muscle. That at least gave them a believable dynamic to work with. The last thing he needed was word getting out that Durik the Pathfinder had been spotted abroad in Forthyn with a handsome old human rogue.

Logan had almost started to relax, flashing a smile at two young women snatching wide-eyed glances at the orc. Then he spotted the castle esplanade ahead. It was a cleared, cobbled space leading up the citadel's crag, a mustering point or kill zone depending on the needs of the town's garrison. To the right of it stood a squat tower, the guardhouse and headquarters of the town watch. Ahead and above, the citadel itself loomed, sheer gray walls above a sheer gray rock face, flanked by circular towers and overhung with machicolations and wooden hoardings. The heraldic pennants of Highmont, Forthyn and the town's guilds and burgesses fluttered from its ramparts, while a silk banner bearing the personal arms of Baroness Adelynn blazed in the autumnal sunlight above the keep that crowned the crag. The gatehouse at the end of the esplanade had its drawbridge lowered over a sheer chasm carved into the approaching slope, and its portcullis was raised. There were, however, rather a lot of men-at-arms and watchmen between them and the open gateway. Logan gulped.

"My travel pass doesn't extend to the damned citadel," he muttered to Durik. "How are we supposed to get in there with only your ruined piece of paper?"

"I thought you would talk us in," Durik said, as though it was the most obvious thing in the world.

"For the love of Fortuna," Logan snapped. "You're the one who received a personal summons from the baroness, not me! I'm just a very wealthy, very retired gentleman of fortune. I don't even know what I'm doing here… Ah, captain!"

The last words were uttered to a man-at-arms who had just stepped out of the guardhouse as they passed by. It was Kloin. He was wearing a smile that looked decidedly unfriendly.

"Well met again, Lord Durik," he said, falling in alongside as they carried on up the esplanade. "It is Durik, is it not? That's the name I seem to recall from your pass. You said you gave it to the orc, but it does belong to you, doesn't it? That's what you said?"

The captain carried on before Logan could conjure a response, his arrogant tone forcing the rogue to wrestle with the urge to lash out at him. "Funny name though, if you don't mind me saying, sir. Sounds a little bit… orcish to me. If you don't mind me saying."

Logan tried to mask his fear with a glare, fishing in his cloak pocket for the pass, pretending to fumble it while he made sure the dirt had fully obscured Durik's name. He'd been regretting traveling under a false identity since reaching Highmont – several rather rampant parties of debt collectors on the road east had made the ruse a necessity. Now it had become over-complicated.

"It's Dur-Roc, captain," he said imperiously. "You should remember a name like that. My mother is second cousin to your baroness. Not that you'd be able to read the name now, thanks to your earlier clumsiness."

He waved the ruined paper in Kloin's face. The captain was still smiling.

"My mistake, sir. It's strange though. Downright unusual. I got back to the wardroom just a few moments ago. It just so happened that the last shift from the town gate had also recently returned. A few of the lads said there was a gentleman who'd just arrived at the town, a curious sort of fellow. His pass said his name was Gelbin. Not from around here either. West Terrinoth type. Wealthy, but not born to it, apparently. A bit vulgar, you know the sort. Almost rogue-like. Come to think of it, the description sounded a lot like you, sir."

The drawbridge was barely a dozen paces away, the portcullis-fanged maw of the gatehouse over it. Kloin put his hand on Ishbel's bridle, bringing her to a stop. A trio of men-at-arms, heavily armored in plate mail and carrying maces, began to approach from the gate's archway.

"This is an outrage," Logan began to say, deciding his only hope was to push the "furious nobleman" trick. Kloin spoke through him.

"I don't think your name is Durik," he said. "That may be your orc friend's name, but it's not yours. As a matter of fact, I don't think it's Gelbin either."

"Trouble, captain?" one of the armored men-at-arms asked as he approached. Kloin's smile broadened and he held Logan's gaze as he answered.

"I hope so."

"Listen, captain," Logan said, dropping the act and leaning over in his saddle, almost conspiratorial. He lowered his voice. "You're on the brink of making a very unfortunate mistake. Unfortunate for you, that is. Not me. Let us pass and we'll forget both this little incident and the one back down in the town."

"I like being intimidated even less than I like being tricked," Kloin replied, his smile disappearing like a spring frost. "I don't know who you are, or what you hope to achieve by talking your way into the citadel, but I fully intend to find out. Probably as slowly and as painfully as possible."

He turned to the men-at-arms who had approached and pointed at Logan.

"Seize them both!"

Logan's hand dropped to the hilt of his sword, and Durik made to draw his dagger, tusks bared. That was as far as anyone got before an angry shout cut the air.

"Kloin!"

Logan saw the captain close his eyes in a look of pure frustration, struggling to contain his own relief as the man turned towards the citadel's open gate. There, flanked by several more men-at-arms, stood an aged woman. She was tall and gaunt, draped in the furs of a thick tusker pelt, the garment drawn over what looked like several layers of thin, gossamer silk. Her hair was silver-gray like her clothing, and she wore it long, hanging down almost to her waist. Her features were severe, haughty, with an air of nobility. Logan suspected that in her youth she had been both very beautiful and very used to having her every word obeyed. He had no doubt that the latter was still the case.

"What are you doing, Captain Kloin?" she demanded in a firm voice, striding out from the gatehouse's shadow and across the drawbridge.

"Lady Damhán!" Kloin exclaimed, forcing a smile. "I

thought you were attending the noon guild council?"

"You make it sound as though you didn't expect to see me, Kloin," the woman said. "Or that you wish you hadn't. Why have you waylaid the baroness's guests?"

"I didn't realize they were the baroness's guests," Kloin said, his expression closing up. It was clear where this was going. Logan couldn't quite keep the smile off his face.

"Did you not show him the pass I gave you?" the woman demanded of Durik. She had reached them across the drawbridge, and, despite her apparent frailty, looked the orc in the eye as she spoke. She was almost as tall as he was.

"The captain struggled to believe we are who we say we are," Logan said, glancing sideways at the helpless Kloin. The woman turned her gaze on him, and it was all he could do to hold it.

"It is difficult to judge just how great a transgression that is, given that I don't know who you are myself," she said. "Though the evidence points towards Logan Lashley, former rogue, now master of Sixspan Hall. Am I correct?"

"At your service, my lady," Logan responded, inclining his head while wondering just what had given him away. He needed to have a word with Durik about sharing his identity too readily with his employers. The last thing he needed was one of those damned debt collectors picking up his trail again.

"My name is Lady Damhán," the woman said. "And if you are quite done being harassed by the captain here, we have a council meeting to interrupt."

Without another word, Damhán turned and strode back across the drawbridge. Logan glanced at Durik, who shrugged.

"Logan Lashley," Kloin said, his voice incredulous. "The Logan Lashley of Sixspan Hall? One of the Borderland Four?"

"If you want to hear some of my adventure stories, captain, you now know where to find me," Logan said, patting Kloin on the helmet before spurring Ishbel forward across the drawbridge. Durik followed him.

"I'll see you again, Logan," Kloin called out after him, his voice dark. Logan didn't turn, but made an obscene gesture over his shoulder. The gatehouse's shadows swallowed him up.

CHAPTER TWO

Durik paused inside the citadel's gatehouse while Logan dismounted. The castle's courtyard was a small square of packed dirt, sloping upwards to the pinnacle rock that bore the central keep. To the right stood a row of wooden stalls – stables and livestock pens, Durik assumed. To the left was a log barracks cut from Forthyn pine, set against the inside of the curtain wall.

A boy from the castle's stables took Logan's horse. Durik waited for Logan to fix his cloak, while Lady Damhán watched.

"I take it Pathfinder Durik has told you why you are here, Master Lashley?" she asked.

"No, actually," Logan responded, refastening the cloak's expensive-looking clasp. "No one's told me anything, more's the pity!"

"I thought it would be best coming from the one who sought me out in the first place," Durik said.

"That may be," Lady Damhán replied, seeming to ponder the orc's words for a moment before turning on her heel and striding towards the keep.

"Come," she called back to them. "Now that your companion has arrived, pathfinder, the baroness will want to see you both in person."

"Didn't that horrid captain say she was sitting in council?" Logan asked, hurrying to catch up.

"He did, and she is," Damhán responded without slowing her pace. "And I should be with her. But her instructions were clear. I was to remain vigilant for your arrival and inform her immediately, council session or not. We have been waiting for you for some time, Master Lashley."

"I won't deny 'master' has a fine ring to it, but please, call me Logan," he said, giving her a winning smile. Damhán didn't respond.

Durik followed behind them both, up the short, steep path to the keep's doorway, wondering as he went if he had done the right thing. Sending letters to Logan, Ulma and Dezra had been a gamble. The task he had been hired for called for speed – delaying over two weeks hadn't pleased the baroness. But Durik had made the inclusion of his old friends a non-negotiable clause of his employment, and thankfully Lady Damhán had spoken in favor of the idea of including them. It seemed that if Baroness Adelynn was willing to purchase the services of the most renowned orc pathfinder in Terrinoth, she was also happy to have the entire Borderland Four working for her. She had already told Durik she would spare nothing for this task.

Damhán led them into the entrance hall of Highmont's keep, a chilly, towering stone space whose upper limits were crisscrossed by spars and a timber walkway. A pair of servants hurried past with baskets full of dirty linen. Damhán carried on to a wooden staircase at the hall's far end and up to a second level. This one had a timber floor covered with pelt rugs, daylight shafting in through a trio of arrow slits in the outer wall. There was a door opposite the stairway, and a fire burned low in a large hearth set across the room, the carved stone roc above it blackened by centuries of smoke.

"Wait here," Lady Damhán ordered. She opened the far door, and Durik caught a snatch of conversation before it thudded shut behind her.

"Well, she's a charmer," Logan said, moving to stand by the fire.

"She is the reason we are here," Durik responded. "The Lady Damhán was the one who recommended my skills to the baroness."

"And who recommended mine?" Logan asked.

"I did. Lady Damhán agreed."

"Does that mean the baroness didn't?"

"I think we're about to find out."

Logan grunted and looked down with a rueful expression at his mud-splattered boots Unnoticed, Durik smiled. He may be silver-haired now, a little thinner and a little more stooped, but Logan Lashley was still the same rogue the orc had known during his adventures across Terrinoth. Those days in Sudanya, in the sunbaked ruins and the dark, creeping, infested tunnels beneath, had bound them, entwined the strands of their fate into a single, strong cord. Durik had known he would come as soon as the letter reached him. Even so, privately he rejoiced at seeing him again. It had been years, and each one had felt longer than the last.

He moved to stand by Logan in front of the fireplace, still

smiling to himself – the physical differences between the two of them had only become more pronounced with age. Logan was the image of self-made Terrinoth wealth, while Durik looked every inch the Broken Plains tracker, still broad and thickly muscled, his thighs and upper arms ringed with Guk'gor knot tattoos, shoulders draped in pelts and feather fetishes. He wondered if Logan had noticed the more subtle changes the years had brought on – his charcoal-gray skin was paler and leatherier, and his topknot had turned snowy white. Then there were the scars. Those, at least, he was proud of.

"We make for unlikely friends, little rogue," he said. Logan looked up at him and narrowed his eyes.

"Don't get maudlin on me, pathfinder. This place is depressing enough as it is."

"You have grown soft."

"Everyone is soft compared to you," Logan responded, his gaze turning to the dying embers before him. He suddenly looked very old. Durik felt a pang of regret. Perhaps it had been wrong to summon him here, to drag him away from his own hearth and home, the place he had earned with gold won all those years ago. Durik suppressed the sudden guilt. He could not do this alone. There were some wildernesses even too vast for him to track, and that was without considering the manmade obstacles he expected to face in the coming days. Orcs were rarely welcome in the region they would be traveling to.

"How is Ulma?" Logan asked abruptly, as though reading his thoughts. "I know we didn't part on the best of terms, but did she really have to go all the way to Upper Forthyn rather than meet me here?"

"I told you, she arrived before you," Durik said. "My letter found her just across the border, in Dhernas."

"Still conducting all sorts of ridiculous experiments, I imagine? I'm truly shocked that she hasn't blown herself to pieces yet."

"She… has not changed a great deal. The baroness requested that she begin investigating while I waited for you. She has gone on ahead."

"Investigating what?" Logan demanded. Before Durik could speak, he heard the sound of a raised voice from beyond the door Lady Damhán had passed through. The words were indistinct, but clearly angry. They both exchanged a glance.

"Sounds like the gray lady is pissing someone off," Logan muttered.

"Lady Damhán is a good ally," Durik said. "Without her counsel none of us would be here."

"I'm not sure that's a good thing, Durik," Logan said. Seconds later the door swung open. A guard in the baroness's livery stepped outside and stood to attention as a stream of figures exited past him. There were about a dozen of them, all aging men, a few of them portly. They were well dressed in padded, embroidered shirts or doublets trimmed with fur, feathered bonnets and chaperons decorating their heads. Logan offered those that glanced his way a bow, while Durik watched them impassively. Their looks were vehement.

"I'm guessing those are the burgesses," Logan hissed to Durik as the last of them began to descend the stairwell.

"They seem… unhappy," Durik responded.

"They are unhappy because I have just curtailed their weekly council hearing with the baroness," Lady Damhán said, standing in the doorway like a gray specter guarding her ancestral home.

"You may enter," she went on, beckoning them inside. Logan glanced up at Durik before following him through the door. The guard closed it behind them.

The chamber beyond was clearly built to impress. A vaulted ceiling soared over a long wooden table flanked by high-backed chairs, carved in the likeness of rampant rocs. The walls were hung with tapestries depicting scenes of hunting and battle alongside instances of Forthyn's history that Durik didn't recognize – an elf and a human being wed beneath a half moon, a dragon struck down by a golden-haired archer, a crooked tower sat high amidst mountain peaks. Daylight shone into the chamber from its far end, where blue drapes half hid what looked like a balcony jutting out from the keep's north face. Durik had been in the chamber once before, when he had first met with Baroness Adelynn. He glanced sideways at Logan. The old rogue didn't seem taken by his new surrounds – his eyes were on the two figures standing at the opposite end of the table.

One was an obese, bearded man clad in a short red jacket that bulged around his ample gut. He wore a gold-embroidered cape over his left shoulder and had a small, fur bonnet perched on the side of his head. He was speaking to the second figure, a woman, as tall and stately as Damhán, clad in a rich brown and gold suircoat and skirts that trailed to the floor. About her shoulders was a heavy mantle of white roc feathers that shone brilliantly in the light streaming between the drapes behind her. Her hair, piled up around her head, was the color of hazelnut dashed through with streaks of white, while her features were pale, full-lipped and strong. There was a sword at her hip. She turned gray eyes on Logan and Durik as Lady Damhán announced them.

Durik bowed, and Logan hurried to do likewise – clearly the rogue had already worked out who he was being addressed to.

"The Baroness Adelynn," Lady Damhán declared.

"Welcome to my halls once again, Pathfinder Durik," the baroness said. Her voice was clear and firm. Like Damhán's, it seemed well accustomed to command. Durik merely nodded.

"And a new welcome to you, Logan Lashley of Sixspan Hall," Adelynn continued. "I understand you have only recently arrived in Highmont? I hope the town and the citadel are both to your liking?"

"A fine break from the travails of the western baronies, my lady," Logan said, offering another bow, this time accompanied by a smile. "I am at your service."

"Then I count myself fortunate indeed," Adelynn said. "No doubt you are weary from your travels. Food and lodgings will be provided for you immediately."

"And they will both be very welcome," Logan said. "Though, if I may, I crave to speak of more pressing matters first."

"You refer to the reason for your being here," Adelynn said. "Is it true you came all this way on just a few words from the pathfinder?"

"A few words from a trusted friend," Logan said. "I would travel beyond the Sea of Smoke for Durik. We have saved each another's lives on more occasions than I could count."

Durik tried not to roll his eyes and set about mentally totaling up how often he'd been saved by Logan. Once.

Twice if he counted the incident with the Uthuk Y'llan in the Thalian Glades. Logan was still speaking.

"I won't deny it though, my lady, the question of just what secretive summons brought me here has been weighing heavily on my mind."

Adelynn nodded. "If you do not yet know what it is then I can only assume the rumors have yet to reach west of the Shadow Peaks," she said. "That, at least, is a comfort to me."

"The rumors, my lady?"

Adelynn glanced at Lady Damhán, then spoke once more to Logan and Durik.

"Come with me." She turned, and, accompanied by the fat, red-clad man, strode out onto the balcony. Durik, Logan and Damhán followed, Durik having to duck through the blue drapes. He realized immediately that the space beyond was less of a balcony, and more of an eyrie.

A large, semi-circular stone platform jutted from the upper north face of Highmont keep, soaring out over the crag the tower was perched upon. Below, the streets of the town sloped away, row after row of rooftops and smoking chimney stacks interspersed with the grander building of the golden dome of the Temple of Kellos. They all gave way in turn to the outer wall, where banners of blue and golden silk fluttered, and beyond it, to the green and brown patchwork quilt of fields and forests that formed central Forthyn. In the far distance, hazed to a dark smudge, stood the southern edge of Blind Muir Forest.

The wind hit the group as they stepped out, snatching at cloaks and hair and ruffling Baroness Adelynn's feather mantle. Only Durik didn't draw his pelt closer, inhaling deeply as he savored the chill. Up here the air was clear and free – Durik hated the stale interior of any building, hated anything that confined him and kept him from the wilderness he called home. The two weeks he'd spent waiting for Logan had been difficult, but up here he could almost taste the freedom.

"You know what this space is for?" Adelynn asked Logan.

"I could guess, my lady," he replied. "It has been many years since I last saw the creature your barony is famed for."

"I suspect that wait will end today," the baroness said, stepping to the edge of the platform. Durik noticed there were things scattered across the stone underfoot – splinters of broken bone. He knelt and picked one up, examining it. A slender rabbit rib, gouged by claws. Or, more accurately, talons.

"You recognize the marks, pathfinder?" Durik realized Adelynn was addressing him. He simply nodded, placing the bone back down and straightening up.

The group stood in silence for a while. Logan caught Durik's eye, clearly trying to prompt him into asking the baroness just how long they would have to stand out in the biting wind. Durik let him wait. It was clear the baroness wanted to make an impression – she wouldn't have dissolved a session with the town's wealthiest burgesses otherwise. Besides, prying ears were plentiful in any barony capital. Anything they said here belonged only to the wind.

After a while he caught a cry on the wind. He looked up. The sound had been too distant for the others to hear but Durik, attuned to the sounds of the wild by decades of tracking, recognized it instantly.

A second cry pierced the autumn wind. This time the others heard it. Logan started to look apprehensive and edged back to where Damhán and the fat man were standing by the council chamber entrance. Durik noticed that Adelynn was smiling, though the expression was a sad one.

A shape, larger than a man, darted around the east face of the keep, razor-fast. Durik heard Logan give out a little yelp of shock as it swooped down towards the balcony. At the last instant it splayed and beat its great wings, the air whipping at Durik's pelts and snatching at the baroness's skirts. The cold sunlight gleamed brilliantly from the golden feathers of the great creature as it alighted on the balcony's edge, its talons latching onto the scarred stone.

"By the glory of Kellos," Logan stammered, cringing back from the avian beast. It resembled a giant golden eagle, its gaze equal parts haughty and curious as it twitched from Durik to Logan. It was a roc, and Durik knew that, despite the fact that it was as large as he was, it was still only an adolescent.

The creature cried out once more, the ear-aching sound carrying out over Highmont. Baroness Adelynn moved to its side and reached up, running her fingers through the thick plumage around its neck.

"Her name is Amara," Adelynn said, looking back at Durik and Logan. "After my grandmother. She is almost fully grown now. In two weeks, maybe three, she will go to the eyries amidst the Howling Giant Hills, and there find a mate. Gerold, come."

The last words she directed at the fat man, who advanced with obvious unease. Durik realized that Amara had something clutched in her talons – a ragged carcass, slowly oozing blood out over the balcony's edge. Judging by the strands of matted wool caught in the roc's lower feathers, the remains belonged to a sheep.

Gerold stooped with some difficulty before the great avian and then, after glancing up as though afraid she was going to decapitate him with a swipe of her beak, began to examine the sheep's remains.

"The blood makes it difficult to say," he muttered, red-faced from the effort of straining forward without getting too close to the roc. Adelynn looked unimpressed, so he dared lean a little nearer. "The wool appears to be blue-dyed, my lady."

"Whose herds are blue-dyed?" Adelynn asked.

"Alderman Dalin's, I believe," Damhán answered before Gerold could speak. Throughout the exchange Amara had remained perfectly still, ignoring Gerold. It was looking unblinkingly at Durik. He returned the creature's gaze steadily, then offered a slight nod. Amara clacked her beak, making Gerold rise sharply and retreat.

"Make a note, Gerold," Adelynn ordered him. "The next livestock reimbursement is to go to Alderman Dalin. Twenty crowns and six ewes, not too old. You may use the citadel's own stock. Be sure the expenditure is fully accounted for, or I will have the burgesses complaining to me again about the misappropriation of the town's market taxes."

"Yes, my lady," Gerold said with a bow. Adelynn patted the roc again.

"Amara, feast," she said.

Durik watched as the roc deposited the sheep's remains on the stone beneath her and snatched it up again in her beak. Throwing her head back, she began to gulp down the carcass whole. Adelynn stepped away from her as she did so, drawing

Durik's and Logan's eyes.

"Since I became baroness, I have helped to raise eight rocs from hatchlings to maturity, continuing the work my family has performed for centuries," she said. "The roc is a sacred creature in Forthyn. They are our friends and our protectors. Those eight hatchlings are like children to me. Do you have any children, Logan Lashley?"

"Probably a few I don't know about," Logan said, clearly still preoccupied by the sight of the roc hacking down its lunch right behind the baroness.

"To lose a child is the cruelest blow a mother can suffer," Adelynn continued. "And I have lately had the misfortune to feel that pain. My child has been stolen away from me."

"Someone has taken one of the rocs?" Logan asked. Durik caught his eye and shook his head. Adelynn's expression was almost unreadable, but Durik could sense a deep-seated, tightly controlled grief as she spoke.

"A roc, dear though they are, I might hope to replace. But not this child. I speak of my own daughter, Master Lashley. My only daughter, Kathryn, heiress to the Barony of Forthyn."

Durik could tell how surprised Logan was by his lack of a sharp response. The baroness continued.

"Last year was the twenty-fifth summer since Kathryn was born. As is tradition, she was granted new estates to oversee in Upper Forthyn. Handling their day-to-day running has been used as a means to prepare the barony's heirs for generations. Three weeks ago, however, Kathryn disappeared. We believe she has been kidnapped."

Silence followed Adelynn's words, before Logan finally found his voice.

"You have my sincerest condolences, my lady. May I ask who is responsible for this outrageous act?"

"We believe the northern clans had a hand in it," Adelynn said. "Relations have become… increasingly strained of late."

Logan looked at Durik, but the orc kept his response to himself. He had already advised the baroness that he didn't believe the clans were responsible – they had nothing to gain from snatching her daughter, and in the weeks since her disappearance no one from the clans had come forward. She was convinced though, and Durik didn't yet have any evidence to prove otherwise.

"If that is true then they will be brought to task," Logan said. "You have my word!"

"Punishment is my prerogative, Master Lashley," the baroness said. "Confine your word to the return of my daughter. That is what truly matters to me."

"Of course, my lady," Logan said, offering another bow. Behind Adelynn, Amara had finished devouring her prey. The great beast clacked down from the edge of the balcony and ruffled her feathers, lowering her head for Adelynn to stroke, like a child seeking attention. Durik resisted the temptation to also reach out and stroke her plumage – such an act would be disrespectful towards the roc's mistress.

"My lady Damhán and a small number of my personal guard will accompany you north," Adelynn said as she ran her fingers through Amara's crest. "She makes no pretense to advise you on the skills that saw you hired, but she will act as my eyes and ears during the search and will report back to me regularly. You may also find her particular abilities of use."

Durik watched Logan struggle to mask his unhappiness at

the prospect of Lady Damhán's companionship. For her own part, Damhán remained inscrutable.

"I suppose it best we discuss the matter of payment," Adelynn went on. "As I have already discussed with Pathfinder Durik, I intend to spare no expense–"

"Baroness, with all due respect," Logan said, daring to interrupt, "being of assistance to you in this gravest of matters is reward enough. Knowing I am serving the future of the barony and of Terrinoth is the greatest prize I could ever hope for."

Durik raised an eyebrow. In his youth Logan had harbored a hunger for wealth that would have given a Dunwarr dwarf pause. The orc supposed that, after years of actually possessing gold, it had lost its allure. Adelynn allowed the merest hint of a smile to break through her controlled expression.

"Very well. If you have no more immediate questions, then Gerold will show you to your chambers. I have ordered lodgings to be prepared within the keep, and a luncheon will be waiting for you. I must ask, however, that you depart tomorrow morning. We have already lost precious time awaiting your arrival, Master Lashley."

"Time I intend to make back with all haste," Logan said. "If you might indulge me, I have one more question though. What estates were given to your daughter in Upper Forthyn? Where was she last seen?"

Adelynn glanced at Lady Damhán. She was the one who responded.

"The town of Fallowhearth, Master Lashley. That is where our search begins."

CHAPTER THREE

Logan had been relieved to hear the baroness was providing personal lodgings in the keep, rather than somewhere out in Highmont's provincial streets. As it was, the chamber proved draughty and damp and the bed coarse, but he still slept better than he had done since leaving Sixspan. Durik had been given a hastily converted guard room next door, a slight which the orc, typically, didn't seem to mind at all. They ate a supper of stewed rabbit together and a breakfast of bread and cheese the next morning, brought by a young servant boy.

It was still dark outside as Logan followed Durik down and out into the castle's courtyard, fastening his cloak as he went. He wasn't relishing the thought of a full day's riding. In fact, he wasn't relishing the thought of doing anything he had promised to do the day before. Turning down the baroness's offer of payment had brought on a gratifying sense of his own wealth, but it was one thing showing off to old money, another agreeing to do their dirty work. He had briefly considered stealing away in the middle of the night, though he had eventually decided against it. Pride truly was a curse, but he also had no desire try to outrun a roc, not at his age.

The roc started to seem like the better bet almost as soon as he reached the courtyard. Damhán was already there and mounted, riding sidesaddle on a great, mottled gray steed. Together they looked like an apparition in the torchlit darkness. Unexpectedly though, Lady Damhán's presence wasn't the worst thing to greet Logan that morning.

"Hello again," Captain Kloin said with a horrid, petty smile that Logan felt was becoming far too familiar. He was mounted alongside Damhán, flanked by half a dozen of his crooked-nosed, pig-stinking men-at-arms. For a split-second Logan thought they were going to arrest him. Then he realized his predicament was even more unfortunate.

"We are to provide a personal guard for Lady Damhán, by order of Baroness Adelynn," Kloin said when he saw the look on Logan's face. "Needless to say, I don't think the baroness trusts her noble advisor with a pair of vagabonds such as yourself. She will have a more fitting escort."

"Truly?" Logan asked, looking at Damhán. "Him, of all people?"

"Play nicely, children," Damhán said without a hint of humor. Kloin urged his horse over to Logan, stopping beside him and looking down at him imperiously.

"I told you I would see you again," he said.

"You must be a prophet, Captain Kloin," Logan answered, injecting every ounce of sarcasm he could into the words. "Perhaps you can tell us what has happened to the baroness's daughter, and save us all a long trip north?"

"Oh, I'm rather looking forward to our little adventure

together. Joining the Borderlands Four. Or three, if the rumors I hear are true. Where's your final companion? That witch the stories all talk so highly of? Dezra the Vile?"

Logan felt Durik's strong hand clamp over his shoulder. He forced himself to take a breath, and then did the most vicious thing he could think of – he smiled back at Kloin.

"We are going to have such fun, you and I," he said.

A horse had been provided for Durik, a heavy black stallion. Usually such mounts didn't mix well with orcs, but then Logan knew Durik was no ordinary orc. The pathfinder spent a few moments murmuring in the ear of the beast and feeding it an apple, and the stallion made no protest when he mounted it. Logan did likewise with Ishbel, gritting his teeth as he hauled himself up into the saddle. His bones were stiff and cold this early in the morning, but damned if he was going to ask for help in front of this particular assembly.

"Kloin, lead us out," Lady Damhán ordered. The captain cast a last venomous look at Logan, then turned his horse towards the gatehouse. The rest fell in behind him – Damhán first, then Durik, Logan, and the remaining men-at-arms, the last leading a packhorse laden with food panniers and a chest that Logan assumed belonged to Damhán.

The streets were deserted, but for a single drunkard who stumbled from an alleyway near the north gate and was almost flattened by Kloin. Beyond the town walls, a rough, rugged countryside was slowly being brought to life by the gathering dawn. Frost bristled across tall grass and skeletal hedgerows and gave recently harvested fields a tough, hardpacked appearance. The clouds were low and gray, and stayed that way throughout the day.

They traveled east first, towards the wicked peaks of the Dunwarr Mountains, then picked up the crossroads between Kellar, Last Haven and Highmont. Their route took them north. Logan could all but feel the chill gnawing into him already.

They rode until the day was wearing thin, and then some more. Logan complained about the lack of lunch, albeit only to Durik, who seemed unfazed. By the time they stopped for the night at a grubby little wayside inn, Logan's whole body ached. It was a struggle just to dismount. He ate a cold dinner and shared a room with Durik, struggling to sleep through the snoring of the big brute. It felt strange to be back on the road again, especially with the orc. Why had he missed this so much? Was he really just unable to accept that his best days were behind him? Surely only a fool would fail to see that if he kept trying to relive his youth, it would catch up with him in the worst possible way?

"You look terrible," Kloin taunted over breakfast the next morning.

"So I look the same as you do every day?"

Durik actually laughed, earning a withering look from them both. The pathfinder had been in a fine mood since they'd left Highmont. Logan wasn't surprised. Brittle autumn air, grubby fields and grubbier taverns, dark northern forests encroaching with ever-greater regularity onto the road, the white caps of the Dunwarrs drawing slowly closer – it was just the sort of bleak, uncomfortable journey Durik had always relished.

On the third day they passed a straggling column of about ten families. They were dirt-poor northerners in drab wool and pelts, and they scrambled to get off the road as they heard the sound of hoofbeats approaching. Damhán stopped the column beside them.

"I come with the authority of Baroness Adelynn," she declared loudly. "Where is this group bound for?"

The peasants exchanged worried glances. Wherever they were going, it certainly looked to be permanent. Mothers had babes strapped to them, and several were wheeling handcarts and barrows heaped with possessions. One stooped, wizened old creature actually had a lamb in a wicker basket mounted on her back. It bleated pitiably.

"Forgive us, my lady," one man said, stepping forward from the stinking, shivering huddle. He dragged back his liripipe's hood, only meeting Damhán's eyes furtively. "We are southward bound, for Highmont."

"You have come from Upper Forthyn?"

"Yes, my lady."

"And why have you abandoned your homes there?"

The commoner glanced back at another man, as though seeking his support – the figure nodded, placing a hand on the shoulder of the first and speaking to the party.

"We are afraid for the lives of our families," he said. "There have been rumors about raiding from the north. The clans are on the move."

"The clans have attacked settlements in Upper Forthyn?"

"As I said, my lady, there are rumors, and there are few enough men capable of bearing arms to protect us at Fallowhearth."

"Have you actually seen any clansfolk recently?" Damhán demanded. Logan saw a little steel enter the man's eyes, drawn out by the adviser's demands.

"I have not, my lady. But the harvest is in, and every village is speaking of the clans coming down out of the Dunwarrs. I will not gamble with the safety of my mother or my partner here. I won't stay. And we won't be the only ones."

Damhán seemed to consider the man's words for a while, then snapped at the man-at-arms leading the packhorse.

"Parchment and ink," she ordered. The guard obeyed, dismounting and bringing her the items from her chest. She leant the scrap of paper on her saddle and scrawled something on it, before folding the slip and handing it back to the man-at-arms.

"Take this to Baroness Adelynn immediately," she ordered. Then, pausing only while a second man-at-arms secured her quill and ink back in the chest, she spurred her horse on up the road. Logan spared a glance at the sorry group of families, apparently forgotten at the side of the road.

"Come," Durik said from beside him. Logan met the eyes of the man who had spoken to Damhán and offered him the smallest of shrugs, before spurring off after the party.

On the third day they turned north of the dark, brooding edge of Blind Muir Forest and stopped outside an inn a few miles short of Fallowhearth. Durik had requested the halt and, to Logan's surprise, Damhán had agreed.

Southern Forthyn had been an unpleasant experience, but as far as Logan was concerned Upper Forthyn was practically wilderness. The land was more forest than field, the soil craggy and infertile. Bristling pine tops were dominated by the vicious white caps of the Dunwarrs, presiding over the cold land from both the north and the east. Logan had never been so far into this particular corner of Terrinoth, and he found its remoteness chilling. The golden fields, ripe orchards, gentle hills and clear brooks that surrounded Sixspan Hall now felt like a slow, lazy dream, one whose warmth was lost with waking.

They passed through a hamlet of squat thatch and unadorned wattle, seemingly deserted but for a few chickens that scattered beneath their hooves, then paused at the roadside inn beyond. From a glance it made what Logan considered to be the unseemly establishments of Highmont appear palatial in comparison. Topped by a thick nest of thatch, its timber walls brittle-looking, its tiny windows crooked and unaligned. On one side of it stood a mossy old marker stone that pointed the way to Fallowhearth, while on the other was a timber barn, barely different in appearance from the inn itself.

"The Forester's Rest," Durik said as they reined in outside. "Last inn on the road to Fallowhearth."

"You say that like it means something," Logan said, looking with distaste at the churned-up mud of the front yard.

"It does," Durik said, dismounting and beckoning to Logan to follow. The old rogue sighed and grunted at the effort it took to get down off Ishbel. Durik was already knocking on the front door as he waded after him.

"Do you smell that?" the orc asked.

"I'm trying not to smell anything," Logan answered, glancing back at Damhán, Kloin and the guards. They were watching in silence on the roadway, still mounted. He sniffed.

Unsurprisingly, the inn's yard stank, but beneath it Logan caught an even more pungent, powerful smell. He recognized it instantly. Sulfur.

"Ah," he said, understanding now.

The door to the inn opened. Logan found himself looking down at a squat, rotund woman, clad in a stained apron. She was almost wider than she was tall, and had a few notable patches of bristle across her flabby, red-cheeked face.

"Whatcha want?" she grunted in an accent that Logan found nigh impenetrable.

"Greetings," Durik said, splaying a hand over his broad chest. "My name is Durik, and this is my companion, Logan."

The woman inhaled hard through her nose, hawked, and spat a wad of slime into the dirt at Logan's feet. Then she nodded past them both, at the retinue still on the road.

"They your companions too, orc? That gray lady looks like trouble."

"Oh, she is," Logan agreed wholeheartedly. Durik frowned. The squat woman continued.

"You're here for the dwarf, in't cha'?"

"Is she still here?" Durik asked.

"Not here," the creature said, then poked her head round the door and pointed. "There."

Logan realized she meant the barn sitting hunched on the inn's flank.

"She wanted more space," the innkeeper explained, then paused. A dark look crossed her face, and her apron twitched. Logan abruptly noticed a small, grimy child pulling on its strings, half hidden by the woman's bulk.

"I told ya to wait inside wiz your brother," the innkeeper hissed, shooing her back into the dark interior.

"Your lady friend," she said, after facing Logan and Durik once more, "said she wanted more space. Didn't say anything 'bout comfort. So I gaves her the barn. My grandnan was a dwarf, see, and she always taughts me to be polite to guests. Hospitable."

She wrestled with the word, and spat again. Logan managed to marshal the faintest of smiles.

"Has she paid up in full?" Durik asked.

"Uh-huh," the woman said, looking at Damhán and the men-at-arms once more, clearly weighing up the threat they posed versus the wealth they potentially had to offer. "Says, do you and your friends want to come in for some refreshments? Shake off the mud from the road? I gots three rooms available. The premium ones."

"Perhaps next time," Logan said, as Durik nodded to the innkeeper and turned towards the barn. Saying nothing of how supposed dwarven hospitality was best secured with an open purse, Logan followed Durik round the side.

"What a delightfully vile specimen," he said once he was certain the sounds of the innkeeper shouting at her children were loud enough to mask his words. "She fits her surroundings so perfectly!"

Durik said nothing. The pair came to a halt in front of the barn doors.

The last thing Logan expected was the explosion which followed.

It blew part of the thatch away and shook the whole rickety structure. Durik caught Logan before he collapsed with fright, ears ringing as straw rained down around them. He thought he was having a heart attack.

The flames followed. They caught in amongst the remains of the barn's roof, leaping hungrily all along the thatch and rearing up like a goaded serpent. More flared from within the structure, licking through the gaps in the rough wall planking. The sight would have been horrifying, were it not for the sudden blaze's two unnatural aspects – firstly, that the flames were purple in color, flaring to violent pink in places, and secondly, that they produced no smoke, and didn't seem to be consuming any part of the building.

"What in the name of Fortuna…" Logan started to say. A further crash cut him off.

The front doors to the barn slammed open, accompanied by a gust of air and a swirl of pink fire. A figure burst from the inferno within, her small frame alight from head to toe, engulfed in the unnatural conflagration.

"Ulma," Logan cried out, torn between the instinctive urge to rush to the dwarf's aid and his equally instinctive fear of the fire.

The burning dwarf, without so much as a cough, came to a halt a few paces beyond the barn's threshold and planted her hands on her hips. Her clothing – two leather smocks over a linen shirt, thick gauntlet-gloves, and steel-capped boots – blazed, the light reflecting in the lenses of the heavy, brass-rimmed goggles she had strapped over her eyes.

"Logan," she said. "Well, this was unexpected."

"You… you're on fire," Logan stammered, trying to work out whether his presence or the flames were what Ulma hadn't been expecting.

"Am I?" she asked, raising one hand and looking at the flames dancing across her glove. "Oh."

She reached into one of the numerous pockets decorating the front of her smock and fished out a small vial of clear liquid, which she proceeded to smash over her head. There was a hissing sound, and the flames died out rapidly, searing down to her boots. One remained alight, and Ulma stomped it in the dirt irritably until it was extinguished.

"Take a note will you, Durik," she asked without otherwise acknowledging the orc, turning to look at the burning barn. "I need to brew up a bigger batch of maltholite before I try this one again."

"You're… you're unharmed," Logan said, aware that he sounded like an idiot. "The fire didn't burn you."

"Obviously," Ulma said, turning back to him. "It isn't a fire as you would understand it, rogue. I brewed these flames very specifically. Two-fifths colix, two-fifths pyrium, one-fifth human urine, or a suitable substitute. A strand of maiden's hair, of any species – my own, in this case – and an ounce of witch's root, freshly chopped. Shake vigorously and…" She extended her arm to encompass the sight of the burning barn.

"But why?" Logan asked. "If it doesn't consume, what does the flame do?"

"I didn't say it didn't consume," Ulma said irritably. "I said it wasn't a fire as you would understand it, a fact you've now kindly demonstrated. It sears away enchantments. Magics. Any curse or spell, anything crafted by sorcerous means or any creature so bound, will be susceptible to these flames. It is, in essence, an artificial reconstruction of the *magi-reducto* incantation. And very difficult to do, I might add. I've been trying to perfect it in that damned barn for the last two days."

She lifted her goggles, revealing a snub-nosed, pretty face

framed by golden braids. She had hardly aged at all in the decades since Logan had last seen her, but then again, she was a dwarf – she was middle-aged at most.

"So you're still practicing your wild tricks," he said, looking past her at the barn. "I'm amazed you haven't blown yourself to bits."

"I have," Ulma said. "At least in part."

She tapped her left boot against her right calf, the metal toes striking hollow. "A pinch too much infernum in a shatter mix. A mistake I won't be making again."

"Well, it seems you've had ample time to perfect your art out here. Did Baroness Adelynn hire you to find her missing daughter as well, or was it just to concoct insane potions for her?"

Ulma glowered up at Logan. "I offered to ride ahead while Durik waited for you, because I didn't think you would come at all. And believe it or not, I've already started making inquiries. There are all sorts of rumors flying around. Things you wouldn't believe. And speaking of disbelief, where's my quicksilver?"

"I don't know what you're talking about," Logan said, foolishly. He suddenly very much regretted swiping the quicksilver elixir she'd spent so long crafting, even if it had been years ago. Ulma rolled her eyes and punched him in the gut.

"I've been waiting twenty years to do that," she said as Logan bent double, wheezing and in pain. "That's for stealing it. I'd give you another, but I'm not in the habit of beating old men."

"Rich old man," Logan managed to correct her as he slowly

recovered. "Thanks to that quicksilver." Despite himself, he grinned. Ulma scowled, but any further blow was interrupted by a horrific wailing sound.

"Sweet mother's stew," came a scream from behind Logan. The innkeeper was standing in the front yard, mouth open and jowls wobbling as she stared with undisguised horror at the purple flames engulfing her barn. "What have you done?"

"The barn is fine," Ulma said, waving her hands. "Leave it to burn out, and it'll be good as new come the morning. Unless you happen to have been casting magical incantations over it recently."

The innkeeper made unintelligible, spluttering noises as Ulma disappeared around the back of the inn and returned with a stocky pony. The creature appeared as unfazed by the nearby flames as she was. Logan dreaded to think what chemical madness the poor beast had witnessed in Ulma's service.

The innkeeper, red-faced, began to scream something far too furious and garbled for Logan to understand. He edged past her, keeping on the other side of Durik, and made for the horses.

"Thank you for your time," Durik said to the innkeeper, offering a short bow as she screamed in his face. By that point Logan was already dragging himself up into Ishbel's saddle.

"I think we should go," he said to Lady Damhán.

"I wondered how long it would be before you managed to come up with something actually intelligent," Ulma said as she fell in with Durik in front of him.

Logan huffed. For a second, struggling to cope with both

Ulma's ire and her alchemical concoctions, it had been just like old times. And not in a particularly good way.

"To Fallowhearth," Damhán said brusquely over the innkeeper's screams.

They rode.

CHAPTER FOUR

In his decades of travel across the length and breadth of the Land of Steel, the Paths had never taken Durik to Fallowhearth. He had been beyond it – he had visited Thelgrim, the Dulder Deeps and had fished the Feldrath Rift, as well as spending five summers living and hunting in an ice cave among the titan-peaks beyond Hadranhold, deep in the Dunwarrs. He had been to the Howling Giant Hills and the lands of central Forthyn as well, seen the rocs soaring and heard the crags resound with their piercing cries. He had even once tracked leonx through the southern reaches of distant, fey Aymhelin. Upper Forthyn though, and Fallowhearth in particular, had slipped by him.

The party came upon the town from the south-west, where a rare tract of tillable land led from Fallowhearth's outskirts to the wild, dark bounds of northern Blind Muir Forest. The houses were timber and thatch, human-built and poor, huddled along muddy tracks and interspersed with small vegetable patches and livestock yards. It was a sight Durik found far preferable to Highmont's claustrophobic, busy streets or, Kurnos forbid, the great cities further west.

The town – if town was the right word – was dominated by a small citadel sited on its northern edge. It had clearly been built by human stonemasons, but bore evidence of the architecture of the dwarf holds of the nearby Dunwarrs, with a squat, thick stone keep and an adjoining wall circling its north-eastern corner. Baroness Adelynn's standard and the half-roc pennant of the local warden flew from its highest turret, caught in a cold wind coming down off the mountains beyond.

The party rode along the main street towards the castle's gate. The town was quiet. A few people, clad mostly in thick woolen pelts, watched them pass from their yards, and Durik saw several banging shut the window boards of their small homes. It was a sight the orc had witnessed a thousand times on his travels – the desire of normal people, in the face of strangers or of authority, to be left alone. It was an attitude he commiserated with.

They arrived before the keep's gate, a barbed portcullis set before two high, heavy oaken doors, studded with black iron. It remained closed, though Durik sensed movements on the ramparts above. A voice called down.

"Who goes there?"

"Lady Damhán, of Highmont," Damhán answered. "I come here on the baroness's business. Send for Seneschal Abelard."

The sentry didn't respond, but after a couple of minutes of uncomfortable silence there came the creak of a locking bar being raised and the clank of the lifting mechanism as the portcullis was hauled slowly up. The doors beyond parted, and a trio of figures strode out – two liveried men-at-arms, flanking a heavy-set man with a bald head and a goatee. He was wearing a blue woolen tunic and hose and with a gray felt bagged hat, folded to one side. Durik noticed a small, golden roc pinned to his breast. It looked as though he'd been drawn away from his luncheon – his goatee was spattered with soup.

"My Lady Damhán," the man said, bowing. "This is an unexpected honor."

"It is," Damhán agreed. "I have come here at the request of Baroness Adelynn. We are to investigate the disappearance of Lady Kathryn. While doing so, I carry the baroness's full authority."

"'We', my lady?" the man asked, casting a pointed glance at Durik, Ulma and Logan.

"They are here to assist with the search," Damhán said. "I will introduce them once our horses have been fed and watered, and once you have shown us to the accommodation you are to provide us within the keep. Followed by luncheon."

The man hesitated only briefly before bowing again. "Of course, my lady. Right away."

A smaller door in the flank of the encircling wall opened for a woman in the horsehair cap of a stable mistress, accompanied by half a dozen young hands. They took the group's horses as they dismounted.

"Well, this is wonderfully rural," Logan said tartly, handing Ishbel's reins to one of the stable girls. "I wonder if the locals here even speak the common tongue?"

"'Mostly," Ulma said, deliberately ignoring the sarcasm. "From what I've heard it's a dialect. Some influences from the northern clans."

"I almost thought they *were* the northern clans," Logan said, casting a glance at one of the fur-clad youths leading the horses away. Durik prodded him and nodded – Lady Damhán was already following the man who had greeted them into the keep, accompanied by Kloin. They did likewise.

Fallowhearth castle was altogether different from Highmont's. Durik found himself in what felt like a suffocatingly low, dark hall, its stone floor spread with heavy pelts. A feasting table carved from northern pine had been laid out with simple wooden bowls and eating irons, while a sallow-faced serving boy was attempting to stoke up a huge fireplace. The hearth was set beneath a stone carving depicting a half-roc carrying a judging stave, the traditional symbol used by the heirs of Forthyn. Hunting trophies lined the walls – the heads of bears, stags, wild tuskers and orids gazed down blankly on the party as they sat at the table. All bar Durik. He paced the length of the hall, looking at each one in turn, pondering their fate. How had the hunts that had ended their lives played out? Had they died a noble death, fighting to the last, or had they given in as the hounds tore at them? Did the one who slew them take note when he sat in this hall, remembering their final moments with pride? Or were their last desperate, bloody breaths forgotten? Durik did not presume to judge. He leaned close to a tusker's horned head, assessing its age. How many decades had this old beast looked down up its conquerors?

"Don't touch the trophies," said the man who had welcomed them to the citadel. His name was Abelard, and he was the seneschal of Fallowhearth castle. He held it in the name of Baroness Adelynn and, until a month before, Lady Kathryn, acting as the local warden and overseeing the town.

To Durik, he seemed like a man grown weary of his lot in life. A strong body was steadily running to fat, the face fleshy and unhealthy, the eyes tainted with bitterness. Durik sat down between Logan and Ulma without responding to him.

Abelard had been in the process of apologizing to Damhán. "It is rustic, my lady," he continued. "But I am afraid that is the nature of things here in Upper Forthyn. Fallowhearth is not Highmont."

"Evidently," Durik heard Logan mutter under his breath. As much as he had privately rejoiced at seeing his old friend again, he really had forgotten how eternally snide the rogue was. He'd barely stopped complaining since they'd left Highmont.

"Comfort is not our concern, seneschal," Damhán said. She was seated at the head of the table, flanked by Abelard and Kloin. As the fire in the hearth behind her slowly rose, it framed her high-backed chair, casting her aged features in hard, flickering lines. "We are here for the sole purpose of locating the baroness's daughter and ensuring her safety."

"Of course," Abelard said. "I can assure both you and the baroness that I have had search parties scouring the countryside for weeks. My own men, local hunters and even volunteers from the town."

"You have put a price on her safe recovery?"

"Of course, my lady."

"Whatever it is, triple it. Make it known to the people that Baroness Adelynn's personal representative is here. Anyone who steps forward with information will be handsomely rewarded."

"Yes, my lady."

The hall's doors groaned open, and a small parade of serving maids entered, carrying platters which they deposited across the table – fish pie, mutton stew and rough gritbread. Durik took a slice of the former and a half loaf, which he began to slowly chew without carving. Ulma filled her bowl with stew, while Logan took a helping of everything. Durik saw Kloin glance at him with disgust. The feeling was mutual, but Durik knew well enough to keep his thoughts towards the captain private. Wise creatures never gave their hunter the satisfaction of seeing their pain. Durik was sure Kurnos would send the captain a reckoning.

"These three will assist your search," Lady Damhán said, nodding towards them. "Their names are Logan Lashley, Pathfinder Durik and Ulma Grimstone."

"We are honored to have them," Abelard said with obvious distaste.

"I hired them personally," Damhán pressed. "You will assist them at all times. That is the baroness's will."

"Yes, my lady," Abelard said, his expression guarded as he met Durik's gaze. "If you are indeed to lead the search, then might I ask where you intend to begin?"

Logan was too busy digging into his food to respond. Ulma spoke before Durik.

"I have been making acquaintances at a roadside inn just outside the town. There are all manner of rumors circulating. Perhaps you can address a few of them before we start looking for the real leads?"

Abelard shifted in his chair and cleared his throat. "There are always rumors, Lady Dunwarr. It is the nature of a frontier town such as this."

"So, talk of the clans attacking and raiding outlying villages is normal?"

"If that is the case, Baroness Adelynn must be informed," Damhán said sharply. "There has not been conflict between the clans and Forthyn for generations. They might live differently to others, but they still owe their allegiances to the baronies. If that has changed, it will have far-reaching consequences."

"I have seen nothing to suggest there have been any attacks," Abelard said, holding up a placatory hand. "But the common folk are certainly unsettled. The migrations have been far greater than usual this year. The harvest is not long in, and it may be threatened."

"If only that was the sole story doing the rounds," Ulma said. "I've heard other tales about what has supposedly become of Lady Kathryn."

"Nothing certain," Abelard said, starting to sound annoyed. "Nothing we could act upon."

"What about the gravedigger?"

Abelard glared at Ulma, and Damhán glared at Abelard.

"What gravedigger?" she asked him, her tone icy. Abelard kept looking at Ulma as he answered.

"The day after Lady Kathryn disappeared, the town's tomb-keeper claimed to have seen her in the cemetery of the Shrine of Nordros. But his story hardly makes any sense. He is little more than a simpleton."

"You've questioned him thoroughly?"

"Yes," Abelard said. Durik got the impression he was lying. That could prove to be a problem if it persisted. He wondered why.

"Where was the Lady Kathryn last seen?" he asked the seneschal.

"In her chambers, on the night of her disappearance," Abelard said brusquely, as though the question was barely worth answering.

"By who?"

"I don't know. One of the servants. You'd have to ask the matron, Mildred. She's in charge of them."

"I'll do that," Durik said. "But I would like to see her chambers as well."

"Now?" Abelard asked incredulously.

"Has the room been sealed since she went missing?"

"Yes. I believe so."

Durik looked hard at the seneschal, considering once more whether he was telling the truth. Clearly the current master of Fallowhearth had hardly covered himself in glory since Lady Kathryn's disappearance. Eventually Durik spoke again.

"The room may still contain valuable evidence of what happened to her that night. I wish to search it. Immediately."

Logan shot Durik a hurt look, his mouth still full of food, but the orc ignored him. Abelard nodded and rose, chair scraping back across the floor.

"Follow me."

CHAPTER FIVE

Kathryn's personal chambers were located in the highest turret of the keep. A claustrophobic spiral staircase of cold stone led Durik up to a landing sealed off by a timber door. Abelard opened it with a heavy set of keys he wore on his belt. Durik followed him into the circular room beyond and made way for the others to crowd in behind him – Logan and Ulma, as well as Damhán and a towering, tree trunk-thick woman Abelard had introduced as Matron Mildred, the castle's chief servant.

The room itself was furnished with a four-poster bed and wardrobe, a small table and a mirror bordered by bronze leaves. The bed was unmade, the linen sheets crumpled, the pale blue drapes suspended from the top of its frame hanging half shut. The wardrobe door was open as well. A stool set before a small fireplace had been overturned.

"Looks to me like there was a struggle," Logan said as soon as he entered.

"Nonsense," Abelard said. "Lady Kathryn was simply… having difficulty becoming accustomed to her new estates.

To be thrown from a sheltered life in Highmont to a northern frontier is difficult."

"The lady took her duties very seriously, sirs," Matron Mildred added. "I would often find her greatly distressed. Especially before..." She trailed off.

"Before she disappeared?" Ulma prompted. Mildred nodded down at the dwarf.

"You think her fragile mental state in the days leading up to her vanishing was solely caused by her duties as the mistress of Fallowhearth?" Logan asked Abelard. "Had she not been fulfilling her role here for almost a year by that point?"

"Fallowhearth is not Highmont, or Frostgate," Abelard said. "Until you have lived here and experienced the difficulties of ruling yourself, I would not hurry to judge what Lady Kathryn was thinking. This is why the heirs of the barony are instated to Upper Forthyn when they come of age. If they can rule in the north, they can rule everywhere. The long winters, the poor harvests, dealing with the clans when they pass through, negotiating with the Dunwarr dwarfs to the north... it is no easy place to govern."

As Abelard spoke, Durik had moved to the side of the bed. He was only half listening to the seneschal's verbose observations, his mind focused on hunting for the tiny telltale signs he had no doubt Abelard and his staff had overlooked. He drew the drapes back and bent over it, examining the covers. He could sense both Abelard and Mildred's displeasure at having a large orc inspect the last place Forthyn's heir had been seen alive, but he had no time for their bigotry. There was something here. He could feel it in his bones.

There was nothing in the bed save for a few strands of dark hair, which Durik left undisturbed. He moved over to her wardrobe, opening the door fully and looking inside.

"What was the last thing Lady Kathryn was seen wearing?" he asked, directing the question at Mildred.

"Her night gown, I think," she answered with a slight frown.

"You think?"

"It was a month ago!"

Durik grunted noncommittally, looking through the arrayed garments. The cupboard didn't look half full. And kidnap victims didn't usually have the luxury of packing. He kept the thought to himself, turning back to Mildred.

"Do you have an inventory of her clothing?" he asked.

"No."

"So, you wouldn't know if any was missing? Her wardrobe seems half empty."

"Are you expecting her to jump out of the cupboard, orc?" Abelard demanded.

"No," Durik said simply. "And my name isn't 'orc,' human."

Abelard glared at Durik but made no response as the pathfinder went on. "You said one of the town's tomb-keepers was the last person to see her?"

"So he claims."

"Where was that?"

"Believe it or not, the cemetery. It is attached to Fallowhearth's Shrine of Nordros."

"We really must be in the north if they're openly worshiping the god of necromancy," Logan said dispassionately.

"Nordros isn't the god of necromancy," Ulma said in an exasperated voice. "He's the god of death and winter. Plenty of people worship him in the north, especially in Upper Forthyn."

Logan didn't voice his thoughts on such cults, though his face spelt out his opinions clearly enough. Durik likewise didn't share a view on the servants of Nordros, though only because he had no desire to add another grievance to Abelard's list – he had known many brave and honest worshipers of the god of death down the years, and plenty of spavined and vile servants of Kellos. Mentioning that wouldn't help anyone right now, though.

"What did the tomb-keeper say she was doing when he saw her?" he asked instead.

"I don't know," Abelard said. "The man is at best a liar, and at worst demented. It would hardly be a surprise given his profession. If it were up to me, the worship of Nordros would be banned in Upper Forthyn, and that shrine would be closed down."

As Abelard was speaking, Durik moved to the center of the room and lifted the fur rug. Nothing hidden, and no trap door. Too obvious. He shifted to the fireplace, pulling a blackened iron poker from the bracket beside it and probing the ash as Abelard trailed off.

"You saw Lady Kathryn in here yourself before she vanished," Ulma said to Matron Mildred as Durik continued to rake through the fireplace, both the matron and the seneschal frowning at him. "Yet no one else in the castle spotted her that night? How did she manage to get out? Surely the gate was barred and guarded?"

"I don't know, my lady," Mildred said. "Your guess is as good as mine."

Durik looked back at her carefully as Ulma continued.

"And how have the servants been taking it? You must be privy to all of the gossip in the lower quarters. Any particular theories? Anyone acting strange, either before or after the disappearance?"

"No, my lady," Mildred said. "Certainly nothing I would put any stock in."

"There was one unusual matter, was there not?" Abelard interjected. "Didn't one of the cooks stop working in the kitchens just before Lady Kathryn disappeared?"

Mildred's heavy features began to flush red. "I'm not sure, sir. I would need to check…

"Tobin, or Toben?" Abelard went on. "One of the recent hires. He came in after Cookmaster Jarrow's promotion."

"As I said, sir, I would have to check," Mildred repeated, by now an odd shade of puce. Durik spoke from beside the fireplace.

"We would like to speak with Tobin, assuming he's still here?"

"The cooks don't stay in the keep," Abelard said. "They're usually seasonally hired. He lives somewhere in the town."

"Do you know where?"

"No, but I'm sure someone will."

"There have to be other people in the citadel who saw her that night," Ulma said. "Does the keep have any sally ports? Any hidden routes or tunnels?"

"Not that I know of," Abelard said. "Another of the servants did mention something about a strange fog in the lower chambers, but it had cleared by the morning. I'm sure you know how the common folk can get. It will have been nothing more than a figment of his imagination, or some dream he failed to separate from reality."

"So if the good lady simply upped and vanished," Logan said slowly, "then why does the baroness believe the northern clans are responsible? Were there any northerners in the town on the night that it happened?"

"I doubt it. I told you, there have been stories of robberies and raids. The clan folk aren't welcome right now."

"But, as you said earlier, you don't have hard evidence of the clans having attacked anyone. Yet you reported to Baroness Adelynn that she had likely been snatched from her bed by them. How in the name of Pollux's great hammer do northern primitives steal into a garrisoned citadel like this and grab the heiress to the barony unnoticed from its tallest tower? And, for that matter, how do we know she was kidnapped at all, northern tribes or not? Unless you're sure her clothes are all accounted for, it seems as though she could quite easily have slipped away of her own accord. Gods know, I've availed myself of enough quick escapes in times of stress. Why isn't anyone considering that a likely lead?"

Durik had only vaguely been listening to Logan. He thought he'd found something – the fire poker had hit an unyielding object amidst the cold embers. He probed it with a thud, causing the rest of the group to look at him before answering Logan. There was something solid, right at the back of the hearth. He tested it again with the iron rod, thinking at first that it was just the brittle remnants of a log that had yet to crumble. It was the wrong shape, though. Placing the poker to one side, he reached into the mound of ash and gripped whatever was buried beneath.

He knew what it was almost immediately. The others crowded round the fireplace to watch as he dragged a heavy book from its tomb of embers.

"A book in a fireplace," Logan said with a smirk. "The northerners probably didn't realize what it was. Thought it was kindling."

Durik blew off the thick layer of ash cladding the book's cover, making Mildred cough and Lady Damhán grimace. It was heavy and leather-bound, though it didn't seem to bear either a title or an author.

He opened it. Despite having been buried in the hearth, its pages showed no sign of damage or befoulment. It was composed of thick yellow parchment, roughly cut. Some pages were larger than others. Durik glanced at the words, rendered in ink in a neat, regular hand. His skin began to prickle.

He understood none of them, but that in itself was no surprise. He handed the book to Ulma, Logan leaning over the top of the dwarf to gaze down at it.

"What is it?" Abelard asked. "What does it say?"

"I don't know," Durik said, standing up. "But I wouldn't advise you to try and translate it."

"It's one of the arcane tongues, isn't it?" Ulma murmured, pausing on a page filled with carefully drawn diagrams and what looked like a heavily annotated chart of constellations. "It's a tome of magic."

"The question is, who put it in there?" Durik asked. "And how long ago?"

"I set a fire in here myself the night Lady Kathryn vanished," Mildred said, beginning to sound upset. "It was burning before I left the chamber! The book couldn't have been there before it!"

"So you're saying someone has broken into this chamber and concealed it there since that fateful night?" Logan demanded.

"Well how else would you explain it? If it had been buried in there when I set the fire it would be nothing but ash by now!"

"How would I explain the survival of the sorcerer's tome in the fireplace?" Logan repeated rhetorically. Then, muttering something about parochial northerners, he took the book off Ulma and put it back in the fireplace.

"Where's the kindling?" he demanded.

"Logan," Ulma said in a warning tone, as the rogue set about throwing a few logs on top of the book and hunting through the table drawers until he found a piece of flint and a striker. "We don't know what that book can do, or what will happen to it."

Durik simply watched, knowing better than to critique his friend's theatrical streak as Logan knelt down with a grunt and began striking sparks. It took an awkwardly long time, but he didn't move to help the rogue – he knew it was best to just let him get on with these sorts of demonstrations. Eventually a scrap of wool caught. A small fire leapt and flared along the logs lying on top of the book.

"Nothing's going to happen to it," Logan said firmly, stabbing the logs with the prong before giving them a few short, sharp kicks, sparks swirling. He scraped the charred remains aside and reached back in, lifting the book free once more.

"Nothing," he said with an air of triumph. The cover and the pages within were wholly unmarked.

Abelard grimaced and Mildred, wide-eyed, made the sign of Kellos's holy flames.

"The book is warded against fire," Ulma said. "But if I had another brew of *magi-reducto* it would probably bring about a conflagration that would destroy it utterly. As well as the keep."

She sounded quite excited at the prospect.

"There's no point in destroying it until we know more about it," Durik said, offering Ulma an apologetic shrug – he knew how much she enjoyed experimenting on artifacts like this. "Could it have been Lady Kathryn's?" he asked Abelard and Mildred.

"Absolutely not," the seneschal said. "The baroness's daughter was no sorceress."

"Well, if not, then someone close to her was," Durik said, looking from Abelard to Mildred. "Or at the very least, someone who knew she was gone and that nobody was going to be entering her room anytime soon. This could have remained hidden here for months, perhaps years."

"It still brings us no closer to finding her, though," Logan pointed out. "Not until we can connect it to someone or something."

"We can only use what we have," Durik said. "There are other leads. I will go and speak with the tomb-keeper who claims to have seen her. Ulma, perhaps you should continue to make enquiries around the town. Take in as much gossip as you can." Ulma nodded.

"And don't tell me," Logan said. "I'm going to have to go and track down the missing cook?"

"Yes," Durik said.

"Leave the most dangerous job to the old, rich man," Logan said, throwing his hands up.

"Finding a cookhouse servant is hardly dangerous," Ulma sneered. "He's probably just contracted a bout of food poisoning."

"Why don't I take the tavern gossip?" Logan said. "I'm far better with people than you are, Ulma." Durik let out a little grunt of laughter and Ulma rolled her eyes.

"Have you seen yourself recently? You dress like a vagrant who's just unearthed a dead dragon's hoard. You'll stick out like an elf in a brewery. No one will want to talk to you. Besides, I'm funnier, prettier and cleverer than you are, so just altogether more qualified."

"I doubt it will take long to find the cook," Durik said before Logan could explode. "Once you have, you can join Ulma."

"I can't imagine anything better," Logan said. Ulma gave him a little curtsey.

"Where does the tomb-keeper live?" Durik asked Abelard while the other two bickered. "And the cook?"

"The tomb-keeper's family are given the gatehouse by the cemetery entrance," Abelard said. "His name is Volbert. As for the cook, I have no idea." Durik looked at Mildred.

"I think he stays in the first house past the Black Crow," the matron said noncommittally. Durik nodded his thanks.

"And that's it?" Abelard asked. "What about the clans? You're not going to investigate them at all?"

"We have no reason to, yet," Durik said. "There is no evidence any of them were here the night Lady Kathryn disappeared. Seeking the nearest clan out and questioning them would be gambling with time we do not have."

"If you wanted help with the clans you should have asked the baroness directly, rather than simply inventing their involvement," Logan added.

"I've invented nothing," Abelard said angrily, but Lady Damhán silenced him.

"A word before you depart, Master Pathfinder," she said to Durik. She had remained silent throughout the discovery of the book and the exchanges that had followed, but Durik had felt the intensity of her eyes on him the whole time. It was rare for a hunter to feel so hunted.

"In private," Damhán added unsubtly to Abelard and Mildred. The former looked unimpressed at being ordered from the chamber, but both bowed and departed, leaving Durik, Ulma and Logan alone with the baroness's gray-clad adviser.

"How familiar are you with Forthyn's laws on the use of magic?" Damhán asked. Durik shook his head while Logan said nothing. It was Ulma who responded.

"Users are expected to register with the sorcerers' guild if they intend to practice within the barony's borders," she said. "There are also a number of forbidden magical arts."

"Correct," Damhán said. "Namely demonancy, necromancy and prophesy. The latter may be practiced by fully accredited members of the guild. The first two are entirely forbidden, under pain of death. Tell me, do you believe that tome might relate to either of those?"

Logan was still holding the book, but appeared to be on the verge of dropping it when the dark magics were mentioned.

"I am no warlock," Durik said. "I cannot decipher it. Such

knowledge is beyond me." Damhán held her hand out to Logan, and the rogue quickly handed her the book.

"I have some ability when it comes to the mystic arts," Damhán said. "I will attempt to decipher the owner or author or, at the very least, make something of its contents. However, if we were indeed to discover that this is a tome of dark magic, it would not do well to imagine it belonged to Lady Kathryn."

"The heiress to the barony can't be outed as a dabbler in the dark arts," Ulma said.

"Regardless of what has become of Lady Kathryn, news of this book does not leave this chamber," Damhán said. "I will be impressing that on both the seneschal and the matron too, individually. If word of the existence of this text somehow does reach beyond this room then there will be consequences, for everyone. Is that clear?"

"It is," Durik said. Logan and Ulma both nodded.

"You may proceed with the investigation you have already outlined, pathfinder," Damhán said. "In the meantime, I will be making my own enquiries."

CHAPTER SIX

On the night of Lady Kathryn's disappearance, the Fulchards had risen from their family crypt and walked out into the graveyard of the Shrine of Nordros, through the lich-gate and out into the town. That, according to Volbert, was one of two options. The other was that a woman with a startlingly similar appearance to Kathryn had entered the crypt and dragged them out, though where to, no one knew.

The markings certainly didn't suggest any dragging had been involved. There were only a few prints left around the Fulchard tomb, partially preserved by the hard frosts that the north experienced at this time of year. Durik studied them intently. Over the past month, hundreds of other footsteps had destroyed the trail elsewhere in the graveyard, and out on the street there was no hope of picking them up whatsoever, but the dark rumors that had swirled in the wake of the night's events had at least kept anyone from daring to approach what should have been the Fulchard family's final resting place.

"How many bodies were in the crypt?" Durik asked Volbert. The tomb-keeper was a sturdy young man, wrapped in the black robes of his profession, his blond hair cropped short. His family had apparently been the tomb-keepers at the Shrine of Nordros for five generations. Normally his duties involved digging and tending to the graves, taking donations from visitors and chasing off potential thieves. He had never, he claimed, come across a case like this.

"There were five bodies," Volbert said outside the Fulchard tomb. "The grandparents, their son and his wife, and their daughter. The pestilence took the younger half of the family three winters ago. They still have a brother living in the town."

"Does he know his relatives have disappeared?" Durik asked.

"Yes, sir. He refuses to come and visit. Says there's a curse."

"And is there?" Durik asked matter-of-factly.

"I don't know, sir," Volbert answered nervously. Durik had caught him casting furtive glances at him from the moment they had met. When he had caught the man's eye Volbert had apologized profusely. He had, he explained, never met an orc before, much less conversed with one. He was clearly a dutiful man though. Durik's word that he served the baroness seemed to be enough to ensure his cooperation.

"Were the caskets opened, or broken?" Durik asked him, standing at the rear of the crypt, where the footprints became impossible to read.

"They were opened," Volbert said. "And the lock on the gate was broken. Shattered."

"Show me."

Volbert led Durik back round the front and into the Fulchard family crypt. It was a low, lichen-covered stone structure, its wrought iron gate cast in the likeness of the bones of Nordros. The space within was cold and damp, lit only by the evening's gloomy light shafting in through a circular hole in the ceiling. It illuminated five stone slabs, their tops cast aside onto the ground. The insides were exposed and empty.

Volbert held up the remains of the gate's lock. It was made of heavy metal, and it had been split clean in half.

"Whoever broke this had great strength," Durik said, taking the lock in his hands and turning it over. "And even greater technique. You have tools for your work, I suppose? Shovels, mallets? Were any stolen?"

"None," Volbert said, his breath frosting in the crypt's icy air. "I have accounted for them all, sir."

Durik grunted and inspected each stone casket in turn. A few held trinkets or memento mori – a twist of old cloth, a small hemp horse stuffed with wool, a few pieces of jewelry. There were no grave shrouds, though. Durik motioned for Volbert to step back outside and followed him out, slipping the lock into his satchel as he went.

"Tell me what you saw that night," he asked.

"I cannot be certain, sir," the young tomb-keeper said. "It was a very dark night. The clouds were low, and there was neither moon nor stars. It was raining…" He trailed off.

"You can speak freely with me, Volbert," Durik said. "Every piece of information you have is valuable, no matter how unimportant it may seem. I am not here to judge you."

"Yes, sir," Volbert said. "I was woken by what I thought was someone passing through the lich-gate. I live adjacent to the yard. Sometimes, especially during this season, we have trouble with thieves. Opportunist graverobbers usually, passing through on their way to Frostgate."

"Clansmen?"

"Sometimes, yes. It is my duty to protect the graves as well as to tend to them. I headed out into the yard to see if there was anyone there. Usually they flee as soon as they are discovered."

"You were alone?"

"Yes. My wife was not awake."

"Go on."

"There was something strange in the air that night," he said, his voice earnest yet uncertain. "I am not sure I can explain it, but I have never felt anything like it before."

"A strange air," Durik prompted. Volbert frowned, speaking carefully.

"You must understand, sir, I have been performing these duties for as long as I can remember. I aided my father as a boy, and now that he has passed on into the Cold Embrace, I performed the tasks as he did, as my family have done for almost two centuries. I have heard that the work of the worshipers of Nordros is frowned upon in some other baronies, but not so here. There are many worshipers in Upper Forthyn who come seeking to thank Nordros, or have the bodies of their loved ones interred in the sight of his servants."

"You do not need to explain your life's work to me, Volbert," Durik said, attempting to sound reassuring. "I have traveled far and seen enough to know that not every worshiper of Nordros is a corpse-disturber."

"No indeed, sir," Volbert said. "The role of tomb-keeper at this shrine comes with a plot of ground by the lich-gate. I will lie there beside my father when my time comes and, Nordros willing, my son will go on tending to these graves. This place is my family's home, sir. There is nothing morbid about it for me, it is simply the duty great Nordros has allotted to me. I have never once felt afraid amongst these headstones, either during day or night. Except…"

"Except on that night," Durik said. "There was something strange at play, and you could sense it. You are wise not to disregard your instincts."

"Thank you, sir," the tomb-keeper said.

"So, you thought at first it was grave robbers. What did you find instead?"

"A woman," Volbert said. "At least, that is what I believe I saw. As I said, it was dark, I had only a torch. But I do believe I saw a woman there, between the headstones."

He pointed to the row nearest to the crypt, a crumbling, jumbled mass of particularly weathered-looking headstones, most of them bearing the grim iconography associated with the god of death and cold – skulls, bones, hourglasses; brittle, frozen leaves and branches.

"She wore a heavy cloak. I saw her only for a second, and I caught nothing of her face before she fled. I will confess sir, for a moment my courage failed me. I thought I had seen a specter."

Durik nodded, letting the man speak. He respected his honesty. He'd shown nothing so far that made Durik doubt anything he had to say. He certainly wasn't the simpleton Abelard, doubtless in his arrogance, had made out.

"It took me a while to find my resolve," he continued, and Durik noted how his eyes lingered on the graves he had indicated. "When I finally approached, I could find no sign of her. But I did notice that the gate to the Fulchard crypt had been opened. And that's when I discovered the empty tomb."

"And the footprints?" Durik asked.

"Yes. I am no tracker like you, sir, but there were definitely a number of people around the tomb that night. Not just one."

As Durik considered his words, Volbert spoke again.

"May I ask you something, sir?"

"Of course," Durik nodded, already guessing what it would be about.

"You must understand how this looks. The stories that have been going around the town for a month now. My wife hasn't had a proper night's sleep since this all began. Do you think ..."

"Do I think dark magic has been practiced here?" Durik finished. "Perhaps necromancy? The truth is, I do not know. There is much about what I have seen and heard here today that I cannot yet explain. But I could not yet say with certainty that a necromancer has been here."

"The seneschal has been considering closing the shrine for a while," Volbert said, looking worried. "If he does, I'm sure he will ban the worship of Nordros soon after. Our religion will be driven to the dark places. Already I know of devout worshipers forced to flee to Blind Muir by the bigotry of some in this town. All it takes is a single rumor about necromancy, and every one of Nordros's faithful becomes a suspect. There have been purges before."

"When I speak to the seneschal I will make it clear that we have no hard evidence of necromancy at work here," Durik said. "But it will be difficult to explain either the disappearance of the bodies, or these prints. The investigations will continue. They have to, until Lady Kathryn is found."

"Even if the shrine remains open, we may be forced to begin cutting the heads from the dead before interring them," Volbert said. "Or even bringing back the heathen practice of cremation. It would make us no better than the northern clans. I pray it does not come to that."

"I will ask the seneschal to do nothing until we know more," Durik repeated, supposing that a return to the old ways of decapitation and cremation would be bad for a tomb-keeper's business. "Until then, if you remember anything more, or discover anything new or unusual, go immediately to the castle and ask for me. I will be there."

"Of course, sir," Volbert said, offering a bow. "Allow me to walk you to the threshold."

Durik nodded and let Volbert accompany him to the yard's lich-gate, a stone arch heavy with moss and tangled creepers.

"Remain on your guard, tomb-keeper," he said, before stepping out into the street. "And pray to Nordros for his help in this matter."

CHAPTER SEVEN

It was getting late. Logan glanced left and right, trying to shake the feeling that he was being watched. He had left Ishbel in the castle stables, partly to stretch his legs during the walk back through town, and partly because he didn't trust the locals not to steal her the moment he left her hitched.

Twilight had settled over Fallowhearth, a gray gloom that left deep shadows festering between the squalid buildings. Angry black clouds were brewing in the east, clambering down from the Dunwarrs to herald the coming night.

Logan felt miserable. He blamed himself. He'd grown senile and foolish. Imagine letting old sentiments drag him out to this far corner of Terrinoth? Now he was up to his neck in it. He should never have come. The rogue grumbled under his breath as he hunted through the streets for the sign of the Black Crow, cloak hitched up so its hem didn't trail in the mud.

People cast strange looks at him, but he ignored them. He was too tired and too stiff from three weeks of near-constant travel to care about fitting in with some northern peasants. He found the tavern, its signpost creaking over a crooked door that opened ahead of him just long enough to spill firelight, a burst of laughter and a half-drunk shepherd in a wool smock out into the dirt. Logan stepped over the groaning man without breaking stride, wondering whether Ulma was inside.

Past the tavern was a tenant's cottage, as squat and nondescript as any of the buildings that lined the street. Its shutters were closed, and there was no sign of movement from within. In fact, besides the faint sounds of the neighboring tavern's patrons, it seemed as though the whole street was deserted. For some reason that made Logan feel even more uncomfortable.

He glanced over his shoulder one more time and tried the latch on the front door. Why didn't he knock first? He wasn't entirely sure, but he didn't question his actions either – he had learned a long time ago to trust his instincts, and his instincts said that he didn't want to alert whatever was inside.

Whoever, he corrected himself. There was nothing more sinister to this than a cook with a bad case of the runs. It might not be as pleasant a task as trawling the local ale houses, but at least it was preferable to checking the cemetery, especially with darkness falling.

The door was locked. Logan hissed through his front teeth and carefully tried one of the shutters. Also locked. He peered around the corner into the narrow, dirty lane between the cottage and the tavern. It was impenetrably dark. Logan swallowed.

Rules, rules, rules. He'd promised never to draw his sword again. His hand was on its expensive pommel now, though.

He straightened up, cleared his throat. Come on, Logan. Surely you aren't afraid of the dark? Ulma would laugh herself silly if she could see him right now.

That settled it. Head up and shoulders back, he marched into the beckoning shadows of the alleyway.

He almost tripped on a broken wheel set against the tavern wall. Edging round it, he emerged into the yard at the rear of the cottage. A back door stood ahead of him. The windows were dark.

He walked to the door, pausing to listen. A few streets across, a dog had started to bark. Laughter and voices swelled inside the tavern. The wind gusted, snatching at his cloak and making the sign on the main street creak.

Logan tried the latch. This time it gave. The door swung slowly, quietly, inwards.

The rules said nothing about daggers. Logan drew his from the inside of his boot, savoring the familiar grip for a second before entering the cottage. Darkness ruled the interior, and he paused for a few seconds on the threshold, letting his eyesight adjust.

He was standing in a back porch, a larder. The place stank, even more than he had expected. Something was turning rancid. There was a closed door to his right and another directly ahead. The darkness was cloying, reeking. He abruptly thought of Dezra – she'd be amused, no doubt, by the thought of him stealing into some foul peasant's back room. He certainly wished he had her scrying abilities right then.

He listened. He could hear something, a low chirring noise. Buzzing, coming from the right. He eased the door open.

That was when the stink really hit him. He gagged, stumbling back and instinctively slamming the door shut as a cloud of flies rose up to greet him.

He should have known it would be like this. He swallowed again, hard, but a clattering noise from deeper inside the cottage banished thoughts of being sick. Without hesitating he lunged through the other door directly ahead and found himself in a low, narrow hallway. Directly in front of him was the front door to the cottage, the one he had initially tried to get in through. A figure, hunched and indistinct in the near-total darkness of the cottage's interior, was fumbling with the door's bolt and latch.

Logan charged it. He still wasn't thinking – he was acting on decades of experience, and his body followed. The thing by the door heard him coming and let out a ghastly shriek.

He tackled it. The door banged open under the impact and they both half spilled out into the street, mud spattering Logan's face. He snarled, trying to bring his knife up, wrestling in the thing's grip. He was damned if it was all going to end here, in the clutches of some Uthuk Y'llan demon-worshiper on the threshold of a peasant abattoir.

Given the twilight's gloom and his own frenzied state of mind, he'd almost hauled the dagger up and plunged it into the thing's face before he realized just what the "thing" really was. A sickly face, white as a death-shroud, stared up at him, eyes wide with terror.

"Hello," Logan said, knife poised inches from the man's throat – for man he was, quivering and weak, with breath that stank of sick, but most definitely a man. Nothing more.

"Stay still," Logan told him.

"P- Please," the man stammered. "Please tell her I can't! Not any more!"

"Tell who?" Logan demanded, deciding against trying to bluff his way through this.

"Mildred! Didn't she send you?"

Logan began to laugh uncontrollably, the adrenaline flushing from his system in a bout of hysteria that then quickly gave way to pain. He flinched and hissed, rolling off the man and clutching his sore back. It seemed the body was no longer willing, no matter how sharp the mind still was.

"Fortuna's glittering gold," he cursed, teeth gritted as the exertions caught up with him. The man, doubtless assuming he'd just been assaulted by a lunatic, wisely decided to stay down.

Logan stood up, very slowly and very tentatively, and stretched each limb in turn. "You're Tobin," he grunted as he did so, letting out a whistle as his back crunched. The man just nodded.

"You're a cook in the castle kitchens," Logan continued, still trying to recover his breath. "You've been missing for weeks."

"I'm sorry! Tell her I'm sorry!"

"You think the matron of your miserable cookhouse hired the most famous rogue alive to force you to go back to work?" Logan asked incredulously. "Come on man, I know I startled you, and you look unwell, but stop and think for a moment!" Tobin just stared up at him.

"If Mildred didn't send you, then why are you here?"

"Uh-uh," Logan said, brandishing his dagger and glancing left and right to ensure the street was still deserted. "I'm the one holding the knife, so I'm the one doing the questioning. Does that sound fair?"

Tobin nodded hastily.

"Why did you run?" Logan asked.

"I thought you were Mildred," the pathetic wretch managed. "Or one of the other cooks."

"You thought I was the matron, come to force you back to work despite the fact that you are gravely ill? If that's the case, why wouldn't Mildred tell us? A sick cook would have saved me a journey to this… delightful part of town. And why did she go so red-faced when the seneschal mentioned you? Also, what in Fortuna's lucky dice is festering next door to your pantry?"

Tobin just whimpered again. Logan motioned to him with the knife. "Get up. And don't think about running. If you do I'll come back here with my bloodhounds, and once they have your scent they'll chase you to Carthridge and beyond. I keep them hungry, much like your matron. Understood?"

The cook managed to nod and pull himself up out of the mud. Logan prodded him back into the cottage with the knife and, after a final glance along the street, closed the front door.

"What's that gods-awful smell in the back room?" Logan repeated.

"It's my last meal. I fell sick about a week ago. I haven't dared leave the house in almost a month."

"It smells like it," Logan said. "I thought you were keeping a rotten body in there."

Tobin looked shocked. "No, sir! The cottage is used by the cooks sometimes during the winter season, so it's well stocked. I haven't been letting anyone in."

Logan tried the door on the right-hand side of the corridor and found himself in a cramped bedroom, the sheets of its small cot unkempt and stained. He grimaced and backed out, trying the door to the left. A small eating room with a table and a single, rickety-looking chair. Another door led back through to what Logan took to be the kitchen with the festering smell.

"You don't mind if I sit?" he asked rhetorically, before easing himself carefully down into the chair. His back was still aching. Tobin stood awkwardly by the door, still dripping with muck and looking like he was about to throw up. Logan was glad he was in no fit state to make a run for it, because he was in no fit state to try and catch him again.

"What's got you so afraid then, Tobin?" he asked, stretching his stiff legs out under the table. "What causes a man to lock himself away in this sty for a whole month? You're practically on your deathbed."

Tobin blanched an even paler shade.

"It's just the bad food, sir!"

"I pray so, for both our sakes," Logan said. "Because if I start breaking out in sores or black welts I'm coming straight back here and putting you out of your misery."

He laconically stabbed his knife into the grubby tabletop, letting it quiver there.

"Start talking."

"I signed on to work the Fallowhearth kitchens at the end of summer," Tobin began hesitantly. "It was my first time."

"Where were you working before?"

"Strangehaven, sir. I got talking to a rotisseur from Skydown who said there were better opportunities in Frostgate during high season. But when I went there the work had all dried up. Fallowhearth was all I could find."

"What a tragic story," Logan said, without a hint of compassion. "Those are dark locks you've got, Tobin, and even darker eyes. You don't look like you're from Strangehaven. In fact you don't look like you're from anywhere north of Tamalir."

"I was born in Summersong, sir," Tobin said, almost apologetically.

"Hah," Logan said. "I knew it! I'm from Summersong originally. That explains our shared good looks. Please, continue."

Tobin seemed to relax fractionally, though Logan made a mental note to get out of the way if he looked like throwing up – his cloak had suffered enough in the past few weeks without adding some destitute cook's bile to the muck.

"So you found work for the winter at the citadel," he said. "And you were in the care of the lovely Matron Mildred. Did something happen between you two?"

"Of a sort, sir," Tobin said unhappily. "She's… something of a hard taskmaster. All the other servants fear her. She threatened to have me caned once for undercooking the seneschal's tusker shank. For what it pays, it's not worth it."

"So why not just quit?"

"I can't, sir. Not with indentured seasonal work. I have to wait until spring, but I can't bear it any more."

"So you're just going to run away," Logan said with a smirk. "Smart man. I do that all the time."

"I'm waiting for the next caravan bound for Frostgate," Tobin said. "As soon as it arrives, I'll be gone."

"I bet you will," Logan said. "So you've been holed up for the last month. Have you heard about the baroness's daughter?"

"Lady Kathryn?" Tobin asked, clearly nonplussed. "I think she took control of the estates here about a year ago. She spends most of her time in the citadel."

"Did you see her often when you were working there?"

"No. I'm lower-kitchen staff. I've only served the food on a few occasions."

"Well, Tobin, you've been delightfully unhelpful. Apologies for nearly murdering you."

Logan plucked out his knife and then, gripping into the edge of the table, hauled himself to his feet.

"You are an absolute coward, my lad, and I respect that. I wish you well, though do excuse me if I don't shake your hand."

He waved Tobin aside as he limped for the front door.

"I'm Logan, by the way," he said as he went, flashing his best winning smile at the unfortunate cook. "Logan Lashley."

Tobin showed no reaction. Logan paused at the door.

"Logan, Hero of Sudanya? Master of Sixspan Hall? One of the Borderlands Four? Most famous rogue of his time?"

Tobin shrugged.

"How can you be from Summersong and not know who Logan Lashley is?" Logan demanded angrily.

"I… I was very young when I left, sir," Tobin said lamely. Logan dismissed him with an angry wave and, sighing, stepped out into the night.

It was dark by the time Durik returned to the keep. He only got as far as the front gate. Logan and Ulma were already there, the rogue on one side of the lowered portcullis arguing furiously with Captain Kloin on the other, while the dwarf just stood, looking too tired to care any more. Kloin gave

Durik his sneering smile when he saw him approaching. The pathfinder noted their belongings, dumped unceremoniously in the dirt outside the gate.

"Well, three is a party," the captain said as Durik came to a stop next to Ulma.

"Durik," Logan said, turning to the orc. "Please restrain me before I stab this bastard. Or better yet, stab him for me. You have a spear, you can definitely reach between the bars."

"I thought the orc was a pacifist," Kloin mocked.

"What's happening?" Durik demanded, ignoring the barb.

"This peasant in armor won't let us into the keep," Logan said, locking eyes with Kloin.

"You have no reason to be in the keep," the captain replied with equal vehemence.

"Apart from the fact it's where my bed is," Logan hissed.

"Not any more. My men are sleeping in those chambers. There was no room in the barrack block."

"Your men are stinking pig-soldiers," Logan said. "We are the Borderland Four!"

"Three," Ulma muttered under her breath.

"Lady Damhán will hardly approve of this when she finds out," Durik said, rather more levelly than Logan.

"Lady Damhán is locked in her room with some ancient book," Kloin said. "She left strict instructions not to be disturbed until dawn. And Seneschal Abelard has retired to his bed, which leaves me acting warden of this keep."

"You really stayed up this late just to spite us?" Ulma asked. "I'm actually quite impressed."

"These are dangerous times," Kloin said, grinning past the portcullis's bars. "And the safety of this citadel is my first and only priority. I'm sure you'll be able to find wonderful accommodation in one of Fallowhearth's inns."

"I will end you!" Logan all but screamed. Sighing, Durik took him by the shoulder and steered him away from the triumphant captain.

"It is late," the orc said. "And Kloin is right. There will be a bed for us somewhere."

"This is why you'll never get on in life," Logan snarled up at him. "Never accept injustice when it's heaped upon you by bitter, inferior men!"

"Quite right, little rogue," Durik said in his most placatory tone, patting Logan as he led him back into town with Ulma in tow. "You can kill the captain in the morning."

It began to rain. Logan's anger turned to surly silence as he found himself back at the Black Crow. Several of Ulma's quarter crowns managed to elicit the fact that there were a few spare beds upstairs. A few more, and the diplomatic purchase of a pot of stew and some flagons of ale, managed to secure the room. There was little demand for accommodation in Fallowhearth these days, the innkeeper admitted, though not before he had pocketed the money.

The three sat at a table in the corner of the taproom, a small, smoky space with a dying fire that hissed and spat as rain fell through the chimney. Only a few hardy patrons remained at the bar, glancing at the unlikely trio and muttering in low voices. One greeted Ulma in passing.

"My, don't you get around," Logan said, shaking the rain from his cloak before sitting down.

"Someone has to," the dwarf answered, taking a long, slow

draught of her ale. "I've heard all sorts of stories tonight."

"Such as?"

"Supposedly there's a half-man, half-crow preying on the townsfolk. Giant spiders, a whole neighboring village that disappeared overnight, buildings and all. The usual mutterings about necromancy. Some of the townsfolk claim in the months leading up to Lady Kathryn's disappearance, a strange woman was in the habit of visiting the castle. According to a few she was a peddler of dark magic. One even claimed she had seduced Lady Kathryn."

"Rustics and their dirty little minds," Logan said, taking a cautious sip from his tankard and grimacing. It tasted rank, but what else should he have expected from a place like this?

"Could this woman they speak of have been from the clans?" Durik asked. "That could have been the source of the rumors about her kidnapping."

"I don't know," Ulma said. "But there's more. Giant crow-man or not, it seems people have been going missing. At first, I assumed it was just folk getting out of town, like those villagers we met on the road north. But everyone I spoke to was adamant. The butcher's daughter is missing, and an old vagrant well known about the town hasn't been seen for weeks."

"How can you tell if someone around here is a vagrant or just a normal townsperson?" Logan asked innocently. The other two ignored him. Typical.

"So, the baroness's daughter isn't the only one to disappear," Durik said. "That complicates things."

"You're overthinking," Logan declared, setting down his tankard and pushing it away from him. "It's obvious what is happening here."

"Feel free to enlighten us, O great investigator," Ulma said as she saw her drink off and signaled to the bar for another.

"Fallowhearth is a miserable northern town presided over by a miserable northern warden, Abelard. The harvest is poor and there are people flocking south looking for a better life. Maybe there are even rumors that the clans are getting more aggressive. The rest of the barony doesn't care. Baroness Adelynn won't intervene to chasten the clans, it's just not worth her while. Coincidentally, the baroness's daughter has just taken up residence. She's a bright child but she's also very much used to being in charge. So how do you solve all those problems? You kidnap her!"

"You think Abelard has taken Kathryn and is hiding her somewhere?" Ulma asked. Logan gestured expansively, trying to make the dwarf understand.

"It all makes sense! How else could she vanish from inside the keep without a trace? Abelard stuffs her in some dungeon he doesn't tell us about, then sends a letter to the baroness saying the northerners have snatched her. He probably expects Adelynn to come north herself and there you have it, he has a personal audience with the baroness and she gets to see how bad it is up here. Maybe she even goes to war with the clans and stops them using Upper Forthyn as a highway to Frostgate every season. That also explains why Abelard looked so unhappy when he realized it was just us and one of the baroness's advisors who had been sent north to deal with this whole mess."

"You have a point," Durik said, mulling the claims over as he helped himself to their shared stew pot.

"I wish it was the most outrageous suggestion I'd heard

tonight, but it doesn't even come close," Ulma added.

"I take it from all this that your missing cook came to nothing?" Durik asked Logan. He scoffed, internally damning the orc's perceptiveness.

"The poor man was in the process of fleeing the town. Apparently, he was tired of Matron Mildred's despotic reign. I almost left with him."

"Told you it would be the easiest lead to follow," Ulma said.

"But your theory doesn't explain everything," Durik pointed out. "How does the book in the fireplace fit in, and why have other people been vanishing? Abelard can't be taking them all?"

"I can't imagine him dressing up as a giant crow either," Ulma added, fishing into her leather smock to tip the barmaid as she brought her a fresh drink. Logan wondered how much the indomitable dwarf had already imbibed that night.

"It doesn't explain what I saw in the cemetery either," Durik went on. "There was a family missing from their crypt. And it looked as though they got up and walked out."

Logan laughed, then realized he was being serious. That was just the sort of story he could do without before going to bed.

"I looked for any sign that I was mistaken. The markings were old, but clear enough. More people came out of that crypt than entered it. And they walked out."

"Was there any sign of Kathryn, though?" Ulma asked.

"Only the tomb-keeper's testimony."

"Bet he was a withered, half-demented old creature," Logan said.

"He was young, and seemed sound of mind, if a little too

earnest. Certainly he was no fool, regardless of what the seneschal's hatred of the cult of Nordros may lead him to think. I believe what the keeper said. Or, I believe he thinks he saw something."

"Two very different things," Ulma mused.

"True. Whatever he saw, the trail goes cold beyond the cemetery gate."

"Which means we're no further forward than we were when we arrived," said Logan. "Except for the evidence that there's someone in this cursed town practicing necromancy."

"Maybe," Durik said. "Necromancy has been unheard of in Forthyn for years. The dark reign of Waiqar is long since ended, and practicing is a capital crime. The tomb-keeper had certainly never come across any cases, and his family have been tending to those graves for generations."

"So what do we do?" Logan asked, his tone surly. Unaccounted-for corpses were just the sort of thing he didn't want to be investigating further. "I'm open to suggestions, including having that bastard Kloin beheaded and mounted on a pike come the morning. That might improve the look of the town."

"We should ask the butcher what has become of his daughter," Durik said. "But not before we tell Lady Damhán about at least some of this. We report to her, after all. And that can wait until we've all had a good night's rest."

"I should be so lucky," Logan grumbled, finishing the last of the stew.

CHAPTER EIGHT

The weather showed no sign of improving the next day – if anything, it got worse. The rain continued to fall, and dark clouds kept gathering. Logan felt sure they were conspiring together about something sinister.

They took some gritbread for breakfast in the Black Crow, then returned to the castle. This time there was no Kloin to waylay them. Lady Damhán received them in the castle's hall, empty but for a serving maid waiting on the lady's breakfast. Damhán seemed unconcerned with Kloin's ousting of the band from their chambers the night before. She informed them she had sent the captain with Abelard earlier that morning to investigate rumors of a clan raid against a village barely an hour's ride east of Fallowhearth. The town garrison – just thirty men-at-arms, not counting the levies – was so small that Abelard had previously been able to do little about stories of attacks, but Lady Damhán's willingness to lend her dozen-strong retinue to the task meant Abelard was now able to ride out. Or, Logan suspected, the seneschal just wanted to seem busy now that the baroness's representatives had arrived.

They presented the previous day's findings to Damhán, minus Logan's theory about Abelard. She chewed slowly on the cold piece of fowl the maid had served to her, listening intently.

"I will pay a visit on the town butcher this afternoon," she said once they had finished. "In the meantime, I wish for you to go after Abelard. Help to track the clansfolk. If possible, capture some and bring them here."

"It is very unlikely the clans are involved in the disappearances, my lady," Durik said.

"I am aware of that, master pathfinder. But the clans may still have heard something, and it is necessary for us to make sure. Once we have one or two, I will send them south to Highmont, to Baroness Adelynn. It will reassure her that we are being proactive and close the line of inquiry leading back to the clans."

"If they aren't willing to come quietly, it would amount to kidnapping," Ulma pointed out.

"Is that a problem?"

The trio looked at each other.

"Well," Logan said, sounding quite unconcerned. "We have kidnapped people before."

"Once," Ulma clarified. "And it was a Uthuk Y'llan, so…"

"If you think it wise, my lady, we will follow after Abelard," Durik said. "But I doubt it will further our search beyond the closure you mention."

"Any luck with the book?" Logan asked.

"A little," Damhán said, looking less than impressed at being questioned by the rogue. "I have sent ravens to the sorcerers' guilds in Highmont and Last Haven seeking their opinion on a number of aspects."

"Is it… safe?"

"Yes," Damhán said. Her tone brooked no more questions. Durik bowed them out of the chamber.

"This is a waste of time," Logan said as they waited outside for their horses to be brought from the stables.

"Mostly, yes," Durik said. "But Lady Damhán's orders do have some merit. The clans may not be responsible for Lady Kathryn's disappearance, but they could have a sighting of her, or more recent knowledge of her whereabouts. And it will help to prove the clans haven't taken her. That should help focus Damhán's attentions elsewhere."

"How will we convince any of them to come to Fallowhearth?" Logan asked. "Relations between the barony and the clansfolk don't exactly seem to be at an all-time high right now."

"We'll have to work that out when we encounter them," Durik said. "And hopefully before either Kloin or Abelard get to them."

The village's name was Barrowdelve. It lay at a confluence of narrow woodland paths east of Fallowhearth, a collection of log cabins, lumber yards and sawmills surrounded by overgrown stumps. Durik claimed that years before such logging communities had been commonplace, when civilized – or, as Logan called them, semi-civilized – people had first started to clear the forests. Once Blind Muir had blanketed all of Upper Forthyn, from the foothills of the Dunwarrs to the walls of Frostgate, but the work of generations had shrunk its thorny borders and left these patches of isolated woodland scattered across the countryside.

It became apparent as the three rode into Barrowdelve's little square that hard times had finally caught up with the forester village. It looked deserted, sitting silent in the rain. Doors and shutters stayed barred, and nothing stirred as Durik reined in his mount and looked around.

"Abelard and his men passed through here recently," he said, judging the flooded hoof prints pockmarking the village square. "Two hours, maybe three."

"The locals are probably just tired of providing welcoming committees for visitors from Fallowhearth," Logan said ruefully, glancing around. Durik noted that, despite the rogue's light tone, he'd thrown his sodden cloak back over his shoulder and had one hand resting on the ridiculously bejeweled pommel of his sword.

Durik sniffed the damp air before dismounting and crouching, inspecting the marks in the thick mud more closely.

"There are other prints beneath the hoof markings," he said. "But they've been trampled on. They're difficult to read in these conditions."

"So, we're dealing with a whole missing village now," Logan said. "Perfect."

"Could the clans have taken them?" Ulma asked.

"I doubt it," Durik said slowly, standing and turning. "But perhaps she can tell us?"

An aged woman had been sheltering in one of the log cabin's doorways, overlooking the square, at least since Durik had dismounted. Silent and still, she'd gone unnoticed by the other two.

"Pollux's hammer," Logan swore as he spotted her, making Ishbel snort with fright.

Durik approached the woman. She made no attempt to draw back from him. She was stooped over and wizened, her hunched shoulders draped in a plaid shawl. Her thick brown hair was tangled, parts of it plaited together into dozens of braids. In her bony hands she grasped a short wooden stave, its top carved in the rudimentary likeness of a snarling dog or wolf. Durik stopped before her door, towering over her, and splayed his fingers over his chest.

"Greetings, elder," he said.

The woman said nothing. Instead, she reached up with her free hand and, slowly, brushed Durik's face. The fingers probed his tusks, edged around his nose, and swept up over his brow.

"You are an orc," the woman said, her voice a dry croak. Durik realized that she was blind.

"I am," he said. "And I mean you no harm. My name is Durik."

"I am Ann Mogg," the woman said.

"My companions and I are seeking those who passed through your village this morning, Ann Mogg."

"I did not speak with them," she replied. "They stopped here only briefly."

"Do you know which way they rode?"

"You will discover that for yourself," Ann Mogg said. "You have the smell of a hunter about you."

"That is true," Durik said. "If I may, I will ask one more question, and then my companions and I will leave you in peace."

"You wish to know where the people have gone," Ann stated.

"Yes. Have the clans taken them?"

Ann Mogg made a hacking sound that Durik eventually realized was laughter.

"No, they have not. I was a clanswoman, once, a long time ago. I married a forester when this village was first planted. I have lived here since that day, but I haven't seen the clans pass through for many years. That was before the gods took my sight from me."

"Then where have the village folk gone?" Durik asked.

"South. Blown away on the wind of a rumor. These days it gusts stronger than ever."

"They thought the clans were going to attack them?"

"I told them such a thing would not happen, but these days ignorance and stupidity are far stronger than the words of an old woman. They left three days ago."

"And they abandoned you?"

"I refused to leave. This is my home."

"Did the clans come in the end?"

Ann Mogg scoffed. "A few youths from the Redferns this morning. They left me alone, took a few chickens. I told them to."

Durik digested the news. It was as he had feared – the clans were simply foraging, not raiding the surrounding countryside, and it made it even less likely that the group they were pursuing had anything to do with Kathryn's disappearance. But Abelard, for starters, wouldn't accept that. He glanced up into the rain. It showed no sign of abating. A few hours more and the tracks would start to become difficult to read.

"Will you be able to take care of yourself out here, alone?" Durik asked. Ann Mogg smiled thinly.

"My husband passed almost twenty winters ago, pathfinder," she said. "I will live twenty winters more, if the gods will it."

"Very well," Durik acknowledged. "We must be on our way. Those we follow will be drawing ahead of us."

"Further than you know," Ann Mogg said. "Farewell, pathfinder."

"A group of clansfolk have passed through here," Durik reported back to Ulma and Logan. "The villagers fled before they arrived."

"They've hardly left the place looted and ravaged," said Logan. "Not that I imagine there's much to steal."

"Because you and I both know the clans have no squabble with the people of Upper Forthyn," Durik said. "But we need to prove that to Damhán, and Adelynn. We need to find these Redferns."

"Presumably before Abelard," Ulma added.

"And how are we going to convince the clansfolk to come with us back to Fallowhearth?" Logan asked. "Or Highmont for that matter?"

"They're hungry," Durik said. "Otherwise they wouldn't be roaming this far south at this time of year. Food can be a powerful motivator."

"Which way, then?" Ulma asked.

"The hooves of Abelard's band continue east, into the forest," Durik said. "I can only assume they are following the tracks of the Redfern. There are traces beneath the more recent prints that suggest a group of four or five, on foot."

"Lead on then, pathfinder," Logan said, pulling his cloak close around his shoulders.

They rode beyond the bounds of the village and in amongst the boughs of the forest. The rain fell in fat, heavy droplets that pattered on the mulch underfoot, creating a continuing, soft susurration. The carpet of autumn leaves made the tracking easy – Durik led them on into the wood, arcing slowly north.

Beside a lightning-blasted ironroot, the tracks diverged. Durik halted and dismounted to inspect them.

"Abelard lost their trail here," he said as Logan and Ulma rode up. "He split the group into three to try and pick it up again."

"How do we find the northerners now, then?" Logan asked.

"Simple," Durik answered. "We follow the group that went the right way."

"You can still read the clansfolk's tracks?"

Durik gave Logan a look, and the rogue shrugged.

"Just checking you really are the greatest pathfinder in Terrinoth."

"Only you would make a claim like that," Durik said, in no mood for Logan's games. He felt as though they were falling behind, and on the hunt there was no feeling he hated more. "They turned hard east again. Five riders following them. They'll catch up with them soon. We must hurry."

It was early afternoon when they heard a cry echo through the trees. It was followed by an angry shout. Durik cast a glance back at Ulma and Logan, then set his stirrups to his horse's flanks, leaning low in the saddle to avoid the branches and twigs that whipped at him. He heard more shouts, and a clash of steel, ringing cold and hard through the wet woodland.

His stallion burst through the undergrowth into a small,

leaf-choked hollow, overhung by a bent old yew. At its center a group of Abelard's horsemen were attacking a huddled trio of clansfolk. Five riders were striking with swords and maces at two of the men, clad in wool and plaid and armed only with staves. As Durik arrived one fell, his skull split by a brutal blow. A fourth was already lying dead beneath the horsemen's hooves, alongside a brace of trampled poultry.

"Stop!" Durik roared and charged into the fray. Kloin was leading the group of riders, and he turned his horse sharply to intercept the orc as another of his men chopped his sword down through the stave of the next clansman, hacking open his throat.

"This is none of your business, orc," Kloin snarled, but Durik wouldn't be denied – without slowing, he barreled past the captain, his large stallion thrusting the smaller mount into a stumbling retreat. As he did so he untied his short boar spear from around his shoulders.

A single clan member remained, a girl with a silver torc around her neck who screamed in terror as the man-at-arms who had cut open her kinsman's throat raised his bloody sword to cut her down in turn. Durik lunged, at full tilt. His spear caught the man in his unprotected armpit as he brought up his arm to strike, and Durik felt the impact judder up the haft as it plunged through heart and lungs and jarred off a rib. The weight and momentum behind the strike lifted the man from his saddle and sent him tumbling into the leaf mulch, still skewered by Durik's spear.

Shock at what had happened gave Durik enough time to dismount and draw his long skinning knife. Kloin was the first to respond – with a cry of rage he swung his sword at Durik.

It rebounded with an ear-aching clang from a second blade. Logan, still mounted, pushed his horse in between Kloin and Durik, raising his sword once more. Ulma had arrived on the other side of the surrounded clanswoman, her mallet in one hand and a vial of fizzing purple liquid in the other.

"You just made me break a promise, captain," Logan said.

For a second, Durik thought the furious men-at-arms were about to fall on them in a hacking, stabbing frenzy. Logan's voice, strong and clear, again cut through the tension.

"Four against three. Not great odds for anyone wanting to take on the Borderland Four. Even less so when you consider the fact that we also have a clanswoman whose kin you've just murdered on our side."

"It'll be three against three if I throw this," Ulma added, shaking her vial menacingly. "Immorlative. Which one among your fine gentlemen wants to burn first?"

"This is an outrage," Kloin shouted. "I won't stand for this, you murdering scum!"

"Look who's talking," Logan shot back at him.

"These people are savages," Kloin fumed, pointing his sword at the girl cowering between the trio.

"They have harmed no one," Durik said. He knelt down beside one of the fallen clansmen. He was only a youth, barely come of age. His pale face seemed strangely peaceful, a cruel contrast to the vicious red gouge in his throat. He was dead.

"Did Abelard give you leave to slaughter these people?" Ulma demanded of Kloin.

"They resisted," the captain said. "My men were only defending themselves."

"Five grown soldiers, armed and armored, forced to defend

themselves by butchering three starving boys and a girl?" Logan responded. "In better circumstances you'd make me laugh, captain."

"You've killed one of the baroness's personal retinue," Kloin said. "Once we return to Fallowhearth you will all be thrown in irons and you, orc, will hang."

"Perhaps," Durik said, standing up and laying a hand on the clan girl's shoulder. She was shaking and terrified, her eyes red with tears. It was all he could do to keep his rage in check and his expression controlled. He didn't want to frighten her further.

"We mean you no harm," he said to her, speaking in Goltacht, the language of the northern clans. "If you come with us, my friends and I will protect you. I swear it by blood oath, on Kurnos's great horn."

He slid his knife quickly along the back of his forearm, drawing a thin stream of blood. He knew enough about the northern clans to understand the importance of a promise made with blood.

The declaration seemed to have the desired effect. The girl sniffed and managed to nod. Durik mounted his horse and helped her up behind him, securing her skinny arms around his broad chest. Then he leaned down and dragged his spear from the body of the man-at-arms he had run through.

"We'll see you in Fallowhearth," he said to Kloin, holding his furious gaze as he walked his horse past him and out of the hollow. He kept the bloody spear in one fist as Logan and Ulma followed.

They rode hard for Fallowhearth. Logan knew he didn't need to stress the importance of speed – Gods only knew what stories Kloin would concoct for Lady Damhán if he arrived back at the castle first.

They were admitted at the main gate, the guards throwing dark glances at the girl still clinging to Durik. He kept her right by him as they dismounted and entered the keep, a protective hand on her shoulder.

"Might want to put the spear away now, Dur'," Logan murmured to him as they waited outside the main hall. Durik didn't seem to have realized he still had it in his grip. With a grunt, he tied it back over his shoulder, its tip still red.

Inside the hall, Lady Damhán was waiting for them. Bar the odd sniff, the clan girl had remained silent as they had ridden through Fallowhearth. Now, however, she let out a little whimper. Logan wondered whether she had somehow met Lady Damhán before.

The advisor watched in silence as Durik led the girl in, Logan and Ulma behind them. Logan realized that the tome they had discovered in Kathryn's chambers was lying open on the banquet table before her. Damhán's expression remained inscrutable as she spoke.

"You made good time with your return."

"We had good reason to get back," Logan said. "Mostly relating to your friend, Captain Kloin."

"Does she understand the common tongue?" Damhán asked, looking at the girl and ignoring Logan. The rogue didn't respond – he wasn't sure any of them had actually paused to consider that question. Durik said something to the girl in a language that he didn't recognize.

"I understand," she said falteringly, her voice tinny in the cold hall.

"Where did you find her?" Damhán asked Durik, as though the girl wasn't standing there.

"We rescued her from your men-at-arms," the orc said stonily. "They had already murdered three of her kinsmen."

"Elaborate."

"We tracked Abelard's little expedition east," Logan said, deciding it was best to interrupt Durik before he said something unwise. He'd rarely seen the stoic orc so angry. "We found Captain Kloin attacking a small group of clansfolk. They were unarmed, but they killed them anyway. We… intervened."

"You convinced Kloin to stand down?"

"I ran one of his men through," Durik said. "Killed him." Logan closed his eyes and sighed, any hope he had harbored of downplaying what had happened in the forest now gone.

Damhán seemed unperturbed by the news. She beckoned the girl with one bony finger.

"Come here, my child."

Logan stayed where he was with Ulma at the far end of the table while Durik accompanied the clan girl to Damhán's side. He almost had to push her the last few yards, though Logan noted he also had his hand on his skinning knife. This day really, really wasn't going the way he had planned it.

"What's your name?" Damhán asked the girl, ignoring Durik's looming threat.

"I am Carys Mogg," the girl said. She seemed afraid of the book resting before Damhán, casting furtive glances at it.

"That is a common name among the Redfern clan, is it not?"

"Yes," Carys said.

"They are your clan?"

"Yes."

"And how old are you, Carys Redfern?"

"Fifteen summers… I think."

Damhán paused, as though considering the information, then placed one hand on the open pages of the tome.

"Do you know what this is?"

Carys shook her head, a little too quickly. Damhán looked at her for what felt like an age, and Logan realized that he was sweating despite the autumn chill. There was something utterly penetrating about Damhán's eyes, something that went beyond merely being discerning or astute. He couldn't help but pity the girl.

"What were you doing in this part of Forthyn?" Damhán continued. "You and your clansfolk?"

"We were on our way to Frostgate for the last of the harvest bartering," Carys said. "The summer has been short and poor. My friends left the camp to go and find food."

"Or steal food?" Damhán wondered.

"The places we came across were all abandoned," Carys protested. "The food was going to waste."

"She speaks the truth," Durik interjected. "The village we rode through, Barrowdelve, was abandoned."

"We were looking for the clan's trail when we were attacked," Carys said, fresh tears welling up.

"Where was Abelard during this?" Damhán asked, directing the question at the trio.

"He lost the trail," Durik said. "So he divided his riders. The group led by Kloin was the one that caught up with the Redferns."

"I will have to corroborate that with both Abelard and Kloin once they return," Damhán said. "In the meantime, I will have this girl conducted to the dungeon." Both Logan and Ulma began to protest, and Durik's voice rose above them.

"She is not a prisoner," Durik said as Carys began to cry again. He was angry, and he was no longer doing much to hide it. "She is a subject of Terrinoth, and she has done nothing wrong!"

Damhán looked at the orc, her expression as cold as the peaks of the Dunwarrs.

"As Captain Kloin has likely already told you, the garrison house is full, and your rooms are taken. There is nowhere else for her to stay besides the dungeon and, prisoner or not, I will not permit her to spend the night beyond the castle walls, not until I have questioned her further."

"There is a spare room," Ulma said abruptly. All eyes turned to the dwarf.

"Lady Kathryn's," she said, her thumbs stuck casually in the pockets of her leather apron. "Why can't she spend the night there?"

Logan expected Damhán to deny the suggestion immediately, but instead she looked at Durik.

"You are certain there is no more you can glean from searching Lady Kathryn's room? No traces of her that you might have missed?"

"I am sure," Durik said. "That chamber has nothing more to offer us."

"Then I will have the servants prepare it for our guest," Damhán said. "And since you seem so concerned with her safety, pathfinder, you can stand watch outside her door. If I awake tomorrow and find that she is gone, you can consider your contracts terminated and your status reduced to outlaws of the barony of Forthyn. Am I clear?"

Logan nodded, followed by Ulma. Durik didn't move, except to take his hand off the hilt of his knife.

CHAPTER NINE

Kloin returned not long after. At some point Abelard had caught up with him. Logan had just finished pilfering food from the castle scullery when he heard raised voices coming from the hall. He considered taking the other way out through the kitchens, but heard the bass tones of Mildred scolding someone just beyond the door. Given Tobin's stories about the matron he decided he'd rather risk the wrath of a force of recently bereaved men-at-arms over being caught in her domain. He climbed the stairs into the hall.

Kloin and Abelard were standing at the far end of the table, flanked by several of their men. They were clearly fresh from the road, cloaks still hanging off their shoulders and their boots and breeches spattered with mud. Damhán was in Abelard's high chair at the far end of the table before the hearth, the tome still opened before her. She looked less than captivated by whatever Kloin or Abelard was saying.

Ulma and Durik had left the castle minutes earlier for the tavern, and Logan abruptly regretted lingering behind to fill his belly. He made an effort to keep to the edge of the hall and work his way around the angry gathering, towards the main door. He got all of three yards before everyone saw him. Kloin transfixed him with an accusatory finger.

"There he is! Murderer!"

"Actually, Durik is the murderer," Logan said, immediately beginning to backpedal towards the scullery stairs. "I, in fact, prevented a double murder being committed when I stopped you from cutting his head off."

"You'll hang," Kloin raged, beginning to move around the table towards Logan. "All three of you!" Logan changed course, keeping the table between him and the advancing men-at-arms. Damhán remained seated, looking decided unimpressed with all around her.

"Seneschal, you won't allow violence in the walls of your own keep, will you?" Logan pleaded with Abelard. The warden looked torn. Clearly he had no desire to get caught up in rivalries imported from Highmont – Logan didn't doubt his first and only priority was to impress Lady Damhán. The seneschal kept his mouth shut.

"My lady," Kloin practically shouted at Damhán. "I don't know what they've told you, but this is the truth. The orc murdered one of my men. He ran him through like a beast at the hunt, like a brute boar!"

"I'm amused that you would say that," Damhán said, her words stilling Kloin's fury. "Very 'boring' indeed. I fear you must learn not to raise your voice in my presence, captain."

Kloin opened his mouth to speak, but no sound came out. A look of surprise replaced the raw anger coloring his face.

"I've never really paid much attention to you, Kloin," Lady Damhán said, still not moving from her seat, like a predator using its stillness to attract prey. "For quite obvious reasons. You are of no importance to me whatsoever. In all honesty, I didn't know who you were until we departed Highmont. You happened to have finished your watch duties when Baroness Adelynn insisted I take protection. That is the extent of how highly you were recommended for this undertaking."

The captain's features had gone white with fear. He tried once more to speak, but the only sound that passed his lips was a low, ugly croak. The hairs on the nape of Logan's neck prickled, and he found himself now edging the opposite way around the table, away from Damhán and closer to the men-at-arms.

"But despite the baroness's directives, I do not need your protection, Captain Kloin," Damhán went on, her voice finding the precise tone of a tutor berating an unruly child. "You are here to give Baroness Adelynn peace of mind. Nothing more. You are certainly *not* here to raise your voice in my presence. Do that again, and I might not give it back."

Damhán tapped a single digit on the open page before her, the smallest of motions. Kloin let out an audible cry, the abrupt sound seeming to surprise even him. He stumbled back, a hand going up to his throat, staring at Damhán. Then, without a word, he turned and fled from the hall. An ugly silence settled in his wake. Logan kept very still.

"My apologies if we have disturbed you, my lady," Abelard said carefully. "Is there anything you require of me?"

"No," Damhán said idly, turning her attention back to the book and slowly turning a page. "I will see you at supper tonight, seneschal."

Abelard bowed and made his own hasty exit, waving the men-at-arms out with him. Logan began to tiptoe after them.

"Master Lashley."

Logan froze and half turned, trying to conjure up a smile. "My lady?"

"I visited the butcher today. The one your dwarf companion mentioned in your report. Unsurprisingly, it seems at least some of the rumors relating to these disappearances were false. His child was healthy and well, and he told me she hasn't been missing for a moment."

"Well, praise Kellos," Logan said, daring to take another step towards the door. "I'll be sure to tell the others!"

Damhán said nothing, turning another page. Holding his breath, Logan edged out of the hall.

"Did you know Lady Damhán is a sorceress?"

"Yes," Ulma said. Logan flailed his arms in exasperation. They were upstairs in their rented room at the Black Crow. Logan had thought it wise to return there immediately, and had spent much of the rest of the day feasting on the food he had liberated from the castle. Now he was pacing while Ulma crushed several ingot fragments into her small pestle. Durik had remained at the citadel, guarding Carys.

"She's a powerful one," Logan went on. "Not just some hedge wizard with a high office!"

"The baroness said she had particular abilities that could help our search," Ulma said, not taking her eyes off her work.

"Since when did that automatically mean skilled sorceress? I haven't seen something like that since…"

He trailed off.

"Since Dezra?" Ulma finished, looking up at him.

"Yes," Logan agreed unhappily, trying to banish the memory of their fourth companion. He had endured enough lost sleep and misery down the years without resurrecting her to haunt him.

"What did Damhán do?"

"She stole Kloin's voice."

Ulma scoffed, placing a sliver of metal in the pestle. "Is that it? Bet you loved that."

"I would if she hadn't given it back. Or if I didn't think she was about to do the same to me."

"Durik said you started off badly with her," Ulma shrugged. "I don't think there's anything wrong with her. You're just the sort of man who doesn't like being told what to do by the opposite sex."

"Durik said I started off badly with her?" Logan asked, sounding betrayed. Ulma sighed.

"I rest my case." The dwarf uncorked a vial of dark liquid and poured it delicately into the pestle. The metal hissed and fizzed as it dissolved. Logan withdrew rapidly.

"That's not going to explode, is it?"

"Probably not."

"Thank the gods," Logan said relaxing fractionally.

"It's more likely to poison the air as we sleep. But it should be fine."

"Maybe I'll go and spend the night on watch with Durik…"

"Be my guest," Ulma said, smiling brightly.

"You just want to get rid of me, don't you?" The rogue scowled. Ulma sighed and set her mortar down.

"I'm sorry, Logan," she said.

"What for?" he asked suspiciously.

"For the way I speak to you."

"Isn't… that how you've always spoken to me?"

"Alright, I'm sorry for the way I've spoken to you since we met again."

"I mean, apology accepted, I suppose," Logan said, offering a slight shrug. "But why now?"

"Because I have a bad feeling about this – all of it – and I don't want you to die thinking I hate you. I just have occasional bouts of strong dislike."

"Who said anything about dying?" Logan asked, alarmed. This was just about the last sort of conversation he had expected to be having with Ulma tonight. What had gotten into her?

"No one, I'm being dramatic."

"How un-Ulma like."

"Logan, why are you here?" Ulma pressed, her expression serious. "I mean, why did you take this job? Do you have debts? Gambling, or worse?"

"What an outrageous thing to ask a gentleman!" Logan huffed, crossing his arms defensively.

"Gambling it is, then."

"I pay a scribe at Greyhaven University a good deal of money to reassure me that my debts are manageable," Logan said. "Especially if I just never go back to Summersong. Besides, I told Baroness Adelynn that I wasn't doing this for a reward, financial or otherwise."

"How very noble of you. But that doesn't answer my first question. Why are you here? Why did you leave that home you go on about and travel halfway across the Land of Steel when you must have expected you'd end up in a place like this?" She nodded at their shabby surrounds. Logan sighed and sat down in the set opposite her.

"You know I worked solo for a while after the group split up," he said, his thoughts wandering as the memories came back. "Tried to make it on my own. Succeeded too, damn it. But it was never quite the same. Not after..." He trailed off. Sudanya loomed large in all their lives. He didn't need to tell Ulma he'd missed the bonds they'd forged in that bleak, desolate place.

"Dezra?" Ulma asked quietly.

"No, not just Dezra. I missed all of you. Yes, even you, dear dwarf."

Ulma smiled and Logan stood up once more, clearing his throat, as though to mask what he'd just said. He paced back over to his bed and grimaced, looking up at the timber rafters above it.

"There's a spider up there," he noted, glaring at the little arachnid in its web.

"Still afraid of them?" Ulma asked, sounding amused.

"After what we went through I don't know how you're not."

"I thought you said you missed the old days. Sudanya. That labyrinth of ruin." Logan shivered slightly, feeling his skin crawl. Too many memories there, of creeping, crawling death.

"I missed some parts of it. The arachyura and their queen aren't included in that."

"Ariad, I'd almost forgotten about her. That spider bitch and her tricks. She nearly lured us all to our doom."

"Durik stuck her," Logan said. "And then the overlord. What a bastard he was. Withered old beast."

"See, happy memories," Ulma said, getting up from the table and joining Logan beside his bed. She clambered up onto it, ignoring his complaints as her boots sank into the straw mattress, and snatched at the web above it. The spider fled, scuttling up onto the rafter and away into the dark.

"There," she said, jumping back down to the floor. "Like you said. Just like old times."

Durik had placed the platter on the table beside the mirror over an hour earlier. It was still full, the bread and chicken untouched.

"You should eat," he said in Goltacht.

Carys didn't reply. She was sitting with her legs crossed in the middle of Kathryn's bed, still wearing her woolen tunic and plaid, the torc around her neck bright in the torchlight. She looked at Durik warily from beneath her unkempt, dark hair. He had seen that look many times before – it was the expression of an animal trying to gauge whether he meant to do it harm or not.

"If you need me, I will be outside," he said, turning towards the door. He had been sitting on the steps by the narrow landing outside since Carys had been taken to it, cleaning the dry blood off his spear's tip and working it out of the haft. He expected it to be a long, slow night.

"Who used to sleep here?" Carys asked abruptly, making Durik pause. "Whose room is this?"

"How do you know it isn't just a spare bedchamber?" he asked, turning back.

"I can still smell her," Carys said. "On the pillows. Who was she?"

"Some were hoping you would already know about that," Durik said. "Her name was Kathryn."

"Where is she now?"

"We don't know. That is why we are here, my friends and I. We were asked to look for her."

"She is someone great? A chieftain?"

"A chieftain's daughter," Durik said. "She was to rule these lands when her mother passed on. But now she has vanished."

"If you are looking for her then why have you taken me?" Carys asked. The tone wasn't accusatory, but it still stung Durik.

"The master of this town blames your people for his troubles. He claims you took Kathryn."

Carys seemed to consider the statement very seriously for a moment before speaking.

"Why? What reason would the Redfern have to take her?"

"I do not know," Durik admitted. He was angry that he couldn't offer the girl greater reassurance, that there wasn't a good reason why she'd been kidnapped and her companions slain. Telling her that he thought it was all folly and madness wouldn't help. "Do you think any of the other clans would?"

"No," Carys said, as though it was a stupid question. "The winter has come early in the north. We only want to make it to Frostgate before the snows do. We have already suffered from the revenants. A war with the southerners would end my people."

"The revenants?" Durik asked.

"*Beò marbh*," Carys said. Durik shook his head.

"*Beò marbh*? I'm sorry, I do not know this phrase."

"It is like… death," Carys said slowly, pronouncing the

words carefully. "Like... Waiqar."

Durik felt a chill at the mention of the great necromancer. Many centuries before Waiqar had betrayed his allies in the war against Llovar's demons and turned to unspeakable magics. His legions of the living dead had terrorized the length and breadth of Terrinoth during the Second Darkness, before he had finally been defeated.

"Waiqar has been dead for centuries," he said. Carys shrugged.

"His children remain. I have seen one myself. It killed my uncle, then made him walk, like a puppet. We had to kill him again, with fire."

Durik was silent for a moment, trying to rationalize what she was describing. A rogue necromancer on the loose in the north? Surely it couldn't be the work of Waiqar. He'd been consigned to myth and legend long ago.

"That's why so many of the clans are coming south so early in the season?" he said slowly. "You are being threatened by dark magics?"

Carys nodded. "I am sorry that your chieftain's daughter is dead," she said. "But we cannot help you find her."

"Why do you think she is dead?" Durik asked, surprised. Carys frowned.

"You said her name was Kathryn. Not her name *is* Kathryn."

"My Goltacht needs practice," Durik lied.

"You speak it well," Carys said. "When they come I will try and to stop them from killing you."

"Who? Who is coming?"

"I'm the daughter of Maelec Morr," she said. "Carys Morr, youngest child of the chieftain of the Redferns. I told your mistress my name was Mogg because I fear what she may do if she discovers she has a chieftain's daughter in her power. But I fear what my father may do even more. When he realizes I am missing, he will send the Son of the Wild to bring me home. I hope you are not the one guarding me when he arrives."

Durik considered her words, his expression unreadable even as his mind raced. This was no mere clan girl lost in the woods. She was of royal blood. Another mistake made by Damhán and that idiot Abelard. He suppressed the news for the moment, pointing at the platter. He needed time to think.

"Eat," he said, and turned to leave.

As he opened the door, Carys called out after him. "I promise, orc. They will come for me."

The voice woke Durik, crashing by like thunder. It boomed through the citadel, accompanied by a flash of white lightning that seared in past the arrow slit in the turret's stairwell.

The pathfinder stood, cursing softly. He'd dozed off – he really was starting to get old. He cracked his back and stretched his arms, trying to work out the cold that had crept into them on the stone steps while he'd been asleep. Rain was trickling in through the arrow slit and running down the stairs below him.

He stood for a while, eyes closed, listening. The storm had broken, a deluge battering at the stone walls of the castle. Thunder growled and snarled again, a little further off this time.

Something was wrong. He had no reason to think so, other than his instincts. His whole body felt charged, as though set alight by the storm.

Then he remembered the voice. That had been what woke him, not the thunder. He couldn't remember exactly what it had said, but he could remember who it had sounded like.

Dezra.

He took a few steps down, then up, to the door that led to the top of the tower. It was locked from the inside – no one could have done so from out on the parapets. No one could have gotten past him to reach it, either.

He returned to the landing, the memory of Volbert's words in the graveyard coming back to him. He had described something unnatural about the night of Kathryn's disappearance, something unsettling. Durik had traveled far enough through Terrinoth and beyond not to dismiss his words, but nor had he fully understood what he was trying to describe. Until now.

He leant closer to the door to Kathryn's room, thinking he had heard something beneath the constant hammering of the rain outside. A sob? A groan? He turned the door's latch and opened it, slowly.

It was dark inside. He let his vision adjust, scenting the air. A detached part of his mind noted how on edge his body was, how his heartbeat was rising, and his muscles tensed. He stepped over the threshold, silently.

The platter was empty, bar a few crumbs. Rain was pattering down into the barren fireplace and rattling at the small window. The bed had its drapes dawn. Another soft sobbing sound came from beyond.

Durik approached the bed. Without realizing it, he'd moved a hand to the hilt of his knife. He reached up, gripped the drapes, and snatched them aside.

A flash of lightning illuminated Carys's pale, tear-streaked face and lit up her wide eyes as she stared up at Durik. She was hunched over in the bed, the sheets wrapped around her.

"You are afraid of the storm?" Durik asked, trying not to sound awkward as he dropped his hand from his knife. She shook her head wordlessly, bowing forward again.

"You feel it too?" he asked, as thunder followed in the lightning's wake. She looked back up at him, an indistinct shape in the darkness. Between the sobs, she managed a single phrase.

"*Beò marbh.*"

Logan had grown to enjoy storms since his retirement. There was something wonderfully relaxing about being inside, ensconced before the blazing hearth at Sixspan, wrapped up in a rich leonx pelt and with a goblet of mulled wine to hand. It was certainly a happy contrast with the misery of being outside in downpours, winter frosts and all the other elemental tribulations he'd endured during his younger days.

There were times, though, when a storm's fury rose to such a fever pitch that, even indoors, he found himself worrying. There was something fierce about this particular storm, something about how it battered at the thatch and rattled on the shutters, like it was trying to gain entry.

Logan lay in bed and listened to it as it hammered against the tavern. When the thunder spoke, it shook the walls. Water was leaking through from above, pattering to the floor in three separate places across the room. A dagger of lightning sliced past the shutters and lit the space, silhouetting the shape of the spider in its web above his bed. It was back. He shivered.

Sleep was elusive. At some point he rose and sat on the edge of his bed. Ulma was sound asleep across from him, snoring with an intensity fit to rival the storm. He'd known her to sleep through far worse. The memories brought a small smile to his face.

The candle they had left lit on the table was guttering amidst a pool of wax, its light small and weak. They were deep into the deadwatches, the darkest hours of the night. He stretched his legs before standing up carefully. He wandered over to the window, avoiding one of the leaks puddling on the timber floor, and edged the shutters open.

The outside was indistinct, almost pitch-black. The street seethed, a river of water and mud churned up by the incessant rainfall, the humped shapes of the thatched buildings opposite looking as though they were soaked through. He stood watching for a few seconds, marveling at the intensity of the storm. He wondered if the ground floor of the tavern was flooded.

Movement caught his eye, not the uniform movement of the water pouring down, but something more singular and deliberate. The merest suggestion of a shape was moving along the street, past the tavern. Logan peered closer. Surely no one was walking outside on a night like this? Even someone as indomitable as Durik would have sought shelter in this weather.

But his eyesight wasn't playing tricks on him – there was someone down there, working their way slowly along the street, pounded every step of the way by the wind and the rain. For a second Logan's natural reservations were overcome by instinctive pity, and he considered calling out of the window to them, offering them shelter.

Then he realized there were more of them. He counted two, then three, following in the wake of the first. Then more, a mass of people, indistinct in the dark, struggling against the ruthless weather.

"What in the name of the gods," Logan breathed, unease prickling across his skin. A sound in the room behind him made him turn.

It's late," Dezra said, standing by the bed, her cowl drawn up, eyes gleaming in the dark. "You should be sleeping, Logan."

"There are people outside," Logan said, glancing back at her and pointing past the shutters. "Out there in the storm! Can you believe it?"

He turned back to the window. The street was full, a mass of figures pouring past the tavern. And as Logan watched, the lightning flared above, illuminating them. The unease the storm had bred in him surged into outright horror.

In that split second, Logan saw rain glistening on pale, rotting flesh and exposed bone, on white eyes and mud-caked, tattered bodies. A hundred corpses, more, standing, walking, dragging themselves with the slow, decrepit gait of old bodies newly awoken.

Logan screamed.

CHAPTER TEN

Logan woke to a powerful grip on his shoulders.

"No," he screamed again, thrashing. The grip relented, accompanied by a worried voice.

"Calm down, you idiot manling! It's me!"

Logan realized the figure standing over him wasn't a rotting corpse. It was Ulma.

He sat up, panting, his heart pounding painfully in his chest. He was in bed, the sheets slicked with sweat.

"Finally," Ulma snapped. "I thought you'd never stop squealing!"

Logan didn't know what to say. He began shaking uncontrollably. Was he still asleep? Had he been asleep at all, or had it all been real? He ran his fingers through his hair, trying to slow his breathing. What in the name of the gods had happened last night?

"You woke me up with all that screaming," Ulma went on. "What's gotten into you?"

"They were all dead," he stammered, trying and failing to order his thoughts into words. "Dead men walking."

"You had a nightmare," Ulma said, her tone turning irritable. "Come on, get up and get changed. It's late."

Logan realized that weak, pallid sunlight was streaming in through the window. The storm had passed. Still shaking, he got out of bed and stumbled to the half-open shutters. He could remember standing there, transfixed by the ghastly parade. He didn't remember going back to bed.

The street outside was deserted. The mud had been churned up, while the houses sat, drenched and dripping. The sky was pale with morning sunlight, only a few scraps of dark cloud remaining, like a bad memory. There was no one – living or dead – in sight. Logan turned back to Ulma.

"I saw them," he said hoarsely. "In the night. The dead were walking. Hundreds of them!"

"You had a nightmare," Ulma repeated. "It's hardly surprising, given how much stress we've all been under."

"I saw Dezra too," Logan said. "It all felt so real."

"Well if you saw her then it was definitely a dream," Ulma replied dismissively, heading over to the table where she was packing away her vials and potions. "Gods only know what far corner of Terrinoth she's in right now."

Logan had just pulled on a fresh tunic when a knock at the door made him jump. He glanced nervously at Ulma, who rolled her eyes and stomped over to the room's entrance.

"Yes?" she demanded of the barmaid who had knocked.

"There's a man downstairs says he wants to see you both," the disinterested-sounding woman said. "He told me to tell you that it was important."

"What sort of man?" Logan asked from behind Ulma.

The woman shrugged. "Looks like he's from the castle."

Logan and Ulma looked at each other.

"Tell him we'll be right down."

Minutes later they met a servant in Abelard's demi-roc livery. He bowed hastily as they descended the stairs into the tavern's taproom. Logan noted the fear in his eyes and felt his heart rate begin to pick up once more.

"Lady Damhán and Seneschal Abelard request your presence at the castle," the man said. "Urgently."

"Why?" Logan demanded.

"I cannot say for sure, sir," the man said, his tone fretful. "But the town's tombkeeper is with the seneschal right now."

"Oh gods," Logan groaned, shuddering. This couldn't be happening.

Durik, Damhán, Abelard and Kloin were in the castle hall when Logan and Ulma arrived. Volbert was with them. The tomb-keeper was sitting in the chair beside Damhán, his hair and black robes unkempt, face as white as a death shroud. He barely glanced at Logan and Ulma as they entered.

"What's happening?" Logan asked, looking from one face to the next. Damhán's expression was as stony as ever, and Kloin just glared at him, but both Durik and Abelard looked uneasy. And an uneasy Durik was never, in Logan's experience, a good sign.

"Something occurred last night," Abelard said delicately, glancing at Volbert, who was now staring blankly across the table. He looked like he was in shock.

"There has been an attack on the town," Damhán said rather less cryptically. "By a practitioner of dark magics."

"Gods," Logan murmured. "It really wasn't a dream. I told

you!" He looked at Ulma, who in turn spoke to Damhán.

"What do you mean by 'an attack'?" the dwarf demanded.

"The Shrine of Nordros has been violated," Damhán went on. "As the tomb-keeper here can attest."

"You're Volbert?" Ulma asked. The man managed to nod, snapping out of his daze.

"Repeat what you told us earlier this morning," Damhán instructed him.

He swallowed hard and, in a thin voice, addressed Logan and Ulma. "It is my duty to attend to the Shrine of Nordros, and the graveyard that adjoins it. I have been the tombkeeper there almost all my life. Recently my job has become… increasingly difficult." He faltered, then rallied, looking from Ulma to Logan with an earnest expression.

"There have been attacks on the shrine, and the graves. Vandalism. Headstones broken and the shrine doors daubed with paint. Bodies have gone missing. I have done what I can to repair and maintain everything under my care but, this morning…"

He trailed off again and this time didn't seem able to continue, shaking so badly one of the legs of his chair began to thud repeatedly against the stone floor.

"This morning he awoke to find the graveyard empty," Durik said.

"Isn't it empty most of the time?" Ulma asked.

"Not of people. Of bodies. Every single grave and tomb currently lies empty. The earth has been ploughed up, and caskets and sarcophagi have been broken open. Hundreds of them." Logan let out a little involuntary groan of fear.

"You've seen this?" Ulma asked Durik. He nodded.

"I went there at first light, as soon as Volbert came to the castle."

"I saw them," Logan said. "Last night! The storm woke me. They were out in the street, all of the bodies. The dead, walking. I thought it was a nightmare."

"Necromancy," Abelard spat, making the sign of Kellos's flames over his breast. "I knew this day would come. I sent letters to Highmont, to Baroness Adelynn, demanding all the shrines of Nordros in Upper Forthyn be closed. This is what happens when people are allowed to openly worship the dark powers!"

"Your letters were all received, seneschal," Damhán said dryly. "And rejected. Forthyn is not Vynclvale or Dawnsmoor, and the cult of Kellos does not hold preeminence over all others. Adherents to Nordros are still the baroness's subjects and outlawing his worship would simply drive it underground. Besides, in case you hadn't noticed, your local tomb-keeper was not the one responsible for the foul magics cast last night."

"Thank you, my lady," Volbert managed. Abelard glared at him.

"We have to assume that this act of desecration is linked to Lady Kathryn's disappearance," Damhán said. "We can also assume that the sorcerer responsible was in or near to Fallowhearth last night. They cannot have gone far since then."

"With respect, my lady, are we really sure whatever monster is responsible for this is likewise behind the Lady Kathryn's loss?" Abelard asked. "We have not begun to fully question the clan prisoner. She may know the one behind this outrage."

"I will speak to the girl today," Damhán said. "But we must act on this now. The fact that Lady Kathryn was spotted in the very same yard that came under attack is unlikely to be a coincidence."

"Carys felt their presence last night," Durik said. "And so did I. This isn't the work of some clan shaman or primalist. The air was rife with dark energy."

"You seem very certain the clans aren't involved in any of this," Abelard said, his tone accusatory.

"And you seem very certain they are, contrary to evidence," Logan retorted, glaring at the seneschal.

"With just that orc guarding her, how do we know the girl wasn't the one responsible for what happened last night?" Kloin added. "She could be a witch! I thought that the moment I happened upon her."

Durik bared his tusks in anger, but Damhán's warning hand stopped him from rounding the table at Kloin.

"Enough," she said sharply. "This discussion is unproductive. Our priority right now is to track whoever was responsible for last night's desecration. Find them and it is likely we will also find a connection to Lady Kathryn."

"Well that should be easy enough," Ulma said, drawing eyes back to her and Logan. "Presumably the necromancer is with the small army of bodies they just raised," she continued. "So, all we need to do is find where are all those bodies are now."

"They left behind hundreds of fresh tracks, and their direction is clear," Durik said. "They walked out of the town and went south-west. Into Blind Muir Forest."

Silence followed the statement. Logan didn't like the worried looks that crossed the faces of Volbert and Abelard.

The seneschal spoke first.

"Blind Muir is another nest of Nordros worshipers, and worse," he said, glancing distastefully down at Volbert. "No wonder the necromancer responsible for this has made it their home."

"You're familiar with the northern tracts of the forest, seneschal?" Damhán asked.

"Barely. I forbid people from the town to go there. The farmers who till the fields closest to its borders request armed guards to accompany them for most of the year."

"That sounds like little more than superstition," Durik said. "I have traveled through Blind Muir on three separate occasions. It is little different to any other deep forest in Terrinoth."

"And have you ever ventured into its northern reaches?" Abelard demanded. "You will find those tracts quite different from the southern edges above Highmont and Frostgate. They are the domain of vagabonds, cultists and worse."

"Do you think you can track the undead through it?" Damhán asked Durik, ignoring the seneschal.

"Yes," the orc said firmly.

"Then do so, and take your companions. Be alert to any trace of Lady Kathryn's presence."

Logan tried to formulate a protest, but couldn't think of anything to say beyond the fact he had no intention of traipsing into some cursed woodland. He closed his eyes briefly as he mastered himself. Everything would be fine. He'd just stop on the edge of the forest and complain about a bad knee or something similar. Let Durik and Ulma go in without him.

"I will not leave the keep without Carys Mogg," Durik said. Damhán let out an acerbic sigh, and Logan shot him a glance. Why did he always insist on making things even more complicated?

"When I recommended you to Baroness Adelynn, I had no idea you would prove to be so sentimental," she said. "It is quite unbecoming for a creature such as you. I will not allow you to leave with the girl."

"If I leave and she stays, these men will harm her," Durik said, an accusatory sweep of his arm encompassing Abelard and Kloin.

"They will do no such thing," Damhán said.

"Seneschal Abelard's hatred for the clans has been evident since we arrived," Durik pressed. "He has been using every means he has to tie them to Lady Kathryn's disappearance."

"Preposterous," Abelard growled. Logan forced himself not to say something snide. Now, more than ever, he wanted to keep a low profile, before he was saddled with some even more ridiculous quest.

"The clan girl will not be harmed," Damhán said firmly. "But if it would help you to focus on more important matters, pathfinder, I will send Seneschal Abelard with you. He and a detachment of his men-at-arms can aid your hunt, and you can rest assured that he isn't here brutalizing your newly adopted human child."

Logan worried that the sarcasm dripping from Damhán's voice would push Durik over the edge, but the orc nodded before speaking.

"And what about Captain Kloin?"

"I think the seneschal will be all the help we need," Logan

interrupted quickly, glaring at Kloin, who grinned back at him. The last thing he wanted was to go into Blind Muir with a man like Kloin for company.

"The captain will remain here as custodian of the castle until your return," Damhán said. "Under my supervision."

"My lady, this is irregular," Abelard said. He was starting to go red in the face. Logan wondered what he was more unhappy about, his temporary ousting or the thought of having to traverse Blind Muir Forest with a trio of old adventurers. "My task is to safeguard Fallowhearth! The town is clearly threatened, if it falls under attack I will be needed here. To leave now would be a dereliction of my duty."

"Your duty is to Baroness Adelynn, by whose grace you yet hold your post as warden of this citadel," Damhán answered. "Make no mistake, Abelard, she is watching events here closely. She is keenly aware of your lethargy when it comes to the matter of her missing daughter. A month has gone by, and you have failed to turn up any tangible leads. You should be thankful you still hold the title of seneschal."

The adviser's words chilled Abelard's anger. He bowed.

"I will take six of my best men, my lady."

"No horses," Durik said. "They will be ill-suited to a deep wood like Blind Muir."

"You wish us to walk?" Abelard demanded. "By the time we've departed we'll be lucky to reach the edge of the forest by nightfall!"

"Then pack for more than a day," Durik said simply. Damhán nodded.

"The pathfinder is right. In my experience, the dead need no sleep. It may take you some time to catch up with them."

• • •

They set out from the town a little after midday. They weren't the only ones. To Logan it looked as though the greater part of those who'd not yet left had decided that enough was enough. The road south was scattered with individuals and small groups, most of them struggling in the mud with what looked like their worldly possessions. They looked at Logan and the rest of the party with a mixture of fear and disgust. One old woman spat in front of Abelard, and Durik had to ward him off from striking her.

"You are all cursed," the crone hissed, shaking her walking stave. "Fallowhearth is doomed!"

"Charming," Logan muttered.

Durik led them off the main road – itself little more than a strip of dirt churned up by the recent rains – and along the narrow track that led through the fields to the south-west. The open farmland was bleak, the fields lately harvested and empty of livestock. Ahead, the shadow of Blind Muir loomed, a dark, dense expanse that grew steadily nearer as the afternoon wore on. Every step Logan took closer to it increased his desire to go in the opposite direction. The shadows beneath the boughs seemed to leer at him, as though mocking his approach. *That's right, you old fool, a little closer.* If Durik had told him in Highmont that they'd be venturing into some cursed-looking woodland, he'd have turned around and ridden back to Sixspan there and then.

He pushed on, silently wishing he had a stave like the old woman's. The mud was dragging at his heels, and the cold air was making him wheeze. He accepted Ulma's arm. Durik was already carrying his pack.

"Still craving adventure, rogue?" Ulma asked him casually as they walked. He managed to laugh.

"You always forget the drudgery," he said. "We must have walked a thousand miles or more back then."

"You used to make fun of my short legs," Ulma said ruefully. "And I used to make fun of you when you couldn't walk for half a day without needing to rest."

"I think it's a bit less than half a day now," Logan admitted. "Help me catch up with Durik."

He didn't add "so we can get away from Abelard." The surly seneschal and his men-at-arms were following behind the trio, a dire presence that was making Logan nervous. He pushed on with Ulma. Durik was striding ahead, inexhaustible. He nodded to the other two as they caught up.

"Enjoying the walk?" Logan asked with sarcastic brightness.

"It is good for the limbs," Durik said noncommittally.

"Not when you're my age."

"I'm older than you."

"Not when you're not the pinnacle of mature, orcish perfection," Logan rephrased. Durik bared his tusks in a grin. The rogue lowered his voice.

"I saw Dezra," he murmured. "Last night. While the dead walked."

"Where?" Durik asked, displaying no surprise.

"In my room. Standing right there by my bed. I thought it was a dream."

"It does sound like something you'd dream about, little rogue."

"I'm not joking," he said, glancing back again at Abelard and his men-at-arms. "I hadn't thought about her for years, and that's Kellos's honest truth! But the moment I received your letter, there's hardly been a day where she hasn't been in my thoughts. And now she's in my dreams too."

"That's hardly surprising," Ulma spoke up beside him. "I think about her too. You'd expect it, with the rest of us united again. As you said, it's just like old times."

"There's something more to it, I'm telling you," Logan said. "It felt… wrong."

"I bet it did," Ulma smirked.

Logan sighed, changing tack. Gods, he'd forgotten how frustrating these two could be, especially when they had their heads turned by some life-or-death quest.

"Is no one pausing to consider why someone would go to the effort of resurrecting half of Fallowhearth's dead in one night? As far as we know, not a single person in the town was harmed. They even left that mad tomb-keeper alive. They could've massacred everyone sleeping outside of the castle last night and more than tripled their own numbers in the process, but they didn't."

"So why does a necromancer want just a couple of hundred undead rather than a thousand?" Ulma followed up. "It isn't as though they're trying to be subtle either, or they wouldn't have raised them from a yard in the middle of the town. It's like they want us to follow them."

"I agree," Durik said. "We could well be walking into a trap."

"Dare I ask why, then?" Logan said.

"To spring it, of course."

The sun was a low, reddish orb by the time they approached the northern edges of Blind Muir. Night already seemed to have fallen beneath the boughs of the forest, the gloom spreading out across the fields and towards the town. Fallowhearth was little more than the distant spikes of the castle's turrets and the two competing spires of the shrines of Nordros and Kellos, soon to be swallowed up by the darkness.

"I will not venture into that place at night," Abelard said as they came to a halt where the track ended, a few hundred yards short of the tree line. "If we had ridden here, we could have been in and out already!"

"The sun sets early at this time of the year in Forthyn," Durik pointed out. "Regardless of how quickly we got here, we would likely have had to set up a camp on the forest's edge. I doubt we will find either Lady Kathryn or the necromancer in a single afternoon."

Abelard grumbled, but agreed to pitch camp in the dead ground between the furthest fields and the forest's northern bounds. Durik led the men-at-arms as they gathered brushwood for fires and lean-tos. Logan sat down gratefully on an old, mossy stump, groaning at the pain in his joints.

"Drink this," Ulma said, pulling a small flask from her smock. Logan eyed it suspiciously.

"Is it going to burn me up from the inside, or make me sprout a second head?"

"One head and one mouth are more than enough to deal with," Ulma said, shaking the flask, making its contents slosh. Logan took it and sniffed it gingerly. The fiery scents of Dunwarr brandy almost scorched his nose off.

"So, it *will* burn me up from the inside," he said with a grin, and knocked his head back. The fiery sensation of the brandy seared down his throat and worked its way steadily out to his limbs. Ulma took it off him before he could drain half the flask.

Twilight turned to darkness. The moons were out, dueling dark, scudding clouds across the sky. It was cold.

The party had built their lean-tos near the last ditch beside the pathway, the shelters composed of undergrowth, old brushwood and the tall grass that grew in the fallow land between the fields and the forest. Logan was sharing one with Ulma, who was already snoring with her flask clutched in one hand. He considered stealing it, but good sense prevailed – the powerful dwarf brew had already given him a thumping headache to go with his loosened limbs.

He bade goodnight to Durik, who seemed content to sleep in his pelts by the small fire they had built, then crawled in beside Ulma with his cloak. The ground had been spread with uprooted grass, but it was still cold and hard. Logan turned half a dozen times before sleep finally began to creep over him, feeling more miserable and wretched than he had at any point since leaving Sixspan. Never again, he vowed. Like he hadn't said that before. As he dozed off, he distinctly heard the sound of a horse's whinny.

"Damn it, Ishbel," he murmured softly. Then he started. Ishbel wasn't with them. She was back in the stables at Fallowhearth. They hadn't brought a single horse.

Cursing to himself, he clambered stiffly out of the lean-to and onto his feet. The little camp was quiet. Durik had been awake when Logan had bedded down, but he looked asleep now. Logan cast around for the two men-at-arms Abelard had left as sentries, eyes straining against the darkness encroaching on the dying campfire. He was about to go and wake Durik when he heard a snort come from the end of the track leading back to Fallowhearth.

He hadn't imagined it. There was a horse out there somewhere. And if there was a horse, damned sure there was a rider. He bit his lower lip, thinking. He couldn't ignore that, but he was also damned sure that if he woke Durik or Ulma, they'd investigate and find it had been nothing at all. More jibes and snide comments relating to senility would follow, and Logan had endured more than enough of that in the past week. Pride truly was a monstrous burden.

He went back into his lean-to and dragged his cloak and belt out. There was only one thing for it, and he consoled himself with the fact that he wasn't exactly unused to creeping around in the dark. After fastening the belt and throwing the cloak over one shoulder, he crept past the shelters housing Abelard and his snoring men-at-arms. The darkness beyond the edge of the encampment seemed absolute, despite the silver lining provided by the moons. He swallowed and edged forward, boots sinking into the mud of the track.

Wind gusted, abrupt and sudden, making him snatch at his cloak. He took a moment to try and calm down, his heart hammering. Something moved in the shadows past the edge of the nearest field. Something pale.

"Dezra?" he murmured.

"Sleep," hissed a voice, like the rattle of dry autumn leaves in the wind. Logan stumbled, his headache redoubling.

"Yes," he mumbled, rubbing his scalp. "Sleep." He turned and wandered slowly back to the fire, dropping his cloak and slumping down into the dirt next to it.

• • •

Durik woke with his knife out. He snarled, tusks bared as he struggled to free himself from his pelts.

Something had woken him, he was sure of it. Just what "it" was, he didn't know. He brought his free hand up to his scalp, cringing. His head was throbbing.

He looked around. The fire was low, almost dead. Logan was slumped beside it, out of his shelter, his cloak abandoned. Durik retrieved the discarded garment from the dirt and placed it over him, followed by his pelt for good measure. In this cold he doubted the old man would otherwise survive.

He paused and looked around the camp. The sentries were missing, but that wasn't the most unsettling thing. The worst part was that Durik couldn't remember falling asleep.

He turned in a semi-circle, eyes traveling past the lean-tos and into the outer dark. There was something out there, something moving between the fire and the edge of the forest. His keen eyesight picked out what looked like moonlight gleaming off a silver torc.

His skin prickled.

"Carys," he hissed, trying not to shout.

There was no response. Nothing stirred. He glanced back at the forms of Abelard and his men-at-arms, undisturbed beneath their shelters. If Carys had somehow made it out of Fallowhearth then the last thing he wanted to do was alert them. It made sense that she would seek shelter in Blind Muir – she could easily evade anyone coming after her. But that forest was no place for a young girl on her own, regardless of whether she was a clan chief's daughter or not. Durik knew well enough the stories of its northern borders, of cannibal cults and ancient predatory creatures woven from dark sorceries. He couldn't abandon her out there.

He stepped out beyond the light of the campfire. It was like walking into the void, into a darkness far more absolute than Durik had known. For a moment, his heart quailed.

Gritting his tusks and keeping his knife unsheathed, he set off towards the forest.

Ulma's grip on Logan's shoulders woke him. He blinked and groaned, opening his eyes groggily. "We have to stop waking up like this," he moaned.

"They're gone," was all Ulma said, letting go of him.

"Who's gone?" he asked, propping himself up on his elbows. "And why does my throat feel like a rat's crawled down it and died?"

"Everyone's bloody gone!" Ulma shouted, her voice startlingly loud in the dark. That finally brought focus.

He was lying by the glowing embers of the fire – though he was sure he'd crawled into his shelter before falling sleep. It was still night time. Darkness had crept up to embrace them – the only light was the red glow from the fire's remnants. Even the moons seemed to have gone out.

All that was worrying, but couldn't compare to the fact that all the lean-tos appeared to be empty. Ulma had stamped over to one and overturned the brushwood, exposing its abandoned inside.

"No Abelard," she said, standing on the edge of darkness. "His men are all gone too."

"And no Durik," Logan added. "He was sitting by the fire when I fell asleep."

"You've got his pelt," Ulma pointed out. Logan realized she was right – it was laid out over his cloak. He set it to one side and fastened the cloak around his shoulders.

"I don't remember leaving our shelter," he said. "How much of that damned brandy did you give me?"

"This isn't the brandy, you idiot," the dwarf snapped. She fumbled beneath the pack laid out beside their shelter and drew out a stubby little torch which she thrust into the fire. After a few tense seconds it took, new flames flaring up around the torch's head.

"We have to find them," she said, her face thrown into light and shadow, her braids blazing like gold shot through with silver. Logan grimaced. Ulma was clearly worried, and on the rare occasions when that happened he'd learned it was best to pay attention.

"But where would they have gone?" he asked, struggling to rise. Ulma helped him up.

"Doesn't take a tracker to work that one out," she said, holding her torch down towards the ground. The patch of dirt it illuminated beyond the smoldering camp fire was stamped with footprints. Logan felt his heart quail.

They all pointed towards Blind Muir Forest.

CHAPTER ELEVEN

Even with Ulma's torch, the darkness was so absolute it was difficult to tell where Blind Muir began. Thick underbrush, thorns and overgrown stumps eventually began to include boughs and branches, the flickering red glow picking out gnarled bark and raggedy autumnal leaves.

They lost the tracks from the camp almost immediately. Logan nearly stopped, overcome with panic.

"We can't go back," Ulma said, gripping his arm firmly. "They wouldn't have just wandered in here of their own will."

"We could wait until dawn," Logan tried.

"We both know it'll be too late by then," Ulma said. "Besides, it doesn't look as if dawn is coming."

They advanced into the forest, Logan drawing his sword. It was painfully slow going. He quickly lost count of the number of times he hurt his lower legs on trunks, stumbled over roots and was snagged by thorns. All the while Ulma steadied him, but he got the distinct impression the doughty dwarf didn't have a plan beyond pressing deeper into the forest.

"Do we know where we're going?" he asked eventually.

"I was following you," Ulma said dryly. Logan came to a halt.

"We could be going in circles," he hissed. "This is madness!"

A cry interrupted him, distant but unmistakably human.

"Well, that's encouraging," he said grimly.

"This way," Ulma said, pointing her torch. They set off again, Logan doing his best to hurry. He was sure he could feel blood trickling down his shin from an encounter with an irontree root.

Another shout pierced the forest, closer this time. Logan's eyes roved amongst the surrounding trees, each one a looming, gaunt shade that seemed to creak with mirth as they struggled past. A wind gusted through the branches, making them rustle and clatter like dry bones in a tomb. The torch guttered, and for a terrifying moment he thought the wind was going to snatch its light away. The flame returned, though, maintaining that small, precious sphere of light around them.

Logan came to a halt again. An angry curse died in this throat as he realized this time it wasn't a log he'd tripped over. Ulma came up short and lowered her torch.

"Fortuna preserve me," Logan murmured. The light picked out a body, one of Abelard's men-at-arms. He was slumped face-down amidst the undergrowth. Ulma crouched beside him and rolled him onto his back.

The man was glassy-eyed and white-faced. His coif had been torn and shattered, leaving part of his throat exposed. The skin there had been marred by what looked like a bite mark, oozing a clear liquid. Even as he watched, Logan noticed the skin around the wound beginning to darken. The sight brought back a sudden surge of memories, none of them welcome. He suppressed them – it couldn't be. It just couldn't.

"He's still breathing," Ulma said. She didn't get any further. A sudden crash made them both jump and scramble for their weapons.

The figure was on Ulma before Logan could fumble his sword free from his cloak, almost bearing the dwarf to the ground. She threw him off and brandished her torch, barking something in the grating Dunwarri tongue. Logan relaxed fractionally, panting, as he realized a second man-at-arms had run into them.

"They're coming," the man gasped, flinching back from the torch's flame. "Hundreds of them!"

"Who's coming," Ulma snapped, gesturing down to the prone form of the other man-at-arms. "Who did this to him?"

"I've got to get out," the man shouted, staggering, eyes wild. "I've got to get out!"

He set off again, pushing past Logan and almost overturning Ulma for a second time.

"Wait, you damned coward," Logan shouted after him, but it was useless. The man's mind was clearly gone. He looked helplessly at Ulma. Despite her stony expression, he could see the fear in her eyes. That didn't make him feel any better. He thought he was about to be sick. He knew he was panicking, and there wasn't a damned thing he could do about it.

"We should probably go in the direction he's going," he said. "Or at the very least, away from whatever he's running from."

"We could be going deeper into the forest," Ulma pointed out.

"We should never have come here."

"It's a bit late to be saying something intelligent now," Ulma snapped back. "What about this man-at-arms here? Are you going to just leave him?"

"Absolutely," Logan said. A further clatter from the direction the second man-at-arms had come running made him jump. The forest rustled, trees squeaking and groaning. Something was definitely coming, something that Logan's gut told him exuded far more malevolence and power than another fleeing man-at-arms.

He looked at Ulma, his body frozen with tension, unable to keep the fear from his expression.

"Run," she said simply.

They followed in the wake of the fleeing man-at-arms. Logan tried to keep up alongside Ulma, cursing again and again as he stumbled. His cloak snagged on something and almost choked him. He grabbed at it and hauled, desperate with fear, ripping the expensive Lorimar-made garment.

The rustling and the creaking grew louder, filling the forest around them. Logan didn't dare glance back. His breathing was labored, and it felt as though his heart was going to split his chest in half. He could barely see, sweat stinging his eyes, branches and low boughs lashing at him like assailants. He fell, got up, fell again, making a terrified, primal moaning noise. Where was Ulma's light? Where was she?

The flames returned. He got up, only to run into something solid and musky. A hand snatched the torn half of his cloak, snagging him and arresting another fall.

"Slow down, little rogue," Durik said.

"Oh gods," Logan groaned, almost breaking down in tears. "Durik, Durik they're right behind–"

The pathfinder shushed him with a finger to the lips. He froze. Ulma, beside them with her torch, did the same.

Logan could hear… nothing. The rushing sound that had been shaking through the forest behind them was gone. The wind moaned softly through the dark canopy above, the branches rattling as though mocking him.

"There was something coming," he whispered to Durik, trying to control his breathing. The big orc was gray and still in the torchlight, like an ancient statue abandoned in the wood.

"No," he murmured back to Logan, still gripping on to him. "Something is already here."

"Where did you go?" Ulma demanded fiercely. "We came looking for you!"

"I don't know," Durik said, eyes on the surrounding trees.

"What do you mean you don't know?" Ulma snapped.

"I woke up here a few minutes ago," Durik said, a rare hint of anger flaring in his voice. "I have no memory of coming here."

He glanced briefly back at Logan.

"Can you stand?"

Logan managed to nod. Durik released him and unlaced his spear from over his shoulder.

"You were running the wrong way," the orc said. "I think. Tracker's instincts."

"What does this look like to you?" Ulma asked. She was holding her torch up to illuminate a strange, sticky white substance that was clinging to the upper branches of the trees all around them.

Logan began to shake uncontrollably. He knew exactly

what it looked like. He'd seen it in Sudanya, and it had almost paralyzed him with fear then. It had done the same in a thousand nightmares since. Something darted through the thick, silken mass, multi-limbed and wickedly fast.

"Oh no," Logan moaned hoarsely. "No, no, no!"

"Can you run?" Durik asked, clutching the side of his head and forcing him not to look up any higher.

"Yes," he whimpered.

"Then run," Durik said. "I'll hold them up."

Logan stood rooted to the spot, too terrified to move. Then, at last, some ingrained instinct kicked in.

He ran.

The previous flight through the trees had been nothing compared to this. Logan ran as he had never run before, too fast for his own thoughts to catch up. He burst through thickets and undergrowth, snarling and panting like a wild animal, his clothing ripped and torn in half a dozen places. He was vaguely aware Ulma was still with him, if only thanks to the wavering torchlight that lit up the web-infested branches all around him. All else was darkness. He felt sick, he felt blind, he felt half mad with fear. And when he finally tripped for the last time, he didn't have the breath to scream.

This time it wasn't a log. It was a furred, eight-limbed monstrosity the size of a hound that now reared up over him with mandibles that glistened in the torchlight.

Now he had the breath to scream.

Ulma lunged back through the undergrowth to him as he grappled with the chittering nightmare.

"*Dol barag,*" she roared in her native tongue, and thrust the head of her torch into the drooling maw and eye clusters that constituted the thing's face. It unleashed an inhuman shriek and recoiled from the burning wound, sparks flying as it flailed. Logan threw it off him with frenzied strength.

"For the love of the ancestors get up, manling," Ulma shouted at Logan, brandishing the torch in the direction of the hissing monster. It had scuttled back to the edge the darkness but stayed there, clacking its mandibles.

"I can't," Logan moaned, rising onto one knee before slumping back down again. When it had tripped him the creature had torn his breeches and slashed his thigh with its jaws. By Ulma's torchlight he could see the same clear liquid that had been oozing from the fallen man-at-arms's throat dribbling from the shallow cut.

"It's going numb," he said. "I can't move it!"

"Maiden Ancestor grant me strength," Ulma growled and handed him the torch. "Hold this!"

Once he had it in his grip, she put her hands under his arms and began to haul him along the forest floor, grunting with the strain.

"Just kill me," Logan begged, unable to process his thoughts rationally any more. He just wanted it all to be over. "Kill me and leave me."

"Shut up," Ulma hissed between gritted teeth. "And keep the torch raised. There's a clearing just beyond these trees."

Logan forced himself to keep the torch up, its light wavering in his grip. There were things all around them now – scuttling, crawling things whose fragmented eyes glittered in the darkness.

"Kellos light my way," Logan moaned in terror as Ulma

hauled on him, oblivious to the scrapes and scratches he was suffering. "Grant me your guiding light!"

"Not helping," the dwarf hissed, then cried out as she fell backwards over something, releasing Logan. He half rolled and dropped the torch.

"No," he shouted, fumbling for it before it went out. He managed to snatch the haft, waving it left and right, those hellish, inhuman eyes bearing down on them from all sides.

"It's going out," he shouted to Ulma. "The flame is going out!"

"Hold it still," the dwarf ordered, giving up on trying to drag Logan. They'd almost made it to the center of a small clearing, the ground underfoot thick with leaves and mulch. Ulma fished in her smock and drew out two vials, pouring the contents of one into the other. She worked with a speed and nimbleness clearly born of experience in dire situations, shaking the vial now holding both liquids before emptying it over the torch head.

"It's going out," Logan repeated in fresh panic as the flames hissed and died. "You've doused it!"

Ulma didn't bother to respond. A second later the flames flared again, though this time the light they emitted was far brighter – white and blinding. Logan was forced to avert his eyes. A chilling shriek went up from all around them as the vile things that had been crowding in on the clearing drew back from the fierce illumination.

"Phosphernum," Ulma said proudly, lowering her goggles over her eyes as she surveyed the blazing brilliance of the torch. "Or star-fire. That should keep them back."

"But for how long?" Logan asked, squinting down at his

leg in the hard, white light. Thank all the gods, the numbness hadn't reached to his crotch, but he still couldn't feel anything lower. He groaned and slumped back as Ulma took the torch off him.

There was a crash of snapping branches and an ugly squeal. Ulma drew her mallet with her free hand just before another great arachnid came hurtling from the darkness. It was followed immediately by Durik. He had run it through with his spear, and it was twitching and spasming, its legs writhing hideously. It was far larger than the one that had brought down Logan, almost big as a fully grown man, with pincers like shortswords and limbs as thick as a human's thigh. It shrieked as Durik planted it on the ground and twisted his spear, before bringing his boot down on its skull. There was an ugly crunch, and it finally went still, its limbs sticking stiffly upwards. Durik hauled his spear free, steaming ichor staining the leaves beneath the monstrosity.

"Arachyura," the orc said, looking at Logan and Ulma. He was panting, and his body was crisscrossed with lacerations, but he didn't appear to have been stuck with any of the creatures' venom. In a lifetime of being relieved to see the orc, Logan couldn't ever remember being more so.

"This can't be happening," Logan moaned, sitting up once more. "There are no arachyura in Blind Muir! I checked with the loremasters in Greyhaven! I would never have come here if I'd known there were going to be giant damned spiders!"

"Now is not the time for panic." Durik joined them in the center of the small clearing. A low chirring was building in the darkness around them, Ulma's star-fire reflecting from hundreds of black eyes and sticky mandibles.

"Just kill me now," Logan wailed again.

"Did you see any of the other men-at-arms?" Ulma asked Durik, ignoring Logan.

"Yes," Durik replied. "One was entangled in a web. I tried to free him, but could not." Logan moaned again.

"What about Abelard?"

"I saw no sign of him."

"What in ancestor's name were any of you thinking, wandering in here at the dead of night?" Ulma demanded.

"I don't believe we did it of our own free will," Durik said. "Some fell sorcery lured us here."

"It's just like Sudanya," Logan said, starting to shiver. "I promised after that I would get over my fear of spiders!"

"Well, now would be an ideal time," Ulma said humorlessly. "Can you use your leg yet?"

Logan gripped his thigh and shook his head. "It won't move!"

"I don't have enough ingredients on hand to make any more phosphernum," Ulma said to Durik. "We should at least try to move, while we still have this light."

"But in which direction?" Durik pointed out. "Even if we could manage the rogue between us, we could walk into a web or nest. I cannot tell the way out of here. Some unspeakable darkness has snared my senses."

"So the master plan is to wait here to die?" Logan demanded, looking at Ulma's torch. The intensity of its illumination had decreased, the flames now little more than a white flicker around its burned-out head.

"Draw your sword, little rogue," Durik said, standing over Logan, spear at the ready. "And prepare to conquer your fears."

Logan whimpered and managed to free his weapon from the tattered remnants of his cloak, its jeweled handle gleaming in the last of the star-fire. Ulma planted her back against Durik's and started to recite a Dunwarri oath. She tossed the torch to the ground, the last of its chemical glare flaring. The chittering from the surrounding forest rose as it did so.

It endured for a moment more, then flickered.

"Gods be with us," Logan said.

The light went out.

CHAPTER TWELVE

Captain Kloin smiled indulgently across the candlelit table and bit deeper into his chicken wing. Opposite him Matron Mildred returned the expression shyly, cheeks a little ruddy. They were sitting alone in the main servants' quarter, long after the rest of the castle's attendants had retired to their beds.

"Tell me more of Highmont, sir," Mildred said, her eyes holding Kloin's. "Tell me what else has changed since I left."

Kloin shrugged and swallowed before wiping poultry grease from his lips with the back of his hand. Finally, everything was beginning to go his way. The bitch Damhán had locked herself up for the night with her new book and, best of all, the three idiots she'd hired had been banished to Blind Muir Forest. He doubted he'd see any of them again. Damhán sending the seneschal with them was an unexpected bonus – now he was master of Fallowhearth in all but name. It had all worked out perfectly, and he was intent on enjoying the victor's spoils.

"You said you moved north with your mother twenty years

ago?" he asked Mildred, doing his best to feign interest in the matron's story.

"Yes, captain," she said enthusiastically. "I have missed Highmont so! I've been meaning to travel back for many years, but duty and circumstance have always prevented me."

"Call me Darrien," Kloin said, before letting out a low belch. "No need for formalities here, Mildred! And in all truth, I wasn't long born when you left Highmont. I couldn't tell you much about how it's changed since you were there last. It has certainly expanded in the last few years though. There is even a sorcerers' guild beneath the castle rock now, twinned with the one in Last Haven."

"I suppose Fallowhearth must seem very small and uninteresting in comparison," Mildred said, sounding embarrassed. Kloin laughed.

"Oh, it has a few charming aspects. In fact, one is sitting across from me right now."

"Oh Darrien, you are too kind by half," Mildred said a little shrilly. Kloin shrugged.

A noise drifted in through the arrow slit in the chamber walls, what sounded like an angry shout. The servants' rooms looked out over the courtyard contained within the curtain wall. Kloin frowned slightly, looking towards the slit.

"Do the young rocs still roost atop the great keep?" Mildred asked, clearly oblivious to the shout from outside. "I used to love watching them when I was a child. My mother always scolded me, though. She said if I wasn't by her side they'd snatch me up and eat me whole!"

"I have seen many up close, even touched one," Kloin lied. "They are magnificent creatures."

Mildred gazed at him wide-eyed, her own platter untouched. Kloin smiled nonchalantly and bit into his wing again.

A hammering at the chamber door made them both jump. Kloin swiveled in his seat, glaring. He was glad he'd locked the door before sitting down.

"Not now, damn it," he snapped irritably. He heard the scrape of mail as whoever it was withdrew.

"I don't want to keep you from your duties," Mildred said anxiously. Kloin scoffed, banishing his scowl with another smile.

"It is the deadwatches, my dear. What could possibly demand my attention at this time of night?"

The door rattled again. Kloin snarled and stood up so fast he almost knocked his chair back.

"What in the name of the gods –" he demanded, unlocking the door and throwing it open "– do you want?"

The man-at-arms he'd left in charge of the night watch, Grubin, came to attention.

"Sorry captain," he said. "But Lady Damhán's horse is missing from the stables and…" he trailed off.

"What, man?" Kloin growled. "Hurry up!"

"We think there's an intruder loose inside the keep."

The arachyura came for them.

Durik met them with a roar. His eyesight wasn't as good as Ulma's in the dark, but it was still keener than any human's, good enough to see the first great spider rear before him with its pincers gaping. He rammed his spear into its maw and up through its skull, stinking ichor arcing through the clearing.

More of the cursed things were coming at him, scrambling over their brood-kin's twitching body. With a vicious twist he dragged his spear free and thrust it into a second, slashing his knife at another before freeing it once more. The wicked, curved blade lopped through a furry limb, spattering him with more of the creatures' internal fluids. It stank, and stung his bare skin, but he barely noticed as another met his spear-tip.

Behind him he could hear Ulma wielding her mallet, while Logan jabbed desperately up from beneath her, the two struggling to keep the wall of arachyura at bay. The whole clearing was infested not only with the great mother-beasts, but millions of smaller arachnids. Durik could feel them swarming up his body, trying to bite their way through his leathery skin. He stomped down with one boot, crushing one the size of a large rat, grinding it into the forest floor.

As he fought to disentangle his spear from another, one crawled in under his guard, latching its mandibles around his wrist. His furred vambrace took the worst of the bite, but he still felt its jaws cut deep before clamping around him. Almost immediately his hand and lower arm started to go numb.

Grunting, he spun the knife in his other hand, reversing the grip and plunging it down into the arachyura's head. Its jaws began to spasm, and he wrenched his arm free, though in the process his dead fingers lost their grip on his spear.

Knife it was, then. He held it in a horizontal back-grip, slashing at compound eyes and every hooked limb that reached for him. The numbness in his arm was reaching up past his elbow now. The deadweight the limb had become made fighting with the other arm all the harder. He gritted his tusks and carried on, cutting open a bulbous torso as a gout of webbing sprayed at him, splattering his left leg. He kicked out, breaking more multi-jointed legs. Despite himself, he began to laugh.

This all really must be Logan's worst nightmare.

"What do you mean you didn't see your attacker?" Kloin snapped at one of his men-at-arms, Havard, as they climbed the staircase to the solar, the main bedchamber directly above the castle hall. "He didn't blind you, did he?"

"He got the drop on me from behind, sir," Havard said apologetically. His scalp was still bleeding. "I heard someone coming at me fast, but I didn't turn quick enough."

"Truly you are Forthyn's finest, Havard," Kloin said bitterly, reaching the door to the solar. He raised his fist, hesitated for a second, then knocked.

Nothing. He glanced at Havard, then spoke.

"My lady? It's Captain Kloin. We… have a situation."

For a few moments there was no sound from behind the door. Then a dull, dry croak finally answered the captain's words.

"Situation, captain?"

"Yes," Kloin said, throwing another angry glance at Havard. He felt like a fool. "It seems as though someone has stolen your horse from the stables. We also may have an intruder within the keep."

"An intruder?"

"I'm not sure yet, my lady. Several of my men have been attacked. I came immediately to check on your personal safety."

"How reassuring, captain," came Damhán's deathly rattle.

She sounded unwell. He found himself hoping she was. "I very much hope this so-called intruder will be in irons come sunrise, for your sake, captain. I also hope that our prisoner is still secure."

Kloin's eyes widened. The little witch! He'd completely forgotten about her. Without answering Damhán he snatched Havard by the hauberk, furious that the man's stupidity was risking his authority.

"Stay here and guard this door," he hissed. "Think you can manage to avoid getting attacked from behind while looking down a stairwell?"

"Yes, sir," Havard said, but Kloin was already clattering down the steps and shouting for Grubin. He met him at the bottom, outside the doors to the main hall, along with two local guards, Abelard's.

"Kellos burn my soul," Kloin swore, gesturing for all four men to follow him. "It could be the clansfolk. They're going to free the girl!"

It was a nightmare. That's what Logan had almost convinced himself of. A terrible, terrible nightmare where he was in pitch blackness, paralyzed, assailed on all sides.

There were things crawling all over him. They were running along his arms and up his back, over his face and through his hair. He couldn't scream or they'd get in his mouth. He screwed his eyes shut, trying not to throw up.

He was partly aware of Ulma standing over him, her stout legs planted against the arachnid onslaught, her mallet cracking down relentlessly. It sounded as though Durik was laughing behind them, though he assumed a part of his mind was just going insane. Ulma's voice reached him over the chittering, scrabbling assault.

"Cut their legs off," she bellowed. He swung his sword desperately. It bit and stuck. He hacked again, a strangled, demented noise rising from inside him. Something gave way. A sticky substance smacked his face. It stank and burned. He swung again, wildly, blindly, hewing at the forest of furred limbs that was threatening to bury them.

He didn't know how long it lasted for. It could've been hours. It could have been minutes. All that he was sure of was that at some point the pressure of the bloated, scurrying things around him began to decrease. He kept hacking, his limbs burning, his whole body numb from a thousand tiny scratches and bites. A scream finally ripped free from his throat, a mangled, feral sound. He beat his face and shoulders with his other arm, crushing and pulping and smearing the things crawling all over him.

"Logan," Ulma shouted breathlessly. "Logan, stop!"

Her hand snatched his, leaving him whimpering and sniveling, twitching at every phantom scuttle he felt across his body.

He opened his eyes, slowly. At first it hardly seemed to make any difference – the clearing was still in darkness. He was vaguely aware of misshapen bodies heaped around them, some still writhing horribly. The most startling thing, though, was the silence. The rustling, the creaking, that awful insect-like chirring, it was all gone. All that remained was the ragged breathing of the trio and his own heartbeat, hammering in his ears. And the snap of a single twig.

That was when he realized there was light in the clearing

after all. Hundreds of tiny pinpricks, each a sickly green-yellow in color, flickering gently like little candle flames. It took him a second more to realize that they were eyes, sunken in the sockets of the hundred or more figures who now surrounded the clearing.

Not men or women, but their corpses. They stood still and silent, rank after rank, their jaws slack or grinning, the deadlights in their skulls flickering. Still more lights joined them as bodies that had seemingly fallen fighting the arachyura clambered slowly, painfully, back to their feet. Every single one was facing towards the trio.

"Oh gods." Memories of the last night in the tavern flooded back. He'd been right, right about all of it. It hadn't been a dream.

"Get up," Ulma whispered to him.

"But my leg…" Logan started to say, but Ulma's hand gripped him by the collar and dragged him to his feet. He found he could stand, just about – his whole body itched and ached from the post-numbing effects of the smaller spiders, but at least the venom in his thigh seemed to be spent.

"Well, at least I'll be able to walk when I'm resurrected as a corpse puppet," he muttered. "I'd hate to be one of those crawling or limping ones."

Regrettably, none of the corpses laughed. The deadlights in their eyes did flare, though. Fire rose up behind them, that rotting, ugly green-yellow flame, and ignited the thick webbing that clad the upper branches of the trees all around the clearing. It took like a conjurer's trick, and in seconds the arachyura nest was a blazing inferno, the light it cast illuminating the maggoty flesh, gleaming bone and ragged, soiled death shrouds of the surrounding undead.

The ranks of the undead parted ahead of Logan. A figure stepped between them, slender and vital next to her awkward, shambling creations. She was clad in tight-fitting black leathers, sewn together with thick stitches of sinew. A ragged black cloak hung about her shoulders, its pointed hood raised. Her upper chest and shoulders were bared above a corset of purple leather and bone, the pale flesh almost white in the balefire. A wisp of that same flame still coiled around her raised left hand. It illuminated the face beneath the hood – sharp and fair with eyes as black as the darkness beyond her flames. She stopped before the trio, who simply stood and stared.

“It can’t be,” Logan breathed, all the aches and pains in his body forgotten.

“Hello, friend,” said Dezra the Vile.

CHAPTER THIRTEEN

"You're here," Logan said in shock. Dezra smiled and made a gesture with her burning hand that encompassed the balefire-lit clearing and the dozens of arachyura bodies heaped across it.

"And not a moment too soon, it seems," she said.

"These resurrected bodies," Ulma said, eyeing the surrounding corpses warily. "You have control over them?"

"I do," Dezra said, and snapped her fingers. The deadlights in the eyes of one of the corpses – the body of a withered old man – flared, and he stumbled forward to Dezra's side before offering a stiff, awkward parody of a bow towards the trio. Logan recoiled, while Ulma and Durik looked on levelly, both masking their shock far more effectively than the rogue.

"Necromancy," Logan said. Merely uttering the word made him feel tainted. "Dezra, don't say you've fallen for such depraved arts!"

"Perhaps I should have left you for the spiders," she responded.

"What are you doing here?" Logan pressed. "And how did you find us?"

"I could ask you the same thing." The undead beside her was still bowed down. Logan eyed it distastefully. "I suspect I've been in this forest a lot longer than you," Dezra continued, noticing Logan's gaze and allowing the corpse to straighten and shuffle back. "I've been treading the paths of Blind Muir for years now."

"Do those paths often include infestations of arachyura?" Logan demanded. "Or was that just unhappy coincidence?"

"These creatures are invasive," Dezra said. "I do not know where they have spawned from, but they do not belong here. I am hunting them."

To emphasize her point she clenched her fist towards the closest spider body. It ignited with the same toxic-looking flames that still burned through the canopy overhead.

"You can thank Nordros that I came upon you when I did," she said, the flames coiled around her. "And thank the screams of your friends. They were the ones who alerted me."

"The men-at-arms," Ulma said. "Have you found any of them?"

"One. Dead when I found him." She pointed across the clearing, and the trio turned to see one of Abelard's soldiers standing amidst the undead gathering. He was still clad in his mail and hauberk, his skin discolored, jaw slack. Long gashes across his stomach spoke of the attentions of razor arachyura mandibles. The wounds were still oozing dark, infected blood.

"There were more," Ulma murmured. "The seneschal of Fallowhearth was with us."

"Not that I've seen," Dezra responded. "If they are still alive, the arachyura have them now. I have yet to unearth where they are spawning from."

"Why are you doing this?" Logan asked. "What brought you to the far corner of Terrinoth?"

"I've always walked in dark places, Logan," she said, as though the answer was obvious. "Here in the north, servants of Nordros can worship without threat of persecution. I might not be accepted still, but at least I am able to go about my life without constant fear and threat."

"It's one thing to worship Nordros, and another to raise the dead and use them like puppets," Logan said, unable to keep the force of the accusation from his voice. "You're avoiding my question; you know necromancy is banned here, yet you practice it anyway. It is wholly unnatural!"

"I didn't save your lives to be interrogated by you, much less judged," Dezra said sharply. "I had enough of that from all of you down the years."

She turned, her undead shuffling out of her way.

"Wait," Logan said, stepping out and immediately regretting it as his wounded leg almost gave way beneath him. Dezra paused and looked back at him.

"You're hurt," she said.

"I am," Logan admitted, then scowled as Dezra pointed past him to Durik.

"I meant him."

Durik shrugged his broad shoulders. He hadn't spoken since Dezra had appeared, his thoughts as guarded as ever. Sometimes, Logan really did find the orc's stoicism infuriating.

"It's just a scratch," he said dismissively.

"I doubt that," Dezra said, picking her way between the arachyura corpses to the center of the clearing. As she went, the fire around her hand snuffed out, though the unnatural flames in the canopy continued to sear the arachyura nest away. Logan had to resist the urge to reach out and touch the sorceress as she passed by – since the sheer terror of the arachyura attack everything had felt so surreal, so unnatural. A part of him was afraid of Dezra, but the greater part simply hadn't come to terms with the fact that he wasn't dreaming.

"Hold out your hand," Dezra ordered Durik. The orc stretched out his right arm. His vambrace was stained with blood. Dezra inspected it for a moment before carefully unbinding it, exposing a gash that ran right around the orc's wrist.

"Clench your fist," she ordered him.

"I can't," he admitted, though he gave no outward sign of the pain he surely felt.

"It may have cut a tendon," Dezra said. "Or the venom has worked deep. Either way, you might never hold your spear again. Keep still and say nothing."

She placed her hand just above Durik's wound, her limb looking ridiculously pale and slender next to his. Durik looked as though he was about to complain about whatever Dezra intended, but words died in his throat as the temperature in the clearing plummeted. Logan's breath started to frost before his eyes, and he began to shiver, even while the flames the sorceress had summoned continued to burn above. He grimaced – the little displays of dark magic were often the worst. Seeing nature usurped made him feel vulnerable, no longer in control.

He watched Dezra's hand, expecting the flesh to suddenly

slough off or more balefire to engulf them both. Instead a shallow red cut began to appear around the sorceress's wrist, a mirror image of Durik's wound. At the same time, the orc's injury seemed to fade, the flesh re-binding itself. Dezra's face was one of tight, controlled pain as the change continued until, suddenly, she drew her hand back with a hiss. Durik's injury still remained, but it looked much shallower. Abruptly, the temperature in the clearing rose again.

"Clench your fist," Dezra said, flexing her own fingers. Durik did so, then gripped his spear still buried in an arachyura corpse and wrenched it free.

"What did you do?" he demanded, sounding more angry than relieved.

"*Participes mortus,*" Dezra said, holding her wrist up to display her new cut. "I shared your wound between us. The venom, too. Half the potency, it will heal in a few days."

"That is powerful magic," Ulma said, watching on. Even she had narrowed her eyes, her stance more defensive. "Dark, powerful magic."

"These are dark times," Dezra countered sharply, looking at the dwarf. "It pays to be powerful." As she spoke, her eyes seemed to glaze for a second and she stumbled, righting herself before Durik reached out instinctively to steady her.

"It comes at a price, though," she added, regaining focus. "That is true for all sorcery."

"How long have you been practicing this… this sort of magic?" Logan asked. She smiled and walked by him once more, to the edge of the clearing.

"You know I practiced it in Sudanya. You know what I have always been. Dezra the Vile."

"Never to us," Logan said. "Your magics were dark, but you were no necromancer. What happened?"

"I see you're still charmingly naive," Dezra said, looking at Logan again. "I am going now. If you wish, I can guide you to the northern borders of the forest. You are free to find your own way, though."

"We would welcome your help, Dezra," Ulma said before Logan could speak. "And perhaps you can explain something to us on the way."

Dezra's flames went ahead of the group, leaping from tree to tree above them. Logan noticed that they didn't seem to burn up the branches themselves, though they scorched away any arachyura webs and left those boughs they did touch look unusually gnarled and ancient.

Even more unsettling was the presence of the undead, who formed a silent, shuffling guard ahead, behind and on either side of them. He tried not to look at them, but couldn't avoid staring at shriveled skin and the exposed body parts that snagged on twigs and underbrush as they passed by. The morbid procession looked even more unnatural in the rancid light cast by Dezra's balefire.

"I had heard Lady Kathryn was ruling in Fallowhearth," the sorceress said as they traversed the forest. "But I did not know she was missing. How long has it been?"

"A month, thereabouts," Ulma said, trudging at her side.

"And that's why you're here? Looking for her."

"Yes. Baroness Adelynn hired Durik to find her, and he called on us. And you."

Dezra let out a short, cold laugh. "Where did you send

messengers?" she asked, looking back at the orc.

"Your brother's dwelling in Rothfeld, your old haunts in Strangehaven and Valdari," the orc responded. "I couldn't wait any longer to find you."

"You wouldn't have anyway," Dezra said. "I have been in Upper Forthyn for nearly five years."

"In this miserable place?" Logan interjected, gesturing at the night-shrouded forest surrounding them. The trees were as dense and as dark as ever, a seemingly impenetrable maze that Dezra walked with confidence.

"Partly," she said. "Upper Forthyn suits my temperament."

"And you haven't seen Lady Kathryn at all in the past month?" Logan asked. "Haven't heard anything through… arcane means?"

Dezra laughed again, the sound at odds with the morbid sight of the stumbling corpses surrounding them.

"I've seen nothing, and been told nothing, but nor have I been looking," she said. "Purging the arachyura has occupied my attention for months now."

"Why are they here?" Logan wondered aloud, his voice bitter as he considered the presence of the huge spiders. "You said yourself, these creatures don't come from Blind Muir."

"Why do creatures of darkness settle in the dark places of the world?" Dezra asked. "You know the answer well enough, Logan. We've been in enough of those dark places together."

Logan had to concede that. For a moment, he almost smiled. This was the Dezra he knew: self-assured, sharp. For all her defiant tone, it was part of her character that he liked the most.

"We have to find the baroness's daughter," Ulma said,

refocusing the conversation. "If we don't, we risk a war between the baronies and the northern clans. They make an easy scapegoat."

"Do you have any evidence they didn't take her?" Dezra asked.

"Not directly, no, but it makes no sense," Ulma said. "It would gain them no political leverage, and if it was just a ransom they wanted then they'd have sent terms to Highmont weeks ago. Sorcery could explain how Kathryn disappeared from her chambers on the night that she did. That, or she departed of her own free will, though we have no clue as to why she'd do something like that. Disappear without a trace."

"Perhaps you could help us solve some of those riddles," Durik said. He'd been walking behind the other three, deep in thought. "Come with us back to Fallowhearth. Use your abilities to help us track down Lady Kathryn. It could avert a war."

"You think I am able to simply walk into Fallowhearth at will?" Dezra asked. "Into the town's keep as well? Logan wasn't lying when he said that necromancy is outlawed in Forthyn, on pain of a lasting death via decapitation and immolation. I have no wish to suffer that fate."

"But you've been to Fallowhearth before," Logan pointed out. "You emptied the graves around the Shrine of Nordros just last night. I saw the bodies being summoned from the town. Fortuna's gold, I saw *you*. I thought it was all a nightmare."

"Illusions and dreams are an unavoidable byproduct of the magnitude of the incantation I used last night," Dezra said.

"I did not send shades to torment you specifically, Logan, if that's what you're accusing me of."

"But why did you steal the town's dead at all?"

"Why do you think?" Dezra demanded. "To help rid this place of the death-damned arachyura. My powers are not sufficient on their own. These things have been festering in here for years, breeding and multiplying. It's a wonder they haven't taken over the entire forest. They could easily begin infesting other parts of Forthyn, even eastern Terrinoth, if that happens."

"We all felt your power that night," Durik said. "It's part of the reason we came here. We were sure that whoever dragged two hundred bodies from Fallowhearth to Blind Muir had to know something about what happened to Lady Kathryn."

"I told you, I don't," Dezra said sharply. Logan knew better than to push the matter, not while they were still lost in the woodland with only Dezra for a guide. They walked on in silence for a while, picking their way between the trees, the shuffling cohort of undead still surrounding them. Logan was at least thankful that their presence was keeping his mind off his own exhaustion – he suspected that if he stopped now and sat down, he wouldn't be able to get back up again.

"You spoke of illusions," Durik said to Dezra. "I met with the tomb-keeper of the Shrine of Nordros, in Fallowhearth. He thought he had seen Lady Kathryn on the night of her disappearance, in among the gravestones. Could that have been another illusion?"

"Possibly," Dezra answered. "If someone was casting an incantation of particular power in the town, it may have created echoes."

"Echoes are different from illusions," Ulma pointed out.

"You are trying to ascribe hard rules to arcane practices," Dezra said. "You should all know by now that all such efforts end in madness. Even I cannot account for the byproducts of my work, let alone what might happen when another practitioner attempts a spell of great magnitude."

"And you haven't come across any other powerful arcanists in Forthyn?" Logan asked. "Someone capable of, say, conjuring Kathryn straight from her chambers?"

"If you hadn't already noticed, I have hardly been mingling with the barony's populace," Dezra said. "Nor do my abilities allow me to scry every magic user in Forthyn, much less those who don't wish to be found."

Logan realized that the way ahead was no longer lit by Dezra's grim balefire. For a moment he began to panic, before noticing that there were no more nests and no more canopy to ignite. They'd reached the edge of Blind Muir. Ahead, the darkness that had once shrouded the dead ground and the fallow fields leading to Fallowhearth was giving way to the first hint of daylight, a slender, golden line that picked out the caps of the Dunwarrs. Logan had seen sunsets from Lorimar to Ru, but right now this was the most beautiful sight he had ever seen.

"Thank you, great Fortuna," he said, stumbling out beyond the tree line.

"You're welcome," Dezra said. Her corpse puppets had halted at the edge of the forest. Logan turned back to her.

"You're sure you won't come with us, then?" Durik asked.

"No," Dezra replied. "I don't belong among the company you keep any more. I have started a task here in this forest, and I will not leave it until it has been completed."

"You won't even come for old times' sake?" Logan said. Dezra let out her dark little chuckle.

"You haven't been acting as though you want my company, Logan Lashley."

Logan scowled to hide his embarrassment in the growing light. Just then he didn't know *what* he wanted, and that, in his long experience, was always a bad thing.

"You caught me at a bad time," he said.

"That almost sounds like an apology."

"You don't think about the good times at all?" Logan asked. "The places we all saw together? The adventures we had?"

"Occasionally," Dezra said, her tone guarded. "But I was younger then. We all were."

"You don't look any different," Logan said. It was true. Durik and Ulma might have aged slower than him, but the signs were there once the rogue had looked hard enough. Dezra, though, appeared the same age she had in Sudanya, just shy of thirty summers. She smiled, and Logan felt twenty years younger again. Until she spoke.

"I wish I could say the same, Logan. Be thankful. This long youth hasn't come cheaply."

"At least you're not worried about your teeth falling out and your hair turning gray. Not that that's a bad look for a necromancer."

Dezra smiled, but there was a hard gleam in her eyes, and the expression faded.

"I've nothing more to offer any of you. I've told you all I know. My advice would be to leave Upper Forthyn. Go home, wherever that may be."

"Why?" Logan asked. It was one thing to refuse to help their search, but to ward them off entirely? "What aren't you telling us, Dezra?"

"I want what's best for all of you," she replied. "No good can come of lingering in a place like this."

Another deflection, but Logan could tell he wasn't going to get any more out of her. He buried a sigh and conjured a half smile.

"Home is overrated," he said. "Besides, I'm sworn to Baroness Adelynn's service until this task is completed. Wouldn't want to become an oath-breaker."

"And change the habit of a lifetime?" Dezra asked. "Go with every ounce of Fortuna's luck, my friends." Logan bowed his head, and Ulma placed a hand on his shoulder, nodding.

"I don't think I've ever called on old Nordros before," the rogue said. "But may that cold bastard not see you in person anytime soon."

Dezra nodded at the off-color blessing. Then Logan turned, and, following Durik and Ulma, began to limp towards the dawn.

The camp they had abandoned the previous night still stood, the lean-tos and their packs undisturbed. Ulma began collecting them, grumbling under her breath. Durik moved further up the track, crouched in the morning half-light.

"What's he doing?" Logan asked as he joined Ulma, taking his pack off her.

"Tracking," Ulma said unhelpfully.

"He's found something?"

"Why don't we ask him?" Ulma said, shucking her own

pack onto her back. Logan followed her towards the track, glancing back one more time at Blind Muir. The dead were still there, a shadowy rank on the edge of the forest, shrouded by twisted boughs, but Dezra had gone.

"There are hoofprints in the dirt," Durik said. He was crouched in the mud of the trackway, his keen eyes apparently unperturbed by the weak dawn light. "A horse rode this way and back, sometime yesterday."

"Back to Fallowhearth?" Logan asked. Durik nodded.

"I thought I heard a horse last night," Logan said, a fragment of a memory stirring within him. "It felt like another of those damned dreams. I don't remember much before Ulma woke me up."

"How can we hope to find Lady Kathryn when every lead turns out to be either false or a trap?" Ulma asked unhappily.

"The air was heavy with illusion that night," Durik said, standing. "Now is no time for despair, my friends. We can only keep going. At the very least, I'm going to find whoever is responsible for this trickery. I am tired of finding more questions every time I look for answers."

"That's you told," Logan said to Ulma. Neither she nor Durik responded.

"Do you hear that?" Durik said, cocking his head to one side like some sort of avian. Logan listened, and eventually managed to detect a faint, distant ringing.

"Bells?" he asked uncertainly. Durik was looking north-east towards Fallowhearth, where the castle turrets and the two shrine spires were just visible on the lightening horizon.

"There are two bells tolling," Durik said slowly. "It has to be the shrines of Kellos and Nordros, ringing together."

"Not like them to be in accord over something," Logan said, smirking at his own observation.

"That's because they're sounding the alarm," Durik responded. "Fallowhearth is under attack."

CHAPTER FOURTEEN

By the time they reached Fallowhearth, both the Shrine of Nordros and the Chapel of the Flame of Kellos Eternal had ceased ringing their bells. Logan wasn't sure whether that was a good thing or not.

There was no immediate sign of an attack being conducted on the town. The streets were empty, with neither refugees nor assailants in sight. The trio strode along the main street towards the keep, wariness battling with exhaustion. Logan felt as though he hadn't slept in days, and his whole body was stiff and aching.

They found the keep's gates barred, and there seemed to be an unusual amount of activity on its battlements.

"What is happening?" Logan called up from the road. He got no response.

"We've returned from Blind Muir, but the seneschal and his men are still in the forest," Durik said, trying a different tack. "Lady Damhán must hear our report. Open the gates immediately."

A coif-clad head appeared above them, the look of

uncertainty evident even from beneath the gatehouse.

"Captain Kloin has ordered us to admit no one," he began to say.

"Not this again," Ulma snarled, pushing her way past Logan and Durik. "Listen to me, manling!" She pointed up at the unfortunate sentinel, then planted both hands on her hips, her expression furious.

"I've just fought my way through a forest full of giant damned spiders looking for, among other things, your idiot seneschal. I've been rescued by a legion of undead corpses, and walked all the way back here from Blind Muir only to find no sign of any threat to this miserable, dung-heap town whatsoever. I'm also all out of brandy, so either you open this sorry, ancestor-damned excuse for a gate right now, or I blow it open. And don't think I can't!"

The sentry had fled out of sight long before Ulma had finished. Logan held his breath, then grinned and patted her on the shoulder when the portcullis began to rise ponderously. Wordlessly she turned her glare on him, and he quickly withdrew his hand.

"Well done," Durik said as the gate swung open behind the rising iron bars. A stonyfaced man-at-arms in a tabard bearing Abelard's half-roc was waiting for them within the entrance hall.

"Is the town under attack or not?" Logan demanded, striding in through the gate as though he owned the citadel.

"Yes, sir," the man said, then hesitated. "Partly, sir."

"Come on man, what's that supposed to mean?"

"Someone broke into the keep last night, sir. They're still here."

"In here?" Logan reiterated, looking past the guard at the stair shaft leading up into the keep's chambers. He suddenly regretted being the first one inside.

"They've been confined to one of the upper bedrooms, sir," the guard said.

"Captured, you mean?"

"Not yet sir. Just contained."

"Just so I understand this correctly," Logan said slowly. "One person broke into the keep last night, was discovered, but they're still here and still successfully resisting capture? Dare I ask what sort of creature our intruder is?"

"A clansman, sir," the man-at-arms said.

"He's in Carys's chamber," Durik added, his voice certain.

"How do you know that?" Logan demanded.

"She said someone would come for her. Someone she called the Son of the Wild."

"And you neglected to tell anyone?" Logan snapped, clearly frustrated. "In what way didn't this seem important?"

"What could one man do?"

"Apparently take on an entire castle's garrison for a whole night," Logan said. "You're far too fond of that girl, Durik!"

"This is madness," Ulma said, her anger clearly still simmering. "Take us to the chamber where he's been cornered."

The guard offered a short bow and led them up through the keep's narrow stairways and passages. Along the way Logan could hear shouts and the clattering of armored bodies from elsewhere within the stone structure. He noted that all the doorways they passed were secured shut. He couldn't help but wonder at the supreme confidence, or supreme stupidity, of the man who decided to infiltrate such a place alone. What sort of mad, brute savage was going to be waiting for them in that bedchamber?

The stairway winding up to Kathryn's tower was choked with the castle's garrison. Their guide shouted at them to make way, and Logan, Durik and Ulma worked their way up to the landing outside Kathryn's old room. As Logan had feared, both Kloin and Lady Damhán were already there.

"Hurry up, man," Kloin was snapping at a sweat-streaked servant who was attempting to waft black smoke from a fitfully smoldering cluster of sticks in under the bedchamber's heavy timber door. The captain turned as the trio arrived, and Logan relished the brief flash of surprise that crossed the man's flushed visage.

"Didn't expect to see us back, Kloin?" he asked. Now it was his turn to wear that infuriating grin. Kloin just scowled.

"Not so soon, anyway," Lady Damhán replied for him. She was standing a few steps up from the landing, on the edge of the stairway's spiral curve, overseeing the attempted smoke-raising like the tall, gaunt idol of some savage religion, clad in her pale robes.

"I take it you found no trace of Lady Kathryn in the Blind Muir?" she asked.

"Nothing relating to the baroness's daughter," Logan said archly. "Blind Muir's a lovely place, by the way. I highly recommend you both visit sometime soon. Preferably at night."

"They've hardly been gone a day," Kloin growled to Damhán. "How thorough could their search have been? You should send them back."

"Where is Seneschal Abelard?" Damhán asked, ignoring the captain.

"He's still looking for Lady Kathryn," Logan said. "In fact I think he'll be looking in there permanently."

"We were attacked," Ulma said, pushing Logan to one side. "There are arachyura infesting the forest. There was no sign of Kathryn. If she fled there, or something took her there, I fear no one will ever find her again."

"There is something else," Durik added. "On our way back here, I noticed hoof prints in the track leading to the town from the south-west. They were fresh, but none of us took any mounts."

Logan expected Kloin to snap something about farmers and plough horses, but instead he cast a glance at Damhán that looked almost apprehensive.

"My horse was stolen last night," Damhán said. "We assumed it was related to this incursion."

"Why would someone break into the castle stables to steal your horse?" Logan asked.

"But one question of many," Damhán said. "And, unfortunately, not the most pressing at the moment."

"How long has he been in there?" Ulma asked, nodding towards the door. The servant was still trying to generate a decent amount of smoke, to little effect. It was making the back of Logan's throat itch.

"Since just before dawn," Damhán said. "We still don't know how he got in."

"How many of the guards has he killed?"

"None that we know of. Yet."

"Getting all this way, only to be trapped like this," Logan

shook his head. "I don't know if I'm impressed or not."

"I doubt he thought he would get Carys out without anyone noticing," Durik said. "I think he always planned on this. He isn't trapped. He wants to negotiate."

"We'll negotiate with him over my dead body," Kloin snarled.

"That sounds quite agreeable," Logan said, still relishing the captain's anger.

"It doesn't look like you're going to be able to smoke him out," Durik said. "And you don't dare set fire to the chamber. The whole tower would go up, and it would put the entire castle at risk. Besides, that chamber has a window. He'll just let the smoke out. This stairway is too narrow to maneuver a decent-sized ram for the door, which I assume he's barricaded. All that leaves is starving them out."

"Don't worry, I brought food," came a muffled voice from the other side of the door. Logan looked incredulously at Kloin and Damhán.

"Oh wonderful, he can hear us too."

"Clearly," Damhán said dryly.

"Have you really tried everything to get him out?" Logan asked her. "And I mean everything? You've got quite the arcane talent, don't you, Lady Damhán? Want to give us a demonstration of the abilities you've been keeping so quiet about?"

"My abilities are not parlor tricks," Damhán said icily. "I did not come here to negotiate with northern savages within my lady's own keep. And besides, my… particular powers are of no use here. The barbarian has some sort of ensorcelled creature for company. A null familiar that drains arcane energies. It is countering my abilities."

"It seems that words are the only weapons we have left," Durik said. Everyone looked at Logan.

"What?" he asked.

"We should send the old man in," Kloin said, his anger giving way to unexpected delight. "You're the finest rogue in all of Terrinoth, aren't you? That *is* what you're always saying. Talking down a feral northerner who's barricaded himself at the top of a tower should be one of the easiest jobs you'll ever do."

"What makes you think he's in the mood to talk?" Logan demanded, refusing to fall into the captain's trap.

"He's been saying he wants to talk since the sun came up."

"Ah."

"If he's the one asking to negotiate then we already have the upper hand," Ulma said.

"Don't encourage them," Logan hissed. "What would I even say? 'Come out and we'll let you both live?' Are we just going to let them go?"

"Despite what Seneschal Abelard may have thought, we did not take that clan girl to strain relations in the north," Damhán said. "We are here to find out where Lady Kathryn is, nothing more and nothing less. Whether or not they took her, I cannot believe the clans have no knowledge at all of her whereabouts."

"And what if they really don't?"

"Then you'll have to think of something else that he can trade for their freedom."

"I don't speak any Goltacht," Logan protested desperately as Kloin snatched his shoulder and maneuvered him towards the door. "I won't understand anything he's saying!"

"He speaks our tongue," the captain reassured him.

"I can introduce you in Goltacht," Durik added helpfully.

"Oh gods," Logan whimpered. The door loomed before him.

Durik called out something that Logan found utterly indecipherable. There was no response.

"Must've climbed out through the window, oh well..." Logan exclaimed, half turning and being turned back again by Kloin. Durik said something else. This time the voice answered him.

"What did he say?" Logan asked nervously. Durik repeated something in Goltacht, then spoke to Logan.

"He's asking if I'm the orc. He says Carys has spoken well of me."

"See, he wants you," Logan said. "You could easily get in there and overpower him!"

"I told you, he speaks the common tongue," Kloin said. "And he can obviously hear us. Good job."

"Send the old man," the voice beyond the door said. Logan scowled.

"That's rich old man to you, barbarian," he snapped at the door, then looked back at the gathering behind him. "Alright, alright, I'll do it. But if I negotiate something you don't like, too bad."

"I told you, our only priority is Lady Kathryn," Damhán said. "Surrender nothing without hard evidence of her whereabouts."

Logan turned back to the door, sniffed, and looked down at himself disparagingly. He was an absolute mess, his cloak torn to strips, his tunic and breeches caked with dirt. There were still autumn leaves stuck in his belt. He didn't dare pause to consider the beating his body had taken in the past day, or think about how physically tired he was. He felt like he could drop down dead at any moment. He'd forgotten how utterly miserable these so-called adventures were. Misadventures was definitely the more accurate term.

"Never again," he said under his breath. That was his new promise to himself, and the only one he intended on keeping.

He knocked on the door.

Something scraped across stone, and the door rattled. The latch clattered before easing open, just a few inches. Logan held his breath.

Something moved low down, at ankle height. He found himself looking into small, black, beady eyes. He yelped and took a sharp step back.

"What is that?" he exclaimed in horror.

"It is Pico," said a gruff, thickly accented voice from beyond the door. "Do not move. He will make sure you are safe."

"What's that supposed to mean?" Logan asked incredulously, staring down at the little creature as it sniffed past the door. It was red-furred, about the size of a cat, with curious, worryingly intelligent eyes.

"That's his familiar," Damhán said darkly. Logan noted she had taken a few more steps back. "It will sniff out any enchantments you are carrying."

"I'm no threat, honestly," Logan said to the animal, holding his hands up slowly and carefully. It didn't respond, but darted back out of sight. Logan waited.

There was another scraping sound, and the door creaked open a little further.

"Come inside," said the voice. "Slowly."

Logan exchanged a last look with Durik and Ulma. They both shrugged. Rolling his eyes, the rogue went side-on, held his breath, and slipped in through the door.

It slammed shut behind him.

Logan stood frozen inside Kathryn's bedchamber, convinced that the slightest movement would see him dead. To his left was the girl, Carys, standing warily on the far side of the bed that had been shifted to block much of the doorway. On the bed itself was the little red-furred beast, its whiskers twitching as it rose up on its hind legs and stared at Logan. Both of them he only noticed with a glance – his attention was taken up by the monster who stood poised over him, a sword in his left fist held ready to run Logan through the gut, his right planted firmly on the door behind him.

He was human, but that came as little relief – he was even bigger than Durik, his arms corded with slabs of muscle, his body twice as broad as Logan's and at least a head taller. An etched metal ring, crafted like a serpent devouring its own tail, was fitted around the bicep of his right arm. He was clad in rustic plaids and wool, a cloak lined with thick brown ruck-bear fur heaped over his shoulders, tied with the dead beast's paws over his chest. His face was bearded and hard-chiseled, stony, with dark northern eyes like Carys, but unlike hers his hair was pale blond, tied into a single heavy braid. His forehead was marked with a blue tattoo, a stylized eagle, some clan marking that Logan didn't recognize. His breath was on Logan's face, heavy, hot and stinking like a wild beast.

"Please don't kill me," Logan said.

The beast remained still and tense, his silver blade – looking like a shortsword in his massive paw – poised a few inches from Logan's unprotected stomach. To the rogue's shock and horror, the man smiled.

"So, they really did just send an old man," he rumbled.

Logan decided to save his favorite retort for some other time. The man withdrew and sheathed his blade before grasping the side of the bed. The heavy, four-poster construct looked as though it would have taken six men to shift, but the man flexed and, with barely a grunt, hauled it back over so that its northern pine frame was fully blocking the door once more.

Logan was trapped. He suddenly felt very much like a hostage.

"What is your name?" the man asked, moving from the bed to the hearth. Logan realized that there was a small fire kindling there.

"Lashley. Logan Lashley."

The man looked at him with surprise. "Logan Lashley of Sixspan Hall? Hero of Sudanya?"

Logan stared at him aghast, before managing to say, "You've… heard of me?"

"All of Terrinoth and beyond has heard the stories of the charming rogue Logan," the man said, sitting on his haunches by the fire. It was like being complimented by a huge wolf. Logan didn't know what to say.

Carys came from around the bed to sit beside her fellow northerner, the red animal scurrying up to perch on her shoulder. It didn't seem to have blinked since Logan had first set eyes on it. He stayed standing awkwardly by the door.

"My name is Ronan. Among my people I am Ronan of the Wilds. It is an honor to know you, Logan Lashley." He placed one huge hand over his chest, fingers splayed in greeting. Logan returned the gesture without thinking.

"So," Ronan went on. "You have been sent to talk me out of here."

It wasn't a question. Logan shrugged.

"I think they just wondered if you would like a light snack, so they threw me in here for you."

Ronan rumbled with laughter and gestured to the stand next to the fire. It was laid out with bread and cold meat.

"I am already well stocked, thanks to your castle pantry," he said. "That's how I got in."

"The servants' quarters?"

"Yes. An empty ale cask. I was able to convince one of the servants not to alert the guards."

"Matron Mildred?" Logan guessed.

"I think that was her name," Ronan said, reaching up for a shank of ham from the table. "A fine woman. Come, why don't you sit with us? Take some food as well, you look hungry."

Being invited to luncheon with a clan giant wasn't exactly what Logan had expected when he'd been forced into the room, but he was in no position to refuse. Besides, he needed to buy time while he ordered his thoughts – Ronan might have looked much as he'd imagined him, but he certainly wasn't acting in the way he had expected. He sat down on the rug across the fireplace from Ronan and Carys, unable to stifle a groan as he eased his joints. Ronan leant forward and passed him a hunk of bread he'd torn off the fresh loaf on the stand. Carys said something to him in what Logan assumed was Goltacht.

"The lady wishes to know where you have been," Ronan said to him. "You appear as though you just completed a long journey."

"Less long than fraught," Logan admitted, trying to decide whether to actually eat any of the food. He wondered if the barbarian had any way of poisoning that bread. Damn those northerners and their clan hospitality.

"She said you have been searching for Baroness Adelynn's daughter, yes?"

"We have," Logan said, wondering how much he should be admitting to the clansman. "Some suspect your kinfolk have taken her."

"So I am told," Ronan said gravely. "I have heard nothing of her among the clans."

"You know that for certain? Which clan do you belong to?"

"None," Ronan said. "And all. I act as a *Fìrinn Bruidhinn* between the clans and between the baronies."

"A *Fìrinn* what?"

"There is no direct translation. It is a word like broker or negotiator. Truth-speaker is the closest meaning. I am one who helps to keep the peace between the clans and Forthyn."

"And as part of that job you break into barony castles in ale casks?"

"Be thankful I did. Carys Morr is the daughter of the chieftain of the Redferns. He took her capture and the killing of her bondsmen to be an act of war. There were five dozen sword-kin ready to descend on this town and put it to the torch last night."

Logan took a second to digest the news, trying to appear unconcerned at the prospect of a warband of savage killers descending on the town. Slowly, he took a bite of the bread and ham. Be confident, he told himself. If this brute wanted you dead, you'd already be in bits scattered across the room.

"Five dozen sword-kin?" he repeated levelly. "And they sent just you?"

Ronan smiled. "Many men often achieve few things. Few men often achieve many. I swore on the spirits of my fathers that I would bring Maelec Morr's daughter back. A blood promise. It will be so, whether anyone else in this castle wishes it or not."

"You seem very confident for one man locked in a bedchamber at the top of a tower." Ronan laughed. "Perhaps, but I am Ronan of the Wilds."

"You sound like me in my younger days, Ronan," Logan said, taking a bite of his bread. "Look just like me, too."

Ronan laughed again, the sound coming free and easy. He seemed completely relaxed. Carys seemed calm too – she was feeding slivers of ham to the red-furred animal, though she rarely took her dark, serious eyes off Logan.

"You know even if she is returned, an act such as this will strain the friendship between Upper Forthyn and my people," Ronan said, his expression becoming more serious. "Times are difficult enough already without the added burden of conflict."

"So everyone keeps telling me," Logan said, finishing the bread. "The local seneschal seems to want a war with the clans."

"I have as few dealings with Abelard as possible," Ronan said, his tone making his feelings towards the seneschal clear enough. "This is not his first act of aggression towards the clans, but it is his boldest yet."

"Well you may not have to deal with him any longer," Logan said. "He was lost last night, in the Blind Muir."

"That's where you have been?" Ronan guessed, looking Logan up and down again. "You think the baroness's daughter has gone there?"

"We don't know," Logan admitted. "There have been a number of complicating factors."

"Such as?"

"The forest is infested with dark creatures, and the undead."

Ronan's familiar, still perched on Carys's shoulder, let out a little shriek, and Ronan spat into the fire.

"Necromancy infects the north," he said grimly. "Everywhere, it brings more death and suffering."

"That certainly seems to be the case," Logan said, deciding it would be unwise to mention Dezra and how her undead revenants had saved them.

"You think a corpse-raiser has taken the daughter?" Ronan asked.

"We thought so at first," Logan said. "But now we are less sure. Her disappearance makes little sense. She vanished one night from this very room."

"It does sound like dark magic," Ronan said, proffering a water skin to Logan, who shook his head. "Can your sorceress not track her?"

"Sorceress?" Logan asked carefully, thinking about Dezra.

"The one in this castle. Pico can sense her. She tried to enchant us into leaving this room, but Pico stopped her."

The little, furry red creature squeaked.

"Pico is a familiar?" Logan asked, looking at it warily. "It can nullify magic, yes?"

"Pico can do many things," Ronan said proudly.

"Well, the only person in this castle with any arcane powers is Lady Damhán, but I do not know the extent of them. She is one of Baroness Adelynn's advisers, come north with us to oversee the search."

"She is powerful," Ronan said, nodding thoughtfully. "Pico hasn't felt such power since the witch in the crooked tower."

"A witch?" Logan asked absently, his thoughts still on Damhán. Just what powers was she hiding from them? Since leaving Highmont his intuition had told him Baroness Adelynn's advisor wasn't all that she seemed, and she had told him that her powers weren't parlor tricks. He'd found no way of questioning her though, and he was sure she'd see straight through anything remotely obvious.

"Further north," Ronan said. "The tower lies between here and Thelgrim, a little over two days' hard ride. It is an old Dunwarr watchtower, abandoned long ago. A foul witch resides there now. The clans give it a wide berth when they travel to the south or west. I tried to slay her myself not long ago, but she is too strong. I could not even approach the tower through the damned spirits her fell voice summoned, even with Pico."

"Abelard said nothing of a witch," Logan said. That only made the seneschal seem more incompetent or, worse, suspicious. He cursed inwardly – they really were in deep on this one now, and getting ever deeper. "How long has she occupied the tower?"

Ronan shook his head.

"I do not know. There have been stories for years, but in times like these it is difficult to separate the truth from the bard's tales."

"And the wisest believe in a little of both," Logan said. His thoughts were racing – neither Abelard nor Damhán had said anything about a witch in the north. Nor, for that matter, had Dezra. Even occupied with her purge of the forests to the south of Fallowhearth, wouldn't she have known of the potential presence of another sorceress to the north of the town? Did this new figure have some sort of hold over the seneschal, perhaps even the baroness's advisor too? And if so, what could a witch want with Lady Kathryn? There was no obvious connection, but Logan also found it difficult to imagine the witch's unexplained presence and Kathryn's disappearance were completely unrelated.

"Perhaps this witch had a hand in Lady Kathryn vanishing," he suggested slowly, trying to fathom if Ronan was also maneuvering for some particular gain.

"Perhaps. If you wish, I could take you to the tower she has occupied?"

"That sounds like a convenient way for you to get out of this particular tower," Logan pointed out, instinctively looking for falsehood in the northerner's suggestion.

"I am a *Fìrinn Bruidhinn,*" Ronan said. "I understand the essence of negotiation. I will help you; you will help me."

"I like your style," Logan said. "But I'm going to need more than a story about a witch and your offer to guide us to her."

"I told Maelec Morr that if I had not returned his daughter to him by tomorrow morning, he was to begin the burnings," Ronan said. "Thanks to the *Fìrinn Bruidhinn* and the mutual respect of our peoples there has not been a war between the clans and the baronies for centuries. We are on the brink of one right now. This castle is stout, but I have seen few warriors since I came here. You said yourself the seneschal is gone. Do you think you can hold these walls against the entire Redfern clan?"

"No," Logan said. "But that still doesn't answer why I should trust you. Depart here with us for the tower and you could slip away with the girl on the first night. Or just murder us all."

"I do not think you are a trusting man, Logan Lashley," Ronan said. "I do not think many people like you are. You need something direct you can negotiate with."

"We certainly seem to understand each other," Logan said. Ronan spoke to Carys in their native tongue. The conversation lasted for some time. Logan did his best to read their expressions and tone of voice, but Pico's unwavering gaze kept distracting him.

"Very well," Ronan said eventually, looking back at Logan. "I have asked Carys and she is in agreement. She will remain here while I ride to the Crooked Tower with you, but on one condition – that the orc named Durik stays with her. She trusts no one else here."

"Durik is one of my closest companions," Logan said hesitantly. "I wouldn't like to ride anywhere in this blighted land without him at my side. I will have to ask him before promising anything."

"I understand," Ronan said. "But I will not leave Carys here unless he is with her. She trusts him, but no one else. That is enough for me."

Carys said something more in her own language, looking at Logan as she did so.

"She says she will not answer any more of the gray witch's questions either."

Logan laughed dryly. “Don’t worry,” he said to her directly. “I don’t speak to Lady Damhán any more than I have to either.” He looked back at Ronan.

“So what do I tell the others that you are offering in exchange for your freedom?”

“I take you to the witch who stole your chief’s daughter.”

“You don’t know it was her for certain,” Logan said.

“But only a powerful user of dark magic could have taken her? To make her disappear the way she did?”

“Perhaps. How do we know you won’t be leading us into a trap?”

“With Maelec Morr’s daughter still in your power? I would never risk her, even without the blood oath I swore to her father.”

“Would you make a blood oath here to me, that you will lead us faithfully to the crooked tower?”

“I do not swear on things lightly,” Ronan said. “And you are not a northerner. Your end of the oath would mean little.”

Logan looked at the hulking barbarian carefully for a moment. He came across as nothing but genuine, but then again, Logan liked to think he managed that often enough too. Right now though he had very few cards to play. He needed to reshuffle the pack.

“I will speak to Durik, and the others,” he said. “And if they are willing, we will ride north.”

“It is settled then. Go and ask your companion. If he agrees, bid your mistress send a horseman to the Lightning Rock, two days south-east. There he will find the Redfern clan, gathered for war. He is to tell Maelec Morr that the Son of the Wild sends his greetings, and says that his daughter is safe. She will be returned to him in nine days' time. Have the messenger give him this, as proof the words are my own." Ronan reached up and slipped the ring from his right arm, leaning forward to hand it to Logan. The weight of the wrought metal took him aback.

"I will ask Durik if he will stay," he said, rising with some difficulty. "And return with his answer. If he does, you will take us north, and show us this witch you speak of."

"By all the gods of north and south, may it be so," Ronan said, standing too, the familiar darting up the side of his leg and onto his shoulders. "I will see you again, Logan Lashley. Let us hope it is in better circumstances."

Outside the bedchamber Logan found himself facing a bristling array of swords and pole arms. The weapons withdrew when the men-at-arms realized it was him – all bar Kloin's, who looked as though he was on the cusp of running Logan through until Damhán cleared her throat pointedly.

"What did he say?" she asked as the chamber door thumped firmly shut behind him. Durik and Ulma looked like the only two who weren't surprised to see him still alive. Logan took a second to collect himself, considering Ronan's claims about the witch.

"He's willing to come out peacefully," he said slowly, affecting a triumphant stance. "And he's also willing to leave the girl here, provided that you stop interrogating her and Durik stays with her at all times."

"And what do we receive in return?"

"He's going to take us to the witch he thinks kidnapped Lady Kathryn."

Everyone stared at Logan. He wondered if he'd made a mistake – saying it now, it sounded far-fetched. But nothing Logan had sensed about Ronan at the time had felt like a lie, and he should know. He was committed now.

"Did he know Lady Kathryn was kidnapped?" Damhán asked.

"Well, no," Logan admitted. "But as he pointed out, it had to have been someone with sorcerous abilities, and we don't know of any other able magic users around Upper Forthyn, yourself excluded, my lady." He smiled at Damhán, who glared at him.

"But then who is this witch?"

"She has been skulking in one of the watchtowers to the north for some time, harassing the clans. Her lair is a two-day ride away. It fits what we're looking for."

"That's all you have to go on?"

"That's all he has to offer. He won't lead us astray as long as we still have the girl. Also, here's a fun little fact – she's not some clan peasant. She's the daughter of the chieftain of the Redferns. And according to Ronan he's on the brink of descending on this town with fire and sword. He wants a messenger sent to delay him."

"You let him outtalk you, idiot," Kloin hissed. "He reeled off some clan fairy story to you about a witch in a tower and you bought it! You have no evidence that she even exists, let alone that she's connected to Lady Kathryn, you gullible old idiot."

"Well, apparently I'm the only gullible, rich old idiot with the courage to walk into that room alone," Logan retorted angrily. "Perhaps if you were able to do your job, *captain*, he wouldn't have even made it inside the castle at all, and we wouldn't have to be negotiating right now. The last time I checked, we didn't have any other viable options, and no good information to work with."

"Did he say how he got in in the first place?" Damhán asked.

"No," Logan lied, deciding now wasn't the time to indict Matron Mildred, as much as Tobin would doubtless have wanted her thrown in the castle dungeon.

"Let me put it this way," Logan went on, placing a hand provocatively on Kloin's shoulder. The man visibly quivered with the urge to knock it aside. "Since breaking in, has the northerner killed any of your men, or any of the castle garrison?"

"Well, no," Kloin said. "But he assaulted half a dozen in his rampage to this bedchamber."

"A deathless rampage," Logan said. "Have you seen the man in question?"

"No," Kloin said. "But I don't see what the point of–"

"Well I'm assuming at least some of your men have," Logan interrupted. "So they'll corroborate when I say that Ronan of the Wilds is a very, *very* big man. He clearly knows how to handle a sword, as well. If he had wanted to, I suspect he could have massacred every person in this castle last night, half of them before they even knew he was here. He could've carried Carys out on his shoulders over your bloody corpses and disappeared out into the night. Instead he simply went to where you were holding her, and waited."

"If he just wanted to negotiate from the start he could've come here like a normal person, and not an assassin in the dead of night," Kloin said.

"And what good would that have done him? My dear

captain, you've been steadfastly refusing to let either me or my companions into this keep for several days, and we are here with the full authority of Baroness Adelynn. Are we really to believe you would have admitted a northern warrior the size of an ox and sat down at the hall's banqueting table to thrash out terms?"

Kloin was red-faced and silent. Logan didn't much bother trying to hide his smugness as he carried on.

"Ronan came here to negotiate from a position of strength, and despite first appearances, he is doing that. He has Carys and we are unable to harm him. His only wish is to bring the girl – a chieftain's daughter, no less – to safety. He is offering to leave her here, though, still in your custody, while he assists us. If you can conceive of a better end to this scenario then I'm sure we'd all love to hear it."

"I will not be outwitted by some northern barbarian," Kloin snarled, moving closer to Logan. Durik shifted too, the threat of his looming bulk giving Kloin pause as Logan continued.

"You already have been. We all have. He is no mere barbarian. He is a *Fìrinn Bruidhinn*. Anyone with an ounce of knowledge regarding the culture of the northern clans would know that he is a born negotiator. He was sent here with a simple task, and he is going to see it through."

"You appear to have least recovered your ability to speak, Master Lashley," Damhán said. "And despite your general ineptitude thus far, I agree that a sorcerer must have been involved in Lady Kathryn's abduction. I have translated several passages from the book discovered in her chamber. It is called the *Cadaveribus*, and it is dark magic indeed. Someone planted it there, possibly to aid them in the ritual that stole the lady away."

"Are you really agreeing with this decrepit jester?" Kloin demanded, glaring fiercely at Logan.

"He makes some accurate points. The northerner is presenting us with a means to end this stalemate, and we can still keep hold of the girl."

"And just why is that important?" Ulma asked. "You seem to have gone to quite some effort to snatch this child seemingly at random. She appears to know nothing of Lady Kathryn. Why insist that we keep her?"

"We negotiate from strength," Damhán said. "That is what this clansman has been sent to do, and that is what we must match. Logan, Ulma and Durik, you will ride north with him tomorrow morning, at first light. Find the witch he speaks of. Bring me back Lady Kathryn, or clear evidence of her whereabouts."

"He wants Durik to stay," Logan pointed out quickly, glancing at the orc.

"Ridiculous," Damhán said. "Durik was first of your group that I hired. He is a tracker without peer. His skills are needed in the hunt."

"I really don't think–" Logan started to say, but Durik interrupted him.

"I will stay," the orc said. "If nothing else, the intrusion has proved she is not safe in this citadel."

"You'll probably spring her free," Kloin growled.

"Let me rephrase," Durik said. "If you think I'm leaving her alone again with you and your men, you are greatly mistaken. I am staying."

"I will be sure to include all of this in my report to Baroness Adelynn," Damhán said.

"Yes," Logan agreed. "Maybe you should lead with how a single northerner was able to infiltrate Fallowhearth castle under Captain Kloin's watch. It may also be wise to inform the baroness that her appointed seneschal is currently missing in Blind Muir Forest, which appears to have been overrun by an infestation of giant bastarding spiders."

"My report will be entirely comprehensive, you may be certain of that," Damhán said coldly. "As for the seneschal, the garrison is now stretched too thinly to attempt to locate him just yet. I will recommend that Baroness Adelynn send more men north to assist us. I will also recommend that I am taking on the duties of seneschal until we have seen through this crisis."

Kloin couldn't quite cover up his crestfallen expression. Logan smirked at him.

"He gave me this, to be sent to the clan chieftain at the Lightning Rock," the rogue said, holding up the arm ring Ronan had given him. "He said it would be sufficient proof that his daughter is safe for now, but that if the Redferns don't hear any further word they will descend on Fallowhearth. He recommended we have the chief's child back with him within the next nine days."

"I will see it sent," Damhán said. "Meanwhile, you and Ulma will ride with the northerner tomorrow. Kloin, put your two best men on this door for the rest of the day, and rotate another four on in the evening. You are not to enter this chamber, nor is anyone else to go in or out until dawn."

"I will stand watch with them tonight," Durik said.

"If you insist."

• • •

Durik and Logan spent most of the rest of the day asleep at the Black Crow. Ulma, indomitable as ever, gave her bed up to the orc while she busied herself with replenishing her alchemical stocks. Logan woke towards evening, cursing himself for sleeping so long.

"Eat," Durik ordered him. He was already awake, sitting at the table with Ulma. It had been partially cleared of the dwarf's potions and beakers, and laid out with food brought from downstairs – bread and spudroot soup.

"Seems dangerous to have it next to half a dozen flasks of toxic brew," Logan pointed out before tucking in regardless. He felt suddenly ravenous.

"You will need your strength," Durik said. "You think you can trust this northerner?"

"You trust the girl, Carys, don't you?"

"She is an innocent, caught up by fate," Durik said.

"Aren't we all?" Logan said with a shrug. "I certainly don't trust Ronan any less than I do the likes of Kloin, or even Damhán for that matter. I thought for a minute she was going to have the whole tower torched when I came back out of that bedchamber."

"I told you, Damhán's more reasonable than you give her credit for," Ulma said, carefully distilling one vial into another, her goggles fastened over her eyes. "You just don't like each other."

"Should we really be sitting here while you do that?" Logan asked around a mouthful of pulped spudroot, eyeing Ulma's bubbling pots nervously.

"If you want me to go to the Northern Watch with just my

mallet then fine. But I'd rather be better equipped than I was in Blind Muir."

"What's the Northern Watch?" Logan asked, seemingly trying to take his mind off Ulma's alchemy.

"You told me the northerner called it the Crooked Tower. I asked the servants at the castle when I was getting food for the road. They say it's the most northerly watchtower on the borders of Upper Forthyn. They were built to keep an eye on the Dunwarrs and act as a waypoint on the road to Thelgrim. I remember visiting one when I was younger, decades ago."

"Was it the one we're traveling to?"

"I can't be sure, but they were all similar anyway," Ulma said, setting down her last beaker. "Half dwarf-built, half manling. They fall under the jurisdiction of the seneschal of Fallowhearth. One of Abelard's responsibilities was to maintain them, but apparently most of them haven't been garrisoned for years."

"Why am I not surprised," Logan said.

"In fairness, Baroness Adelynn hasn't exactly been pouring silver into Upper Forthyn's coffers."

"So the garrison was recalled to Fallowhearth, and something else took up residence," Logan surmised, deciding to say nothing about the veracity of servants' quarters gossip over the state of Forthyn's treasury.

"Seems like it."

"And how big do you think the likelihood is that said something took Kathryn? I don't think Ronan was lying, but there must be a connection somewhere. Something we've overlooked. There's still the possibility that Kathryn left of her own accord, and was taken later. Perhaps the witch was spying on her, or happened across her?"

"Only the ancestors know that," Ulma responded. "It could be any of those possibilities. But everything we've tried so far has turned up a dead end. We have to strike gold at some point."

"Spoken like a true Dunwarr prospector's daughter," Logan said.

"Actually my father was an alchemist. One of the foremost in his guild."

"And you're not a part of that same guild?"

"I'm not," Ulma said, her tone growing heavier. "It astounds me that in all the years you've known me, Logan, you've never wondered about that before today."

"You Dunwarr are a secretive people," Logan said with a shrug, not wanting to admit that he'd never really paused to consider what could have led a brilliant dwarven alchemist to fall in with a gang of adventurers.

"Let's just say my guild didn't approve of every last experiment I undertook in my younger days," Ulma said. "The guilds control the better part of Dunwarr society – fall out with a guild and it's usually best to hit the road."

"And that's how you ended up joining us?" Logan wondered aloud. Ulma's reply was cut short by Durik, who clearly already knew the tale.

"The guards outside Kathryn's chamber will change soon," the orc said, finishing off his soup. "I am going to join the new watch. I don't want to leave Carys alone near Kloin for any length of time."

"You sure you'll be safe here while we're gone?" Logan asked.

“Yes, I’m sure the veteran Broken Plains tracker needs the geriatric human vagabond to keep him safe,” Ulma chuckled. Logan scowled.

“Pay no thought to me, little rogue,” Durik said, smiling. “I’m not the one riding north with a wild clansman to hound a witch from her lair.”

CHAPTER FIFTEEN

They rode north the next day. Logan almost considered not going. His body felt broken, and the encounters in Blind Muir and his meeting with Ronan had drained him emotionally. How stupid he had been, to imagine any of this would be like it once was. How stupid to forget how difficult and desperate it had all been in the first place. But when he started making his excuses to Ulma, he couldn't make them add up to himself, let alone her. All that was left to do was admit he was a sad, spent old man, and Kellos burn his eyes if he ever did that.

"You can take word back to Baroness Adelynn," Ulma said as she packed fresh tinctures into her smock. "Tell her everything we've seen and found up here. I'm sure she'll be willing to unbind your oath when she hears about what we've all been through."

She was only trying to be helpful, but it annoyed Logan. He'd had enough help lately.

"Damhán will have sent enough messengers to keep the baroness informed," he said. "You're not giving up, Durik's not giving up, so I won't either. Besides, I'm not letting you go north on your own with that barbarian."

"Think I can't handle the big ones?" Ulma grinned. Logan chuckled.

The big one in question met them outside the castle stables. He was mounted on Durik's black stallion, the hefty beast looking altogether regular-sized with the clansman on his back. His red-furred familiar was perched behind him on the back of his saddle, looking somewhat unimpressed by the mode of transport.

"Well met, friends," Ronan called heartily as Logan and Ulma approached. The latter had her stocky pony, Ransom. Logan retrieved Ishbel, fondling the horse's nose and patting her neck reassuringly. He'd missed her.

"How long before you dig back your heels and give us the slip then, Ronan?" he asked as he mounted up with some effort beside the northerner. Ronan laughed, the sound drawing glares from the men-at-arms on the walls overlooking the stables.

"Oaths might count for little for a crafty man like you, but they are more than life and death for the clans. They are reputation itself, and reputation is everything. Besides, I would not have abandoned the daughter of Maelec Morr if I intended to make good my escape. Her father will not act rashly while he knows I am still on the hunt."

"Not going to ride back to the Redferns and tell them we've got her locked up and it's time to burn the town down?"

"And appear before Maelec Morr without his heiress? I would like to keep my head for a little while longer!"

The northerner accompanied his words with a heavy slap on Logan's back, nearly unhorsing him.

"Who would have imagined this day?" the man continued, voice booming. "Ronan of the Wilds joining with the Borderlands Four, off to slay a witch!"

"The Borderlands Four is currently the Borderlands Two," Logan pointed out.

"Off to slay a witch," Ronan repeated, grinning.

"We'll see about the slaying part. The most important thing is to find Lady Kathryn. Fortuna knows, she's led us on a merry chase so far."

"Find the witch and we will find her. By all the gods may it be so!"

They rode north. If Logan had thought the grim forests and stony fields that surrounded Fallowhearth were bleak, he gained a new appreciation for the word on the first day of travel. It seemed half the houses in Fallowhearth as they rode out were now boarded up, but Logan found himself soon missing even their inhospitable presence. By late afternoon any remote sense of cultivation or civilization had given way to sweeping heath and moorland. In the rugged, featureless expanse of heather and peat, only the pinnacles of the Dunwarrs provided a point of reference. The track they followed – though Logan considered the word far too grandiose – was little more than a vague trail leading between heather and particularly swampy areas of low ground.

They camped the first night on a small, rocky plateau that seemed infested with a billion minuscule flies. *Mij*, Ronan called them, claiming they were drawn to the flames of the fire. Logan strongly considered stamping it out – he batted at them in vain all night, infuriated by the itching sensation caused by their bites. Eventually he resorted to wrapping his whole head in his cloak, but even that didn't seem to stop them. Ronan, his huge arms bared, appeared not to mind them, and laughed heartily at Logan's obvious discomfort. The creatures seemed to avoid Ulma altogether.

"Skin's too thick," she quipped.

The second day added a dramatic flourish to the surrounding landscape. The moorland rose up into steep-sided glens, purple and dark brown, the colors brilliant in the cold sunlight that broke through around midday. Ronan sang a song as he rode, something in his native Goltacht, a steady, strong ballad that Logan took to be an ode to the foothills they now traveled through.

"A fine sight, is it not?" he asked as they crested a rise, the rugged terrain laid out before them.

"It's a little bleak," Logan said.

"You should see further east," Ulma pointed out.

"I was born near here," Ronan said. "Not far to the east."

"You were born inside Upper Forthyn's borders?"

"As were many of my kin. You southerners never seem to realize how common it is. My mother was from Strangehaven. She met my father at the markets in Frostgate. The blood of the baronies is as strong as the blood of the clans in my veins. Many can say the same. I have always believed we are one people."

"Is that why you became a… negotiator?" Logan asked, forgetting the proper name.

"*Fìrinn Bruidhinn,*" Ronan said helpfully. "Yes, in part. My parents left my tribe when I was young. We often traveled between the clans and Forthyn. I grew accustomed to north and south at an early age. I even served for a while in the Forthyn militia. That is where I earned my *aon buaidh*."

"What's that?"

"It would be like… my first glory, or triumph. My band were hunting lawless cattle thieves, out on the eastern border, beyond the banks of the Lothan River. We encamped near a system of caves we believed the rustlers were using as a hideout. As it turned out, something else had already claimed it, and them. That night a storm rose up. After we took shelter we were attacked."

"By what?" Logan asked, drawn irresistibly into the northerner's tale. He caught Ulma rolling her eyes, clearly far less enchanted.

"Deep elves," Ronan said. "Vicious, heartless creatures. White-fleshed and half blind. They took most of the militia as captives. I was absent when they struck. When I returned I pursued them into the deeps. Eventually I was able to free all of my friends, along with a few of the cattle thieves the elves had taken."

"Then witches are easy pickings for you?" Logan asked, half joking, half hopeful. Ronan laughed.

"We will see. I am sure you have faced worse than I down the years!"

"Well, I don't like to brag," Logan said.

"He really does," Ulma added.

"We shall make a story worthy of the bards," Ronan said confidently, urging his horse down into the next sweeping glen.

That night they encamped in a sparse, woody outcrop

overlooking a small brook that wound its way between the hills. Here at least the damnable insects which infested the undergrowth seemed less prevalent. It had grown colder, though, a northerly wind tugging at the last few gold and brown leaves clinging to the branches above them.

Ronan entertained them for much of the evening with epic stories of life as a *Fìrinn Bruidhinn*, wandering between the clans and the baronies. Logan couldn't help but be drawn in by Ronan's adventures too. The clansman was, among other things, an excellent storyteller.

"It seems strange to me, sitting here around the kin-fire with Logan Lashley and Ulma Grimstone, and not hearing their own adventures," Ronan said eventually. "Come, enough of my foolishness! Tell me, what is your homeland like, Logan Lashley?"

Ronan insisted on using his full name, despite having been told that Logan was fine – he assumed it was some sort of clan thing.

"I don't really remember," Logan admitted. "I left when I was young and haven't been back a great deal since. I have… quite a few debts in Summersong that I'd rather avoid."

"Then where do you call home?" Ronan asked. "Even the Wandering Clans have their native glens."

"I have a townhouse in Greyhaven," Logan said. "A fine city, if you can stand the scholars at the university, but I like the bustle. And a country hall, Sixspan, on the borders of the Greatwood. It is a beautiful place. Lush forests, fertile, rolling hills, gentle streams. I thought I had found peace there. Too much peace, as it turned out."

Ronan laughed. "You have the heart of a northerner! Your

soul cannot settle. You are a *spiorad krith*. A wandering spirit."

"I'd rather hoped I *would* settle someday," Logan said wistfully. "Wandering, in my experience, seems to bring with it rather a good deal of danger."

"Danger is the forge of legends," Ronan said. "Is that not so, Ulma Grimstone?"

"In my experience combining legends and danger adds up to a high body count," Ulma said. "I don't think I've done a single thing for the sake of glory. Not many Dunwarr can say that."

"Your work is what drives you," Ronan said sagely.

"Consumes, more like," Logan said, looking at Ulma through the flames of the campfire.

"It's what I live for," the dwarf said unapologetically. "Alchemy is a path to countless powers and abilities. I could perform a dozen acts before the sun sets today that most people in Terrinoth would call miracles of the gods."

"But it isn't the power you crave," Ronan hypothesized. "It's the excitement of each new discovery. That is what you enjoy the most."

"How you haven't blown yourself into little bits yet is beyond me," Logan said.

"There's time yet," Ulma said. "The only thing more exciting than mixing up a new concoction is actually testing it."

"It is a great boon, to have knowledge such as yours," Ronan said. "I hope we will see a display of your power before we part ways."

"Be careful what you wish for," Logan said. "Or you'll have bits blown off you too."

Ulma let that one go. They lapsed into silence for a while,

Logan gazing into the flames, listening to the wind rattling the branches above them. In truth, such sudden bouts of introspection left him feeling morose. He found himself wondering what his life would have been like had he settled down sooner. What if he had overcome that adventurous itch, took on honest employment? Would he still have won the comfortable life he had enjoyed at Sixspan Hall? Would he be more than just an old man living in a secluded manse, reminiscing about the sorts of adventures he was now so desperately attempting to relive?

"It must be lonely, the duties of a *Fìrinn Bruidhinn*," he said eventually, trying to ease his mind off his own resurgent unhappiness. To his surprise, Ronan let out a chuckle.

"I have a partner with the Bluestone clan, Morghelm the Swordspinner," he said. "Truly, he is a king among men."

"Do you see him often?"

"No," Ronan admitted. "But he has his own duties to attend to. He is the Bluestone's warrior-champion. Clan feuds are settled through his martial prowess."

"Sounds fearsome," Logan said.

"He is," Ronan said, smiling into the flames. "I am truly blessed by the gods. And besides, when I am not with him I am too busy to be lonely, Logan Lashley. These glens make for good company."

"You sound like Durik," Ulma commented.

"The famed pathfinder? I saw him when I left the castle, but I would like to meet him properly someday. Carys Morr told me much of him."

"I'm sure you could spend days talking about deer tracks or the different fauna of northern trees," Logan said.

"I hope so. But what about you? Do you have a loved one waiting for you in your western hall?"

"I'd hate to have to share the wealth I've risked my neck assembling down the years," Logan said. He laughed, but it sounded as hollow as he felt. Ronan looked at him with an expression that bordered on pitying.

"As you said, we all have things which drive us," Ulma said. "I suppose those same things also tend to drive us away from settling down with a spouse and children."

"You do not wish for heirs?" Ronan asked, sounding puzzled.

"I'm not sure I would have been best qualified to be a father in my younger days," Logan answered, voicing the unhappy truths that had started to creep up on him. "And now, well…"

"The fates work in strange ways," Ronan said, nodding. "What can any of us do but travel the path ahead?" They lapsed once more into silence, before Logan broke it.

"It's late," he said. "And I assume we won't want to reach your Crooked Tower during the hours of darkness, Ronan. We should leave with the dawn and hope to arrive as early as possible."

"I agree," Ulma said. "You should both sleep. I'll take the first watch."

CHAPTER SIXTEEN

Dawn came, cold and gray. A mist clung about the valleys between the high sides of the glens, leaving the scattered trees and undergrowth thickly beaded with dewdrops. Logan awoke stiff and damp. Ronan had taken his part of the night watch, letting him sleep. He was long past feeling aggrieved about that sort of thing any more. They refilled their water skins in the stream nearby and continued northwards as a cold autumn sun slowly burned off the morning fog.

They spoke little as they rode. Logan's thoughts were even more morose than before, lingering on his failure to find proper direction in life. Ronan had no more songs – a gloom seemed to have fallen not only over the small expedition, but over the land itself. The terrain round about became more like scrubland, the bushes sparser and the soil rockier. A brief shower passed over about midmorning, dampening Logan's spirits further.

Around midday he set eyes on the Crooked Tower. It sat upon a crag rising up out of the surrounding moorland, a silent, dark sentinel framed against the titanic purple and white slopes of the Dunwarrs beyond. Its foundations were the squat, angular stonework of dwarven masons, while the upper parapets were like those of Fallowhearth castle, humanbuilt. Those latter works had fallen into disrepair, half tumbled down and jagged. The collapse of the upper masonry had left the whole structure leaning precipitously over the edge of the crag, earning it the name the clans knew it by.

"Looks about as inviting a place as any I've seen since I came north," Logan said.

"Let us go," Ronan said. "Every minute of daylight is precious."

They rode towards the eminence. It had seemed small set against the great mountain range behind it, but the closer they got the higher it loomed and the more jagged its rocky mount seemed. Logan felt a chill creeping over them even before he reached its long, bent shadow.

"Last time I came here, I wasn't assailed until I reached the bottom of the rock," Ronan said as they reined in at the foot of the steep path leading up to the tower's arching doorway.

"That's good to know," said Logan. "By the way, do your people believe in omens? Do you think any of your horses do too?"

He pointed at the base of the track. A dead horse was lying there, its carcass split and near skeletal.

"If I was an omen teller, then that would not be what worried me," Ronan said, dismounting near the carcass. "What worries me is that there are fresh hoof prints leading to these remains. Fresher than the age this body suggests."

"Another phantom steed," Logan said. "And this one isn't Lady Damhán's missing one."

"The tower's curse," Ronan murmured, dragging a clan amulet out from under his wool tunic and kissing it.

"Well, if it's a premature aging curse, at least I won't have long to wait before it puts me out of my misery," Logan said with false cheerfulness, kicking his boots free of Ishbel's stirrups. "You may have to wait a few minutes longer than me though, Ulma."

The dwarf didn't respond. She was still sitting atop her pony, Ransom, gazing up at the tower's broken crown.

"There's something moving up there," she said. "Or there was a minute ago."

"I'd hope so," Logan exclaimed. "If we came all this way for an empty tower you'd be coming straight back to Fallowhearth with us, Ronan. Lady Damhán would be wanting words with all of us, and I'd rather you answered her than me."

"The tower is not empty," the northerner assured them. "Come, before the witch escapes."

"Speaking of, is that the only entrance?" Ulma asked, pointing at the open archway of the main door, leering down at them like a cyclopean eye. Ronan hesitated.

"I do not know," he admitted. "There is only one path up the rock, though."

"That doesn't mean there isn't another *through* the rock," Ulma said. "The servants I spoke to in Fallowhearth said these towers were partly built with the aid of the Dunwarr. That much is clear just by looking at them. It's likely the tower extends at least partly underground, and that there is a secondary route that can be used for sallies or as a means of escape."

"Could you find such a passage from the outside?" Logan

asked, silently praying the answer would be "no." Ever since Sudanya he'd endured bouts of claustrophobia whenever he went underground. A tunnel beneath a cursed tower definitely didn't seem like the time to try to fight his fear.

"Possibly," Ulma replied. "I'll have to ride around it and look."

"You do that, then. We'll wait here."

"We should go up immediately," Ronan said. "Before the witch can prepare her defenses. She will already know of our presence."

"Fine," Logan said, trying not to think about exactly what might be waiting for them, either above or below. Ulma clicked her tongue and urged Ransom to the right, moving around the tower crag from the east. Ronan dismounted and led his borrowed steed to a single, withered tree that stood forlornly next to the start of the path leading up the crag to the tower's door. He tied the stallion's reins to one of the lower branches. Logan did the same with Ishbel, trying not to look at the horse carcass as he passed by.

"We won't be here long, I promise," he murmured to Ishbel, stroking her muzzle. She snorted, clearly spooked. That was never a good sign. There was a whisper of sharp steel as Ronan drew his sword.

"Are you ready?" he asked. Logan looked up at the tower, his expression dark.

"Let's just get this over with."

The path to the tower was hard going. In places the stone gave way to yielding, slipping mud, and at times it seemed almost vertical. It also wound around larger boulders and sections of the crag that were sheer cliff face. Ronan, of course, ate it all up seemingly without even getting short of breath. He paused to help Logan along particularly treacherous sections.

"I'd welcome the undead if they'd only attack us as far down the slope as possible," he wheezed, clutching onto one of the northerner's titanic biceps. Ronan only grunted. His good cheer appeared to have left him.

For his own part, Logan kept his eyes on the track, partly to avoid slipping, and partly because it seemed whenever he glanced up at the crooked tower, it didn't look any nearer. He cursed the foolishness that had led him here, sweating despite the cold wind that was blowing across the moor.

The gusts died for a brief spell, and Logan heard a whinny come from back down the track. He turned, almost losing his footing in the process, to look down at the base of the rock. Ishbel and Ronan's commandeered mount were both still lashed to the withered tree, though they were pulling furiously on their reins, bending the dead trunk. The third horse seemed to be the source of their distress – it was standing, unmoving, near the start of the track. Logan assumed Ulma had doubled back to join them, before realizing that the third animal definitely wasn't the dwarf's tough little pony.

"Ronan," Logan said quietly, his heart feeling as though it was about to stop. "Ronan!"

The dead, rotting horse they'd discovered at the base of the crag had gotten up. Ronan hurried back to Logan's side, his expression grim.

"It has begun," he said as he noticed the decaying cadaver. The thing's near-skeletal skull swung to one side, as though it was looking up at them.

"Don't say it like that." Logan stared at the horrid undead.

A shriek pierced the air, making Logan jump so suddenly that he almost went tumbling back down the pathway. They both swiveled as more screams echoed out from the broken tower.

Logan had heard plenty of screams in his time. They came from all manner of emotions – anger, agony, horror. The worst, in Logan's experience, were those drawn from despair. They cut to the core of his being, reminded him of everything that had gone wrong – was going wrong – with his life. That was what the screams rising up from the crooked tower did now. They tore out memories of loss, of futility, of abandonment. They made him want to lie down and curl up in the dirt, to cry and never stop. They made him want to end it all. Despair, that all-conquering, irresistible void, swallowed him up and snuffed out every clever word and every cunning thought he'd ever had. There, briefly, in the shadow of the crooked tower, he ceased to be.

It was Ronan who drew him from his horrified stupor. The northerner was chanting something rapidly under his breath while clutching the amulet around his neck. Though the words were foreign and unintelligible, the sound of them alone rekindled something like hope in Logan's soul. He wasn't alone. There was other life on this bleak, wind-lashed moor – strong, vital life.

"Kellos, light my way," he snarled as his courage returned. "And Fortuna, guide my steps."

He'd never been one for praying, not seriously, but the defiant words seemed to have the desired effect. He felt part of the black, smothering shroud of oppression that had blanketed his soul lift. He took a step further along the track, then another, no longer rooted to the spot. Ronan too was advancing, body hunched forward slightly as though stepping out into a storm.

And then, as suddenly as it had started, the screaming stopped. Logan was so relieved he almost tripped, letting out a stupid little laugh as he did so.

The relief passed as quickly as the despair had. The tower still soared above them, unmoved by their defiance. Logan shivered.

"There will be worse," Ronan said to him. "Let us push on while we can."

Logan almost quailed at that, but drew strength from the northerner's huge presence. He couldn't go back, he told himself. After all, there was an undead horse waiting for them at the bottom of the track.

"Damned racket," Ulma grumbled under her breath, easing Ransom around the base of the tower rock. She had stopped when the air had filled with an unearthly wailing, picking her ears irritably. Ransom seemed unperturbed by it, and she was considering going back to see if Logan or the northerner needed help, but the sound had cut off again. Now the only thing she could hear was the wind sighing through the heather round about her.

She went back to inspecting the rock she was riding past, her eyes roving over the dark, moss-clad stone. She was no prospector or mason – like her father, she had not been drawn to the mining or mason guilds of her people, preferring the limitless wonders of alchemy – but she knew dwarven craftsmanship well enough. The secrets of stone were no secret to her.

"Where are you?" she wondered aloud, taking her time with her observations as she led Ransom on. The base of the tower was directly above her, still stout and untouched by the elements. The same certainly couldn't be said of the upper half of the structure, which had half collapsed. Ulma almost expected a loose piece of masonry to come tumbling down as she passed beneath its leaning side. Typical shoddy manling workmanship.

She had passed almost three-quarters of the way around the crag when she finally spotted what she was looking for. A break in the moss. Looking at the stonework alone the crack would have been almost imperceptible; a trick of tight, clever angles that made it look like nothing more than a slight fissure. The derelict state of the tower, however, meant thick lichen and small, hardy bushes had taken up residence on the flanks of the crag, and they were absent from that slender section of it. Absent because really there was no rock there at all.

Ulma dismounted and patted Ransom on the shoulder, smiling as she did so. She'd been doubtful about Ronan's story of a witch – it all sounded too convenient. She found herself glad to be here, though, rather than festering in Fallowhearth, where there seemed to be nothing for them except suspicious townsfolk and unhelpful officials. Even just being back in a place touched by her kindred felt like an improvement.

"Stay here," she told Ransom. The pony snorted and lowered her head placidly before beginning to graze.

Ulma settled her smock, adjusted her goggles and stepped into the narrow, dank passageway carved into the crag's base.

It turned immediately left, then right, aiding the illusion that it was simply a short cleft in the rockface. Ulma could barely fit, and she growled as she went side-on, careful not to damage any of the potions stored in her smock. She got a face full of cobwebs and was thankful for her goggles. Another turn to the right, and a fissure in the rocky passage opened up directly ahead, almost pitch black. She let her eyesight adjust, thankful that dwarves were naturally capable of seeing in the darkness of mines and tunnels. Even though her family had never worked the deep seams in the Dunwarrs, such confined spaces held no fear for her.

She pressed on, the spiked soles of her steel-shod boots clacking on stone. The tunnel continued to rise sharply. As she went, she checked her tinctures for steelburner. She had enough to sear away one, possibly two locks, should she be presented with a barred door. A grate or subterranean portcullis might be a trickier proposition.

She heard a noise and paused. More screams, faint and smothered by the rock. She pulled her mallet free, with some difficulty in the confined space, before carrying on.

The passage ended up ahead. An iron grate, as she had feared. She could probably burn through enough of it to work her way past, but it would take her longer. Beyond it she could vaguely make out heaped detritus – the old, abandoned contents of the tower's cellar, she assumed. She was directly beneath the Northern Watch now.

She was about to reach for the steelburner when movement on the other side of the grate caught her eye. Not the abrupt movement of another living person, nor indeed the jerky puppet-motions of an undead. She realized that there was something coiling and seeping along the floor. It was a low, dense fog, passing between the iron bars of the grate. Its tendrils reached Ulma's boots and began to swirl around them, passing by her and down into the steep tunnel.

Ulma suspected she would have been subjected to all manner of nightmare visions and unnatural chills at this point, were it not for her race's natural resistance to the arcane.

"Oh no you don't," she growled at the fog, before snatching a vial from one of her smock pockets and smashing it on the ground. Purple fire flared and ignited the creeping miasma. It shrieked, screamed like a living thing, and immediately withdrew, rapidly coalescing and solidifying into the shape of a human.

The figure stumbled back, its left arm still consumed by Ulma's flames as it half collapsed up against the grate, trapped.

Ulma raised her mallet, dragging a sliver of volatile drakesmetal free in the other hand, the concoction capable of turning any organic being into unyielding, lifeless ferrum.

"Don't move," she ordered. "And whatever you do, don't even think about trying any incantations."

They were over halfway up the path. Logan had spotted movement through the gaping, broken-toothed maw of the doorway moments earlier. He was too out of breath to tell Ronan.

In the end, he didn't have to anyway. Something was visibly coalescing around the old stonework up ahead. At first Logan thought it was smoke, or steam. It moved too coherently, though, with too much purpose, swirling together from around the tower's base to create the impression of limbs, then a body, then a head. Logan stumbled to a halt just behind Ronan.

"A spectral ward," Ronan hissed. "This is the unquiet spirit that forced me back last time. It is summoned to defend the tower's mistress."

"Oh gods," Logan groaned. "How are we supposed to fight something like that?"

"Stand firm." Ronan drew his sword. Pico had risen up on his shoulder and was hissing and spitting, its fur bristling. Logan didn't bother to unsheath his own weapon. He didn't know what harm it could do to a wraith. He'd be as well just accepting his fate.

The thing let out a soul-shuddering howl and fell on them. Logan found himself staring into its gaping, skeletal face, its spectral jaw distended unnaturally, its eye sockets blazing with phantom fire. He couldn't so much as raise an arm to ward it away as it streaked down from the tower like a freshly unbound demon of the Uthuk Y'llan. He screwed his eyes tight shut as it shot towards him, its ethereal body passing through him. Everything went cold, his breath ripped from his lungs. For a moment he felt as though his heart had stopped beating. He fell to his knees, desperately trying to draw breath, his whole body numb with that abrupt, terrible cold.

It had hit Ronan as well, though either the northerner's greater physique or the presence of his familiar had allowed him to shrug off the violating effects of its passage. He managed to drag Logan back to his feet, white-faced and shaking.

"Without Pico it will freeze our souls," Ronan said. "We have to reach the tower before it returns."

The clansman half carried, half dragged Logan up the last, steep stretch of track. The wraith had split apart after tearing through them both, but now appeared to be reforming once more around the tower door it was bound to.

"Courage, Logan Lashley," Ronan panted. Logan moaned again, not wanting to be dragged any closer to the cursed tower. The closer they got to the door, though, the more the spirit seemed to dissipate, its form unravelling back into smoke.

"It's weakening," Ronan shouted, charging the doorway. "The tower's curse is unbinding!"

Logan stumbled in his wake, belatedly struggling to draw his sword. By the time he reached the archway Ronan was already there, staring inside, seemingly transfixed. Logan dreaded to think what he had found beyond. Some cursed sorceress, some withered crone, more demented spirits, a legion of cannibal ghouls. Gods preserve him, it could be all of those at once! For a second he almost turned tail and started heading back down the path.

No, Logan, he told himself angrily. Just because it's shocking to a huge barbarian northman, doesn't mean it need frighten you. Trying to take comfort from the ridiculous notion, he tightened his grip on his sword and stepped around the stock-still Ronan.

In the end, it wasn't what he was expecting at all. It was Ulma and Dezra.

CHAPTER SEVENTEEN

The sorceress was sitting on a fallen mound of masonry just inside the tower door. The chamber beyond had two sets of stairways, one leading through a passage that descended into the tower's foundations, the other climbing towards its broken battlements. Ulma was standing beside Dezra, scowling, her mallet in one hand and a shard of bright metal in the other.

"You two took your time," the dwarf said as Ronan and Logan entered the tower, both panting.

"I take it you found the other way in?" Logan asked, leaning on the side of the door arch as he tried to recover. A part of him was relieved to find the necromancer before them, but for the most part he was shocked and, as ever, trying to mask it. There had to be a rational explanation, he told himself.

"I told you," Ulma said with a shrug, apparently better at hiding how surprised she was than Logan. "Only a fool would build something with only one way in or out. I caught her trying to escape through the lower passage."

"Dezra," Logan said, looking at the sorceress. "Perhaps I shouldn't be so shocked."

"Why have you come here?" she demanded. She was in visible pain, clutching her left arm to her chest. Logan realized that it was badly withered and bony, a sharp contrast to the rest of her smooth, pale skin.

"Did you attack Ulma?"

"She tried to get past me," Ulma said. "Some sort of mist illusion. I didn't know it was her."

"Your damned alchemy scorched away part of my enchantments," Dezra said. "I could have died."

"If it's only the enchantments holding you together, I worry for you," Logan said.

"You can save your worries," Dezra replied and, with a grimace, extended her left arm. She began muttering something under her breath, words that made Logan's skin crawl. Ronan's familiar squeaked, and the northerner raised his sword, but Logan put a staying hand to his shoulder.

A sickly light suffused Dezra's upper arm, traveling down as far as her wrist. As it went it left behind unblemished skin in place of the wrinkled, mottled flesh. It petered out before it reached her wrist, though, leaving the hand bony and claw-like. It almost looked like it belonged to a corpse. Logan looked away.

"I can do no more in the presence of that creature," Dezra said, glaring at Ronan's familiar as it half hid behind his shoulder.

"This is the witch," Ronan said, seemingly prompted into action by the sight of Dezra's balefire, his expression fierce as he gestured at her with his sword. "We must attack, before she beguiles us all!"

"Don't worry," Logan said. "This witch and I go far back."

"I don't understand," Ronan said, Pico still hissing at Dezra.

"This is the final member of the Borderlands Four," Ulma said. "Dezra."

"Dezra the Vile," Ronan said, making Logan wince. "The great sorceress?"

"Who's the brute?" Dezra demanded. "And why are you all here? Didn't you distract me enough in the Blind Muir? I told you, I can't help you, not any more."

"Oh, I think you can," Logan said. "There are questions that need to be answered."

"Witch hunting doesn't suit you, Logan," she said.

"Perhaps not, but humor me. How long have you been living in this tower?"

"I don't know," Dezra said. "Perhaps a year?"

"Do you mind if we search it?"

"Well, I don't seem to have the power to stop you."

Ulma led the group up the tower's spiral stairs. The old guard room lay halfway up, where the Dunwarr foundations gave way to the remains of the human masonry. The south-facing wall was half open to the elements, the rubble filling part of the circular chamber. The rest of it had been converted from an old garrison room into what Logan assumed was now Dezra's lair. An old Al-Kalim rug had been hung across the crack in the wall, while the former guard bunks had been converted into a cot and table. Clothing hung from abandoned weapon racks, and a small metal cage stood incongruously beside the stairs that led to the tower's battlement – stairs which now led nowhere.

"Homely," Logan said dryly as he surveyed the chamber. It was as cold and miserable-looking a place as he had imagined on the journey from Fallowhearth. It was just its denizen he'd been wrong about. Dezra didn't respond, taking a seat beside a table heaped with musty-looking tomes and scrolls. Ulma headed over to the clothing rack, while Ronan stayed warily by the door with Pico on his shoulder. He still had his sword drawn.

"Well, you certainly have quite the view," Logan went on, peering past the rug hung across the broken wall. The moorland stretched away, rugged and unbroken, from the foot of the crag below to the distant horizon. He turned back to Dezra.

"How in Fortuna's name did you end up all the way out here? You're living like some sort of vagrant."

"That's just the sort of question you would ask," Dezra replied. "The reasons would never occur to you. You could never imagine the stigma attached to my life. The doors closed in my face, the shelter and warmth and comfort denied to me because of what I am. Because of what I'm capable of."

"You should have stayed with us," Logan said. "We all accepted you for what you were. Gods know, none of us are any better. A mad dwarf, a loner orc and the most handsome, wealthy rogue in all of Terrinoth."

The jest fell flat. Dezra glared at him.

"So, acceptance depends on you, Logan? Just stay and surrender any dreams I might have beyond the Borderlands Four? Nordros help me if I seek a life and a purpose outside of your idiot adventures."

"I never wanted to hold you back, Dezra," Logan said, moving over to the cage set by the stairs. A dead bluecrest lay among the litter at its bottom, its plumage dusty. "But see where your path has led you?"

"Whose are these?" Ulma asked. She was standing by the clothing draped over the empty weapons racks, the sleeve of a long, pale blue dragonweave dress in her hand. It was one of several expensive-looking garments hanging off the rack.

"Doesn't really seem your style," Logan pointed out. Dezra didn't answer.

"You took her, didn't you?" he asked, biting back his anger. All the danger and discomfort he'd endured, all the fear and worry, just to discover Dezra had been behind it all.

"No," she said firmly. "I played no part in Kathryn's disappearance."

"Well, someone did," Logan snapped, his anger unabated. "Someone with arcane abilities. And they were likely using dark magic, at that. How many people do you know in Upper Forthyn who fit that description?"

"You've been looking for her too, haven't you?" Ulma asked her.

"You won't find her here," Dezra said. Her expression was cold, hard. Logan had seen that look before. She was trying to mask her emotions, but inside she was torn up and angry.

"What have you done with her?" he asked. He refused to believe she hadn't played a part in this.

"Nothing," Dezra snarled. "And by Nordros, if you ask me one more time I'll curserip the skin from your bones! The Baroness's daughter is a grown woman who had been managing these lands for months! Did you never stop to think she could have left of her own accord?"

"But she was here. That, or you stole clothes from her wardrobe. Which is it?"

"It's none of your business," Dezra snapped, her eyes glimmering dangerously. Logan felt Ronan tensing even further, but he was beyond trying to talk the northerner down. He was too angry himself.

"Baroness Adelynn has made it our business." He glared at the necromancer. "So, one last time. Which is it?"

Dezra paused, and for a second Logan thought she was going to lash out. Instead, she spoke. "She would visit from time to time. In secret."

"All the way out here? Alone?"

"I… used my magics to help her," Dezra went on, slowly. She was still tense, defensive, holding the same dangerous poise Logan had witnessed on so many occasions in fraught situations the length and breadth of Terrinoth. "She was never gone for more than a night or two."

"But why? Why was she meeting with you? Did she know you were a necromancer? Did you use your reputation as an adventurer to gain her trust?"

"You don't know what you're talking about," she snapped.

"You're right, I don't. So, explain."

Dezra looked about, almost as though trying to find a way out of the chamber. Ulma crossed her arms, while Ronan remained tense by the stairs leading back down to the tower's entrance. The sorceress sighed and closed her eyes, and Logan was shocked to see tears on her cheeks.

"She told me about this place," she said, her voice low and heavy with emotion. Her stance had lost its aggressive edge, arms at her sides now, shoulders slightly stooped, looking like a condemned woman. "This tower."

"Lady Kathryn?"

"Yes. I was living rough in Blind Muir. She was visiting the forest, and she was about to be attacked by… something. I still think it's linked to the arachyura. I was hunting it when I came across her."

"So she knew about your powers from the beginning?"

"To a degree. I bade her leave Blind Muir and not return, but she did. She found me again, and she told me about this place."

"She took pity on you and told you the northern watchtowers were no longer used by the Fallowhearth garrison?" Logan asked.

"Yes. She knew nowhere in the town would take me in. That if they discovered what I was I would be hounded out, or worse. Necromancy carries the death penalty in this barony, and the local seneschal hates the ways of Nordros."

"So, she always knew who you were?" Logan asked. "What you were?"

"Yes. She wasn't afraid. Just curious. She wanted to know about Sudanya."

"Don't they always?" Logan said, smiling humorlessly.

"You gave her a tome," Ulma said, nodding towards the book-laden table. "A dark text. We found it in her chambers, in the castle."

"The *Cadaveribus*," Dezra said. "And I did not give it. She took it without my knowledge. She was desperate to learn the arcane arts. I taught her simple tricks at first, but I refused to teach necromancy. Given the laws of Forthyn, how could I teach the black arts to the heir and daughter of its baroness?"

"Then how did she come by the book?" Logan demanded.

"I don't know much about the arcane ways, but it clearly contains dark, powerful knowledge."

"She learned quickly. As we grew closer, I allowed her to read small extracts of the *Cadaveribus*, under my supervision. It felt like the least I could do. She gave me this place. She came whenever she could, brought me food, clothing, ink and parchment. But one morning, after she had visited, I realized the book was gone."

"And you didn't confront her?" Logan asked.

"Of course I did. But I didn't want to drive her away, and I couldn't exactly storm Fallowhearth castle looking for it. She admitted she'd been rash taking it. She was going to return it to me. I believe that's what she was going to do when she disappeared."

"Did you help her in other ways?" Ulma asked. "She was the ruler of Upper Forthyn. Not long of age, newly appointed. Did she ask for your help administering her new holdings?"

"I advised her when I could," Dezra admitted. "But you underestimate her abilities. She is a clever administrator. Her mother taught her well. It did not take her long to become accustomed to ruling."

"And while she ruled, you led her astray," Logan accused. He felt like an idiot, like he'd been played for a fool ever since leaving Sixspan. The sense of betrayal had made his tongue sharp, but he didn't care. "Intentionally or not, you said it yourself, what you practice now is punishable by death. It would ruin Forthyn. By the flames of Kellos, it could rip apart the whole of Terrinoth!"

"I loved her!" Dezra shouted, and for the briefest moment balefire flared in her eyes, casting ugly, skeletal shadows across the room. Ronan shuddered at the uncontrolled display, but it seemed even his hatred of dark sorcery had been wrong-footed. In the silence that followed Dezra wiped her tears away, her cold reserve gone now. She was angry, and she was no longer trying to hide it.

"I would have given it all up for her. All of the knowledge I have spent my life acquiring, the powers I have gained, the long youth I have enjoyed. I would have cast it to the wind and burned up every one of these books in an instant if I thought we could have been together. But how could we have been? I am Dezra the Vile, the dark sorceress, famed across Terrinoth and beyond! I could never be seen publicly with Kathryn, let alone be introduced in polite circles at Highmont or at Adelynn's court. Even if I renounced what I am now, her mother would still have me beheaded and burned!"

Logan didn't know what to say. He had never seen Dezra so vulnerable, so anguished. The sight of her misery crushed him, even as her words stoked his anger. She had changed so much, had embraced unspeakable magics that had turned her into even more of an outcast than she had been before. He couldn't see how he could help her, couldn't imagine how she could do what she had described and turn back from the path she had chosen. Without Kathryn that seemed even more impossible.

His thoughts were interrupted by a tinny, chirruping noise. He looked towards the cage by the stairs, and a shiver ran up his spine. The bluecrest that had been lying dead in it was up and hopping about.

"I have seen enough," Ronan barked from the door. "She is a necromancer! She must die!"

Dezra stood up sharply, balefire igniting in her eyes, then sputtering as Ronan's familiar snarled. Before he realized what he was doing, Logan had positioned himself between the hulking northerner and the sorceress, feeling as surprised as either of them at his intrusion.

"Don't," he said to Ronan. "Not now."

"This witch has been a scourge on the clans," Ronan growled. "I have not come all this way just to let her live."

"I've done nothing to your damned clans," Dezra retorted. "I just want to be left in peace!"

"You defile our dead and torture the spirits of our ancestors," Ronan shouted.

Logan quailed at the huge man's anger, but didn't move from between the two.

"You won't lay a hand on her, not while we're here," he said to Ronan, trying to sound firm in front of the furious northerner. "She's our friend."

"You neglected to mention that part when we set out from Fallowhearth," Ronan growled.

"We didn't know that she was your witch."

"I will not bandy words with this damned creature!"

"Then you can leave," Ulma said, moving to stand beside Logan. "We never claimed we were coming here to help your clans, and you never said anything about killing witches. You said she could lead us to Lady Kathryn. That's the only reason any of us are here."

"She's right, for once," Logan said, looking back at Dezra. "Please. You have to know something that can help us. She couldn't have just vanished from her chambers. You mentioned she might have left of her own accord. Why? You said you argued about the book, how do you know she was going to return it that night?"

"Because I sensed it," Dezra said slowly, her voice riven with pain and regret. "She… I think she tried an incantation alone. She wanted to use the book before returning to me with it. She raised a family from the Shrine of Nordros, but she couldn't control them. They pursued her to Blind Muir. I don't know what happened after that."

Ronan growled at the mention of necromancy, but made no move to get past Logan.

"Durik spoke of bodies missing from the shrine's graveyard," Ulma said.

"How did she get out of the castle without being seen?" Logan pressed.

"I suspect it was the same way I tried to leave this tower, before Ulma's little alchemy trick," Dezra said, looking bitterly at her withered hand. "The *hex nebulum*. The mist shroud."

"Sounds like you taught her well after all."

"I told you, she's clever. More so than any of us. She taught herself far more than I ever told her. If I had truly tried to instruct her, she would have become more powerful than me. Far more powerful. Her potential is vast."

"And now she's lost somewhere in the Blind Muir. Lost, or worse."

"I've been looking for her every day since she left," Dezra said.

"That's what you were doing when you found us. Not just hunting arachyura. Looking for Kathryn."

"Is that why you raised Fallowhearth's dead?" Ulma asked.

"Yes," Dezra said. "I was getting desperate. It's been over

a month, and I've found no sign of her, either through my undead or any form of scrying."

"You said she tried to perform an act of resurrection and lost control," Ulma said. "Is it possible that she might have fallen foul of her own undead?"

"Perhaps," Dezra said. "But the arachyura are a far greater threat. You saw that for yourselves."

"No one could survive for more than a day in that place," Logan said, unable to quell a shiver as he remembered the infested, nightmarish forest. "Not unless they already possessed powers as great as yours."

"She is inexperienced and untrained," Dezra said. "But there's no reason to assume she's dead. I have to find her. I came here to perform another scrying rite. And now you're wasting precious minutes for a second time in almost as many days."

"Very well," Logan said, turning as though to leave. His anger had burned out. He wasn't wasting his time here any more. "It's clear you have no intention of helping us to find her. If she did indeed flee into Blind Muir Forest, then there's nothing more we can do." He paused and looked at Ulma.

"I suggest we return to Fallowhearth and retrieve our belongings, then ride south and report these events directly to Baroness Adelynn."

"I agree," Ulma said. "I would rather tell her in person than leave it to Lady Damhán. Doing so might see us released from our oath."

"You're not going back into the forest?" Dezra asked. "I swear to you, that's where she has gone! We can still get her out!"

Logan turned back to her, his own anger rising. "A small group cannot enter that forest and hope to survive long enough to find any trace of her. It would take an army to march into Blind Muir and cleanse it."

"So you're just going to give up?" Dezra demanded. "You're many things, Logan, but I didn't take you for a coward. Age has that effect on some, I suppose."

Logan turned on her, then paused, fighting back his resurgent anger. "You know nothing of growing old, Dezra, and I pity you for that. I am no coward. I am doing the logical thing. I would return to the baroness and explain to her what has happened here. We need the resources she has at her command. This isn't a job for a small group of aging adventurers. And besides, don't you think the baroness has a right to know? She's her mother, for Fortuna's sake!"

"You would condemn her," Dezra hissed. "Think about what you're saying! If she is found safe and whole, her mother will be forced to confront her necromancy. She'll either pardon her and fatally undermine her barony's laws, or she'll execute her! And that's without even considering the political damage it will do to her house, to Forthyn, to all of Terrinoth! A necromancer set to inherit one of the twelve baronies? As though the times we live in now aren't fraught enough. At best, she'll be disowned and forced to give up her land and titles."

Logan had no immediate answer. To his surprise, Ulma spoke for him.

"Logan's right. We can't do any more for Lady Kathryn here. It is our duty to report all that has happened since we came north. Even if we could somehow find her and save her, she will still have to explain herself to Baroness Adelynn. I believe she would rather renounce her rulership entirely than sign the execution order for her own daughter. As for the turmoil that would bring, well, that wasn't our doing."

Dezra was silent, her eyes shut. Logan sighed.

"Think of it this way," he said. "If Ulma, Durik and I didn't take this news to the baroness, we'd be guilty of breaking our oath to seek out Lady Kathryn. As Ulma said, it's our duty to tell her everything we've discovered. We're not abandoning her daughter."

"That's a coward's answer, and you know it," Dezra said, eyes still shut, her voice a harsh rasp.

"But it's also the truth," Logan replied. "And it might be her last hope."

Dezra said nothing more. Logan looked at her, pity and regret warring with anger. Before leaving Sixspan he hadn't seriously imagined he would ever see her again. Now this, a bitter parting that made their decades of friendship seem like a cruel joke. What had she become? Or what had he become?

"Your path is your own," he said eventually. "But I would strongly recommend leaving this tower as soon as possible, and not returning. I doubt you'll be safe here for much longer."

"Thanks to you," Dezra said. "Again."

"Yes. I'm sorry."

"Your sorrow has never been worth anything."

They departed as the sun lowered over the moorland, trudging back down the track to the foot of the crag. Nobody spoke. Ronan was glowering, and Logan was half afraid he would rush back and try to put Dezra to the sword – he was just glad they'd made it this far without blood being shed. At the bottom of the track they found her undead mount lying still once more, insects swarming over its carcass. Ulma went and retrieved Ransom, who had remained grazing serenely on the moorland grass.

"We're going back to Fallowhearth," Logan said to Ronan. "We'll make our report to Lady Damhán and then turn south. I'll make sure she frees Carys Morr and hands her over to you before we depart."

"I will not go back to the castle immediately," Ronan said. "I will join the Redfern. Maelec Morr may not have believed the messenger sent from the castle, and I would not want him to attack any of the nearby villages because he has no news from me. I also do not trust your mistress to hand over his daughter without anyone to exchange."

"I told you, we'll see she goes free," Logan said, but Ronan shook his head.

"This time I need to be sure. I will bring thirty of Maelec Morr's bondsmen back to the castle with me."

"You think that's enough to threaten Damhán and Kloin?"

"I know their weaknesses now, and their castle's. The size of the garrison, the number of their supplies. If we wish, we could take the citadel in a single night, or simply burn the town."

"Sounds like an extreme form of negotiation for a *Fìrinn Bruidhinn*."

"These are extreme times, Logan Lashley."

Logan couldn't disagree with that. He glanced at Ulma, who shrugged.

"Very well, then," he said to the northerner. "We will wait three days on your return, and try to convince Damhán in the meantime. If you haven't come by then, I'm going south with or without the rest of you. I've had enough adventures now for this lifetime."

CHAPTER EIGHTEEN

It was a morose ride south. Ronan departed after the first night and turned west, intending to skirt south around Fallowhearth, along the borders of Blind Muir, and search out the Redferns on the far side of the town.

Ulma and Logan barely spoke over the remaining day and a half of the journey. What she thought about Dezra and Kathryn, Logan didn't know, but he didn't care either. It had all fallen apart, and Logan had had his fill. For the first time in his life, he just wanted to go home.

They reached Fallowhearth in the late afternoon. The town was quiet, a few figures hurrying past shuttered homes and businesses. The air had turned cold, and the clouds were a low, gray blanket, threatening snow.

"Gods, I'll be glad to never see this place again," Logan said as they rode into town, as much to himself as to Ulma. "I hope the Redfern do burn it down."

Ulma said nothing. Logan assumed she was just being taciturn, until he realized she wasn't actually riding alongside him any more. He twisted in the saddle and saw her a dozen paces behind. She'd brought Ransom to a stop and was gazing up at a storefront across the street.

"What is it?" Logan asked, turning Ishbel back to join her.

"This used to be the town butcher's," she said. Logan looked at the timber building properly for the first time, noticing the boarded-up windows, door and the sign hanging above them.

"Well done," he said. "You can read the common tongue."

"Gods, you're an idiot," she said. "Don't you remember what Damhán said? I told her about the stories relating to the butcher's daughter. How she had disappeared."

"So?" Logan said defensively. "She said that they were just tavern rumors. That the girl had never been missing at all. She told me she checked herself."

"But what if she didn't?" Ulma said. "This place was boarded up before we rode north. What if it's been like this for weeks? What if the butcher left, or has disappeared as well?"

"For Fortuna's sake, Ulma," Logan said. "Why would you make these sorts of suggestions just when I'm on the cusp of getting out of this gods-forsaken town?"

Instead of answering, Ulma dismounted and tied Ransom to a hitching post. Then she crossed the street to the butcher's door.

"Don't do this," Logan called after her, in no mood to be dragged into another of the dwarf's investigations.

"Go if you want," she snapped back. "Go and tell Damhán we're giving up, or just hide in the Black Crow until the northerner gets back. You're rarely any use anyway."

Logan bristled and tied Ishbel next to Ransom. Ulma was testing the planks that had been nailed over the door.

"They look fresh to me," Logan said as he joined her. "Like

they were only put up days ago. You realize by far the most plausible story is that the butcher and his daughter have decided to get out of this festering wound of a town while they still can? A decision, by the way, that I think we should be seeking to emulate."

"Well, we're here now," said Ulma, pulling out her mallet. "Hold the top plank firm."

Logan sighed, but did as he was instructed. Standing on her tiptoes, Ulma hammered the top of the uppermost board of wood until it splintered around the nails and the length came clattering down.

"That's one," she said, before setting to work on the next one.

Logan held them firm, flinching at each strike of the mallet that came close to his fingers. He glanced occasionally over his shoulder. The few people that passed by glanced their way, but none stopped. Clearly a raggedy human and an angry-looking dwarf breaking into an abandoned shop wasn't worth anybody's time.

The last plank rattled free. The door behind was locked.

"I suppose you have some sort of potion for burning through the wood," Logan said. "Or one that solidifies when you pour it into a lock and forms a key? That would be impressive."

Ulma looked at him impassively for a second before leaning back and delivering an almighty kick right to the center of the door's frame. With a crash the timber gave way beneath her steel-shod boot.

"Or you could do it that way," Logan shrugged. He followed the dwarf inside.

The first thing that hit him was the stench. It was totally overpowering, far worse than even the ungodly stink of Tobin's festering kitchen. He recoiled back out into the street, his guts churning.

"You pathetic manling," Ulma called from inside the shop.

"What in the name of all that's sacred is that?" Logan demanded, breathing deep and slow through his nose as he tried to recover. Ulma's answer didn't help much.

"I think we've found Lady Damhán's missing horse."

Logan wrapped the edge of his cloak up around his mouth and, after taking a deep breath, stepped back inside.

It was almost dark within, the only light filtering through the broken doorway and the cracks between the boarded-up windows. Logan made out a wooden counter and walls lined with empty rows of hooks that he assumed had once been hung with the butcher's stock. A flight of stairs led up to a closed door, while a second doorway lay behind the counter.

Ulma was standing beside it. Logan edged round the counter to join her, desperately battling his nausea.

He realized that the dwarf was right. Damhán's heavy gray horse lay behind the store front. It seemed curiously deflated, and stinking pink slurry was congealing around all of its orifices. The skin around its nose, eyes and mouth was shriveled up, the veins black. It looked as though its insides had been liquidated.

"Arachyura," Ulma murmured.

"Here?" Logan asked, his pulse quickening. "In the middle of the town? That can't be."

"Remember the Northern Watch was half Dunwarr built?" Ulma said. "Remember it had a passage beneath it? Well, we

Dunwarr didn't just help the baronies build the watchtowers. We helped to build Fallowhearth castle as well."

"I don't like where this is going," Logan said.

Ulma eased open the door behind the counter without answering, having some difficulty bending one of the carcass's legs.

"We should go back," Logan said, watching as the dwarf peered through into the rear of the shop. He felt uncomfortable, penned in. He realized it was the same sensation he got when he journeyed underground, the same phobia he'd been dealing with ever since Sudanya's labyrinths.

"Ancestor's golden beard," she murmured.

"What? What is it?"

Ulma forced the door a little wider and, against his better judgment, Logan looked over her head and into the room beyond.

What light had made it through the storefront illuminated what looked to have been an abattoir adjoining the rear of the shop. Heavy sides of meat hung on dozens of hooks suspended from the low, heavy beams of the ceiling. Something, however, had clearly taken up residence in the butcher's absence. Glistening strands of thick webbing hung between the sides of dangling meat, with some of it wrapped up in the thousands of cloying threads. The web was so dense Logan couldn't see the back of the room.

"I think I agree," Ulma said quietly. "We should go."

Before Logan could respond, the light shining in behind them flickered. They both turned. Something was moving in the shop's open front door. An arachyura, poised above the entrance – it could have been there from the moment they'd broken in. Its limbs were jerking and twisting with an almost rhythmic regularity, and Logan realized with a surge of horror that it was spinning. Spinning a web, right over the door.

"Move!" Ulma shouted, shoving him aside and delving into her smock. Logan yelled in pure horror, trying to draw his sword, his hands shaking so badly he could hardly grip the weapon. As he did so, he realized with a plummeting feeling that the arachyura wasn't alone. The entire ceiling was crawling with spiders, great and small, hundreds of them infesting the rafters overhead. They exploded into frenzied motion as Ulma pulled out a vial and hurled it at the doorway.

The glass shattered and burst into flame. It seared away the freshly spun web and ignited both the arachyura and the doorframe.

"Get out!" Ulma bellowed at Logan and made a run for the door. He followed just as the horse's corpse started to distend and burst. Long, multi-jointed legs ripped free from the remains and thousands of smaller spiders came pouring out of the carcass.

Logan dashed across the store, screaming. He could already feel spiders dropping on him from above. Ulma was ahead, about to duck through the flames framing the door, when a burst of webbing sprayed her, causing her to trip and sprawl across the floorboards. Logan reached down to help, wildly grabbing at the edge of her smock and unintentionally spilling several vials out onto the floor. He got her onto her knees in time to receive a second blast of webbing that dragged them both to the floor.

Ahead, a black carpet of scuttling bodies was actually

smothering the fire that had engulfed the doorway, burning themselves in their efforts to douse the flames. Ulma was fumbling with a trio of vials, pouring them together into a spherical glass orb which she stoppered firmly.

"Why aren't you using it?" Logan screamed at her, trying to haul himself clear of the sticky webbing that had engulfed half of his body.

"Because I want to live a bit longer," Ulma said.

A weight slammed into Logan's back. He yelled and twisted, thrusting his sword up into something with far too many legs. It squeaked and spurted a foul, stinking ichor.

They were all over him. It was even worse than Blind Muir – claustrophobic, maddening. He slashed viciously, but more damned webbing snagged his arm and made his blows useless. Something was digging pincers into his thigh and another into his side. His body had already started to numb.

His panicked mind unable to think of anything else, he tried to pray out loud, but more webbing struck his face. Limbs dug into his side, turning him over. He realized the arachyura weren't trying to kill him. They were trapping him. More webbing clung like fish glue to his sides, pinning his arms to his body, his sword still gripped uselessly in one hand. Webbing over his mouth stopped him screaming. Things were biting his legs all over now. He was losing feeling everywhere. He couldn't see Ulma.

The last thing he saw was the fat, deformed body of an especially large arachyura dragging itself over him, its mandibles oozing. Then the threads splattered and bound his upper face, and he saw no more.

• • •

Durik stood by the window, looking out over Fallowhearth. Darkness was beginning to fall, creeping between the narrow streets and extending out over the fields and forests beyond. In the distance Blind Muir was already swathed in shadow, a brooding, oppressive presence on the town's doorstep.

"What is it?" Carys asked. She was sipping at a bowl of boiled root vegetables, perched on the edge of the four-poster bed. Durik had dragged it back to its place against the wall, leaving the door unblocked. There was no need for barricades while he was here.

Durik continued to gaze into the encroaching night. The wind gusted, rattling the window's small, murky crosshatch panes. The draught was working its way relentlessly into the castle chambers. He moved over to the fireplace, doing his best not to pace. It was almost impossible.

"They're late, aren't they?" Carys went on, looking at the orc over the brim of her bowl. "Ronan and your friends."

"They are," Durik agreed, placing a fresh log in the hearth. He didn't want to have this conversation, didn't want to admit how difficult it was to be trapped in the tower with the clan girl.

"You expected them this afternoon. Three days to the tower and three back."

"Logan Lashley is often late."

"But Ronan of the Wilds isn't."

Durik probed the hearth with the blackened fire poker, getting the fire sparking again, before returning to the window. He was struggling silently with a monstrous restlessness – a hunter required patience, but staying patient was easier said than done when he found himself helpless in the face of his friends' unknown fate. Every moment since their departure seemed to have dragged on agonizingly.

"If you wish to go and look for them, I won't stop you," Carys said.

"I cannot leave you here alone. Not with the likes of the captain still here."

"Maybe I can come with you?"

"Lady Damhán won't allow that."

Carys lapsed into silence. Durik scanned the streets below once more, looking for any sign of Logan, Ulma or the northerner in the dying light. Perhaps they had found the crooked tower simply unoccupied? Perhaps they had chosen to spend the night there? He tried to accept the unknown, to come to terms with the fact that he couldn't be sure until they returned, but the possibilities played out endlessly in his mind, each one darker than the last.

"Lady Damhán scares me," Carys said after a while.

"Why?" Durik asked, not taking his eyes off the gathering twilight.

"I don't know. I feel as though her eyes are always on me, even when she isn't here."

"She is a sorceress," Durik said. "I'm sure she has many unsettling abilities."

"It's more than that. She looks at me like a hunter."

"Don't I? I would have thought I was more a hunter than one of Baroness Adelynn's court advisors."

"That is the wrong word then. Not a hunter, a... *creachadair*."

"A predator?"

"Yes, I think. A creature-that-hunts."

"Perhaps," Durik said, the girl's words taking his mind off his anxiety. What she said had a ring of truth to it. "I have known many such creatures in my time. But I do not see that in Damhán."

"Did you ever find one that could disguise itself? So it did not seem like what it was."

"Some, yes," Durik said. "There are many cunning beasts across Terrinoth and beyond. But I have rarely known any with an ability to seem like an old woman."

"But you have never been to this corner of Terrinoth."

Durik said nothing, still standing post at the window. Outside, night fell.

Logan tried to scream. The realization that he couldn't made him try to scream harder.

Was he awake? He couldn't see, though he was sure his eyes were open. He couldn't feel, either. His body was gone. He tried to reach out, to twist, to turn. Nothing.

It was warm. He could feel moisture on his face. Sweat, he realized. So he still had a face, at least. He tried to open his mouth, but it was sealed. He could only breathe through his nose. For a while he thought he was going to suffocate.

It took time for the worst of the panic to recede. He gave up trying to struggle. His thoughts raced. Arachyura. That was all he could remember. Thousands and thousands of bastard arachyura. Something scuttled across his face. He tried to scream again, but could only get out a low, throaty moan.

Gradually, more memories came back. The butcher's shop. Ulma. The fire she had kindled. Had she made it out? Had the arachyura managed to put out the flames, or had the shop burned down? Was anyone looking for them? And where in the names of all the gods was he now?

His body shifted. Something around him was vibrating, bouncing. The sensation made him queasy and caused him to instinctively try to put his arms out to steady himself. He couldn't, though he felt the fingers in his left hand twitch. Feeling – slow, aching and painful – was beginning to return to his body.

He flexed the hand, tried to move his arm too. It was pinned to his side. The other one wasn't any better. The fingers of his right hand seemed fixed in place. He realized that was because they were locked around something solid, something that was trapped against the right side of his body alongside his arm.

His sword. The rest of his memories returned, rushing back with ugly clarity. The arachyura swarming him. Their horrific webs snagging and snaring him, pinning his whole body, including his blade. That's where he had to be now. Wrapped and trapped in a huge spider's web.

He tried to scream again, but still couldn't. Another wave of panic flooded his thoughts, and he felt the bindings holding him vibrate once more as something large shifted and scurried past him.

This time it took far longer to regain control. He wasn't sure if he had passed in and out of consciousness at some point – deprived of his senses, it was difficult to tell. He tried to regulate his breathing through his nose. It was so damnably hot.

Then the voice spoke to him.

"You wake," it murmured.

Hope filled Logan – unreasoning, heart-pounding hope. He wasn't alone. He wasn't going to die here blind and dumb amidst these scuttling monstrosities.

He tried desperately to speak but could only force out a muffled grunt.

"Good," said the voice. It was slow and rattling, at once familiar but alien to him. "You are first," it went on. "I hoped you would be. I am glad."

The web around him vibrated again, as though dozens of creatures were scuttling over its taut threads. Logan made an ugly, mewling noise. He felt something probing the side of his face, all questing, hooked, hairy limbs. Abruptly the webbing binding his mouth was ripped away. He gasped, panting in the humid, stinking air, trying to find his voice.

"W- Who are you?" he managed.

"You do not recognize?" croaked the voice in the darkness. "Let me help."

More spiders' legs snatched and groped his face. This time Logan was able to scream. He made the most of it.

More webbing unraveled and fell from his eyes. He blinked, but it did him no good, not at first anyway – it was pitch black, wherever he was. Slowly, however, a hot, golden light started to glow ahead of him. He made out fingers, splayed beneath the tiny, coruscating ball of illumination, then a full hand, then an arm. The light grew, like an Al-Kalim dawn, until it had illuminated the entirety of the figure who had conjured it.

Lady Damhán stood before Logan, the light in her hand making her thin gray robes seem almost translucent. Her whole body was suffused with the glow. She looked at Logan, but her expression was unmoving, as emotionless as a mask. Her eyes were black and held only hunger.

"Do you know me yet, Logan Lashley?" she hissed in a rattling, deathly voice.

Logan didn't respond. His mind was racing like a sparrow's heartbeat, too fast for conscious thoughts. She raised her arms up straight, the orb of light floating until it was above her, her palms touching above her head. As though snatched by a sudden wind, her gossamer robes bolted against her body, moving of their own accord. They tightened and overlapped, until Damhán was no longer clad in thin, loose gray robes, but in a lattice of web-like bindings that hugged her entire form. The last remnants of her cloak wove about her gaunt face, wrapping over and over, completely covering her. As the last piece was snatched into place, a burst of light as bright as the midday sun dazzled Logan. When his sight returned, Damhán's mummified face was shielded by a golden mask, young, feminine and expressionless. For a second he thought he could feel the heat of the desert.

"Now you know me, don't you?" hissed the voice from behind unmoving golden lips.

"Ariad," Logan stammered. "Spawn of Arachne, Goddess of Spiders."

"Yes," the creature that had been masquerading as Lady Damhán said. Its speech was jerky and disjointed now that it had stopped trying to mimic its human prey. It let out a hideous ticking noise.

"I see you forget not. It has been long since Sudanya."

"You were stabbed by Durik," Logan said, not believing what he was seeing. "And then crushed when the temple fell. You had transformed by then. You… you couldn't have survived!"

"Naive fool," Ariad hissed. "It will take more than a savage's spear to cut the thread of my life." She indicated her left side, where the web-like rags that bound her body were knotted and twisted. "I repay that soon. When my children bring the savage."

The mention of Durik gave Logan a moment's hope. It didn't have him yet.

"Where is Ulma?" he demanded. The arachyura queen raised a hand, and the golden light above her head floated towards Logan, then went right.

"Oh gods," Logan breathed. The light picked out the thousands of strands of webbing that surrounded him, and not only exposed the thick wrap of threads that tightly bound his own body, but also the remnants of other beings pinned to the thread. He counted a dozen or more all around him, most of them skeletal remains half-wrapped in mummifying silk. He realized a few were still clad in armor, and spotted a golden roc pinned to the chest of one slack-jawed corpse, gleaming in Ariad's light. Abelard. He shuddered uncontrollably, his thoughts in turmoil. The creatures had gotten to everyone. Nobody was safe. Were they even now picking off the last of Fallowhearth's inhabitants? What about Durik and Carys?

Close to the seneschal's corpse was a smaller cocoon. The only part of the person within that was visible was a snub nose, and the end of one blond braid poking through next to it. It had to be Ulma.

Ariad's light traveled on, illuminating part of what looked

like a subterranean cavern and, as it did so, glittered back from thousands upon thousands of black eyes, infesting the great web all around them. Despite the heat, Logan started to shiver uncontrollably.

"I have waited for this," hissed Ariad. "A long time."

"Was there ever a real Damhán?" Logan demanded, trying not to give way to a third surge of panic. "Or has she always been just an illusion?"

The web-clad figure again made a low, ominous ticking sound. Logan found he couldn't look at that chillingly expressionless mask for any length of time.

"Lady Damhán has served the baroness for many decades. That is what the baroness believes. What all believe. So easily tricked."

Abruptly, the pallid figure moved, almost blindingly fast. It was at the bottom of the great web holding Logan before he could even cry out, darting up it with a rapid, disjointed gait, any trace of Lady Damhán gone. It snatched him by his bound shoulders, its golden mask inches from his face. Despite its inhuman pose, it seemed perfectly balanced and weightless on its silken trap.

"Long time have I waited, Logan Lashley. I remember Sudanya. Remember the pain. Now you will know that pain. I tried to show it to you in the forest, but you are too strong together. All together like Sudanya. Not now. Now I pick you and pin you one by one. Soon you will see friends again. Soon, you will suffer together."

CHAPTER NINETEEN

There was a storm building over the glens. Dezra could feel it in her heart as much as she could feel it in the charged air. A scream waiting to tear free, a thunderclap ready to roll out. She had spent much of the day roving back and forth through the tower, snatching up a book or scroll, reading a few lines, throwing it back down again. In her time she had acquired many potent texts, some from the libraries of Greyhaven itself – the powers of Umbros and Mortos, the elemental powers of shadow and death, sat heavy within dusty pages and cracked rolls of parchment scattered throughout the tower. None of it, however, was what she sought.

Kathryn's ghosts were all around her. She could see her sitting at the table, her expression serious as she read through one of Dezra's parchments. Laughing by the door as she took in the mud on her dress, fresh from her journey from the town. By the jagged split in the tower's wall, looking out across the blasted moorland one breezy summer's eve, the wind in her hair as they shared their first kiss.

Dezra would find her. If she had to rip her own soul from

her body and throw it into the abyss, she was going to find her.

The passage she needed wasn't here. It was in the tome Kathryn had taken from her, the *Cadaveribus*. One last, cruel irony. She threw the other, useless, books aside and snatched up a dagger from the table, its blade long, curved, and as serrated as her soul. With it in hand she stalked downstairs and out into the night.

When she had first met her, Kathryn had hated the dark. Dezra had taught her there was nothing to be feared, nothing inherently terrifying about the cycles of the world. Life and death, summer and winter, night and day, they all had their place. It hadn't taken Kathryn long to lose her fear.

The wind was picking up outside. It clawed at her cloak, trying to rip it off. She walked down the steep, winding track to the base of the tower crag, her every step assured despite the darkness. Just beyond the bottom of the path her corpse-steed waited with its eternal patience. She whispered it back to its uneasy rest. She had no need of it tonight.

Beyond the carcass was the tree. During summer Kathryn had gathered up its blossom and woven a small crown from it, one she had insisted on Dezra wearing. She'd waited until Kathryn had left before withering it, so she wouldn't make her wear it again next time. When Kathryn had visited her again Dezra had teased her about it.

The tree was skeletal now, the wind whipping at it as Dezra approached. Its gnarled branches creaked and groaned as she reached up, running her fingers along one low, bent bough. She raised the knife and, hissing black words, began to saw.

With the severed branch in her hands, she climbed once

more up the crag's path, the tower above her pointing like a broken finger to where the storm was coalescing above. Rain began to fall. She felt the first drops on her skin before she stepped inside – icy, stinging, bitter.

She climbed the stairs to the guard chamber and tore the rug from the crack in the wall, letting the wind and rain in, banishing the memory of when she and Kathryn had last stood in that same spot. Her balefire had returned, lighting her eyes beneath the cowl of her cloak and coruscating around her fingers. The bluecrest in the cage had started to go wild, flitting backwards and forwards, slamming against the bars.

She sat, cross-legged, in the center of the chamber, the dagger in one hand and the broken branch in the other. The words she spoke seemed to raise the tempo of the wind, as though it railed against the ancient, cursed language. Scrolls and loose sheaves of paper were snatched up and flung across the chamber, whipping in a circle around the dark sorceress. The volume of her voice rose as the tone deepened, unnaturally so, shuddering the stonework around her and causing loose masonry to cascade from the tower's flank. Lightning flared and the thunder answered it, crashing above, shuddering the crag to its core. Still Dezra chanted, her eyes glowing like dying stars.

She knew that this time the magic was going to do more than simply drain her – it could break her forever. But there would be no going back. That no longer troubled her. The doubts and fears that had plagued her were being seared away by the icy burning of her anger.

The lightning struck again, slamming the broken tip of the tower. With a crash that rivalled the accompanying thunder, the whole structure finally came down, stone hammering against stone, the Dunwarr foundations giving out with a crack, like the ending of the world. Dezra's chamber was crushed, its contents pulverized, every book and belonging utterly destroyed.

But by then, Dezra the Vile was far away.

Before

Light was streaming in between the leafy boughs, a warm summertime glow that made the forest seem drowsy and dreamlike. Kathryn was glad of it – she disliked the dark, especially the blackness that haunted the depths of Blind Muir. Today, as she rode through the trees along the forest's edge, the woodland's threat seemed to slumber rather than lurk.

She had been waiting for a day like this, a day when the darkness crept back to the heart of the forest, when it didn't feel like unfriendly eyes were spying on her from behind every trunk and bough. Growing up in Highmont her experiences of Blind Muir had been relegated to the darker bedtime stories told by her night nurse. She'd gazed upon it often from the keep's eyrie, when the days were clear and cloudless, exposing its brooding southern border as a dark line on the horizon. She'd known from a young age that a time would come when she would be expected to rule Upper Forthyn, to govern its places and peoples. And that duty would include Blind Muir.

The seneschal had warned her against visiting today. Ever since she'd arrived in Fallowhearth and assumed control of the upper part of the barony, Seneschal Abelard had spoken darkly of Blind Muir. His views seemed barely removed from those of Kathryn's old nurse – surely, she'd tried to reason, the stories couldn't be true. He'd had the decency to look embarrassed, but hadn't ceased advising her against visiting the forest.

She had the power to disregard his warnings. This was her land, and she could go where she pleased. She knew, however, that Abelard would likely report her trip to her mother, and that was the last thing she wanted. She'd come along today, telling Abelard she was riding to Blackfinch, a little west of Fallowhearth, to visit its newly built shrine of Kellos. He'd offered an escort, but she'd been able to convince him that a single servant would be sufficient accompaniment. That servant had, in turn, required only a small sum of coin to be convinced to stay at Blackfinch while she turned south to Blind Muir, alone.

She paused her mount besides a heavy-set old redbark, leaning over in the saddle to place her fingers against its gnarled, knotted trunk. She wasn't sure why she had felt such an urge to investigate this place. A part of her had always been drawn to the forbidden and the arcane. She supposed it was all part of being the heir of a baroness. In her early teens she had used servants' cast-offs to disguise herself as a stall seller's helper and loitered outside the sorcerers' guild in Highmont. Once she had even snuck into a lecture run by one of Greyhaven University's foremost lecturers on the elemental arts, taking a screed of notes that were later discovered by one of the castle maids stuffed under her bed. Magic had always fascinated her, and in her childhood she had daydreamed of escaping the duty-bound life preordained for her and enrolling as a student at Greyhaven.

The snap of a breaking twig caused her to draw her hand away from the redbark. She looked around, startled. Clouds had shrouded the sun, leaving the space beneath the trees in a dulled, gray haze. How long had she been lost in her thoughts? Surely it had only been a few moments? Where had the light gone?

She turned her mount, looking towards where the tree line had been moments before. Had she not been able to see open fields between the branches? Where were they now? She realized that her heart was racing. There was something wrong, something subtly off about the forest now. Its malignancy had awoken.

The light returned. At first her hopes leapt, and she almost scolded herself. The sun had simply hidden its face for a few moments behind the clouds, and now it had come back to lead her out. But no. This light was contained, throwing back the creeping gray shadows in in the vicinity behind her, like a torch but without the flickering inconsistency of a flame. She half twisted in her saddle, urging her mount about once again.

There was the light – not a torch but an orb, perhaps the size of a fist, glowing deep and hot, like a tiny star. It bobbed slightly in the air, accompanied by a low, clicking susurration that made her hairs stand up. And it was coming towards her.

She tried to turn away. It was bright, but somehow unwholesome. Her eyes ached to look at it, yet she found her gaze locked into its core, unable to look away, almost blinded by it. She wanted to shout out, to dig her heels in, to race away from that unnatural orb, but she was captive, paralyzed, the clicking noise rising to a storm in her ears. For a moment she witnessed an avalanche of twitching, furred limbs and unblinking, multi-segmented eyes.

And then the light was gone. Darkness engulfed it, not a shadow, but something truly and utterly black. The void closed over the light like a fist, crushing it, snuffing it out before being dragged away into nothingness. When it vanished the light had gone with it, and the chittering had been replaced once more by the soft, low creaking of the forest.

Kathryn sat very still upon her steed, her heart hammering. The sunlight returned, banishing the cloying shade that had been creeping in beneath the boughs. The moment had passed, and for a second she wondered if she had imagined it. But that seemed unlikely – there were still eyes on her.

She looked left. There a cloaked figure stood watching, framed by two bent old mirewood trees. Before Kathryn could react, the figure lowered her hood, revealing a pale face framed by black locks and eyes that seemed as dark as the void she'd just seen extinguish the orb.

Kathryn finally found she could move. Her hand went down to the shortsword she had strapped to her waist, hidden from Abelard under her riding cloak before she'd left Fallowhearth. The figure raised a single hand.

"You won't need that," she said. "I am not a threat."

Kathryn left the sword undrawn, but her hand remained on the hilt.

"What was that thing?" she demanded, still struggling to slow her heart and ease her breathing.

"Nothing good," the figure said.

"And who are you?" she went on.

"Nothing good," the woman repeated, though this time with the slightest hint of a smile.

"That was magic, wasn't it?" Kathryn asked, her mind racing. "The orb, the blackness. Where did it come from?"

"On the first count, I wish I knew for sure," the woman said. "On the second, the blackness was all mine. Did you like it?"

The question caught Kathryn off guard. She frowned.

"It was dark magic," she said. "I doubt it's legal in Forthyn."

"Dark magic that saved your life," the woman pointed out. She took a step forward. Kathryn's grip tightened once more on her sword's hilt.

"Don't come any closer," she said. The woman stopped, a placatory hand raised again.

"I mean you no harm," she reiterated. "Though I can't say the same for everything in this forest. It isn't often that Blind Muir gets visitors, especially ones with good mounts, expensive cloaks and fine swords."

Kathryn's frown deepened. "Blind Muir is part of my domain. That means I can visit it when I please."

"Then you are the Lady Kathryn," the woman said. "Daughter of Baroness Adelynn. The spirits have been whispering to me about your arrival in Upper Forthyn."

"Spirits?" Kathryn wondered. "More dark magics. If you are a necromancer, my mother would likely have your head on a roadside stake."

"Then let us hope I never meet your mother," the woman said, the ghost of a smile returning. "But now I have you at an unfair disadvantage, Lady Kathryn. My name is Dezra."

"You live in these woods, Dezra?" Kathryn asked. Dezra shook her head.

"For the time being. I am hunting something here."

"Hunting what?"

"I cannot say for sure, and besides, it isn't something that concerns you. This prey is deadly, and cares not for social station."

"Did it summon the orb?"

"Perhaps. Sometimes there is darkness in the heart of the light, light in the heart of darkness Your mother would do well to learn that."

Kathryn hesitated, caught between the instinctive urge to defend her mother and a deep-set desire to know more.

"Where did you learn it?"

This time it was Dezra's turn to look surprised. She smiled again, more openly now. "My abilities? Books, mostly. And I had a good teacher."

"When I was younger I wanted to learn magic," Kathryn admitted. "At Greyhaven."

"Why didn't you?"

Kathryn smirked. "You think the firstborn heir of a barony is free to do as she pleases?"

"It would seem that way to those who don't know many firstborn barony heirs," Dezra said, making a small, strange gesture with her raised hand. A flame, yellow-green in color, sprang out of nothingness around her slender fingers. Kathryn's eyes widened slightly.

"I thought magic required incantations," she said. "Words. You didn't say anything there."

"You clearly have much to learn about magic, then," Dezra

said, turning her hand so it was facing palm upwards, the flame dancing around it like a fire-insect. Kathryn watched it for a second longer, then urged her mount towards the sorceress, stopping next to her.

"Can you teach me?" she asked. Dezra clenched her fist, and the fire went out.

"No," she said. "You said it yourself. You are a baroness's daughter. Your destiny is as a ruler, not a practitioner of magics. Certainly not the magics I know."

"How am I to judge that until you show me more?" Kathryn asked. "Besides, I know enough about magic to know its uses go beyond the arcane. The more I learn, the better I can serve the peoples of this barony when my time comes to rule. I was sent to Upper Forthyn to hone my abilities. I will never get a better opportunity to learn than this."

"You'd put your trust in a strange sorceress you just found wandering in the woods?"

"Are you calling me a poor judge of character?" Kathryn asked with a slight smirk. "If you meant me harm, you would already have done it. If you intend to manipulate me, well, you will soon learn I am not so easily led."

"Not an ideal characteristic in a student," Dezra said, reigniting the small flame and holding it out. "Give me your hand, and do not flinch."

Kathryn hesitated, then did so, extending one hand from her mount's reins. Dezra's stopped inches from it, and the flame jumped, like a leaping insect. Regardless of the sorceress's instruction, Kathryn was too amazed to flinch. She stared at the yellowish fire as it flickered an inch above her upturned palm. There was no heat – if anything, it made her hand feel cold.

"Concentrate on it," Dezra instructed as she removed her own hand. "It's guttering."

Kathryn frowned, but the more she focused the more the sorcerous little flame seemed to flicker. After a few seconds it vanished, leaving behind no trace of its existence.

"Not bad," Dezra said, smiling. "Longer than my first soul-light, anyway."

Kathryn didn't know what to say. Dezra's expression seemed to harden for a moment, as though she was catching herself doing something she shouldn't have been.

"You have been here too long," she said, an abrupt tone edging into her voice. "Go. This is no place for a baroness's daughter."

"I am more than my mother's heir," Kathryn said firmly. "And I already told you, I can visit whenever I please. This is my domain."

"Then I suppose that makes me your subject," Dezra said with the barest hint of a bow. "But nevertheless, if you come here again you may not be as lucky as you were today."

"Then I'll have to hope you're on hand again," Kathryn said. "Dark magics or not."

For the briefest moment, a troubled look returned to Dezra's face. Then she raised her hood and gestured to the tree line.

"May Nordros protect you, Lady Kathryn. Until we meet again."

Now

Ulma woke up not long after Ariad had revealed herself to Logan. Either the web binding her wasn't as tight, or dwarf jaws were considerably stronger than human ones, because she began to rage and shout oaths as she struggled with her bindings, shaking the web they were both trapped in.

"Shut up," Logan hissed, but too late. A chittering sound went up around them, and he felt the threads vibrating as the arachyura swarmed them. He screwed his eyes shut instinctively, though he needn't have bothered – Ariad had departed earlier, and her golden, magical illumination had gone with her. They were in humid, stygian darkness.

"Get off me, beast," Ulma bellowed, clearly taking no heed of Logan's warning as she tried to wrestle the arachyura pouring over her with both arms bound to her sides.

"That won't help," he snapped.

"Logan? What's happening?"

Logan considered not answering, terrified by the thought of attracting the arachyura's attention again. But he remembered the panic-inducing nightmare of thinking he was alone in the darkness – he couldn't do that to Ulma.

"Don't try to struggle," he hissed. "You'll just attract more of them."

"Where are we?"

"I have no idea. Underground, I think."

"Why… why haven't they killed us yet?"

Logan tried to turn his head, eyes straining against the darkness, but he could make out nothing. Were they beneath the town? The castle? The Shrine of Nordros?

"It was Ariad," he said. "It was Ariad all along."

"Who was?" Ulma asked. "Ariad, that spider bitch?"

"From Sudanya," Logan said, speaking urgently now. Every time either of them said the name Ariad a susurrating hiss rose up from the swarm infesting the surrounding darkness. "She's Lady Damhán. She's behind all this. It was all a trap to lure us here!"

"Are you insane?" Ulma snapped, and he felt the webbing vibrate again as she started struggling once more. "You think Lady Damhán is that giant damned spider we killed back in Sudanya? You've gone mad!"

"I'm telling you," Logan said. "Stop struggling and keep your voice down. Now isn't the time for a shouting match. We're in the middle of an arachyura nest!"

"Why should I stop?" Ulma demanded, not lowering her voice. "If what you're saying is true you might not even be Logan. This could all be a trick! One of her illusions!"

Logan didn't answer. He could feel something probing his head again, more horrid multi-jointed limbs. He whimpered.

The light was back too, that smoldering orb. It floated through the darkness and came to a stop above Ulma. The arachyura had pulled the webbing away from her head. She turned to look at Logan. There was fear in her eyes, as much fear as there was defiance. That was never a good sign.

"By the ancestors, you look terrible," she managed to say as she took in the sight of his own web-bound body.

"Is there one on my head?" he asked her slowly, not daring to move.

"Not any more."

"I can still feel it. I can feel them all over me."

"Well you're not far wrong," Ulma said, looking past Logan at the surrounding web. He refused to do the same – he didn't want to see the bodies, or the black eyes of the thousands of unnatural insects surrounding them. He kept his eyes on Ulma.

The light pulsed brighter, and the chittering grew louder.

"She's here," he whispered hoarsely. "Ariad's here."

The swarm closed in. Logan realized they didn't fear the hot, desert light the way they had done Ulma's phosphernum. They formed a circle around the two prisoners, their mandibles clacking and drooling. Logan closed his eyes again.

"Children hunger." The sound of the sick, dry croak – like a vile parody of Damhán's voice – made him shudder. It drew closer.

"The other wakes. Now only one left."

"Hammers of the ancestors, it's true," he heard Ulma breathe. He felt a presence before him, and couldn't help but open his eyes.

Ariad had mounted the web once more, crouched at its bottom, that blank, golden mask staring up at them with chilling indifference.

"We killed you," Ulma said, her anger warring with her dismay. "You can't be real!"

"Stupid Dunwarr," the creature hissed, the spiders surrounding them closing in a little more. "That is what I made you think. This web took long to build. So many lies. Woven above and below. But now, like all good webs, it catches its prey."

The golden orb moved from Ulma across to Logan, making him flinch with its heat. Ariad made her ticking noise once again.

"You feel the desert heat, Logan Lashley? You feel where I was born? You do not like my light? You prefer the true sun." She spat the last words like an accusation, clambering lithely up the web until she was almost on top of him again.

"When I am finished, no more sun. That is what he has promised me. I will take A'tar and wrap him up in my threads. I will keep him like this little orb. That is what I was born to do. I spin and weave the eternal night, as I spun and wove the tricks that led you here. And now here you are, just as I designed. Pulled by my threads."

"You're insane," Logan said, unable to fathom what the creature was talking about. She ticked as though in amusement, and the golden orb drifted on to Logan's left.

"Here with the one you came all this way seeking."

"No," Logan said in dismay. The light had illuminated a third shape, wrapped like Logan and Ulma, though her head was already uncovered. She was either unconscious or dead, her beautiful features as pale as the threads that bound her like a tightly wrapped corpse shroud. Her hair was long and dark, splayed on the web around her. Though he had never met her, she had enough of her mother about her to leave Logan in no doubt.

"Lady Kathryn," he whispered, surprise warring with fear and anger. All this time, and Ariad had her in her clutches. What a dance she had led them all on. Logan would almost have been impressed, had he not been riven with equal parts terror and outrage.

"A pretty little fly," Ariad chittered, moving past Logan to the woman's side. "She fell so easily into my web. The witch could not save her."

"You took her when she fled to the Blind Muir," Logan said, his tone almost accusatory.

"Children took her," Ariad hissed. "Good children. They were hungry, but did not feed."

"Is she dead?" Ulma demanded, trying to see past Logan.

"Not dead, no," Ariad said. "She has duties still to perform. Her own web to spin. There are still more flies to catch."

The creature pulled herself along the web until she was crouched right over Kathryn, her mummified fingers running along the noblewoman's cocoon as she lowered her masked face to her ear. Logan got the impression she was whispering in it, though the only sounds he caught were those low, spine-chilling ticking noises. He tried desperately to work out what she was doing, how he could counter it. He tested his bonds again, but it was no use. The orb glowed brighter and the Arachyura chirred and rustled once more.

Kathryn opened her eyes. She stared blankly up for a moment, then turned her head to look at the golden mask just inches from her face.

"Oh mother," she murmured, her voice filled with relief. "I… I just had the most terrible nightmare."

Ariad ticked something else, backing away from the pinned woman. A cascade of smaller spiders, rippling like black liquid, flowed down the web and over her cocoon, unpicking it. She seemed totally oblivious to both them and Ariad's true form, smiling sleepily up at her.

"Yes," she murmured. "You're right, mother. A walk would do me good."

The spiders withdrew as the now-freed Kathryn clambered slowly down from the web, the traveling cloak she wore still draped with wafting, ethereal strands of thread. She reached the ground beyond the light of the orb and turned back towards Ariad, still poised on the web.

"You're sure it's safe to go outside? Alone?"

"You are never alone, pretty little fly," Ariad chittered. Kathryn smiled and turned away.

"Kathryn!" Logan shouted. "Lady Kathryn, stop! Please!" She showed no sign of having heard him, wandering like a sleepwalker into the darkness beyond Ariad's light. Logan redoubled his efforts to free himself from the web, no longer caring if Ariad saw what he was doing.

"Where is she going?" Logan demanded, straining vainly against the sticky bindings. "Where are you sending her?"

"To be with the one she loves," Ariad said. "To bring her here, so that this feast might be truly memorable."

Volbert started awake, a cry on his lips. His wife clutched him.

"What is it?" she whispered urgently. "Vol?"

"The shrine," he whispered. He'd never experienced a more vivid dream. Someone, *something,* was in the shrine. He'd felt its unwelcome presence, like an intruder in his own home.

He dressed quickly in the dark, fumbling his robes on over his head then pulling the keys from their peg beside the bed. After a brief hesitation he took a torch from the fire basket and thrust it into the embers still smoldering in the kitchen hearth. It took, throwing weird, flickering light across the tomb-keeper's small home.

"It's the dead of night," his wife said, standing pale-faced in the bedroom door.

"I have to go," Volbert said, with more firmness than he really felt. The apparition in his nightmare had been insubstantial, but its presence was wholly real – he could feel it even now, waiting for him, the manifestation, he was sure, of all the troubles that had been plaguing Fallowhearth. "Lock and bar the door behind me, and do not unlock it for anyone but me. And make sure it really is me before you open it."

The plaintive cry of a child came from the bedroom.

"Look after him, for us both," Volbert said. "I won't be long."

Outside the wind was picking up. Dark clouds scudded across the pale faces of the moons, making shutters rattle and signs creak along the street. Volbert drew his robes tight and turned the corner of his house, to the front gate of the Shrine of Nordros. It stood, a grim block of arching, unyielding stone in the darkness, edged in silver moonlight. Its windows seemed to glare accusingly down at Volbert as he fumbled for the heavy key to the front door, the light of his torch reflecting off the murky glass panes of the tall windows flanking it.

The key turned, and the lock gave way with a thud. He eased the door open, the old pinewood timbers groaning.

Darkness reigned within. He stepped inside, holding his torch aloft. The flames seemed unwilling to light the shrine's interior, picking out the rows of benches and the statue of Nordros – with his dagger and his withered branch – only with the greatest reluctance. Volbert's eyes lingered on them for just a second, before he realized the pool of shadow lying before the statue was more than the mere absence of light. The was a woman sitting there, at the head of the shrine.

She was cross-legged and hooded. Her head was bowed. In her right hand was a dagger, in her left a broken, dead branch, a mirror image of the idol of Nordros that loomed over her. Volbert stopped short, his heart hammering. Why had she come here on this dark, storm-racked night?

The figure looked up at him, sickly lights playing beneath the edge of her cowl. She spoke, and her words were like the first, biting frost of winter.

"You dare bring the spawn of Kellos into this sacred house of Nordros?"

As she spoke, the wind howled. It blasted the door to the shrine wide open and snuffed out the flames of Volbert's torch. In the darkness that followed the tomb-keeper stood shivering, too terrified to move. He heard the sounds of the intruder rising, pacing towards him, the un-light of her eyes like the pinprick gaze of a nocturnal predator as it prowled around its prey.

"You are the keeper of this shrine?" she asked, the words seeming to reverberate from every corner of the vaulted space.

"Yes," Volbert whispered. He closed his eyes, his whole body shaking, and felt icy breath on his face.

"Stand guard upon this door," whispered the voice in his ear. "And watch for my return."

He felt the chill presence pass him by, out of the shrine. Unbidden, words spilled from his lips.

"Who are you?"

He sensed the presence pause before answering.

"Tonight, I am the shadow of Nordros. Rejoice, tomb-keeper, for your god walks abroad in Fallowhearth."

For a second Durik thought Carys had woken him. He'd been lying asleep on his pelts beside the fireplace. At some point she'd gotten off the bed and crouched down next to him.

Then he realized that it hadn't been her at all. It had been a woman, insubstantial, cloaked in the remnants of Durik's dreams.

He sat up, swiftly and silently drawing his knife.

"You felt it too, didn't you," Carys whispered, her earnest young face underlit by the dying embers of the fireplace.

"Yes," Durik murmured, standing and looking around the bedchamber. All was still and silent, but for the wind and the rain knocking at the window.

"It happened just now?" Durik asked, noting how the hairs along his forearms had risen.

"Yes, I think so."

Durik was silent for a while, his eyes closed. There had still been no sign of Logan and Ulma. He could wait no longer. He had to act.

"What do we do?" Carys asked.

"You will do nothing."

"Are you going to leave?"

"Perhaps." He opened his eyes and walked over to the window. A storm had risen during the night. It was impossible to see anything beyond the sheeting rain that was battering at the window. Fallowhearth lay swallowed in darkness.

"Something is out there," Durik said, pondering the dark presence that had woken him. It had reeked of grief and remorse, shot through with a resolve Durik found chilling in its intensity. "And it's coming this way."

CHAPTER TWENTY
Before

Kathryn stood at the top of the stairs, the helm of her cloak rippling in the wind blowing in through the tower's broken wall. Except for the bluecrest twittering in its cage across from her, the chamber seemed to be deserted. The breeze made the pages of the books and scrolls scattered around her rustle.

She stepped fully inside the room and lowered her hood, smiling. The bluecrest trilled louder, fluttering its little wings. It was hungry. She picked up a bag of seed from the table and paced to the cage, her senses on edge the whole time. Where? Where was she? As she poured a small amount of seed into the cage, she felt the hairs on the nape of her neck rising. She could almost hear Dezra's voice. Trust your instincts.

She turned sharply and raised her right hand, speaking loudly and clearly as she did so.

"Ostendum!"

The wall near the crack in the tower's shell seemed to flicker and shimmer, revealing a figure standing there with a smile on her face – Dezra.

"Got you," Kathryn said, snapping her fingers. Dezra laughed and paced over to her, the last of the illusion spell sloughing from her form.

"Not bad," the sorceress said, and kissed her. Kathryn placed a hand on her waist, savoring the moment before Dezra broke it off to continue. "You're getting better."

"At the unmasking spells, or the kissing?" Kathryn asked with faux seriousness, gazing up into Dezra's eyes. The sorceress laughed again and stepped away.

"I'll let you decide. You're early. I wasn't expecting you until sundown."

"I told Abelard I was going to visit the border markers. He knows better than to question me now. He doesn't even demand I take a maid with me any more."

"So you're learning how to impose your will," Dezra said, looking down at Kathryn a moment more before pacing over to the broken wall to gaze out at the moorland. "I'm glad. And I'm sure your mother would be proud."

"I'm less sure of that," Kathryn said, watching Dezra for a moment before walking over to the table, her gaze wandering across the jumble of texts and parchments heaped there, as though seeking inspiration. "There are so many duties I have to attend to. So many problems that needed fixing on the spot. Boundary disputes, tax avoidance, tithe relief, the northern tribes migrating. I can only get away from it all when I'm here. Every time I leave this place, all I think about is coming back."

"You have your duties," Dezra said, turning from the view to look back at Kathryn. "You know you cannot escape them. I will always be here for you, but you cannot abandon your noble house. Or your mother."

"Perhaps I can just learn to disappear for a few minutes," Kathryn said, her smile more cautious now as she laid a hand on a particularly heavy-looking tome. "Won't you teach me that one? What's the point in being able to sense it and dispel it if I can't cast it in the first place?"

"A cloaking spell like that takes years of practice," Dezra said. "And besides, the only one I can teach you is a part of the darker arts, the elements of Umbros. I told you I wouldn't show you anything beyond the simplest magics. And especially not the lessons of the Cadaveribus." She looked pointed at the book Kathryn had her hand on. She raised it with a shrug.

"But you will keep teaching me the basic incantations?" the baroness's daughter pressed hopefully. Dezra smiled.

"I will. It helps give me a purpose. Focus is something I haven't known for years. What would you learn of tonight? And don't say a cloaking spell!"

"Well, do you have something that can convince Abelard to stop worrying about the northern tribes," Kathryn asked, clearly only half joking. Dezra scoffed.

"Is he still complaining about them?"

"Constantly. I need something to take my mind off his constant worrying. Tell me one of your stories. One of the tales from your days as an adventurer." Dezra tutted, moving behind Kathryn and helping her out of her traveling cloak.

"I think you've heard all the best ones already," she said as she did so. Kathryn shook her head, sitting down on the edge of the table.

"What about Sudanya?" she asked. "You never finished that one. How does it all end?"

Now

Ariad moved languidly across the web, her head and limbs twitching. Logan noticed that the threads vibrated whenever he or Ulma struggled, or whenever the arachyura moved close by, but the spider queen's motions seemed to do nothing to disturb the slender weave.

"You won't take Durik," Ulma said to her as she prowled around them. "He speared you once and he'll do it again."

Ariad hissed, moving closer to the dwarf.

"His pet, the girl. It will distract. Why else do you think I allowed her to stay? I will have both. She will be a tasty treat for my younglings."

The surrounding arachyura chirred in apparent excitement.

"And you think you can lure Dezra down here using Kathryn?" Ulma demanded. "You would be a fool to do so. She's far more powerful than she was in Sudanya. More powerful than you."

The arachyura clacked their pincers aggressively. Ariad clutched the web binding Ulma.

"You know nothing of power, Dunwarr. I have tricked the masters of this land. I have hidden before their very eyes. My nests are many. My children breed and multiply in places far and near."

"It must have taken you years," Logan said, trying to take some of the spider queen's attention off Ulma. How typical, to be the one having to talk her out of a scrape. Ariad's mask turned towards him and he immediately wished he hadn't spoken.

"My kind are patient," she clicked, crawling slowly over to

him. "If a web is made with care, it lasts. Long enough for prey to wander by. Wander in."

"Well, I do love a lady who can hold a grudge," Logan said, forcing himself not to flinch as she loomed over him.

"Shame none love you, Logan Lashley," she hissed. "Grudge or not."

She clamped a hand down over his mouth, almost crushing his jaw. The web beneath him went into spasms as both he and Ulma began struggling, the dwarf crying out. The pressure on his skull caused tears to well up in his eyes. That wasn't the worst thing though – in front of him, the webbing that bound Ariad's hand began to come away, peeling down and extending from her fingers to his mouth. In just a few moments his lips were bound shut again, his jaw sealed. Ariad released him.

"Your strength is words," she said, turning away from him. "So you speak no more. Do not fear though. When the time comes, I will make sure you can still scream."

CHAPTER TWENTY-ONE

Rain. She felt rain on her skin, stinging and cold. Wind too, snatching at her clothes. It woke something in her, refreshed thoughts that had lain smothered and suffocated for too long.

Her head ached. Her throat was dry. She felt weak. It was dark – she was used to that – but it was a different sort of darkness. Something far removed from the hot, stony depths she had known. There was cold mud oozing beneath her feet. A banging sound, loose shutters. A creaking noise, like an old ship at sea.

She stumbled, her hand going out and finding a wall. Wattle. A sturdy doorframe and windows. She looked around as the rain fell, trying to better discern her surroundings in the dark.

She was standing in a street, an open street. She knew this place. Fallowhearth. She had come to it… when? How long ago? A few weeks, she thought. Mother had sent her. It was her duty to go to Fallowhearth, to assume her duties as the future ruler of Forthyn, to show that she had the capacity to lead, to command – the skills she had so admired in her mother. She was a great woman, truly. She had told her that when she had seen her last, just recently.

Her mother was in Fallowhearth, she was sure. She had to find her. And if not, well, the witch would help her.

"The witch," Kathryn said aloud, wiping long, wet hair from her eyes. Who was the witch? It felt important. Why was she so confused? Her headache made thinking difficult. It pounded like a drum between her temples, making her stumble slightly as she tried to take a few more paces.

There was the creaking noise again, and a rattle she took to be a latch. One of the doors facing out onto the street had opened and a figure was emerging, sluggish and slow. Kathryn walked towards it, calling out.

"Hello?"

The figure turned and Kathryn came to an abrupt halt. Though still indistinct in darkness, she caught an impression of a hideously disfigured face, and a torso that had been dealt a grievous wound. The figure, a dire shape in the dark, let out a low moan.

"Oh, great Kellos," Kathryn exclaimed, stumbling back. She heard footfalls in the mud behind her and turned sharply. Two more figures were shuffling towards her, a man and a woman. The man was missing his jaw, and the woman half her skull. The nearest walking corpse reached out, slowly, shakily.

Kathryn struck the hand away with a shriek and ran, thrusting past the undead. There were more ahead, emerging from the houses out onto the street, their groaning filling the air. She had done this, she was sure. Just as the witch had warned her. Terror gripped her heart.

Overhead, with a great crash, the storm's fury broke.

• • •

Low mist coiled across the street, seemingly unaffected by the wind and rain pelting Fallowhearth. To Dezra it was like walking in a dream – she was weightless, immaterial and numb. All around she could feel the nightmares of the townspeople in their beds, raw, bloody and dark. She could feel too the sharp jolts as they awoke, sweating and panting and crying. Fallowhearth was riddled with fear tonight.

She had never gone this far with her powers before. She had felt as though she was about to throw up when she had first materialized in the shrine to Nordros, and the gravekeeper had found her. Something had happened since then, though – she had pushed through the draining discomfort that spellwork always brought on, finding an inner core of strength, a reservoir of power that wasn't yet showing signs of running out.

The magic took its toll in other ways, though. Right now it seemed as though Dezra's fears and doubts were manifesting in the minds of Fallowhearth's remaining townspeople. Some stumbled from their homes, half-dressed, drawn out by the unknowable forces at play. Dezra heard shouts and the wet slap of running feet in the mud. She was invisible to them, though, her presence passing around and through shivering bodies as she made her way through the black streets towards Fallowhearth castle, and the light that shone in the single window near the top of its tallest tower.

Just short of the gate she heard more voices, this time raised in anger rather than fear or confusion. Bodies stumbled past, indistinct in the dark. A flame flickered ahead as a torch was struck. For a second her consciousness wandered, her mind forming an impression of a gathering of people, townsfolk, pointing and shouting among themselves. One broke free from the press and ran from them with a shriek. Shouting, they pursued. Dezra's heart seemed to stop and her enchantment unraveled as she saw that one fleeing figure, clad in a traveling cloak that seemed to be covered in strands of gossamer thread.

It was Kathryn.

"No," Dezra shouted, her shock manifesting in the word as it ripped through the nightmares of everyone still asleep in Fallowhearth, dragging them screaming into wakefulness. The fog that was prowling the streets turned an ugly, angry black, whipping together with the rising wind, taking on shape and form. Dezra materialized in front of Kathryn, snatching her slender body and holding her firm as she tried to break free.

"It's me," she said, a desperate edge to the soothing tone. "Kathryn, it's Dezra!" She dragged back her hood, looking desperately into Kathryn's eyes. A foul, golden light, visible only to Dezra's witch sight, was suffusing her, but she saw recognition in her eyes. Kathryn stopped struggling.

"Oh gods," Kathryn said, and collapsed into Dezra's arms, burying her face in her shoulder.

"It's alright." Dezra hugged her fiercely. A part of her was exultant, triumphant. She'd been right not to give up hope. All the fear and misery of the past month had fallen away. "I'm with you now."

"The undead," Kathryn said, looking up at her with panic in her eyes. "The corpses are coming! The town is overrun! What have I done?"

"There are no undead," Dezra tried to reassure her. Now she had her back, nothing was going to separate them again. She was surrounded by danger and threat, but all of those things she could fight. The uncertainty was gone. "You've been hexed. I need to get you somewhere safe, where I can break it. Then everything will become clearer."

"Who in Kellos's name are you?" shouted a gruff voice. Dezra looked up to see the townsfolk who had been pursuing Kathryn gathering around them. They were an ugly, vicious-looking group in the light of their torches, half afraid, half angry, made sick by the fear they had been enduring for so many weeks. Dezra had seen that look too many times before.

"She's the witch," one woman cried out. "Just look at her! She's driven the Lady Kathryn mad!"

There was no time for explanation, even less for negotiation. Dezra had long ago given up trying either when faced with the ignorance and prejudice of the people of Terrinoth. She hissed a curse-phrase, and the townsfolk that had started to surround her let up a wail as their most primal fears intruded abruptly onto their consciousness, momentarily breaking their grasp on reality.

Holding Kathryn by the hand, Dezra steered her free of the screaming mob. The girl was weeping with sheer terror, whatever hex had infected her mind clearly convincing her that everyone in the town she encountered was a rotting, reanimated corpse. Dezra had never known magic like it. Seeing Kathryn driven on by such fear made her angry, the emotion counteracted by more rational fears of her own – what being could have done this to her?

She led her to the Shrine of Nordros. She needed somewhere to break the hex, and quickly, or it could tighten its grip on Kathryn, and Dezra might never get her out of Fallowhearth. Rain was sheeting down now, churning the streets into a stream of muck. Kathryn was soaked through. Dezra kept her hand in hers, right up the steps to the shrine's main doors.

The tomb-keeper was still there, kneeling before the idol of Nordros. He started when they entered and Dezra's balefire lit the braziers around the walls, his eyes darting from the cloaked sorceress to the dazed and terrified woman in her grasp.

"Bar the door," Dezra snarled. The man hurried to obey as she gently took Kathryn to one of the pews, making her sit.

"It's all gone wrong, Dezra," she mumbled, her eyes glazed. "Please forgive me! Please!"

"There's nothing to forgive," Dezra said, placing her hand on the side of Kathryn's head and planting a soft kiss on her brow, trying to bring calm and clarity to her. "I told you, you've been hexed. Try and clear your mind, while I unbind you from it."

She knelt before her and closed her eyes, gently taking both of Kathryn's hands in hers as she sought the words that would break the curse. Almost as soon as she began, she felt the resistance – the incantation came only slowly, each utterance forced. Whoever had placed the spell on Kathryn had been immensely powerful. Breaking it could be painful, for both of them. For a second Dezra quailed at the thought of hurting her, but she knew she had no choice. She continued to chant.

Kathryn began to groan and tried to rise back to her feet. Dezra eased her back down, breaking the recital for a moment to snap at the tomb-keeper as he finished sealing the shrine's doors.

"Get over here and help me with her!"

The man ran to her side and gripped Kathryn by her shoulders, partially pinning her in place as Dezra began to chant once more.

Kathryn began to scream and struggle. Dezra couldn't tell whether it was because she thought the tomb-keeper holding her down was a decaying undead, or because removing the hex was causing her pain. She suspected it was both, and the realization caused her to falter. Seeing Kathryn like this was almost unbearable. Dezra forced herself to continue, chanting louder and faster as she rose and placed a hand on Kathryn's sweat-streaked brow.

"*Syath nex rath,*" she hissed, then gasped as a shock traveled through her body. Golden light flowed from Kathryn's eyes, then faded as she stopped struggling and slumped back against the pew. Dezra knelt before her again, her limbs trembling with the aftereffect of the spell, taking Kathryn's hands in hers as the tomb-keeper took an uncertain step back. She looked up at Kathryn, her heart racing, searching desperately for lucidity in her eyes, for any sign that the hex was broken.

"Kathryn?" she said slowly. Kathryn's eyes rolled as she gazed around the shrine before fixing on Dezra's. Dezra saw recognition there.

"Dezra?"

Dezra embraced her, kissing her softly. It was over. She

had Kathryn back, and nothing else mattered. She laughed, Kathryn smiling back at her, before drawing her in for another kiss.

"It's going to be alright," Dezra said.

"I know," Kathryn answered.

There was a shuddering blow against the shrine doors. Voices rose up from outside. The moment of sanctuary, of pure relief, evaporated.

"I've been dreaming, Dezra," Kathryn said urgently. "Terrible dreams. I don't know what was real and what wasn't."

"You were cursed by something," Dezra said, looking into Kathryn's eyes, looking for any last traces of that golden light. "A powerful practitioner. Their magic is old and dark, older and darker than mine, but foreign to me. I do not know from which elements it draws its powers, but it is strong with the ways of Umbros, and possibly Lumos."

Fear gripped Kathryn's expression as the memories came back hard and fast. She said a single word, shivering. "Arachyura."

Dezra nodded. "Where?"

"Beneath the town. Tunnels. I don't know where exactly. They took me after… after I tried the Black Invocation. I'm so sorry, Dezra. Can you forgive me?"

"I am the one who should be asking for forgiveness," Dezra said, gripping her hands once more and trying to reassure her with a smile. "From the day we met you were nothing but kind to me. I have repaid you by leading you down a dark path."

"No," Kathryn said, planting her forehead softly against Dezra's, looking into her black eyes. "It isn't a dark path. It's simply a different path. Your path. Let no one tell you otherwise. I have seen you heal wounds and make scars disappear. I have seen you cure diseases and give comfort to the grieving. Nothing about that is dark, or wrong."

Dezra closed her eyes, fighting the turmoil within. Every word Kathryn said lightened her soul and gave her hope, but hope had been a stranger to her for so long that it felt unnatural. It had started to grow difficult for Dezra to view the paths she trod as a positive force any more, not when everywhere she turned she was met by hatred and disgust. Even if what Kathryn said was true, that wasn't how others would see it.

"You have your whole life ahead of you," she told her. "You will be the wisest, greatest ruler Forthyn has ever had. These lands need you. Terrinoth needs you."

"And I need you," Kathryn said. "I love you."

There was another crash, and the doors to the shrine shuddered. Dezra heard an imperious voice shouting at the townsfolk to make way. She opened her eyes and looked at the tomb-keeper.

"Is there another way out?" she demanded. "A back door?"

"Yes," he said. "The yard entrance. But the only way beyond that is the lich-gate, and it leads onto the street. You will be seen."

"No, we won't," Dezra said, turning back to Kathryn and grasping her shoulder. "Do you remember the *hex nebulum*?" she asked. "The mist shroud?"

"Yes," Kathryn said, with a smile. "It's how I made it out of the castle last time."

"I thought as much," Dezra said, feeling an unexpected jolt of pride. "Speak the incantation with me. We'll get out of this together."

Before she could begin, there was a great cracking sound. The shrine doors crashed inwards, the lock shattered, the timber bar splintered into pieces. Kathryn and Dezra surged to their feet as bodies flooded in through the open door, chain mail, helmets and blades gleaming in the light of Dezra's flames.

These were men-at-arms, not townsfolk. They thrust the tomb-keeper to one side, and he fell to the stone floor with a cry. The wind rushed in with them, billowing Dezra's cloak and Kathryn's gown as the sorceress pushed her lover protectively behind her.

The onrushing men came to a clattering halt as Dezra raised her hand, her green-yellow flames igniting around her clenched fist. Her racing heart caused the exhaustion brought on by her recent spellcasting to burn away in an instant.

"If you value your immortal souls, you won't take another step closer," she snarled.

Fear and anger, the same looks she'd endured all her life. The looks she wanted nothing more than to protect Kathryn from. They wouldn't take her, not after what they'd both been through. She wouldn't lose her now.

One of the men was smirking. He thrust past the others until he was standing directly in front of Dezra.

"So, the three idiots were right after all," he declared, voice echoing back from the shrine's ceiling. "The Lady Kathryn was abducted by a fell sorceress. And a pretty one at that."

"There was no abduction," Kathryn declared loudly, half pushing past Dezra. "And this is no fell sorceress. She is my mentor, and I love her!"

"My lady," the man said, offering a short, meaningless

bow. "My name is Captain Kloin. I've been sent by Baroness Adelynn to retrieve you and return you safely to Highmont. Immediately."

"I won't go," Kathryn said, moving past Dezra, her posture tall and commanding. "You can go back to Highmont and tell my mother that. Tell her I renounce my titles, and the heirship to Forthyn. Tell her I am leaving these lands and that I won't be returning."

Kloin looked unmoved by her words, his expression sneering and dismissive. Dezra didn't try to move in front of her again – she had seen this on rare occasions before, the flash of her abilities to command. The strength and conviction of her noble lineage shining through. It only made her love Kathryn more.

"With all due respect, my lady, you are not yourself. You have been snatched away by this witch, held Kellos-only-knows where for the past month, and are no doubt possessed by some sort of curse or delusion cast by this monstrous creature. My duty is clear. I have no choice other than to take you back to the baroness. I pray you will not make me use force."

"If you lay a hand on her, you die," Dezra said, her icy glare fixed on Kloin. "And that'll just be the beginning of your suffering."

"Don't make this mistake, captain," Kathryn urged. "You serve my family, so you serve me. Do as I say and stand your men down. Let us pass in peace and this will all be forgotten."

"You are not yourself, my lady," Kloin repeated, not breaking eye contact with Dezra. "I'm sorry it has come to this, but you'll thank me later. As will the baroness."

For a second, absolute stillness settled over the shrine. Then Kloin spoke again.

"Take them."

Dezra shouted a curse-word as the wall of armored men surged in on them, once more conjuring nightmares into the thoughts of the onrushing figures. These weren't tired, confused townspeople, though, and their shock lasted only a few heartbeats. Dezra snatched Kathryn's wrist, throwing her towards the back of the shrine, shouting at her to find the door to the graveyard as Kloin charged them, his sword drawn. She wasn't going to let him reach Kathryn. Men like him had tormented her for long enough.

She brought her knife up, another short incantation on her lips, but this time she was too slow. Kloin was on her, hatred in his eyes as he thrust his sword home. The blade jarred off the rib bones that decorated the exterior of her corset and plunged into her stomach, a lance of icy pain that forced her to bend forward and scream. Kathryn staggered, the disbelief on her face giving way to horror.

"No," Dezra heard her shout. Kloin's face was inches from hers, his breath rancid, his eyes burning with a fierce triumph.

"Unless I'm much mistaken, I've just become the first man to kill one of the Borderland Four," he said, grinning before twisting his sword and ripping it free. Dezra's legs gave way and she fell. Pain paralyzed her thoughts. Her hands clutched at the wound in her stomach, the pale flesh turning a bright, vital red as blood pumped out between her fingers. More choked her throat, spilling from her dark lips.

Then Kathryn was with her, kneeling by her side, clutching her in her arms. The movement drew a fresh, strangled cry.

She tried desperately to form words through the blood gagging her, looking up at Kathryn with terrified eyes.

"Step away from the witch, my lady," Kloin ordered, standing over the fallen couple. Blood, running thickly from his sword, had started to flow through the cracks between the shrine's flagstones. He reached out a hand to snatch Kathryn's shoulder, but she snapped a phrase at him, and he took a step backwards with a yelp of pain, as though he'd been stung or shocked. None of his men moved, uncertain whether they should try to seize Kathryn by force or not.

"Don't speak," Kathryn told Dezra urgently, ignoring Kloin and clutching her close. "Just hold on. Hold on to me for a few more moments, and it'll all be alright. I promise you. I promise."

Dezra could only let out a deep moan, hands slippery and red. It hurt, by all the gods, how it hurt, a pain deep inside her, like a shard of pure ice that she couldn't pull free, no matter how she clutched and grasped at it. Her mind knew that she was dying, but her body was in panic, still desperately fighting against what was coming.

Her vision blurred. She was vaguely aware of Kathryn saying something, holding her close. Everything sounded as though it was underwater, or coming from another room, muffled and woolly. She managed to drag a breath in through her nose, spitting more blood, the taste bitter and choking at the back of her throat. The pain made her writhe, driving out her thoughts, her fears, her regrets. Kathryn was still holding on, a white-knuckled death-grip.

It was too soon. That was one of the only things Dezra was able to focus on. Too soon, after so many years alone, to be torn away from the woman she loved. The ache of it was as great as the agony of her wound – she didn't know where one ended and the other began. She felt betrayed by the fates themselves, the subject of a sick jest. To have found Kathryn again and be torn away was more than her thoughts could bear.

And then something strange began to happen. Her vision cleared. She could see Kathryn's face above her, grief-stricken but determined, her lips still moving. Her body stopped shaking and she realized, little by little, that the pain that had been so overwhelming before was receding. At first, she thought it was the final stage before death, that slow, numb moment where eyes glazed and struggles grew still. But her body wasn't giving up. She could breathe again. Blood was no longer clogging her mouth. Her hearing returned with a pop, and with it she caught the tail end of what Kathryn was saying, the last words of an incantation Dezra had once, reluctantly, taught her.

Blood pattered down on Dezra's face, blood that was now falling from Kathryn's lips. Horror filled her as she realized what was happening. She tried to speak, to beg Kathryn to stop, but her voice had deserted her. Kathryn smiled down at her and slumped backwards.

Dezra scrambled up onto her knees. Her hands were still sticky with her own blood, and her body felt weak and drained, but the pain was gone – only echoes of it remained now, in her mind and in the core of her being. The wound, she realized, was closed.

And, like a cruel joke, it had opened up in Kathryn. Blood was spreading in a crimson stain across the center of her cloak and the white tunic beneath, blossoming like a brilliant red flower. More blood ran from her mouth, streaking down her perfect, pale cheek.

"Kathryn," Dezra said, now kneeling in turn over her, grasping her. "You didn't! How could you?"

"I told you," the baroness's daughter whispered, a small smile on her red lips. "I told you it would be alright."

"This isn't alright," Dezra said, snatching the front of the bloody tunic and ripping it open. The wound in Kathryn's midriff pulsed, fresh and fatal, identical to Dezra's. Stolen from her.

"The *participes mortus*," Dezra said, her mind racing, horror even greater than before besetting her. "You can't use it like this! It's too much! It will kill you!"

Now Kathryn was the one struggling for words. She clutched Dezra's wrist, grip like a vice.

"You taught me so much," she managed. "But ... the greatest lesson, was that death is never an end. Only a beginning."

"No," Dezra choked, her eyes filled with tears. "I love you, Kathryn. Don't leave me. Don't go to Nordros without me."

Kathryn's voice had dropped to a struggling whisper. Dezra leant her forehead against hers, hearing that last, dying breath. "Light, in the heart of darkness."

The grip on Dezra's wrist loosened, and her eyes unfocused. She slumped in Dezra's arms.

For a while there was nothing, nothing but the sound of sobbing, echoing back from cold, uncaring stone.

Then Kloin spoke.

"By all the gods," he spat, taking a step forward. "You vile witch! What have you done to her?"

Dezra stayed bowed over Kathryn's body, shaking, her sobs turning to silence. An agony worse than any she had felt before had gripped her, a shard of ice driven into her body and her soul. It ached, ached worse than the fatal wound she had been dealt, and she didn't know how to make it stop. She leant forwards, planting her lips on Kathryn's forehead, a soft, unwilling goodbye. Kloin raised his sword.

"Answer me!" the captain barked.

Before the blow could fall, Dezra rose. She looked up, eyes meeting the captain's once more, and even his arrogance and his anger quailed. Her face was a tearful, bloody mask of pure hatred.

She raised her hands and screamed. The sound transcended the mortal plane – it was a roar of purest, unadulterated agony, and it ripped through the shrine with a force far greater than the storm. It struck Kloin and his men-at-arms head on, like a million wicked razors. Their flesh was slammed against the far wall in a gory shower – only the bones remained untouched. As Dezra's howl peaked, the doors to the shrine, banged shut by the sorceress's unleashed power, exploded into a million splinters.

The remains of Kloin and his retinue collapsed. The scream died in Dezra's throat, leaving it raw, her whole body shaking. The soft matter that had once clad the bodies of the men-at-arms dripped slowly down the walls on either side of the obliterated doorway.

In the terrible stillness which followed a single body moved – the tomb-keeper. Perhaps shielded by his faith in Nordros, he had been flung back against the wall. He was alive, though, and seemed dazed but unharmed.

Dezra lowered her arms, panting. Her whole body ached with the aftereffects of the vicious spell, but she no longer noticed – the pain went far deeper now. She tried to still the shaking as she looked at the annihilation she had unleashed, a razor-curse of titanic power. Then she cast her eyes down at Kathryn. She was laid out on the floor as though for burial, her face white and peaceful, a contrast to the red that stained her stomach.

"Forgive me," Dezra said to her. That icy shard of sorrow was still buried within, still aching, but in the last few minutes it had become something more. Its chill had spread, the cold death-grip of Nordros empowering her. If her lover was gone, her god had given her the strength to avenge her. That was what mattered now. She raised her hands once more.

The bodies of the men-at-arms shuddered. They were nothing but red, raw bones now, but at Dezra's unspoken command they reknitted, standing up with an awkward gait. Their armor and clothes hung from them, still dripping. Then, with a clatter, they came to attention, grasping swords and polearms that moments earlier had been posed to hack Dezra to pieces.

Kloin was still at the forefront, his red skull grinning at Dezra, flecked with scraps of meat. Dezra stood before him, looking at his sword, at her blood that still glistened on its edge. Then, slowly, she smiled at him.

"You are right, Captain Kloin," she said to the crimson skeleton. "I am vile. Dezra the Vile. And your soul will serve mine now, for the rest of eternity."

"I'm going to find Lady Damhán," Durik told Carys. He could wait no longer, but nor did he wish to abandon his post undeclared. At the very least, the baroness's advisor needed to know that there was something dark afoot in the town, if she hadn't sensed it herself already. "Promise to me that you'll stay here?"

"The clans make no promises except on blood," Carys said. "I thought you would know that by now." Durik bit back an angry reply – he was on edge, he realized. That wouldn't do. He forced himself to be calm, to embody the skills of a hunter. He was increasingly sure he'd need them before the night was out.

"Then… just please stay here. Lock the door behind me. I will return soon."

"Fine," Carys said unhappily.

Durik took his spear and headed down to the main hall. It was deserted, the fire out, the torches burning low. The abandonment only increased his unease. He took the stairs to Lady Damhán's chamber.

There was no response to his first knock. His second drew an ugly croak from within.

"I'm asleep, fool. What is it?"

"There is something happening in the town," Durik said against the door, wondering at how ill Lady Damhán sounded. Had she fallen under some sort of sickness in the past day? Durik felt his skin prickle. "Something dark walks abroad in Fallowhearth at this very moment. I fear the castle may be threatened."

"I have felt nothing," Damhán's voice answered. "I did not know you were a warlock as well as a pathfinder, Durik."

"We can both feel it. Carys and I," he said, again forcing down an angry retort. He needed to focus.

"You're only still here because you insisted on staying with that idiot clan girl. Perhaps she should be your first priority, rather than wandering the castle halls and passages in the dead of night."

Durik fought the urge to smash the bedchamber door down. Without another word, he turned on his heel and descended towards the front doors of the keep. It was clear Damhán intended to be as unhelpful as usual. He had to find someone, anyone, who could at least explain why the castle seemed practically deserted.

At the gate he found two hastily dressed men-at-arms from the local garrison, blearyeyed and unhappy-looking as they conversed in hushed tones. The doors themselves were open and the portcullis had been raised. Outside Durik could make out a vague impression of a rain-slashed, stormy night.

The two men stopped talking and stiffened as Durik approached, eyeing him warily.

"Where is everyone?" Durik asked. They exchanged a glance, clearly weighing up what to tell him.

"There's been a disturbance in the town," one said. "Captain Kloin has taken most of the garrison to subdue it."

"Should the doors be open like that?"

"The captain ordered us to keep them open. He said it wouldn't take long and he didn't want to have to wait out in the rain." Durik decided it was best not to give his opinion on Kloin or his orders – the fact that the bitter captain had left the castle vulnerable for his own convenience was no surprise. Durik found himself imagining catching him alone in a dark, rain-slashed alleyway that night.

"And how long ago did he leave?" he asked. Neither men answered.

"I would close them for now," he said. "And set a watch on the battlements, if there isn't one already." Every one of his instincts was on edge, convinced Fallowhearth was in the grip of something far darker than just the encroaching night. He had to speak with Damhán about whatever was going on, face-to-face, before the situation deteriorated any further.

"You can hardly see five feet in this weather," one protested.

"Five feet is better than none," Durik said. "Between you and I, something is coming this way. I'd rather we didn't welcome it with an open gate and no sentries."

"Have you spoken to the baroness's advisor?" the other man asked.

"Briefly. She… does not wish to be disturbed, but I doubt she would be happy knowing we're compromising the safety of this castle by leaving the doors open."

That seemed to be enough. Together, the men closed the entrance and hefted the locking bar back into place.

"Winch down the portcullis as well," Durik advised, turning back towards the stairs leading to Kathryn's chamber. "I will return soon."

Dezra knelt beside Kathryn, her hand resting on her head. She could feel death in its final act of triumph. The last processes of Kathryn's life were breaking down, the light that had once been her soul now a tiny, guttering flicker, too small for any magic or artifice to reignite.

The sorceress wiped fresh tears from her eyes and, slowly, removed her hand. The horror of what had happened, the icy chill of shock and despair, was gone now. A deeper pain had replaced it, driving out all other emotions. She stood and looked at the tomb-keeper. The man had managed to stand, though he was still splattered in gore.

"Go to your home," she told him. "Retrieve one of your shovels and dig a pit beside the arch of the lich-gate inside your graveyard. Do not stop until dawn. When the sun has risen, bury Lady Kathryn. I will return to see that the work has been done properly."

"Yes, my lady," the bloodied man managed to say, not daring to meet Dezra's eyes. She swept past him and out of the shrine's splintered doors, her undead retinue following her.

Outside, a crowd had gathered in the rain, their torches spluttering. A gasp went up as Dezra appeared, then cries of horror as she was followed by her skeletal guard. She halted on the steps to the shrine, the wind lashing her cloak and hood. Her sorrow and her anger were so potent they made the skeletons flanking her shiver and rattle.

A multitude of words assailed her thoughts, desperate for release, all of them bitter and cruel. For a moment she wanted nothing more than to destroy these blind, oafish people as she had the guards, to punish them for the misery they had heaped on her and Kathryn. But the words never left her throat. She was not a murderer, and becoming one, even in the face of such hatred, would simply prove that their bigotry had foundation.

She had a task to do now, one that didn't involve unleashing herself on this town. Whatever person or creature had hexed Kathryn, it had to be close by. There wasn't an easier explanation for her reappearance, though whether Kathryn had escaped or been let loose, Dezra couldn't yet tell. Either way, she needed reinforcements.

Dezra raised her arms and began to say the words of the Black Invocation. Screams went up and panic struck the crowd in front of her, people scrambling and pushing through the rain and the mud as they attempted to scatter before her. She continued, the wind picking up around her, deadlights playing in the howling air, orbs of corposant that shone with deathly light. They built and multiplied, swirling about the necromancer as her voice rose. As the final words knifed out into the storm, the lights rose together, as though swirled up on the eddying wind. Then they shot away, darting like meteorites southwards, over the shrine and the graveyard and across the rooftops of the town.

"Run while you still can," Dezra said as she watched the stampeding townsfolk. "Your doom is already on its way."

She advanced down the steps, her guard closing around her. Still ignoring the people desperately trying to escape, she glared up at Fallowhearth castle, its ramparts rising through the storm, over the thatched roofs ahead. She thrust her consciousness into the skulls of her undead, hissing a simple imperative.

"Bring me the book."

CHAPTER TWENTY-TWO

Ronan's sleep was troubled. When he woke, he thought at first that he was still dreaming.

It was dark. Clouds hid the moon and stars. A wind was blowing hard from the north. Pico had woken him with its hissing – the familiar's red fur was on end. Those were the first four things he noticed. The fifth was that he was surrounded. There were figures moving all around him in the dark.

He surged to his feet, his sword drawn in a heartbeat, as Pico scrambled up the folds of his cloak and onto his shoulder. He'd lain down for the night on top of a low boulder, just east of the fields that ran between Fallowhearth and Blind Muir. That boulder was now surrounded by shapes discernible only by the filthy flames that kindled in their empty sockets or dead eyes. Rotting flesh, dry bone and wet forest mulch assailed Ronan's senses.

"Kurnos preserve me," the northerner muttered, clutching his amulet. Pico growled in agreement, its small body a warm, reassuring weight on his shoulder. Both of their hearts were racing, Ronan's whole body flooded with adrenaline. How had this happened? And why weren't they already on him?

He turned in a tight circle, sword ready, tensed to hack through any bony arms or fingers that sought to quest over the edge of the rock. None did. After a heart-pounding minute, Ronan realized that the undead were all shuffling in the same direction, moving around the rock rather than attempting to get on top of it. They were headed north and had parted like a foul ocean swell around the stony outcrop.

Ronan heard a shriek from nearby, and thought for a second it was the cry of another hideous wraith, before recognizing it as his stallion's distress. He had tied the unnamed beast for the night close to the boulder. It was down there, amongst the living dead.

He didn't hesitate. He leapt from the rock's edge and, bellowing a clan war cry, fell amongst the undead. His sword cleft a skull then almost bisected a torso, the gaunt shapes indistinct in the night's darkness. Horrific, slack-jawed, worm-eaten faces leered at him all around, lit by their terrible eyes, but to Ronan's dismay none attacked him. They didn't even seem to notice him. They just carried on past, even when he hacked off one's arm and jammed his blade between the ribs of another.

"What is this trickery?" Ronan snarled to Pico, shouldering another limping corpse out of his way. Pico leapt briefly onto its shoulder, causing its magic to collapse and its remains to slump to the dirt. The familiar rejoined Ronan as he reached his mount's side.

The horse was clearly distressed by the ungainly creatures dragging themselves past, but he seemed otherwise unharmed. Ronan untied the stallion and mounted him, kicking the steed into the press without hesitation. More bodies collapsed as rider, mount and familiar fought their way free of the mass, but still none turned on them. It was as though they didn't exist.

Soon Ronan could discern open ground beneath the stallion's hooves, rather than more bodies. He eased him down to a trot, patting his neck reassuringly as he turned to look back the way they had come.

The bodies formed one long, shambling mass, nearly indiscernible in the dark but for the balefire that burned in their eyes. The ugly little lights were like a constellation of unwholesome stars, clustered together in the dark. They spread all the way south to the black edge of Blind Muir Forest, a column of walking corpses stretching across the fields from the thorny treeline, all headed north. The dead were on the march, and Fallowhearth lay directly in their path.

Ronan turned his horse towards the town and dug his heels in.

Fallowhearth castle towered above Dezra, its ramparts and hoardings glistening in the rain. There was no movement on the walls, and the doors and portcullis were shut.

She halted, her skeletal companions at her back. The rain was running pink off their bones and armor. Dezra waited, half expecting a challenge.

None came. Glaring, she reached out and laid her hands on the iron bars of the portcullis.

"*Mille en una,*" she whispered, channeling the dark rage that had blossomed in her soul. At first, nothing happened.

Then, slowly, the metal under her hands began to change. It darkened and deformed, growing a thick crust of brown rust that seemed to eat away at the iron. Beneath Dezra's fingers hundreds of years passed in only a few seconds – the decay spread, gnawing away at the metal frame, reducing it to dust that was whipped away by the storm. As it crumbled and gave way, Dezra pushed her hands on through to the iron-studded door behind. The wood suffered the same fate – timber rotted and mulched at her touch, yellow worms and thick knots of lice blossoming beneath her hands. The door sagged before her, reduced to a mound of wet, writhing pulp. Dezra stepped over it and into the castle.

Half a dozen men were waiting for her, the last of the town's men-at-arms, armed and armored, their eyes wide with fear in the flickering light of the torches that lined the entrance hall.

Dezra smiled at them and, wordlessly, spread her arms. The skeletal remains of the men's comrades marched past her, their own weapons raised. Without breaking step, they attacked.

The sorceress advanced through the melee, ignoring the struggle of the living and the dead. The largest passage lay on the far right-hand corner of the hall, the spiral stairs appearing to lead directly to the keep's highest tower. She went up them, leaving the battle in the hall behind without a thought.

She didn't get far. There were footsteps coming down to meet her. A heavy figure rounded the central pillar, his spear at the ready. With whiplash reflexes, Dezra grasped the weapon just beneath its tip.

"Durik," she said, looking up at the orc towering over her.

"Dezra," Durik grunted. He relaxed the pressure on the

spear but didn't remove it from where she had stopped it, inches from her chest.

"You've left Blind Muir?" he asked, the orc for once unable to mask his emotions as a mixture of surprise and consternation flitted across his face

"Don't worry, I'll be back there soon enough."

"What's happening down below?" the orc demanded, hearing the clash of weapons and the shouts of the men-at-arms echoing up from the entrance hall.

"Nothing that concerns you. Get out of my way."

"It isn't here."

"What isn't?"

"You're here for the book, aren't you? The enchanted tome hidden in Lady Kathryn's fireplace. I thought you might have a connection to it after our meeting in the forest."

"Where is it?" Dezra asked angrily. She didn't have time for Durik's stoicism. Anything that blocked her path was running a very real risk, and not even her oldest friends were exempt. All that mattered now was the book.

"If you tell me what you've done with Logan and Ulma, I'll tell you where it is," Durik said.

"I haven't done anything with the idiot and the dwarf," Dezra said, trying her best to match the orc's apparent calm. She couldn't lose control now. In her current state, she didn't know what damage she could do. "Haven't they returned yet?"

"No," Durik said darkly. "Perhaps you can explain why."

"Don't make me break this spear, pathfinder," Dezra said, the balefire in her eyes flaring.

"Durik?"

The voice came from behind the orc, his body and the narrow stairs combining to obscure Dezra's view of the speaker. Durik didn't turn.

"I told you to stay in the room," he said.

"She is dark, Durik," the voice said. "Be careful." Dezra attempted to look past the orc.

"Replacing me already?" she asked, trying to get a sense of the power behind the voice she'd heard.

"If you want the book, I can take you to the one who has it," Durik said. "But something tells me she'll be more than reluctant to part with it. Nor is she the sort of person you would wish to anger."

"We'll see," Dezra said. "Taking me to her is certainly a wiser option than the alternative."

"Which is?"

"I tear the souls from every living being in this castle and torture them until they give up the location of the book."

"Let's avoid that, then. Just for old times' sake."

Durik raised his spear and Dezra backed off a few steps.

"Show me," she said.

Durik led Dezra to the castle's entrance hall. Carys came with him, refusing to return to Kathryn's bedchamber. She eyed Dezra with a mixture of fear and curiosity, while for her own part Dezra seemed surprised to find the girl was so young.

"Who is she?" the sorceress asked Durik, as though Carys wasn't walking right behind him.

"A clan chieftain's daughter," he said, glancing back reassuringly at Carys. "We thought her kindred might have taken Kathryn. We… wanted to make sure they hadn't."

"She's a hostage?"

"Not exactly."

"She's the reason the northerner was with Logan and Ulma, then."

"You met them," Durik said, stopping at the foot of the tower stairs. His hand was back on the handle of his knife. "What did you do to them?"

"I told you, nothing," Dezra said firmly. "They came to me demanding to know where Kathryn was. I didn't know."

"She knows more than she's admitting," Carys said, half hidden behind Durik. Dezra glared at her.

"The girl has the witch-sight," she said. "Be careful. You know more than you admit as well."

Durik looked between the two, before stepping out into the entrance hall. Bodies littered the floor, most of them belonging to the castle's garrison, the rest nothing but bones and armor. There were two skeletons as well, standing impassively, skulls grinning as Dezra passed them by. They reacted to a short gesture by the sorceress, turning and walking unsteadily back through the broken gate and out into the night. Durik realized one of the corpses had still been clad in a bloody tabard bearing Forthyn's golden roc, the same tabard Captain Kloin had worn.

"How many more have you killed on the way here?" he demanded of Dezra.

"None who didn't try to impede me," she answered defensively. "I have been merciful, for now. The dead are coming from Blind Muir. They will help my hunt for the monster that cursed Kathryn. They will be here by the time the sun rises."

"Call them off."

"Not until I have the book."

"Why? Why is it so important?"

"I can't perform the spells it contains without it."

"And what spells would they be?"

"You'll see once I have the book."

Durik blocked her way once more. "You've only gotten this far because of who you are, Dezra. Or who you used to be. Don't betray what trust I still have in you. If your only intention is to steal back your book and slaughter this town, we stop here."

"Kathryn is dead," Dezra said, facing Durik. Just speaking the words brought back that icy feeling in her gut, that pain that transcended mere emotion. It made her want to flinch. She forced herself to keep speaking, not to show how much agony she was in. Now was not the time to break down. "She was killed by a man named Kloin."

"What?" Durik's tone faltered. She saw sadness in his expression, an emotional response that she forced herself not to snap back at – this wasn't the moment for pity. She wanted none of it.

"When? Where?" the orc asked.

"Moments ago, in the Shrine of Nordros."

"You were there? Where has she been this past month?"

"That's what I intend to find out. I discovered her wandering in the streets before we were attacked. It looked as though she had just been released, though from where I don't know. She mentioned the arachyura. If Logan, Ulma and that northerner are missing as well, I suspect that whoever or whatever took Kathryn also took them."

"And your book of spells will help lead you to them?"

"That's what I'm hoping."

Durik looked down at Dezra for a heartbeat, then gestured past her at the stairs. "They lead to Lady Damhán's chamber. She has your book."

They climbed up to the castle's solar, directly above the main hall. Durik paused on the landing and knocked at the door, hard.

"I told you I was not to be disturbed," barked an angry voice from within.

"That isn't her," Dezra said before Durik could answer. He frowned at her.

"How do you know? You've never met her."

"That isn't someone answering us," Dezra elaborated irritably, clearly in no mood for explanations. "It's a mimicry illusion. I can sense it. Someone has enchanted this door to answer questions and ward off attention. It's a very subtle, complex spell, but a spell nevertheless. Whoever you think is answering you isn't actually in that chamber."

"Lady Damhán is Baroness Adelynn's advisor," Durik said, thoughts racing. Of all his suspicions involving Kathryn, none had involved Damhán. She'd been an unsettling presence, yes, but he had never conceived of her as anything other than a stern enforcer of Baroness Adelynn's will. "She rode north with us. She has no reason to deceive us."

"We'll see," Dezra said, planting her hands on the door. "Stand back."

Durik did so, still disbelieving. The words Dezra chanted made Carys go white-faced with fear. The woodwork began to disintegrate, the iron studs rusting before their eyes. Carys hid behind Durik as the door collapsed in on itself, now-ancient timber splitting and cracking apart under the slightest pressure.

The room beyond no longer resembled the solar of Fallowhearth castle. The furniture within was shrouded in thick strands of webbing, and a hundred compound eyes glittered back at them from the dark.

"I don't think your baroness's advisor is quite who she says she is," Dezra said, deadlights flickering into being around her as she drew a long, serrated dagger. Durik said nothing, hefting his spear. He hadn't wanted to accept that his own instincts had so spectacularly failed to detect the predator in their midst. But the evidence was right before his eyes now. Damhán was not what she had appeared to be. He looked down at Carys, who returned his gaze fiercely – he already knew what she would say if he told her to wait outside.

"Here," he muttered, drawing his skinning dagger and giving it to her. As he did so he tried to banish the sudden uncertainties that had beset him. "Just stay behind me."

The girl took the blade and nodded solemnly. Dezra was grinning cruelly, standing on the edge of the infested room.

"Just like old times," she said to Durik, and stepped over the threshold.

CHAPTER TWENTY-THREE

Ronan found Fallowhearth in turmoil. People were stumbling through the dark, wind lashed streets, dashing to and from their homes as they desperately tried to collect together their worldly goods, family and friends. Ronan shouted for them to make way, hardly slowing his mount as he urged the beast on up to the castle.

He slowed as he approached the gate. It had been broken open – how, it was difficult to tell in the darkness. Two figures stood outside it, their blades bared. Ronan assumed they were the castle's garrison, and was about to call out to them when his instincts stopped him.

Something was wrong. A flash of lightning lit up the two sentinels, exposing their grinning skulls and magic-infused bones.

"She's already here," Ronan said to Pico, drawing his sword. The familiar squeaked in agreement. A sense of grim finality gripped the northerner, stoked by a fiery anger. He had been right to distrust the necromancer. Now, finally, he would break her curse.

He dismounted, striding through the swirling wind and rain towards the broken gates. Torchlight glowed beyond the stone archway. The witch had to still be inside, somewhere.

The two corpses moved in from either side, the lights in their eye sockets flaring as they seemed to take notice of Ronan. He picked the one on the left and charged.

It brought up a pole arm to block his first strike, Ronan's sword shivering splinters from the haft. It didn't get an opportunity to deflect the northerner's second strike – Pico leapt onto its bare skull. These skeletons were more tightly bound than the Blind Muir horde; contact from the familiar wasn't enough to cause it to collapse, but it weakened the fell magic binding it enough for Ronan to shatter its rib cage with a hard blow of his sword's pommel, causing it to stumble back.

He turned to the next one as it came at him with a raised sword. The blades clashed, sparking in the rain. Ronan tried to go low, burying his weapon in the body's rib cage, but the thing seemed unaffected by what should have been a fatal strike. It raised its own sword again, and Ronan was forced to clutch its wrist to stop the overhead swing from splitting his head open. Muscle strained against arcana-fueled bone for a few seconds, before Pico bit the corpse's bared femur. The magic binding it weakened, and bones crunched and snapped loudly in Ronan's vice-like grip. He snapped the sword arm clean off and, with a roar, forced his blade up through its rib cage, splitting it in half. It came apart.

The first undead had recovered its pole arm but was still clearly struggling in Pico's presence. Ronan kicked it into the mud and delivered one, two, three further kicks to its skull, shattering it. Like the first one, it came undone. Panting,

Ronan shook rainwater off his blade and stepped into the castle's gatehouse.

Bodies were waiting for him in the entrance hall – men-at-arms and heaps of bone and armor bearing witness to a struggle between the living and the dead that appeared to have left both sides eternally equal. The northerner cast about, expecting more skeletons to advance on him from the spiral stairs that led deeper into the castle, but all he caught was what sounded like fighting in the higher levels. He shared a look with Pico and started to climb.

Durik wrenched his spear from the last arachyura's corpse, kicking its spasming, bloated body for good measure. Dezra stood across the room from him, her serrated dagger hanging in the air before her, dripping ichor. Carys was next to him, Durik's own knife similarly bloodied.

They had hacked away the worst of the webbing, Dezra's balefire scorching the last of it from the chamber. A dozen or more dead arachyura carpeted the floor, some still twitching. Durik went from one to another, piercing their skulls with his spear.

"Watch the door," he told Carys as he moved between the bodies. There could only be one creature behind this, one being he knew capable of weaving so deadly a web of deceit around them. If he was right, he knew it may already be too late to save themselves, let alone any of the others. "If these monsters are in here, they could be anywhere inside the castle. Nowhere is safe."

Dezra appeared to have no interest in making sure all of the arachyura were dead. She had moved to the corner of the room furthest from the door, where the remnants of the webbing that had once shrouded the whole chamber was still hanging. The strands were wrapped around what Durik realized was Dezra's tome. The witch engulfed the book in her dirty, cold flames, freeing it from the last of the threads and catching it neatly.

"What now?" Durik asked as he speared the final arachyura. Dezra walked past him, stepping over the bodies without looking down at them as she began leafing urgently through the book. The knife was still floating alongside her.

"Now, you stand in the corner and say nothing," she said, moving to the center of the room and shoving one of the smaller arachyura aside with her boot. She sat down, crosslegged, the book propped open in her lap. Durik did as she had suggested without question, giving her space.

Dezra began to chant. The temperature in the room plummeted, and the hairs across Durik's body rose. More deadlights flickered into existence around the necromancer. Her eyes rolled into the back of her head, and her body started to tremble.

There was movement in the doorway. A shadow obscured the light beyond it. Durik thought for a second it was just Carys, before realizing the shape was far too thickset. The girl was standing to one side within the solar, eyes wide as she looked from the intruder to Durik. Dezra's fires guttered and her eyes snapped back into focus.

It was the northerner, Ronan. He was drenched through, and his expression was angry and warlike. His sword was drawn, and his small, red familiar was perched on his shoulder, hissing softly at Dezra. Durik appreciated the fiery gaze of a fellow warrior, but the fact that it was directed at his old companion put him on edge.

"Your reign of terror is at an end, witch," the northerner said.

"Oh, not this again," Dezra responded irritably. "Don't make me hurt you, clansman. I'm in a deadly mood."

"You can try," Ronan said, striding into the chamber. Durik moved to intercept him, intending to stop such foolishness before it could escalate any further. Their eyes met, less than a foot apart.

"Stand aside, pathfinder," Ronan said. "I have no quarrel with you."

"You have no quarrel with Dezra either," he pointed out, his voice firm.

"She is a necromancer. She does not deserve your protection."

"So I have been told, many times before," Durik said. "In my experience, someone willing to harm a witch would harm an orc too."

"Ronan," said Carys. She had followed him into the room, and now clutched urgently onto his wrist. "Do not fight them. Durik is a friend of the clans, and he has vouched for the witch. I trust him, so we can both trust her."

"Tell them," Ronan said, looking beyond Durik at Dezra. "Tell them of the legion of corpses that marches here this very moment from the Blind Muir. Tell them how you have massacred the town's garrison and resurrected them as your puppets."

"They already know," Dezra said. "Look around you, oaf. Are spiders this size a common nuisance in the north? Do you often find arachyura infestations in the castles of Upper Forthyn? I am trying to unearth the root of this taint, so that I can rip it all up. If I don't, then every house and home in this miserable town will look like this chamber."

"You sit there performing forbidden magics, yet you still expect me to believe you?"

"Believe your girl. She has the witch-sight too."

Ronan looked down at Carys, her grip still on his arm.

"Is that true?" he asked her. The familiar let out a little screech.

"You rode north with Logan and Ulma," Durik said, drawing his attention away from the girl. "Where are they now?"

"I thought they would have already returned," Ronan said, defensive now. "We parted company after finding this witch in the Crooked Tower. I was riding on to the Redferns when I stumbled across her undead horde."

"The arachyura might have taken the others," Durik said. "Lady Damhán has also been captured, or is somehow involved with them. There is something dark at work in this town. Far darker than my companion here."

"Charmed," Dezra said. Ronan grimaced before taking a step back from Durik.

"You said you would find the root of the infestation," Ronan said. "So find it. I will be waiting."

"Get that thing away from me first," Dezra snapped, glaring at the familiar. Ronan glared back, but retreated with the creature to the far side of the door. Dezra cast a final, withering look at the pair before turning her gaze back to her book.

Balefire reignited around her and swept through the

chamber. Durik shivered at its touch, but its flames twisted away from him, coming together to form the flickering phantoms of shapes across the floor. It had been a long time since Durik had seen Dezra deploy her powers in a scrying – he'd forgotten how much he hated the surreal sense of time dislocation that accompanied them. He recognized the shapes formed by the balefire though. They were the arachyura. Dezra's magics had created shades of the giant spiders killed by the three of them.

Like flickering shadows cast upon a wall by firelight, the phantom spiders rose and began to move. They scuttled under the bed, into the fireplace, into the tiniest cracks in the stone walls. They poured down and away, fleeing the room via a dozen or more different points, their fire-forms dissipating as they went.

"If they move like that, they could be anywhere in the castle," Durik murmured.

"But they aren't," Dezra said hoarsely, taking him by surprise. He had thought she was completely lost in her trance.

"These ones came from the main swarm," she went on, her voice sounding raspy and dry. Her eyes had rolled back again, seeing far more than Durik's were capable of. "There is a nest… nearby. In the castle."

"Where?" Durik asked, tightening his grip on his spear.

"Down," Dezra replied. "We go down."

CHAPTER TWENTY-FOUR

Ulma spoke, making Logan whimper at the thought of her voice attracting the attention of the surrounding spiders.

"How long have we been here?"

At first, he thought that she had forgotten that his mouth was bound. Then he realized she was actually addressing Ariad.

The spider queen had come and gone from the small sphere of light that continued to burn just above the web. Her motions were even more jerky and scuttling than before. Logan got the impression she was waiting for someone or something to arrive.

Ulma's words drew her back up the thread. Her golden mask gazed up at her impassively for a while.

"Am I speaking in Dunwarri?" Ulma said. "I asked you how long you've been keeping us here. Since the butcher's shop."

"That does not matter," Ariad hissed. "When my children feast, you will miss these precious moments."

"I'd say it matters a lot," Ulma said. "For you, for me, for your children."

Ariad clambered closer.

"Why?"

"Because when you took me, I had just mixed pyrium, colix and vitrolium. The first two are the basis of what I call *magi-reducto,* an anti-arcana act of alchemy. You will have seen it already, if you really are Lady Damhán. The barn outside the Forester's Rest, just before we reached Fallowhearth."

"So?" Ariad demanded. "It is stoppered, and you are bound. Your little metal tricks have no power here."

"True, it is stoppered, and I am bound," Ulma admitted. "But I told you, I mixed the *magi-reducto* with vitrolium. If you knew your alchemy, you'd know that particular 'little metal trick' causes whatever elements it's mixed with to become increasingly volatile as time goes by. Speaking the language of a non-alchemist, I have a vial in my smock that, judging by the vibrations and the heat I can feel against my chest right now, is about to explode into a magic-consuming fireball."

Ariad hissed and scurried back from Ulma, pointing one gaunt, web-wrapped limb at her. The arachyura flooded in from all sides, some scrambling over Logan as they swarmed the dwarf. He moaned in muffled terror, thinking he was going to be crushed or suffocated. In that moment he was convinced Ulma's brash plan would only hasten their demise – at the very best, they'd tear him apart before her flames took hold.

Ulma didn't react to the onrushing tide of spiders. Ariad's golden light illuminated the creatures as they tore at her cocoon, stripping away the silk they had woven tightly around her. It was immediately clear that she hadn't been bluffing –

a bubbling, purple liquid was overflowing from one of the pockets of her smock, steaming where it spilled down her front. Logan saw her grin.

"By the ancestor's prized brew, I sure hope I got the ingredients right in this one."

The concoction exploded. A purple fireball roared over Ulma, immediately igniting the hundreds of spiders, great and small, that were scrambling over and around her. Their bloated bodies shielded Logan from the blast, but he still instinctively flinched away, the web beneath him vibrating. When he looked back, eyes stinging from the intensity of the glare, everything between him and the dwarf was on fire.

Ariad's arachyura were clearly infused with enough arcana to be affected by the *magi-reducto*. That, or Ulma had indeed gotten her ingredients wrong. A dreadful cacophony of shrieks filled the air, along with the hideous reek of burning bodies. Arachyura swarmed over one another as they sought to escape the purple flames, only serving to spread them further. The great web holding them had itself ignited, burning fitfully as the fire danced along each thread in turn, expanding rapidly. Logan twisted and struggled in desperation, trying to claw himself free of his bonds and get away from the conflagration.

Then he saw Ulma. She was rising up in the midst of the fire, tearing herself free of the last of the webbing that had once bound her. She was lit head to foot in flames, just as she had been when Logan had first met her again outside the Forester's Rest. And she was laughing. Around her the arachyura burned, their body-sacs bursting in foul, stinking geysers of steaming ichor.

The crazed dwarf snatched onto the still burning web and half dragged, half climbed her way to Logan.

Despite the furious shaking of his head, she clutched at him, the flames coursing over her body. The purple fire ignited the cocoon holding Logan, burning through it in seconds and leaving behind only a sticky residue. He ripped his arms free, sword in one hand, then freed his mouth as the fire engulfed him. There was no pain, though, nothing but a prickling sensation across his body.

"This is insane!" Logan yelled, his further protestations interrupted by the dwarf.

"Hold on!" Ulma shouted, clutching his forearm as he tried to get a grip on the burning web around him. He realized why almost immediately – fatally weakened, the last of the threads gave way and they fell, together, still burning.

The impact drove the breath from Logan's lungs and doused most of the flames that had engulfed him. He rolled and scrabbled against black dirt and cold stone, finally dragging in a mouthful of humid, stinking air. He got onto his knees, looking around in a daze. Ulma was next to him, already standing.

They had fallen to the cavern floor, their descent partly arrested by the last of the burning-up strands of webbing. Ariad's golden light was high above them now, like a tiny star surrounded by a halo of purple flames, as the *magi-reducto* ate away the last of the great web around it. Of Ariad herself, Logan could find no sign. It was too dark across the cavern floor to see with any degree of certainty, but the flicker of movement and a rising, rustling sound made him shudder and turn left and right, his sword extended, its point quivering. A high-pitched screech rose and reverberated from somewhere in the echoing space.

"Whatever your plan is, please hurry," he hissed at Ulma. "They're coming."

"Hold them off, then," Ulma said urgently as she upended the front of her smock and dumped the contents in the dirt. She knelt and started frantically unstoppering bottles.

Logan didn't have time to argue. The first arachyura flung itself at him from out of the dark so hard it impaled itself on his sword, running itself through. Logan kicked at it repeatedly, its writhing limbs still trying to claw at him as more of its kin swarmed forward from all sides. He got it dislodged and thrust hard into the open maw of another, right between the pincers, ichor gouting across his sword. He withdrew the blade and turned the movement into a slash that burst the eye clusters of a third. He felt a surge of exhilaration as he fought, an angry defiance he hadn't known in a long time. He wasn't going to die here, in the dirt and the dark, down among these monsters. He'd live, as he always did. This would be just another story for the fireside.

Then he saw Ariad. Her orb had descended down over her head. She strode across the cavern floor towards them between a scuttling tide as her children parted around her. Golden power coursed like liquid brilliance around her body and made her mask shine radiantly. She extended both hands, claw-like, towards Logan. His sword faltered.

Daylight was on his face, a warm desert wind. He felt a hand grasp onto his shoulder, tight and insistent. He turned around and found Dezra beside him.

"Why are you here?" he stammered, trying to focus.

His thoughts had turned sluggish and slow, the edge that his anger had given him bleeding away. He looked around, almost blinded by the heat and the light. "Where are we? The arachyura…"

"This is an illusion," Dezra said. "A web for your mind. I'm not here. Fight, or you will die."

"Dezra, I'm sorry," Logan began to say, but her grip tightened, painfully, making him flinch. He tried to pull his shoulder away, but couldn't free it.

Dezra was gone. An arachyura had latched onto his shoulder, its pincers digging into his flesh. He cried out, trying to shake it off, desperately switching his sword over to his other hand so that he could stab it. The angle was bad – all he could manage was a glancing slash across its skull, but it clung on, its mandibles locked. His arm was going numb.

He could still feel the heat on his face, and the light. It poured from Ariad, from her golden visage and the corona of power that crackled around her. She was right in front of Logan now, reaching out to snap his neck and turn his body into a husk for her feeding young. Another arachyura had clamped onto his calf, a third, smaller one hanging off his left forearm.

"I bring you my light, Logan Lashley," Ariad hissed. "Embrace it."

Something slammed into his back, almost thrusting him forward into the monstrous queen. Roaring in Dunwarri, Ulma threw herself between Logan and Ariad, a vial of broiling alchemical liquid in each fist. She flung them straight at the arachyura queen, barely a foot away.

The vials struck and shattered, their volatile contents

splashing over her. The reaction was instantaneous. The liquids combusted, and a roaring fireball exploded between Ulma and Ariad.

Logan was blinded by the flash and thrown backwards. Ulma, directly in front of him, took the worst of the blast. She was flung into Logan, driving them both into the dirt. Arachyura bodies snapped beneath them. Logan tried to roll over, gasping for breath, the afterglow of the explosion seared into his vision. He found his hands on Ulma's shoulders and managed to free himself. All around the arachyura were twitching and shrieking, the force of the detonation breaking the swarm's coherence. The space directly ahead had been reduced to a crater, splattered with the devastated remains of spiders. Some were on fire, the flames adding filthy smoke and hellish light to the chamber. Others, hideously wounded, were trying to drag themselves away from the devastation. Ariad was gone.

Logan realized Ulma was on fire. She was sprawled next to him, semi-conscious. The corner of her smock was burning. It was only as Logan beat out the flames that he saw how badly she'd been hit by the explosion. Her goggles were shattered, one eye bloody, and part of her stomach was charred and exposed. She coughed as Logan tried to extinguish her, spitting blood. Logan felt an upsurge of horror as he realized the extent of her injuries, coupled with the urgent need not to let her see. He tried to still his shaking hands.

"Did I get the bitch?" she grunted.

"I think so," Logan said, glancing around the chamber. The arachyura were scrambling all over one another, their predatory instincts and swarm intelligence apparently gone.

Logan wondered if their sensitive eyes had been blinded by the blast.

"I never knew what would happen if I mixed the liquid drakesmetal and vitrolium," Ulma said, grinning bloodily. "I do love a good explosion."

"We've got to get out," Logan said, trying to apply some focus to the dazed, injured dwarf. To himself as well. He had to keep it together now, for both of them. They could still get out of this. "Do you think you can walk?"

"What do you think, you dumb bastard manling," Ulma said, looking down. Logan realized that much of the upper thigh on her left leg had also been burned away. It was a grisly sight.

"Guess that wasn't the wooden one?" he asked. Ulma slumped back, closing her one good eye.

"Leave me," she said, her voice firm and clear despite the undoubted pain of her injuries.

"Absolutely not," Logan said. "Either we both leave, or neither of us do. I'll carry you out if I have to."

Ulma scoffed. "Well that would make a change."

"Hold on," Logan said, shifting his stance so he could get his arm in under Ulma's shoulder. She hissed with pain.

"I thought you'd really lost it earlier," she managed to say. "You just stopped. I was about to get my mallet out and bash the back of your skull."

"More of Ariad's illusions," Logan said, trying to shake off the memory of the monster's tricks. He felt like a fool, as though all this was his fault. If he wasn't so weakwilled, perhaps Ulma wouldn't have had to save him. He forced himself to stay focused. "Dezra pulled me out of it."

"You're really obsessed," Ulma said before spitting more blood.

"Stop talking. Save your strength."

"Convenient for you to say."

Logan didn't answer. Ariad's golden light had returned.

Dezra said nothing as she descended through Fallowhearth castle. Her eyes were as white as those of a freshly raised corpse and her movements were sluggish and dream-like. Her book floated seemingly of its own accord before her, the pages turning in a wind none of the others could feel. Durik had seen her in a similar state before, during a desperate flight from the Uthuk Y'llan through Thalian Glades, guided only by the necromancer's death-scrying. She was spirit walking, drawn on by the whispers of the dead.

Apparently, they had much to tell her. She took the steps to the dungeon, Durik and Carys behind her. Ronan followed a dozen paces further behind, so that his familiar's nullifying aura didn't interrupt the trance. Durik could still sense the hostility radiating from the northerner.

As Dezra passed, the braziers lining the walls ignited with her balefire, one after the other, casting their descent in a pallid corpse-light. Durik heard noises rising from below – voices. They became silent as the group stepped through an open grate out into the single, subterranean chamber that constituted the castle's dungeon.

To Durik's surprise, they found the dank space already occupied. Dezra's lights lit a dozen white, terrified faces that stared back at the group as they entered. It took him a while to recognize them as the castle's complement of servants. Mildred stood before the rest, staring at Dezra with undisguised terror.

"She means you no harm," Durik said, realizing how ridiculous that claim must sound. "How did you come to be down here?"

"We heard fighting at the front gate," she stammered. "The servants' quarters are right above. We didn't know where else to go."

"You may be in greater danger here than anywhere else," Durik said as Dezra advanced towards them. "I would advise you to stand aside."

The servants hurried to obey, throwing themselves out of Dezra's path. She passed between them seemingly without even noticing they were there and came to a stop right in front of the rough-cut wall. Her deadlights strengthened, illuminating the rock face.

"They passed through here," she said in a deep, unnatural tone, like a dozen voices speaking together. The death-tongue. She was channeling spirits, multiple ones. Durik moved closer to peer at the rock. It was riven with cracks, fissures that he supposed were large enough for an average-sized arachyura to crawl though sideways, but impossible for a biped to traverse.

"If they had Kathryn, she couldn't have fitted through any of these," he pointed out.

"She did not come through here," Dezra said. "But that does not mean she could not have. The entire town is riven with enchantments and illusions. This place is no different."

She made a series of scything motions with her hands and the pages of the tome still floating before her rustled. Her deadlights convened at a particular point in the wall, just one of the slender cracks that ran through the rock. As Durik looked on, the wall seemed to run and melt like candle wax. The servants gasped and muttered fearfully as Dezra's orbs ate away the stone, until what had been an unassuming split was a narrow passage, leading away into the dark.

Durik peered into it, eyes straining. Without Dezra's magics there was no way any of them could have located the illusion-cloaked entrance. The air was dry and still, with an underlying stink that made his hairs bristle. A part of him was afraid, he realized. He suppressed it, as he always did. There were others counting on him. He didn't have the luxury of fear.

"They are close," Dezra intoned and, without so much as a glance back at Durik, advanced into the opened earth, her deadlights bobbing ahead. Durik looked back at Ronan, who was holding off with Carys. The northerner's expression was impassive. Durik nodded to him. There was no turning back now. They had to press on and tear out the root of the evil that had lodged itself in this place, before it was too late.

They followed Dezra in.

A golden light transplanted the glow of Ulma's flames. Logan groaned as he recognized it.

Ariad had returned. She had risen back up from amidst the arachyura and was limping towards them. Ulma's blast had fused and melted the webbing that clad much of her left side, and her golden mask was split, a crack running like a lightning bolt from her left temple down through the eye to the chin. Her left arm hung uselessly at her side, but her right was outstretched. Wicked black talons had burst from the webbing cladding her fingertips.

"Don't suppose you've got any more tricks in those pockets?" Logan asked Ulma urgently as she bore down on them. With some effort, the dwarf shook her head.

"I'm all out."

"I'll be honest," Logan said, testing the arm and the leg that had been bitten by the arachyura earlier. "I don't think I can stand up on my own, let alone with you."

"Useless right to the end, you old rogue," Ulma said, grinning at him with red teeth. Despite himself, Logan laughed.

Ariad was upon them. The swarm had rallied in her presence, moving with purpose once more as they surrounded Ulma and Logan. He managed to get up onto his feet, slowly, Ulma still lying beside him.

"You know, I've just realized something."

"What?" Ulma asked, her one undamaged eye now closed.

"I'm not scared of spiders any more."

He'd barely spoken the words before a flash of lightning bolted from the darkness around the edge of the chamber and earthed hard into Ariad's right side. The arachyura queen stumbled back and hissed a flurry of un-words as the pale energy coursed over her. It flickered and died out, just in time for another burst to hammer her. A fresh wail rose up from the arachnid swarm.

More light was growing in the far corner of the chasm, yellow flames tainted green, as though a form of necrosis had somehow infected the fire. It burned from a crack in the jagged wall, writhing fitfully around the figure who had stepped through into the underground chamber.

"Dezra," Logan said, as much for his own benefit as for Ulma's. He hardly dared believe his eyes any more.

The necromancer hurled another blast of ethereal corpse energy that slammed into Ariad. The queen was reeling, her swarm churning around her in fresh disunity. Dezra continued to advance, an open book floating at her left hand, her long knife at her right. Balefire blazed about her feet and the orbs of deadlights danced around her head, deathly energies arcing between them. Despite the salvation she represented, Logan still felt a cloying, primal fear at the sight of such dark powers unleashed. In all their years together, he had never seen her so naturally embody the terrible majesty of Nordros.

Durik was moving forward in her wake, the pathfinder's spear levelled. After him was the clan girl, Carys, clutching Durik's knife, and then Ronan with his sword drawn, his familiar perched on his shoulder.

"We're going to make it," Logan shouted exultantly as he saw the group pushing towards them, Dezra's flames rising up to illuminate the whole cavern. "By all the gods, Ulma, I knew we'd get through this!"

The dwarf didn't respond. Ariad seemed to have rallied, the golden glow of her mask intensifying once more as she turned from Logan to face the new threat. He only wished her children had done the same – the arachyura around him hissed and lunged in once more, a rising flood of bristling black bodies. Teeth gritted against the effort of forcing his own numb muscles to obey, Logan raised his sword once more.

CHAPTER TWENTY-FIVE

"The queen," Dezra's unnatural voice intoned, booming through the cavernous space. She was marching towards its center, her energies lashing at a web-bound, humanoid figure in the golden mask, surrounded by the largest arachyura Durik had ever seen. Malice oozed from the creature, a weight of dread that conjured up dark memories. Sudanya. A warren of stone ruins and temples, baking in the borderlands sun. An impenetrable web of tunnels below, infested with horrors ruled over by a masked predator. He remembered what Carys had said in the tower. A beast that wore a human guise.

It was all clear now. It was Ariad.

Durik had feared as much. The arachyura infestation, the web of illusions. It had been so long he'd refused to countenance that the ancient creature had survived and escaped the labyrinth, much less entrapped them all these years later. But the evidence was right before his eyes. Some predators were truly patient.

Dezra seemed intent on destroying the arachyura queen singlehandedly. Still in her trance, she pressed onwards, her flames igniting every spider that tried to block her path. All Durik could do was follow, spearing the shrieking creatures as they shriveled up in the necromancer's unnatural fires.

He cast a glance back to the fissure they'd struggled through from the dungeon, hoping Carys and Ronan were holding back from entering the cave. They weren't. Ronan was slaughtering arachyura seeking to rush in behind Dezra's advance, fighting with a controlled, brutal efficiency. Short chops of his blade severed limbs and stabs burst swollen abdomens, his face a stony mask of concentrated effort. Durik found himself admiring the northerner's fighting style.

Carys stayed in his shadow, guarding his back. The familiar was perched on her shoulder, aiding the thrusts of Durik's borrowed knife – the arachyura recoiled from its presence, legs twitching frantically as they struggled in the arcane void it created.

"Keep the passage back to the castle clear," Durik shouted at them, signaling to the crack in the wall behind. Ronan offered a nod of understanding as he continued his butcher's work.

Ahead of Durik, Dezra had nearly reached the brood of giant arachyura protecting Ariad. The burning glow being emitted by the queen clashed explosively with Dezra's deadlights, searing away the darkness of the chasm and throwing great, struggling shadows across the uneven walls. Durik saw Dezra stumble. The competing energies blew out in a shockwave that scattered the nearest spiders and almost knocked Durik onto his back.

Dezra fell to her knees, her book and dagger tumbling to the ground on either side of her. Durik rushed to her side.

"She's powerful," the necromancer gasped, her voice her own again, eyes refocusing as she looked up at Durik. "Even more powerful than she was in Sudanya."

"We can still beat her," Durik said firmly, helping Dezra back to her feet. She clutched at her book with one hand, pointing with the other.

"Logan," she said.

Durik followed the gesture and realized that balefire wasn't all that suffused the cavern's darkness. More natural flames were burning beyond where Ariad was still marshalling her monsters, picking out a frail, human figure beset by another wave of arachyura. He was standing over a prone body that Durik assumed had to be Ulma.

Hope leapt in Durik, combined with a surge of resolve. Logan was still fighting, and Ulma may yet be alive. Someone had to try and reach them.

The arachyura nearest to them had recovered from the sorcerous backlash. They rushed in, a chittering carpet of fat insectoid bodies and snapping maws. Durik speared one with a grunt, his tusks gritted, body burning with fresh adrenaline.

"Get to them," he shouted, nodding to Logan and Ulma as he disentangled his weapon. "I'll buy you time!"

Dezra didn't argue. With a flurry of curses she summoned her balefire once more, spreading it in an arc around where Ariad was controlling her brood.

"That will hold her," she spat, before striding out towards Logan.

There were too many. Logan managed to hack into the compound eyes of one arachyura, stinking, gray jelly-like liquid spurting out of its ruined membrane. Blind, it grappled with him, ploughing its pincers into his stomach. He grunted and managed to reverse his sword, plunging it down into the monster's midsection and nearly bisecting it. The thing fell away, suddenly limp, and he went down with it.

Bodies pressed in around him, warm, stinking, bristling. Mandibles clacked and drooled. With a final burst of strength he struggled up, roaring, driving his ichor-slick blade into one unnatural body after another, drenched in their steaming viscera. This couldn't be the end. It just couldn't.

He fell again. There was a dull ache in his stomach. Dimly, he remembered the arachyura he had blinded driving its pincers into his gut. He realized that the creature's numbing, paralytic venom had dulled the sensation of being grievously wounded.

"Ulma," he groaned. The dwarf was still next to him. The arachyura hadn't reached her. He managed to sit up, weakly knocking aside a questing leg, trying with all of his strength to get his sword back up.

Fire broiled, sickly and cold, the flames of Nordros. The nearest arachyura squealed as they shriveled up, aged a century in a second by the sorcerous inferno.

Dezra strode through the flames, untouched by them. She ran to Logan's side and knelt, supporting him in a sitting position before he collapsed back.

"Ulma," was all he managed to choke, blood spilling from his mouth. Dezra placed her hand on the dwarf's head, seeking out her soul flame. She found none.

"Her spirit is gone, Logan," she said, fighting a tremor in her voice. To even admit it felt like a betrayal. "Ulma's dead."

Logan closed his eyes. Dezra pulled his bloody hands away from his stomach and immediately wished she hadn't. Her mind raced, seeking out the words to the *participes mortus*, wondering how much she could channel, how much more pain she could take.

"Don't," Logan said. She realized he was looking up at her again. "I know what you're thinking. No magic."

The old rogue's breathing was shallow. She could feel his flame guttering. Tears stung her eyes as she glanced over at Ulma's body, lying still beside him.

"I'm sorry," he managed to say, his expression tight with pain as he followed her gaze. "She saved me, but I couldn't manage the same for her. Without her, I'd already be dead."

"She's given her life freely for us," Dezra said. "As have you, Logan. You're a good man. You always have been." She almost expected some witty reply, something about it all making a pretty good story for the alehouses. But Logan said nothing. Dezra bowed her head.

Her balefire was almost spent. The surrounding arachyura were coming again, clawing through the embers, limbs questing towards her. She laid Logan slowly down beside Ulma and stood.

She didn't need the words, not any more. The arachyura fell at her feet as she opened up to the rage and agony within her, the loss of Kathryn, Ulma and Logan reforming that shard of ice; bitter and unyielding. She grasped it, flinging it with all her strength into the realm of the arcana.

The razor wind answered her cry. It ripped out from her like a shockwave, an invisible gale that struck the hundreds upon hundreds of spiders surrounding her head-on. Their screeches were torn away as the storm shredded them, ripping off exoskeletons. A wave of arachnid remains exploded across the cavern, the air misting with pulverized organic matter.

Dezra staggered, pain suffusing her body. She looked down at the lacerations that had appeared across her skin. Summoning the razor wind for a second time had almost cut her to pieces. She was bleeding, and her body felt drained of energy.

Focus. If she lost control, the manifestation of her own grief would destroy her utterly. Now was no time to dwell on loss – she had to use it to drive her, to reach Ariad before she grew any weaker. She looked down at Logan and Ulma, both lying still, their lifeflames nearly gone. The sight of them reawakened the pain that gave her power.

Summoning her flames once more, she turned back towards the heart of the cavern.

Ronan heard Carys shout and spun with his sword raised. The pressure of the arachyura assault was less fierce near the edge of the cavern, but he was still having to hack and slash relentlessly to keep them at bay. Still more had gotten past him. As he turned, he saw a pair of the monstrosities grappling with Carys, their struggle lit by the witch fires taking hold across the cavern. The girl's dagger was lodged in the torso of one, while Pico had been knocked from her shoulder. The familiar was laid out, unmoving, amidst the bodies.

The northerner bellowed and lunged to Carys's aid. His sword hacked down the first creature, and he kicked the second off the girl. She was bleeding from several gashes across her back.

"I can't feel them," she said, almost in a panic as she reached behind and found her fingers bloody.

"The venom," Ronan surmised, ripping the dagger from the arachyura body and handing it back to her. This desperate, heart-racing slaughter in the near-darkness was testing every ounce of his skills. A part of him wanted to forge after Durik towards the melee at the heart of the cavern, but his first priority was Carys. He wouldn't let them take her.

The northerner turned in time to cleave open another giant spider as it sprang at him, before kneeling quickly at Pico's side. He could see the little creature's furry chest still rising and falling.

"Try to wake him," he told Carys as he stood back up and turned towards the swarm. "If you cannot, these creatures will overwhelm us."

Durik fought harder than he had ever fought before. He stabbed and swung with his spear, using the haft to crack and parry hook-limbs and the base to pulverize eye clusters. He punched and kicked, headbutted and bit with his tusks. Every muscle in his body burned, a sharp counterpoint to the numbing effects of the dozens of bites and grazes that covered his body.

Ariad was right ahead. The arachyura protecting her were huge, larger than Durik, but he waded in amongst them regardless, stabbing and thrusting them aside. He'd lost sight of Dezra in the press, and he didn't have any time to turn and look for Ronan or Carys. That didn't matter any more. Nothing did, beyond reaching the center of the cavern and plunging his spear into the arachyura queen.

She came to meet him. She was already wounded, her mask cracked and much of her left side torn and oozing black ichor. Power still suffused her, though, the golden light of the Al-Kalim twilight she had been born under. She was the first of that desert realm's daughters to sup of Arachne's corrupting poison and fall under the sway of the spider goddess of Zanaga. She would not be denied her prey. She lunged at Durik.

His spear blocked her claws, the black talons raking off the haft. He drove into her, seeking to use his greater size and power to force her back and open her guard. She pushed back, though, her spindly body at odds with her own unnatural strength. Durik felt her claws slash across his stomach and grunted as pain surged through his body, quickly turning numb. She didn't have to kill him, he realized. She only had to leave him paralyzed.

He tried to give ground, needing more space to use his spear, trying to focus on her wounded left side. She was too slow to avoid the ungainly jab, but Durik couldn't do more than graze her flank. Then she was coming back in again, inside his guard, claws ripping at him. He cried out as they drew blood along his chest and thigh, making him stumble. The golden mask gazed at him with chilling indifference.

He recovered once more, slamming the haft of his weapon up into that serene visage, further cracking it. Something dark and hideous glittered behind the metal. Ariad hissed incomprehensibly and rained blows on Durik. He parried with the spear, using its sturdy ironroot timber. On the third strike it splintered and broke. The end spun away into the crush of arachnid bodies surrounding him, the tip still in his hand.

He fell. Ariad was on him instantly, her talons tearing down his back as he tried to turn protectively away from her. He cried out, hunched over in the dirt, his bruised, bloody body finally refusing to answer to his will.

"I could have killed you in the forest," Ariad hissed, leaning forward over Durik, as if relishing his weakness as she drew a claw slowly down the back of his head. "Or in the castle. I am glad I waited. Your death will be the sweetest treat, pathfinder."

Durik closed his eyes, took a breath, and roared. He turned and rose as he did so, forcing his body to obey, forcing tired, aching limbs and muscles numbed by dozens of cuts and gashes to work one last time. With every ounce of his remaining strength he slammed his right fist forward, his broken spear still grasped in it.

The tip, along with the remaining foot of splintered haft, plunged through the crack in Ariad's golden eye and punched out through the back of her skull. Viscous black liquid squirted from the exit wound. The arachyura queen staggered back, her body rigid, her spine arching horribly. A keening noise rose from her throat. Then, abruptly, her head exploded, the mask shattering, its golden luster drenched in black ichor and foul gray matter. Durik took a step back.

"That's twice I've killed you, monster," he panted.

A chilling wail rose throughout the cavern, reverberating back from the jagged stone. The arachyura were screaming and twitching, seemingly in pain.

Ariad's headless body, still frozen in its agonized death-stance, remained standing. One of the nearest fat arachyura threw itself on her, latching itself against her bent back. Another clamped itself to her left leg, and another her right.

Durik staggered and fell to his knees as more arachyura rushed all around him, every single living spider in the cavern swarming towards their queen.

Within seconds, Ariad's body had been lost from sight, buried beneath the swarm. Durik could only stare, his strength spent, as hundreds upon hundreds of arachnids piled one on top of the other, a writhing, ugly mass that swelled with each passing second. Gradually, underlit by the fires that still burned across the cavern, the churning mound began to resolve itself into a shape. Like a cruel joke, the swarm was merging together into a gigantic spider, a vast creature that grew to such a height it seemed as though it would brush the ceiling. It towered over him, a thrashing mound of limbs that swept down, as though to look at him.

"*Fool*," shrieked an inhuman voice, issued from the maws of a thousand chittering, melded arachyura. "*No orc savage can kill me*!"

Durik had no more weapons and no more strength. Just defiance. He glared up at the composite monstrosity and spat. It wouldn't win. With the certainty of finality, he knew Dezra would beat it.

Then, with a howl, the creature swept down and engulfed him.

Dezra saw Durik's death, buried by the insect mass. She had been forcing her way towards him, but faltered as the reborn Ariad rose up and screeched in triumph.

Despair filled her. She slumped to her knees while around her the balefire died away, doused by her exhaustion and grief. She had lost everything. Everyone she had cared about, who had cared about her. Despair gripped her thoughts, draining and paralyzing her. It was over. Ariad had triumphed utterly. The great mass of arachyura seemed to sense her sudden weakness. It turned and began to drag itself towards her, a roiling, sentient wave of bristling limbs, mandibles and eye clusters.

She bowed her head, searching for strength, trying to harness her pain. One final incantation. One more act of resistance. But she couldn't find the words. She was alone, and she had nothing left to give.

Dezra.

At first, she thought the voice was her own. It came again, soft but insistent, like someone trying to coax her out of a sleep riven by nightmares. Finally, she recognized it, and when she did, the guttering flames surrounding her began to rise again.

It was Logan. He was with her. She looked up, into the approaching morass of wicked bodies that was sweeping across the cavern. Right before her, three deadlights had blinked into existence. She knew them instantly, knew their energy. Had known them almost all of her life. Despite the pain, despite the exhaustion, she smiled.

You should know better than anyone, you're never alone.

She was standing. Power arced from the three orbs, earthing into her body. She felt her strength returning, the cuts healing, the exhaustion burning up. Their spirits were rejuvenating her, lending strength from beyond the realm of the living. The tangible, conscious energies they possessed gave them a potency she could use. She raised her hands, fires bright once more. She looked at the souls of her old friends, still bright and coherent around her sorcerous aura.

"Destroy her," she said.

Like hounds unleashed to the hunt, the pale energy shot away, meeting the onrushing swarm head-on. They slammed into Ariad, arachyura exploding from the triple points of impact. The malformed giant juddered, its momentum slowing as the deadlights tore all the way through and came back around, hammering it from three sides.

The sense of exultation Dezra felt didn't last for long. A glow began to shine from deep within the swarm, that cursed, golden light, an echo of the sun that Ariad had been born to bind into darkness. It grew more powerful, and when the deadlights next smashed into the chirring horde, they rebounded with enough force to shake soil and loose rock from the cavern ceiling. Dezra felt the force of the blow in her core, making her stumble.

Ariad's advance resumed, the ticking of the hundreds of arachyura redoubling. It sounded as though they were laughing. The light within them burned, repelling the orbs whenever they approached. They were growing dimmer and weaker with each passing moment. Dezra held her hand back, drawing them to her once more.

"Go," she said, her voice shaking. "All three of you. You can do no more for me."

"But I can," said a voice next to her. She closed her eyes, and Kathryn was standing before her. She was full, corporeal, her eyes shining brightly in the dying firelight, traveling cloak wafting in a phantom wind, unblemished by blood. In her hands she was carrying the *Cadaveribus,* its pages opened. Dezra stared at her as Kathryn gave her the book. She was smiling.

The sight shook her more deeply than anything she'd witnessed before. A swelling of hope crashed against the cold sea of her misery, shame and uncertainty at war within her. Kathryn was still with her, but her presence only reminded Dezra that she was lost.

"I've failed," Dezra said, her voice raw and broken. "Cross over while you still can, with the others. Don't wait for me. Ariad will not relinquish my soul." Kathryn shook her head.

"I told you," she said. "Death is only a beginning."

Ariad screeched once more, arching above them both. Dezra flinched instinctively and in that instant, Kathryn was gone. She looked down at the *Cadaveribus*, confused, riven with regret. The book lay open at its foremost incantation, the first and last act of dark magic performed by each and every necromancer. The Black Invocation.

Realization struck her, and in an instant her mind was free. The fear, pain, doubt and sorrow fell away as she picked up the heavy tome. The words flowed easily from the page, uninhibited by the mind-aching presence of the arachyura queen. The *Cadaveribus* propped open against the crook of her elbow, Dezra extended her right arm, her voice rising with each syllable, riven with the power of death.

In the far corner of the cavern, one of the arachyura twitched. It had been hideously burned by Ulma's flames, but now it began to move once again, jerking round onto its fleet. It started to scurry towards the center of the chamber. One by ones, others joined it. Spiders that had been hacked down by Logan, Ronan and Carys, run through by Durik, burned by Ulma, started to rise up and move. Greatest of all was the phalanx of arachyura that had been ripped apart by

Dezra's razor wind. Hundreds strong, their shattered limbs and carapaces reformed as they poured towards Ariad, the balefire burning in the many sockets of their eyes.

Dezra finished the incantation, drawing the final word out into a hard, echoing scream. The sheer force of it halted Ariad, throwing her swarm into confusion. Seconds later, the tide of reanimated spiders crashed into it, like two opposing waves. Hundreds upon hundreds of resurrected monsters assailed Ariad's melded horde. Some of them were wreathed in Dezra's fires, carrying them to the heart of the brood. They ripped and tore and stabbed, swarming down the maw of the great composite monstrosity Ariad had crafted, choking her, burying her, crushing her, tearing her apart from the inside.

"You left your children hungry, Ariad," Dezra snarled. "Now, they feed."

The deadlights struck once more, resurgent as the golden power within the brood flickered. They crashed through the arachyura, both the living and the dead, their fury pulverizing them relentlessly. Dezra's body shook as she channeled their energy, her whole body ablaze, corpse light shining from her eyes and her open mouth.

The deadlights spun over the chaos and coalesced, a single, crackling orb of dark magic that slammed down with the force of a meteorite. It plunged directly into Ariad's core. The golden light went out, and the mass exploded. Dezra was thrown to the cavern floor as broken, burning arachyura rained down around her. Her consciousness faltered. By the time she had recovered, silence and darkness had fallen in the great cavern, the contrast utterly shocking.

It was over.

• • •

Dezra picked her way through the great mountain of carcasses, the deadlights illuminating the thousands of broken monstrosities surrounding her. She let her mind quest about, hunting through the cavern for any trace of that cursed golden light, any hint that Ariad had survived. But there was nothing. The place was empty, but for the dead.

She felt a presence next to her and stopped. A fourth deadlight had joined the three, pulsing right above her head. Slowly, she smiled.

"Will you find your way?" she asked.

The pathfinder is with us, Kathryn's voice whispered softly. *He will lead us true. And the other two have plenty of stories for the journey. They're already arguing.*

"I don't envy you," Dezra said, laughing. Then came the tears, finally free from bitterness.

Do not weep for me, my love. Be thankful. You, more than anyone, must know we will meet again.

"When?" Dezra managed.

That is not for either of us to know. But you will find me again, as you did before. You will never be truly alone, Dezra.

She couldn't find the words to answer – hunched over, she gave vent to her grief. As she did so she felt Kathryn's presence behind her, embracing her, a soothing aura that whispered to her of their times together. The others were there too, silent but reassuring, the stillness that surrounded them like the calm wake that followed a terrible storm.

She didn't know exactly when Kathryn, Ulma, Durik and Logan left, but at some point, when she reached out, they were gone. Eventually the tears subsided.

"Who were you talking to?"

The voice startled her. She rounded, a hand raised to summon back her balefire. A man stood facing her, a child next to him. It was the northerner, Ronan. She had forgotten about him. Both he and the girl were wounded and splattered with ichor, foul fluids still oozing from their blades. The girl was carrying the man's familiar. It was unconscious, but Dezra could still sense its life-force burning bright.

"Still intending to slay me, northman?" Dezra demanded. Right then she didn't care if he still meant her malice. Compared to what had just happened, he meant nothing. The battlescarred clansman remained impassive as he spoke.

"The others?"

"Dead," Dezra replied, unable to keep the sting from her voice. A part of it still felt like some dark, strange nightmare. "Along with Lady Kathryn."

"Are they still here?"

"No. They've gone."

Ronan glanced at the girl before speaking once more to Dezra.

"You said Carys Morr has the witch-sight?"

"She does," Dezra said, looking at the girl too. Carys returned her gaze solemnly.

"You know, don't you?" Dezra asked her. She nodded, once.

"A great deal will change," Ronan said, his tone thoughtful. "A seer hasn't inherited the leadership of one of the clans for many generations."

"You will be a great leader, Carys Morr," Dezra said, speaking to her directly. The girl smiled. "I have seen your type before."

"We go back to the surface," Ronan said. "Can you seal this place behind us with your magics?"

"So you're not going to kill the cursed witch?" Dezra asked him, spreading her arms wide, mockingly. Ronan returned her gaze with a stony expression.

"If I did, I would have to slay the daughter of Maelec Morr as well. I would rather die than do that."

"See, you're already convincing warriors to die for you," Dezra said to Carys, winking at her. "You'll go far."

"Do you wish to retrieve the bodies of your friends?" Ronan asked. "I will help carry them."

"No," said Dezra, casting one more glance over the devastation around her. "No burial I could give them would be as fitting as this. Terrinoth will know of their deeds and, one day, if any come looking for them, they will find them surrounded by the thousand monstrosities they vanquished."

Ronan nodded and, to Dezra's surprise, smiled sadly.

"What more could any hero wish for?" he asked.

EPILOGUE

The storm had passed. Fallowhearth lay still in its wake, battered and dripping in the early morning light. The air was cold. The streets were silent. From atop the castle, the lonely banner of the roc still flew.

A congregation had amassed in and around the graveyard of the Shrine of Nordros, a gathering of the faithful. There were hundreds of them, and they stood in absolute silence, rank upon rank of gray shapes in the dawn. They were dead, all but two. The balefire smoldered low in their eyes, like the embers of a hearth that had blazed with great power the night before.

Dezra stood by the lich-gate to the yard, next to a mound of freshly turned earth. Beside her was Volbert, dressed in his full ceremonial robes and cap, his eyes fixed firmly on the ground. A shovel lay against the black iron railings nearby. The man's hands were still caked with mud.

The sorceress had recovered the dead branch she had removed from the tree outside the watchtower. She had found it lying in the shrine and had planted it at the head of the newly dug grave. She reached out one hand, slowly, the slightest glow suffusing her fingertips. The length of bent wood shuddered slightly, and creaked.

"Have you ever seen a dead tree grow, tomb-keeper?" she asked Volbert. The man shook his head, still not daring to look up.

"This one will," she went on. "When it is mature, carve her name into it. That will be her marker."

"Yes, my lady," Volbert said quietly.

Dezra looked down at the grave for a while longer, her mind at peace. Nordros had given her so much. A part of her was thankful that, in the taking, he hadn't severed her love entirely. She believed the words Kathryn had spoken to her – they would meet again. Her god would make sure of that.

She turned her gaze to the congregation. The dead stared back at her blankly in the new light. She smiled sadly at them, then gestured with her right hand. As one the undead responded to her will, turning and shuffling through the packed graveyard. They walked to the hundreds of unearthed graves and opened tombs and, with painful slowness, clambered back down into them. One by one, they lay in the earth, and one by one the flames in their eyes snuffed out. A final low moan drifted through Fallowhearth's deserted streets. Then, at last, there was peace.

"My apologies," Dezra said to Volbert. "It will take you a while to cover them all up again." Volbert said nothing.

She took her leave, glancing one more time at the fresh grave before stepping out beyond the gate. Logan's horse was tied there, one pannier bearing the *Cadaveribus*, the others filled with food taken from the castle's storerooms. Dezra had discovered both the steed and Ulma's pony hitched outside what looked like the remains of the town butcher's shop. She had freed the latter and taken the former. The horse didn't seem to mind.

Turning her back on Fallowhearth's graveyard and the castle beyond, she climbed into the saddle and rode out of the town. Two figures were waiting for her on its southern edge, both mounted. Ronan nodded a greeting as she rode up.

"Not gone yet?" she asked, also acknowledging Carys, sitting on one of the horses taken from the castle stables. The familiar was awake once more, clutching onto her shoulder as it glared warily at Dezra.

"I wanted to say that you should come with us," Ronan replied. "To the Redfern."

"Why?" Dezra asked.

"To teach Carys. To teach us all. There is a great deal the clans do not understand about your ways. A great deal they should learn."

Dezra smiled. "I'll take that as a compliment, Ronan, but you are mistaken. I am no teacher. I discovered that recently at great cost. It is not a mistake I wish to repeat anytime soon. You will walk your own path, Carys Morr, and you will excel. Let there be no doubt of that."

The words were more than mere encouragement – Dezra could see the same iron in the girl that she had seen in Kathryn. Carys already had an intuitive grasp of the arcana. A part of Dezra was drawn to helping her realize her potential, but her place wasn't amongst the northern tribes. Their paths diverged for now, of that she was sure.

"What will you do, then?" Carys asked her. "Where will you go?"

"South," Dezra said. "To Highmont. I am going to tell Baroness Adelynn what happened here. All of it. And after that I'm going to ask for her forgiveness."

"But they'll kill you," Carys said. "Isn't dark magic forbidden there?"

"If that is what must happen, then so be it. I owe it to Kathryn to tell her story. Her mother deserves to know the truth of what happened to her. How she saved me. How she saved all of us."

"As you wish," Ronan said. "But know that if you ever come north again, you will have a home with at least one of the clans."

"Don't stop using your abilities, Dezra," Carys said. "Show that they can be turned to good."

"Maelec Morr's daughter speaks the truth," Ronan added. "I fear a time is soon coming when these lands will need every hero they have, regardless of the path they walk."

"When it does, you'll find me ready," Dezra said. "May Nordros lead you true."

"*Seagh fortan,*" Ronan said. "And may Kurnos guide your path."

Dezra bowed her head and turned her horse south.

ACKNOWLEDGMENTS

A huge thank you is due to the Acontye Books team, especially my endlessly patient editor, Lottie. Likewise to Jeff Chen, the talented artist responsible for that brilliant cover, and the Fantasy Flight Games gang behind the *Descent: Journeys in the Dark* RPG book that provided so much of the inspiration for this novel.